NO HEARTS, NO ROSES

NO HEARTS, NO ROSES

Colin Murray

This first world edition published 2011
in Great Britain and the USA by
SEVERN HOUSE PUBLISHERS LTD of
9–15 High Street, Sutton, Surrey, England, SM1 1DF.
Trade paperback edition first published
in Great Britain and the USA 2011 by
SEVERN HOUSE PUBLISHERS LTD.

British Library Cataloguing in Publication Data

Murray, Colin, 1949-
  No hearts, no roses.
  1. Motion picture industry–Employees–Fiction.
  2. Missing persons–Investigation–Fiction. 3. London
  (England)–History–1951- –Fiction. 4. Suspense
  fiction.
  I. Title
  823.9'2-dc22

ISBN-13: 978-0-7278-6998-2 (cased)
ISBN-13: 978-1-84751-328-1 (trade paper)

All Severn House titles are printed on acid-free paper.

Severn House Publishers support The Forest Stewardship Council [FSC],
the leading international forest certification organisation. All our titles that
are printed on Greenpeace-approved FSC-certified paper carry the FSC logo.

Typeset by Palimpsest Book Production Ltd.,
Falkirk, Stirlingshire, Scotland.
Printed and bound in Great Britain by
MPG Books Ltd., Bodmin, Cornwall.

Voici le soir charmant, ami du criminel;
Il vient comme un complice, à pas de loup; le ciel
Se ferment lentement comme un grand alcôve,
Et l'homme impatient se change en bête fauve...

From: 'Le Crepuscule du soir',
Charles Baudelaire (1821–67)

ONE

Beverley Beaumont wasn't the most glamorous star at Hoxton Films – that was probably Dolores Hart, who Les Jackson was touting as Hoxton's answer to Diana Dors – but she added a touch of elegance to my drab office. Although Miss Beaumont was gracious enough not to look around disapprovingly at the bare floorboards, dirty paintwork and grubby window, it was clear this was not her natural habitat, though malicious studio gossip suggested otherwise.

'Just moved in,' I said, which was a lie. 'Haven't had time to sort the place out yet,' I added, which was true, sort of. Well, it was true if you substituted 'couldn't be bothered' for 'haven't had time'. 'Can I offer you anything? Tea?'

A little wave of one white-gloved hand dismissed the very idea of any refreshments.

'Mr Jackson suggested I talk to you,' she said, lifting her head slightly to look in my direction. 'I have a problem.' Her voice was husky, and I suspected that she'd modelled it on Joan Greenwood's. When I didn't reply she continued, 'It's a delicate matter, and Mr Jackson recommended you highly.'

Well, he would. It'd been months since I'd come close to earning my retainer.

I smiled at her encouragingly, but she probably misunderstood and thought that I was beaming with pleasure at Les Jackson's approval.

She lowered her head and contemplated the neat, white handbag that nestled, like a small animal, on the dove-grey skirt of what had to be the very latest Chanel or Christian Dior suit, the new A line perhaps – whatever that was. She hesitated, then undid the clasp of the handbag and slid her hand in. She placed a slim lighter on my desk and extracted a cigarette from a silver case. She reached into her bag again and took out an ebony cigarette holder and inserted the cigarette. She looked at me expectantly.

Most – well, all – of the women I knew used Bryant and May's finest, and it took me a moment to cotton on but, as soon as I understood, I leaned forward, clumsily clicked the lighter into life and nervously held the flame out for her. She placed her hand on mine to steady it and brought it nearer to her face. It was a strangely intimate moment. I could see the powder that lightly dusted her cheeks and a small mole on her neck. Her perfume – I couldn't think of it as scent – was almost overwhelming up so close. She held on to my hand long after the cigarette was alight and then, abruptly, nodded her thanks.

I resumed my seat and pushed the glass ashtray towards her. She breathed a thin, blue-grey stream of smoke out of her mouth, and I watched it writhe slowly in the weak beam of sunlight that insinuated its way through the window behind her.

She was a very attractive woman in a slim, Tallulah Bankhead kind of way, but she was curiously unanimated, carefully restrained. It was difficult to imagine her sharing La Bankhead's disdain for underwear.

'It's about my brother,' she said, looking straight at me.

'Tell me about him,' I said.

'What do you want to know?' she said. She seemed a little surprised, evidently unprepared for anything that deviated from the script she had carefully rehearsed.

'Name, age, that kind of thing,' I said, reaching for my pad and pencil.

'Jonathan Harrison. He's twenty. I call him Jon. Without an aitch.'

I diligently wrote everything down. 'And where does he live?'

'He was at Cambridge, Downing College, studying – I mean, reading English. We were all proud of him. The first in the family to go to university.' She had become a little animated, obviously back to her prepared script. 'But he's left and come to London.'

'And you want me to find him?' I said.

'I just want to know that he's all right.' She sounded like she meant it. Rather unkindly I thought of the rehearsal time that must have gone into that. 'And –' she placed her cigarette in the ashtray and rummaged in her bag again – 'I'd like to give him this.' She pulled out a bulky brown envelope that I could see was stuffed with cash.

I ignored the proffered envelope. 'How do you know he's in London?'

'He wrote to me,' she said, putting the brown envelope on the desk.

The little handbag was proving to be one of the wonders of modern science. From its apparently infinite interior she produced another envelope.

This one I did take from her. It was off-white and creased, with a brown stain that looked like beer or gravy on one corner. It was addressed to her care of Hoxton Films' Wardour Street office. The blue ink was slightly smudged. There was no stamp, so it had been delivered by hand. Inside there was a small card. It read:

Bev,
Don't worry about me. I'm going to be all right!
Stony broke though. I'll be in touch.
Love, Jon

I flipped it over. It was the card from an Old Compton Street drinking club. It wasn't much, but it was a start. It was undated.

'When did you get this?' I said.

'My agent picked it up this morning,' she said. 'With all the other post.'

'Do you know when it arrived?'

'No,' she said. 'He picks up the post once a week.'

'So this could have arrived any time in the last week?'

She nodded.

Oh well, it was still a start – just even less of one than I'd thought. 'Do you have a photograph?' I said.

She handed over a small snapshot of her standing next to a solemn, good-looking young man. It had been taken at the coast somewhere. The sea stretched out behind them, and the end of an ornate pier jutted into the right-hand side. Brighton perhaps . . .

'Will you give him this?' she said, pushing the brown envelope towards me.

I shook my head. 'If I find him, you can give it to him yourself.' I'd been caught like that before. 'Money?' says the recipient. 'He never give me no money.'

'I'm filming for the rest of the week. Mr Jackson will know how to contact me,' she said, standing up.

I walked her to the door. Jerry was, as he had done twice a day since he'd heard of his death, playing something by Charlie Parker, which meant that there was no one in the shop. Jerry's clientele leaned towards the Teresa Brewer, Dickie Valentine end of the market. It was a source of great unhappiness to him.

'What's the film?' I asked as I opened the door for her. She looked at me blankly. 'The picture you're making at the moment?'

'Oh,' she said, 'a romantic comedy. Something with "Champagne" or "Chocolates" in the title.' She paused and looked thoughtful. 'Maybe it's both.'

'*Champagne and Chocolates*,' I said. 'It's not the best title I've come across.'

'No, that isn't it,' she said vaguely. Then she turned and placed a foot on the top step of the steep, dingy staircase. I followed her down.

The old Roller, Les's pride and joy, was parked, appropriately enough, outside the Gaumont. Where else would Hoxton's managing director, or whatever Les called himself, like to see the old dear? She must have been nearly as old as me, but the elegant, black machine was wearing better and looked clean and sharp against the pale-yellow stone of the cinema.

Ten small boys were waiting for the Tarzan film to begin – or, more likely, they were waiting for their mate to open the side door and sneak them in – and, in the meantime, they were clustered around the car. The corner of Lea Bridge Road didn't see too many Rollers. How not to arouse curiosity in Leyton!

We walked slowly across the road in the surprisingly warm afternoon sunshine. The morning's cloud had all but disappeared.

'This your car, mister?' one of the little boys piped up.

'That's right,' I said. 'We're just driving over to France to meet up with my yacht.'

Charlie Lomax, Les's driver, saw us coming and heaved his considerable bulk out of the car, hastily forcing his cap down over his unruly hair. As always, his dark suit and white shirt looked slightly too small for him, every seam straining.

'Clear off, you lot,' he said and scowled at the boys. They ran for it. Charlie had been a boxer in the thirties and had then had a couple of bit parts in films after he'd retired from the ring. His acting career hadn't come to anything, but Les found him useful to have around and, although he's over fifty, he's still big and, with his battered face, scary-looking. The kids weren't to know that he's one of the most genial men you'd ever meet.

He put his finger to his cap and opened the rear door for Beverley Beaumont. She turned and looked at me, put her hand on my forearm and said, huskily, 'Thank you for your time, Mr Gérard.' I was used to my name being pronounced to rhyme with Herod, and usually I scarcely noticed, but this time I was mildly disappointed. I'd expected her to recognize its French origins.

'I'll be in touch if I find anything out, Miss Beaumont,' I said.

There was the soft whisper of silk stockings as she slid on to the leather seat and then the satisfying clunk of the car door, and I was left standing next to Charlie. His meaty paw thumped into my shoulder.

'Good to see you, Tone,' he said. 'It's been a while.'

'You keeping well?'

'Yeah, and Mr Jackson keeps me busy.' He looked around a little nervously. 'Listen, Tone, can I buy you a drink some time? I'd like to pick your brains.'

'Sure.' I nodded at the car. 'I'm going to be busy for a day or three but . . .'

'Friday lunchtime sound good? Your pub's the Antelope, ain't it?'

I nodded, and his right cross came in again and pounded my shoulder.

'One o'clock then,' he said.

I waited until the Roller had pulled away before rubbing at the bruise.

I watched a trolley bus make the perilous turn into Church Road in a crackle of blue electricity, then I ambled back across the road.

I made my way up to my office to the sound of Rosemary Clooney singing 'The Blues in the Night'. A customer must have sneaked into the shop while I'd been out. If he'd been on his own, Jerry would have played the Artie Shaw version. He didn't care for the Woody Herman recording.

My office depressed me even more than usual: the bare dusty floor cried out for a rug, the dingy brown walls ached for a fresh coat of paint and the entire space begged me to replace the kitchen table with a proper, polished desk.

Beverley Beaumont had forgotten her lighter and the envelope of money. They lay next to the ashtray where her cigarette continued to smoulder, smoke rising from it in a thin, blue-grey plume. Her perfume lingered too. It was subtle and delicate. I didn't recognize it, so it obviously wasn't Evening in Paris. I stubbed out the cigarette.

I picked up the lighter, envelope and cigarette holder and drifted into my other room, where I usually slept, sometimes ate and occasionally lived.

Fluffy, Jerry's ironically named, huge, pale-orange cat, was curled up in the centre of my bed. The scars on my forearms from the last time I tried to move him itched a warning, and I decided to leave him be.

I sank into my grandfather's old leather armchair and listened to the distant voice of Rosemary Clooney as she tried – unconvincingly – to sound like the whistle of a train.

The envelope contained seven fivers, four oncers and two ten-bob notes, so it wasn't as stuffed as I'd thought. The cash had just been crammed in. The lighter was inscribed 'To Bev from Jon with love Christmas 1954'.

A student who could afford to give his sister a silver lighter for Christmas shouldn't need forty quid from her less than four months later. On the other hand, I could think of plenty of blokes who went from broke to flush and back again in less time than that. Of course, they were usually petty criminals with little understanding of even the most elementary principles of sound domestic economic theory as set out by WC Fields in *David Copperfield*.

The music stopped, and there was a refreshing silence. Rather sourly, I guessed that the customer must have insisted on buying 'Mambo Italiano' and Jerry was sulking. He'd probably play 'Lonely Ballerina' by Mantovani soon, just to really depress himself. There are times when living above a record shop can be a little wearing.

Careful not to disturb the slumbering feline, I slipped out

of the room and down the stairs, and then, knocking lightly on the door off the narrow passageway, I went into the shop.

It was messier than usual, with sheet music in little heaps all over the floor and opened boxes of records blocking the entrance. Jerry, of course, was as dapper as ever. He was standing in the centre of the room, thoughtfully stroking his black goatee, in black trousers, black leather waistcoat and charcoal-grey shirt (even Jerry couldn't ignore the associations of a black shirt) with a yellow tie splashed across it. He'd taken to wearing mainly black back in February. He inclined his head in a small bow.

'Tony,' he said. 'How goes it, my friend?' He threw his hands up in a little gesture of despair. 'Two deliveries in one morning. When troubles come, they come not single spies but in battalions.' He gave me a sly smile. 'But what was with the high-class car and the even higher-class broad?'

Jerry had gone to one of the better public schools, but he'd discovered jazz when the GIs arrived and had decided to use a small inheritance to spread the word. Why he'd chosen Leyton to do it in is anyone's guess.

'You noticed that, did you?'

He raised his eyebrows. He and probably everyone in a three-mile radius.

'Work, Jerry,' I said, 'just work. Which is why I came down. Can I put these –' I showed him the envelope, the cigarette holder and the lighter – 'in your safe?'

'Sure,' he said, 'you know where the key is.'

I did and, as I went behind the counter and retrieved it from the brown teapot on the filing cabinet, I wondered how many other people did. Still, he hadn't been robbed in the two years I'd been living there.

'Fancy a coffee?' he said.

'Yeah,' I said, 'that'd be good.'

I stooped down, opened the safe and pushed the stuff to the back of the empty space. No wonder Jerry was so casual about the key. There was nothing in there to take. Which probably explained why he'd never been robbed.

Jerry leaned over the boxes blocking the entrance and flipped the shop sign to 'Closed'. We left by the side entrance.

Costello's isn't much of a café, but it is just opposite us in the little terrace of shops by the Gaumont and it does have an Italian machine – complete with gurgles, steam and froth – and a genuinely lugubrious owner.

He was standing by the door, looking morosely at the sky, his hands stuffed in the pocket of his grubby apron. 'It's gonna rain,' he said by way of greeting.

'I don't think so, Enzo,' Jerry said.

'Bloody country,' Enzo said. 'No papers, and always it rains.' He turned and walked back into the café. 'What can I do you for?'

'Coffee for me, Enzo,' Jerry said.

'And for me,' I said.

'Anything else?' Enzo tried successfully to keep any trace of hope out of his voice as he turned to his gleaming coffee machine.

We both shook our heads. We'd ordered Enzo's egg sandwiches in the past.

We sat at one of the small wooden tables, and Jerry told me about an early recording of Thelonius Monk playing with Coleman Hawkins that he'd acquired. Enzo's machine growled and roiled like an uneasy bowel, and *Mrs Dale's Diary* whispered out from the wireless. Mrs Dale was apparently worried about Jim.

I was worried about Beverley Beaumont. I didn't think I'd find her brother.

'Fancy coming up West tonight?' I said to Jerry as Enzo plonked our cups down on the table. Coffee had slopped on to his thumbs, and he licked it off.

'What for?' Jerry said.

'It's the job,' I said. 'It'll mean a few drinks in a couple of pubs . . .'

He beamed. 'Ah,' he said, 'London's answer to Sam Spade is on a case.'

'Jerry,' I said, 'I am not a private investigator.'

'Of course not. You're an accountant.' He left a beat. 'Just a very strange one.'

We've had this conversation a number of times, and there didn't seem any point in continuing it. 'Seven OK?' I said.

'Sure,' he said. He finished his coffee and stood up. 'So, the sophisticated dame is an actress, eh?'

I nodded.

He smiled and left me to pay for the coffees.

I brooded in Enzo's for a while and then trudged across the road to the doubtful delights of home.

It amuses Jerry to think that I'm something glamorous like a gumshoe. But I'm not.

An accountant is closer because that's what I trained as after school. But, somehow, after the war, I never settled to it again. I do look at the books for the local tradesmen, to check their figures, make sure they haven't made any egregious mistakes, and they slip me a fiver or two, but that doesn't pay the bills and I have to be careful that no one finds out. Impersonating an accountant, apparently, is as heinous a crime as pretending to be a policeman. The profession doesn't like it. So it was a godsend when Les Jackson tracked me down a couple of years ago and put me on a retainer so that he could call on my 'specialist skills'.

Les's brother met me in France back in 1944, and Les had probably heard some colourful accounts of my exploits. My only real skills – surviving, and speaking French like a native because of the accident of birth – are ones that he'll never have a use for.

In the time I've worked for Les, I've found myself negotiating with a bookie on behalf of a sleazy second-rate matinée idol with a gambling habit and an appalling taste in dogs. And there have been two minor blackmailing schemes involving starlets and compromising photographs. Tame stuff, really, and easily dealt with.

Keeping stories of stars' drinking habits or sexual activities out of the papers is not so difficult either. Reporters just have to be reminded about libel laws and then be given 'exclusive' access to the stars. The exclusivity lasts until another star is caught misbehaving – so not that long.

The newspaper strike meant that Les's boys and girls could get up to whatever they liked for a few weeks.

After a plate of bacon and eggs – all that my limited larder had on offer – I shaved at the scullery sink, put on a clean white shirt, my decent blue suit and a blue tie, and I was ready for a long evening.

TWO

Jerry hadn't changed his clothes. He'd just added a black corduroy jacket and a racy black fedora to the outfit he'd been wearing.

He always made me feel old and staid. But, then, we were separated by more than the six years between us. I was from another generation, the one that had fought. The one that had got a little row of coloured ribbons and a demob suit to put it on.

Jerry had done his National Service, of course, but that had been afterwards and he hadn't seen action. In fact, the way he told it, his two years had been a series of beer-sodden escapades separated from each other by weeks of boredom broken only by the ripe insults hurled at him by NCOs. That was not how I remembered my time.

There were other, more profound, differences too. It mystified him that the Goons left me completely cold. He had long since given up greeting me with the cry, 'You deaded me,' because he knew that the smile I managed to twitch at him was forced.

He spent the entire Underground journey from Leyton to Tottenham Court Road reading *The Old Man and the Sea*. He was well prepared for our journey. Which was more than I was. I'd forgotten that there'd be no discarded *Evening News* to pick up, and so I sat and stared through the fug of other people's cigarette smoke at my distorted reflection in the filthy window opposite, thinking about the mole on Beverley Beaumont's otherwise flawless neck.

We walked quickly down Charing Cross Road, though Jerry, like some saucer-eyed urchin outside Hamleys, did press his nose up against the window of a record shop that specialized in imported jazz and blues and stare into the gloom.

I'd decided on a short itinerary: a couple of pubs and then on to the Imperial Club. But it was just an itinerary – I wasn't fooling myself that I had a plan – and to be honest I would rather have skipped one of the pubs and the Imperial Club.

The Bear and Ragged Staff wasn't as popular with the arty, bohemian crowd as the Coach and Horses or the Fitzroy Tavern, but it did try. Situated in one of the dark, gloomy alleyways off the Charing Cross Road, it wasn't quite in Soho (and was nowhere near Fitzrovia) so it attracted a few actors and even fewer musicians from the Opera House and that made it just colourful enough to attract out-of-towners.

It was its usual mid-evening self. An impressive haze of cigarette smoke softened the raw edge of the place, and the ripe smell of stale, spilt beer almost made me gag as we sidled around clumps of drinkers scattered haphazardly across the bare wooden floor.

A raucous group of younger men and one woman by the bar stopped talking for a few seconds and glanced at us as we materialized next to them, but we excited no interest and they resumed their loud conversation and harsh laughter almost immediately.

Incongruously, there was a solitary Scot, in full fig – kilt, sporran, a little dagger stuffed in his sock – standing at the far end of the bar, muttering thickly into his beer. I decided not to approach too close.

The young man behind the wooden counter was dressed in tweed jacket, carefully pressed grey flannels and neatly knotted tie. He looked across at us and then deliberately carried on polishing the glass he was holding. He held it up to the light, then polished it some more before finally putting it down and sauntering over to us.

'Didn't I bar you?' he said amiably.

'Probably, Alf,' I said, 'but that was for being boring. I've become much more interesting since then.'

'All right,' he said, 'you can have one drink, but if you don't say something entertaining then you're barred again.' He looked at Jerry. 'Who's he?'

'Jerry, Alf,' I said, making what passed for a formal introduction on the outskirts of Soho.

He eyed Jerry suspiciously. 'All right, make your minds up, I haven't got all night.'

'Scotch for me,' I said. 'Pint of your best horse piss for him.'

I looked around the room. There wasn't anyone I knew in tonight, though a couple of the faces were familiar from somewhere.

Jonathan Harrison wasn't among them. I hadn't expected him to be, but you can always hope.

Alf returned with our drinks, and I gave him a ten-shilling note.

'Have one yourself, Alf,' I said.

'Don't think you can get round me,' he said. 'You're still barred after this one.'

But he pulled a half-pint anyway. Then he rang up the sale and shoved a small mountain of coppers and silver across the beer-sodden counter towards me. I pocketed the damp coins.

'I don't suppose you've seen this bloke?' I said, showing him the snapshot Beverley Beaumont had given me.

He took it from me and looked at it very carefully. 'Might have done,' he said. 'I get a lot of little pansies like this coming in.' He paused. 'I usually bar 'em.'

'Yeah,' I said. 'But you bar most people sooner or later.'

He looked resolutely unamused, but studied the photograph again. 'He might have been in last week – Thursday – with a couple of other sissies. They drank their gins and orange –' he sniffed dismissively – 'and left.' He looked at the photograph longingly once more before handing it back. 'Nice-looking tart, though.' He stared off into one of the darker corners of the pub, looking young and vulnerable for a few seconds, perhaps recalling someone like Beverley Beaumont, but then he recollected where he was and quickly adopted his usual persona. 'Now, drink up sharpish and clear off,' he said and marched off to insult another customer.

'Nice bloke,' Jerry said, drinking some beer.

'Trying to be famous for it,' I said.

So Alf had Beverley Beaumont's brother down as a wrong 'un. I decided not to attach too much importance to it. Alf wasn't always right, and he did tend to throw insults around indiscriminately. He'd probably describe Jerry and me as sissies to the next people who came in.

I swallowed half my whisky, wishing that I'd had the sense, and temerity, to brave Alf's contempt and ask for some water to go with it. I squinted at the bottle it had been poured from and decided I'd avoid King George IV Old Scotch Whisky in the future. Jerry sipped contentedly at his beer.

The Scot looked across at us and grunted. He moved a foot or two closer, and I braced myself.

'By the way,' he said, 'that Stanley Matthews is a useful player.'

I nodded and relaxed a little. So that was it. He had come down for Saturday's match and couldn't yet face going back.

'Unstoppable on his day,' I said in as neutral a tone as I could manage. A man can be a little sensitive after a 7–2 drubbing.

'You can say that again,' he said, shaking his head. He looked me up and down. 'What outfit were you in?' he said.

'Special Ops,' I said, noting the ribbons on his kilt jacket. 'You?'

'The Argyll and Sutherland Highlanders,' he said, shambling to something that, in his inebriated state, approximated to attention.

'France?' I said.

'Sicily,' he said.

'Good men, the Argylls,' I said. 'Those I came across.'

'Aye,' he said, lifting his beer. 'Here's to those who didnae come back.'

I lifted my glass. He nodded at me and turned away with a quiet dignity, no doubt to face down some of the horrors that gnawed at his soul.

I stared at the mirrored glass behind the bar and glimpsed some of my own.

Jerry kept a respectful silence for a few seconds then put his glass down on the bar. 'I didn't know you were in Special Ops,' he said.

'I've never made a secret of it.'

'I just never knew, is all,' he said, picking his glass up and taking a delicate sip of beer. 'I knew you'd been in France. I assumed you were in the poor bloody infantry.'

'What difference does it make?'

He shrugged. 'I don't know. I just didn't realize. They must have taught you all sorts of things.'

'All right, so I learnt a few useless skills. I expect they tried to teach you how to stand to attention, but I haven't noticed you doing it much since you were back in mufti. Well, I don't use much of what I was taught either.'

He sniffed and took another quick drink and then changed the subject. 'So,' he said, 'do you think mein affable host is right and he saw your prey?'

I shrugged in a non-committal way.

'If he did, shouldn't we be hot on his trail?'

'We can hardly be hot on his trail if he came in last Thursday,' I said. I looked around the pub and was almost swept away by a great wave of *ennui*. 'But I suppose you're right. We ought to be on our way.' I sighed and finished my whisky. The second half went down no easier than the first. I placed my empty glass carefully on the counter and turned to the door. 'Drink up.'

Jerry looked at his nearly full pint. 'Give me a minute,' he said plaintively, but I was already on my way towards the door. I didn't care all that much for the Bear and Ragged Staff and its dyspeptic and irritating landlord.

I waited for Jerry in the cool gloom, watching the traffic charging up and down the Charing Cross Road, breathing in the damp air and staring moodily off at the narrow, paved street opposite. It reminded me of my grandfather. He had told me that, when he'd first come to London from Paris, Cecil Court had been known as Flicker Alley because of its associations with the kinematograph trade.

A little flock of Teds, a couple of achingly young girls fluttering along with them, drifted up from Trafalgar Square. One of them stopped and stared insolently at me. He was sixteen or seventeen with a rich crop of blackheads around his nose.

'You looking at me?' he said, thrusting his face at me. His crooked teeth were yellowish, but his breath had a minty freshness.

'Not me,' I said. 'I'm just minding my own business.'

He looked back at his mates.

'I think you was,' he said.

'No,' I said, 'you're mistaken.'

I took a couple of paces back, but he followed me. I smiled at him and leaned forward so I could whisper in his ear. 'I don't particularly want to break your arm,' I said, 'but, if you force me to, I will.'

A little shadow of uncertainty crossed his face. He looked across to his mates again, and his tongue flicked out and licked his upper lip.

'All right,' he said loudly, 'I'll believe you this time. Thousands wouldn't.' And he hurried back to join the others, and they all continued up Charing Cross Road, laughing and yelling. Some of their riper comments were directed at me.

Jerry emerged after a few minutes with beer on his breath and a burp at the back of his throat, and we walked slowly back up towards Shaftesbury Avenue.

The French was packed, which is as it should be. If I have a favourite drinking spot in the West End, it has to be the French. But then I don't drink beer. I like wine – French wine – and it isn't that easy to find in this insular city. It's also, of course, the case that the French is the only pub I know that has a photograph of me on the wall. Well, it's not really of me. It's of someone more important. I just happened to be in the background. It's fame of a sort.

On the other hand, Jerry doesn't have his photograph on the wall, drinks beer and yet he still enjoys the French. So maybe the place has something about it.

After a little patience at the bar, I bought him a bottle of something dark and evil-looking and myself a glass of Brouilly. Gaston was busy, his impressive soup-strainer moustache hovering thoughtfully over a bottle of Ricard, so I didn't get a chance to show him the photograph of Jonathan Harrison.

As I struggled through the crowd, back towards the window where Jerry stood, someone touched me lightly on the shoulder.

'Antoine?' she said.

No one has called me that in years and I knew who it was instantly. 'Ghislaine,' I said.

She beamed at me. She was ten years older, of course, but the years had been kind to her. She was as small and slim as I remembered her, still quivering with good humour and nervous energy. There were some lines around her mouth and eyes, but her black hair was still thick and lustrous. Her teeth were perhaps a little greyer from the thousands of foul French cigarettes she must have smoked in the last decade, but she still looked wonderful. She was dressed in a belted grey raincoat and had a red beret perched insouciantly on top of her curls and managed to be the epitome of chic.

'You know,' she said in her hesitant English, 'I only arrive today. I hope someone here knows where you are. And then, here you are, just like that.' She snapped her fingers and then she reached up and kissed me on both cheeks.

'Speak French,' I said. 'Your English was never any good.'
I'd always teased her about it.

'Then I must practise,' she said imperiously.

Jerry moved a pace or two towards us and looked at me
quizzically.

'Jerry,' I said, handing him his beer, 'meet an old friend of
mine. Jerry Payne, Ghislaine Michel.'

She smiled. 'No, Antoine,' she said. 'My name is Rieux
now. I marry Robert.'

'Ah,' I said. 'Jerry Payne, meet Ghislaine Rieux.'

Jerry bowed slightly. '*Enchanté, Madame*,' he said, which
was probably all the French he could muster. 'Antoine?' he
whispered at me with a big smile on his face.

I ignored him. 'Where is Robert?' I said, warily. Robert is
the man in the foreground of the photograph on the wall of
the French. He's charming, handsome and witty. He's also the
most frighteningly ruthless person I have ever met.

Ghislaine scowled. 'With his –' she hesitated – '*petite
poularde*.'

I raised my eyebrows.

'So I come to England to find you.' She smiled shyly. 'So
we can be together, like before.'

'Not like before,' I said.

Jerry was looking at me with an irritating, would-be knowing
smile on his face. I glared at him disapprovingly, and he dutifully took an obsessive interest in his beer.

Ghislaine pursed her lips and looked down at the straps on
her elegant black shoes.

'Listen,' I said, speaking French, 'I'm your friend, Ghislaine,
but we haven't seen each other in a long time. It was different
then. You weren't married to Robert. There was a war. We
were younger.'

'We were,' she said, putting her hand lightly on my arm
and smiling sadly. 'We were more passionate too?'

'Perhaps,' I said, 'but now you are married to Robert.'

She shrugged extravagantly. 'Dear Antoine! Always
concerned to do the correct thing. How English of you!'

'And just when did the little country girl become quite so
Parisian and casual about wedding vows?'

'Not long after she moved to Paris and married a man who
can't live without two mistresses,' she said.

'But you must have known that before you married him,' I said.

She shook her head.

'Then you should have asked me.'

'And you would have told me?'

'Probably,' I said.

'Pah!' she said and hit me gently on the shoulder. 'I have a hotel for tonight,' she said, looking thoughtful, 'but I don't have much money . . .'

'You can stay with me,' I said, 'but my flat isn't the Ritz. Well, it isn't even a comfortable pension.' I looked at my watch. 'There is something I have to do this evening, though. You can wait here with Jerry.'

'Well,' she said, 'he is chic, for an Englishman. And handsome.' Then she shook her head. 'But he is young and too much the bohemian.' She made it sound as if both were crimes against good taste. 'And, above all, dear Antoine, he isn't you. I prefer to come with you.'

'OK,' I said, reverting to English, 'you'd both better come.'

Jerry managed to drag his gaze away from the window. 'Can I finish my beer first this time?' he said truculently.

'Of course,' I said, the excellent glass of wine in my hand making me magnanimous.

It was ten o'clock when we found the Imperial Club. It was above a bakery, and the open side door led to a shabby set of stairs lit by a forty-watt bulb that dangled from a wire protruding from a ragged hole in the ceiling. Ghislaine wrinkled her nose and strode towards the staircase, throwing eerie shadows on the walls.

The broad-shouldered woman perched on a stool by the entrance to the club was as formidable as any French concierge. She was dressed in the sort of frilly cream frock that Italian Renaissance artists thought angels manifested themselves in but, in the yellowish light, she bore more of a resemblance to a pale, stone gargoyle thrusting powerfully out from the roof of a cathedral.

'You're not members,' she said suspiciously. Her voice was deep, and she had a strong middle-European accent. Thick make-up couldn't disguise the square jaw and broken nose, but it did highlight the malicious little eyes that stared brightly out, like currents in an uncooked spotted dick.

'No,' I said, 'but I thought we could get some kind of temporary membership . . .'

'Ten bob each,' she said.

I looked at her with raised eyebrows.

'We don't have temporary memberships,' she said. 'This is
good for a year.'

I nodded reluctantly and pulled out my wallet, which seemed
to be much lighter than it had been when I'd left home, and
took out two one-pound notes.

She reached behind her and took an old Oxo tin off a shelf.
She carefully counted out four half-crowns, which she pressed
into my hand. She took a fountain pen and three small, thick
cards from a pocket in the dress and, with great concentration,
wrote a number and a date on each and handed them to us.

'Show the barman and tell her Connie said it was all right.'

She smiled at Jerry as he passed her. '*She's* pretty,' she said,
arching her plucked and painted eyebrows. She blew him a
kiss.

It was as well that the light wasn't good. Jerry was definitely
blushing. I decided not to let him in on my suspicions about
Connie.

THREE

The club was divided into two large rooms. The first had a small bar along one wall. As I entered, I could see, through open double doors to my left, that the other had a billiard table taking up most of the available space.

Light seemed to be on ration. In the billiard room, it was pooled over the table; in the main room, there were five little lamps with fringed shades glowing quietly among the deep shadows. In contrast, the bar blazed like a beacon.

There were only about a dozen people in, which probably explained why Connie had been so happy to accommodate us. They were mostly men, although there were a couple of women. It was difficult to make much out in the gloom, but the members of the Imperial Club seemed to range from the rough-looking to the louche.

It was just a cheap drinking joint, with a few sturdy tables and chairs scattered about, but someone had taken some trouble with the décor. The golden oak of the bar glowed in the light of a couple of Tiffany lamps, and the walls were covered with dozens of framed pencil sketches. Almost all of them were portraits: several were recognizably Connie, staring out maliciously, Gorgon-like.

There was no disguising, even from a relative innocent like Jerry, that the barman was not as other men. He glided sensuously from one end of the bar to the other as we approached, his right hand poised artfully above his hip. But he didn't overdo it.

'You're new,' he said with obvious relish in a fruity Home Counties accent. He was older than I'd thought. And plumper than he probably liked.

'Yes,' I said. 'Connie said to tell you that she said it was all right.'

'Of course you're all right, dear,' he said. 'If you weren't, she wouldn't have let you in. Welcome to Roger's little home from home. What's it to be?'

'Do you have any wine?' I said.

He looked up to the heavens – well, towards the nicotine-stained ceiling – and tutted a 'what *have* we got here?' tut.

'I've port – tawny – and some sherry. Cream. Otherwise it's all beer and spirits.'

'A beer and two cognacs,' I said, looking at Jerry and Ghislaine, who nodded their agreement.

'Light ale or brown?' he said.

'Light,' said Jerry.

'Right you are,' he said and spun elegantly around, on the balls of his feet, like a ballroom dancer.

Within seconds, our drinks were on the bar.

The barman raised a glass of his own. 'To the end of an era,' he said. 'We won't see his like again.'

Jerry nodded gloomily and lifted his own glass. 'I'll drink to that,' he said. 'To the most innovative talent of recent years.'

The barman looked puzzled. 'He was what we needed at the time, but I don't know about innovative . . .'

'Of course he was innovative,' Jerry said fiercely. 'You only have to listen to "Ornithology" to appreciate that his approach to melody, rhythm and harmony changed the way jazz is played.'

'I didn't know Mr Churchill found time to play jazz,' the barman said blankly.

'What's Mr Churchill got to do with it?' Jerry said.

'He resigned today,' the barman said.

'Oh,' Jerry said and walked off to the other side of the room. Ghislaine followed.

'What's he going on about?' the barman said.

'He's still upset about the death of Charlie Parker,' I said, adding, 'the jazz musician,' when I registered that the name meant nothing. 'There are only so many world events a man can grieve over at the same time.'

'It takes all sorts,' he said sniffily.

'So, Churchill resigned today, did he? I missed that,' I said.

'Well,' he said, 'it was only a matter of time after his illness.' He leaned forward conspiratorially. 'Some bloke who comes in says that it was a serious stroke. So he couldn't carry on.'

'I suppose not,' I said and paused. We both stared over each other's shoulder for a moment, reflecting on mortality and, in my case, on the grim early days of the war. Then, since we'd struck up a relationship, I thought I might as well go ahead and ask: 'I'm looking for someone.'

'Aren't we all, dear?'

'Well,' I said, 'I was just wondering if you've seen this chap. I was told he came in here sometimes.'

I handed him the photograph. He gave it a quick glance. Then he moved away to serve a lean, good-looking man with fair hair who had materialized at the bar while we'd been talking. The man rested his cigarette in the ashtray on the bar and asked Roger for a whisky. His dark suit fitted perfectly, and his crisp blue shirt and carefully knotted red and blue striped tie gave the impression of effortless, but expensive, elegance. I thought I might have seen him before, but I couldn't be sure. When he saw me looking at him, his eyes narrowed, his mouth tightened and his good looks took on a mean and vicious cast.

'You're staring at me,' he said.

'Sorry,' I said, 'I just thought I recognized you.'

'I doubt that,' he said. 'I don't know nobodies.'

'That's enough of that, Mr Cavendish,' Roger said. 'I don't want to have to fetch Connie again.'

Cavendish threw some coins on the counter, splashed some soda in his whisky, picked up his cigarette and slid away to the other end of the bar.

Roger rolled his eyes at me and picked up the photograph. 'That's that film star, isn't it? Beverley something. I saw her in *The Shadow of the Sword* a couple of weeks ago.'

'Yes,' I said, 'that is her. But I'm interested in the boy she's with.'

'That's Jon,' he said. 'He started coming in a couple of weeks ago. Was as regular as my morning bowel movement for a week or so. In at half past ten every night. But I haven't seen him for, ooh, nearly a week now. Still, they're like that, the young ones. Flighty. They just don't understand that they're much better off with Auntie Roger.'

'You don't know where I might find him, I suppose,' I said.

'I'll ask around if you like. See if anyone knows anything.'

'Thanks,' I said and gave him one of the smart business cards that Les had insisted he have printed up for me. 'I can be reached on that number. During office hours.' It was the phone in Jerry's shop.

He looked at the card. 'So, Mr Tony Gérard, what's a Producer's Assistant when it's at home then, eh?'

'A boring title for a boring job,' I said.

He put the card by the till. 'So, any chance of you getting me into films? I've always fancied myself flitting across the old silver screen.'

I shook my head. 'Don't have anything to with casting, I'm afraid,' I said. 'But I would be very grateful if you let me know if the boy in the picture turns up.'

'I'll see what I can do,' he said. 'What's that naughty Jon been up to? And what's he doing hobnobbing it with famous film stars?'

'He hasn't done anything, as far as I know. It's a personal matter.'

'Oh,' he said, giving me a long, appraising look. 'In that case, if you'll excuse me, I have to prepare for the evening rush.' He went into a small storage area behind the bar and started hauling crates of beer around one handed. He was remarkably strong.

Jerry and Ghislaine had found a table as far away from the bar as possible.

'Are we staying here long?' Jerry said nervously.

Ghislaine smiled. 'Jerry is a little worried,' she said, 'about the big woman on the door.'

'It's OK, Jerry,' I said. 'Ghislaine will protect you.'

'Seriously,' he said, 'can we just drink up and go?'

'Give it half an hour,' I said.

He slumped down in his chair.

I watched the good-looking but short-tempered Cavendish settle at a table on the far side of the room, careful not to let him catch me looking.

Poor Jerry was very uncomfortable. Cavendish apart, I was at ease, but then I'd been in clubs like this and I knew that the last thing anyone wanted was trouble. Some of the clientele had reputations to protect, and the others – even the rougher ones – would prefer not to arouse the interest of the police. An appearance in Bow Street on the charges they would face could have consequences.

Anyway, it was by no means the queerest bar I'd ever been in. Charlie and I had once had to chaperone one of Les's visiting American stars – actually, he was a washed-up character actor trying to exhume his long-dead career by appearing in British B movies – as he rampaged around London. He was a nice enough guy, full of funny stories, but, after his first few shots of whisky and his first sniffs of cocaine, he went wild. Our job was to make sure that he didn't appear in any of the papers and to have him in the make-up girl's chair by six every morning. It hadn't been easy, and we were both in need of a good night's sleep after ten days, but we had been successful. Reporters finally tracked him down about nine months later when he was working for another studio. Les chortled maliciously. Charlie and I didn't. We'd grown fond of the old reprobate, as Charlie put it, 'his tendencies notwithstanding'. I'd discovered a reservoir of sympathy and tolerance that I hadn't suspected I had.

As people, men and women, started to trickle in, some with little dribbles of paint on their shoes and turn-ups, the women wearing brightly coloured scarves, ostentatious jewellery and flamboyant cotton skirts, I decided that this was more of an artists' club than a pick-up joint for men of a certain persuasion. That would explain the sketches.

The half an hour I'd allowed us was nearly up when an intense young man in a brown corduroy jacket and grey flannels approached us.

'Roger said that you're looking for Jon,' he said nervously.

I leaned forward. 'That's right,' I said. 'Can you help?'

'Not really,' he said. 'But I know where he's been staying for the past fortnight. But he hasn't been there for nearly a week. I was hoping to find him in here tonight.' He looked around wanly and then shrugged. 'He said he'd be back by now.'

I pulled out one of my posh business cards again and then spoiled the effect by rummaging around for something to write with and only coming up with a stub of pencil. 'Here,' I said, handing them to him. 'Write the address down on the back of this.'

He printed it out very carefully in tiny capital letters, meticulously formed.

'Thanks,' I said as he handed it to me. Of course it was south of the river. Kennington Park. I handed him another card. 'That's me,' I said, 'and that's a phone number where I can be contacted. Now, what's your name and how do you know Jon?'

'Richard Ellis,' he said.

'Pleased to meet you, Richard. Like it says on the card, I'm Tony Gérard. This is Jerry, and this is Ghislaine. Sit down and tell me about you and Jon.'

'First of all,' he said, 'will you tell me why you want to find him?'

'His sister asked me to look out for him.'

'His sister?' he said, sitting down. 'I didn't know he had a sister.'

'Well, he has,' I said. 'How well do you know him?'

'We're at Cambridge together,' he said. 'We met when we first arrived.'

I was suddenly aware of another man looking at us from the bar, although looking doesn't do justice to the intensity with which he studied us. The skin on his face had the polished quality of scar tissue and, although it was difficult to tell in that light, he didn't appear to have any eyebrows or eyelashes and he hadn't removed his old battered brown trilby. I had him down as a burn victim, an airman perhaps, one of McIndoe's Army, a fully paid up member of the Guinea Pig Club.

His interest in us was so unnerving that I didn't pay much attention to Richard Ellis's account of his relationship with Jonathan Harrison, which seemed to involve a lot of punting and quantities of champagne. I did notice that he didn't refer much to lectures. I wondered if the university authorities had decided that, since such things played merry hell with a gentleman's social life, they would no longer offer them. Eventually, I interrupted the litany of pubs, clubs, parties, balls and dinners.

'Don't turn around,' I said to him quietly, 'but there's a man at the bar showing a lot of interest in us. I wondered if you know who he is.'

Needless to say, he, Jerry and Ghislaine all shifted their positions for a better view of the bar. The man immediately started like a nervous horse and bolted towards the door.

Richard turned back to me. '*Caramba!* That was Jameson,' he said. 'But I don't know what he'd be doing here.'

'Jameson?' I said, thinking, *Caramba.*

'One of the dons at college. David Jameson. He's the Augustan man.'

I looked at him blankly.

'An expert on the Augustan poets.'

I tried to look less blank.

'Pope, Addison, Steele,' he said. 'Swift.'

I nodded sagely. I'd heard of Swift. And the pope, of course.

'Something of a war hero, Jameson. Shot down over Kent in the Battle of Britain.' He paused. 'Not that he talks about it.'

No, I thought, being engulfed in flame, watching your fingers char, feeling and smelling your face as it burns, inhaling nothing but scorching heat, wondering how long the agony will last, is probably not something you talk about much.

'And that was him, was it?' I said.

'Difficult to say,' he said.

Yes, I thought, a man with no eyebrows or eyelashes and a reconstructed face must be difficult to recognize.

'Does he teach Jon?' I said.

'He's his tutor,' he said casually, as if that answered everything.

I assumed that meant they had a lot to do with each other.

Richard Ellis drank his beer, and I got him another when I bought a round. I took the opportunity to consolidate my relationship with Roger by buying him a drink too.

Richard talked a lot. He was happy to. But it was all to little purpose. Or, at least, he couldn't tell me anything that I wanted to know. He didn't know why Jonathan Harrison had wanted to come to London before the end of term. He didn't even seem to know why he'd agreed to accompany him. It was all just a bit of a lark. He was one of those young men with a glib tongue and an empty head. He'd probably become a Tory MP after working in the City.

Ghislaine could barely conceal her boredom, smoking Gauloises constantly and yawning not too discreetly. Jerry, on the other hand, was as nervous as a Leyton Orient supporter with the team winning 1–0 and five minutes to the final whistle. Admittedly, it was no more frequently than every three seconds, but he kept casting anxious looks at the door. I was as bored with Richard Ellis as Ghislaine. But then I had more cause. I understood every word he said. I decided to put us all out of our collective misery and announced that it was time for us to leave.

I thanked Richard for Jon's address and for sparing the time to fill me in, finished my drink and stood up. Jerry and Ghislaine

moved with more alacrity and were at the door before I
stood up.

Roger, ever the avuncular, efficient barman, came over to
clear the table. 'You off, then?' he said, but didn't wait for a
reply before continuing in a whisper, as he clinked glasses
together, 'Two blokes were watching your table, dear. One was
of a military bearing. Suit, fawn mack, smart brown titfer. Big,
sensible shoes.' He pursed his lips. 'If you get my drift.'

I got his drift all right. 'Thanks,' I said. 'And the other one?'

'Mr Cavendish, looking even more disagreeable than usual,'
he whispered. Then he smiled brightly. 'Come back and see
us soon,' he said, at his normal pitch again.

'I will, Roger,' I said.

He bustled off back to the bar, carrying our glasses.

I rolled my shoulders, stretched and looked around the room
as nonchalantly as possible. But I couldn't see anyone who
looked like Special Branch. Cavendish was looking at me,
though, his eyes narrowed and his lips pinched together.

The city at night is a beautiful place. The gentle light from the
ornate lamp-posts is reflected on the damp pavement in golden
pools and hangs in the smoky air in wispy haloes. It's eerie
too, though. Yellowish fog drifts off the river and licks at the
shadowed doorways of darkened buildings. It's a place of clandestine encounters, hushed whispers and secrets. I like the
city at night.

It was getting on for midnight when we emerged on to Old
Compton Street. No wonder Ghislaine had been bored.

The pubs, dance halls and cinemas had long since closed,
and most of the girls in their bright dresses and the boys in
their shiny hand-me-down suits had hurried off to catch the
last buses and Underground trains to Hackney and Clapham.
There were still a few ragged groups of stragglers, boisterously failing to hail one of the few taxicabs that occasionally
puttered by, but this wasn't the roaring city of a few hours
before. It was a dozing city, and it was very quiet.

As we walked up the Charing Cross Road towards Bloomsbury
and Ghislaine's little boarding house, our footsteps echoed dully
in the relative silence.

And so did those of the man following us.

I didn't say anything to the others, and I didn't look back.

Oddly, recognizing and dealing with someone following you was not one of the skills I was taught in the army. But I have been followed before. Pretending I didn't know he was there was probably the best option for the moment.

He followed us all the way to New Oxford Street and was still with us when, after another corner or two, we turned into Great Russell Street. We passed a shuttered shop that stood directly opposite the British Museum. There were old coins in the window. Ghislaine gave me a knowing look. I should have realized that she had long since clocked our follower. We came up to a scruffy publisher's office, and Ghislaine grabbed me and drew me into the doorway. She put her arms around my neck.

'You do know we are being followed,' she whispered in French.

'Yes,' I said. 'He's been following us since we left the club.'

'What are you going to do?' she said.

'Nothing,' I said.

'Why?'

'This is London.'

'That's not the Antoine I remember,' she said, teasing and challenging at the same time.

It was sly of her, but I responded as she probably knew I would. Danger always excited her and, being foolishly brave herself, she only respected the bold and courageous. It was why Robert, the boldest and most courageous of us all, had fascinated her. She was always going to end up with him.

'All right,' I said. 'Let's see who he is.'

'Right,' she said and pulled me out of the doorway and back on to the pavement.

Jerry was looking faintly embarrassed. 'Don't mind me,' he said.

'Jerry,' I said, fumbling in my pocket, 'here's a quid. Go back to Oxford Street and find a cab. Then come and pick us up. If you can't find us, don't worry. Just go on home.'

'You sure?' he said, pocketing the money and looking relieved. It was far more than he should need, but cabbies sometimes required an inducement to head for Leyton.

He didn't wait to be told again, but set off back the way we had come. Ghislaine and I turned and waved him off. Our pursuer was standing outside the coin shop, pretending to peer into the window.

Ghislaine took my arm, and we hurried along the road while our pursuer was wondering what Jerry was up to. We slipped into a side road and waited. It seemed strange to be standing so close to Ghislaine, listening to her rapid breathing, her body taut and tensed, staring across at the bulk of the British Museum. We should have been in a wood in France, listening for breaking twigs, the bark of a fox, hoping that clouds would dim the moon, waiting to spring an ambush. If Great Russell Street had been a railway line we were planning to blow up and our follower a German soldier the illusion would have been complete.

After about twenty seconds we heard footsteps and then he appeared, striding across the road, tension and anxiety apparent in his stiff movements.

'Hello,' I said, and Ghislaine giggled.

The man turned, and I looked into the ruined face of David Jameson.

He stood still. The skin grafts he had undergone meant that his expression was difficult to read, but his open mouth and rapidly moving eyes suggested confusion.

'Why are you following us, Mr Jameson?' I said.

'Doctor,' he said.

It was my turn to be confused. 'What?' I said.

'It's Dr Jameson,' he said.

'Well, why are you following us, *Dr* Jameson?'

Ghislaine giggled again.

'To be honest, I don't really know. I suppose I was hoping that you would know where to find Jon,' he said. 'Jon Harrison. He's one of my students.' He paused. 'I'm worried about him. I saw you talking to Ellis and I thought . . .'

I looked up and down the street. There was no one about. If Jameson wasn't on his own, then his back-up was very professional. But Jameson didn't seem to me to be Special Branch material. For one thing, Special Branch officers needed to be able to use their hands.

'Sorry to disappoint you,' I said, 'but I'm looking for him too.' I took another look back along Great Russell Street and relaxed. 'I'm Tony Gérard, Dr Jameson. This is an old friend of mine, Ghislaine Rieux.'

'Excuse me for not shaking hands,' he said, looking down at his mittened claws, 'but it's not really possible.' He inclined his head slightly. 'Madame Rieux, Mr Gérard.' He looked at Ghislaine. 'Are you by any chance related to Robert Rieux? I know him slightly.'

'He is my husband,' she said very quietly.

'Walk with us back to Madame Rieux's hotel,' I said. 'Tell me why you're worried about Jon Harrison.'

'It's a longish story,' he said.

'We'll walk slowly,' I said.

FOUR

As I had promised, we ambled slowly along and listened to Dr Jameson. The story he had to tell was not so very long. Nor was it particularly illuminating. He was, though, easy to listen to. He had a reassuringly deep voice, but there was a huskiness in the lower register and a crack in it that reminded you that, although beauty may be only on the surface, burn damage went much, much deeper.

'It's no secret,' he said, 'that Cambridge before the war was a hotbed of communist sympathizers. Most were idealistic young men excited at the prospect of changing our class-ridden society into something fairer. Few joined the Communist Party or did more than attend a meeting or two where Marxism was discussed. However, some were more committed. And it's widely rumoured in the senior common rooms that a few of those went even further and were working for the Russian government. Well, you must remember that ghastly business a few years back. We hoped that that was it. But it's possible that one or two still work for them, recruiting bright and susceptible students.' He paused and looked up at the murky sky. I followed his gaze. It was difficult to tell if there was dark cloud gathering or if the murk was just the usual cocktail of coal smoke and other industrial effluent. There was a sickly yellowish edge to it.

'I don't know the truth of it,' he continued, 'but I do know that Jon is exactly the kind of brilliant, vulnerable boy such men might look at. He comes from a modest background and is encountering privilege for the first time. And I do know that his whole demeanour changed a while ago. He became withdrawn, less forthcoming. I assumed that it was a girl. Then he stopped attending lectures. And two weeks later he disappeared.' He paused again. 'I received a letter from him saying that he had to talk about his studies and that he was in the Imperial Club most nights. This was the first opportunity I had to come to London. I saw you with Ellis and thought it just possible that you would lead me to Jon.'

We walked on in silence for a few moments. We were approaching Ghislaine's boarding house, and I slowed down even more. I suddenly realized that I'd been thinking more about Dr Jameson and what he must have suffered than what he'd been saying.

Like most people, I suppose, I'd read all the stuff in the papers about Burgess and Maclean and was vaguely aware that the story was still rumbling on with sensational headlines about 'The Third Man', but I hadn't thought much about it. So, two minor diplomats had been spying for Russia. Shocking, of course, but I don't know that I've ever expected much from my social betters. It's probably the revolutionary inheritance from my staunchly republican and egalitarian grandfather. His view of the Foreign Office, and the British upper class in general, allowed that while they might not have been quite as bad as the hated Boche, they had raised deceit to an art form.

I met a young, seriously drunk lieutenant in a drab bar in the Boul' Mich' after the Liberation. I was well on the way to being seriously drunk myself, but I do still remember a lot of what he said. He had spoken in unflattering terms about Cambridge and its fellow travellers, expressing the view that some of them were in Military Intelligence and passing secrets to the Ruskies. 'OK,' he'd said, 'they're our allies now, but what about when they're bloody well not?' He'd added that I should never take what a Cambridge man said at face value. They were all devious and dishonest. Of course, that had been the booze talking, and he had been at Oxford, so I assumed that he was not an impartial observer, but his words had stayed with me.

I hadn't knowingly come across too many Cambridge scholars in the intervening years. But David Jameson seemed honest and straightforward enough. The fact that he had been one of Churchill's few counted in his favour. And Richard Ellis, the only other Cambridge man I'd encountered recently, had been like an unmuddied pool.

A new, dark Humber Super Snipe, gleaming under a street light, swept grandly towards us, catching Ghislaine in its headlamps. She was looking thoughtful. It was difficult to tell how much she had followed, but she had been paying close attention.

'How do you know Robert?' she suddenly said.

'What?' Jameson said airily. 'Oh, I met him at a conference,

I expect.' He gave the impression of vagueness, but I thought
he was being evasive. Maybe my lieutenant had been on to
something.

Ghislaine pursed her lips. 'Yes,' she said carefully, 'he
attends many conferences.'

We had arrived at Ghislaine's boarding house. It was in a
little terrace sandwiched between two university buildings and
it looked very closed. The black front door was firmly locked,
and there was no light leaking from any of the windows. I
suspected that it would have a proprietor bloody-minded
enough to lock out any guest who had the temerity to stay
out after ten o'clock.

Jameson took out a small notebook and, clutching the pen
awkwardly in the claw of his right hand, laboriously wrote
the telephone number of his college in it, handed it to me and
asked me to call him with any news. I gave him one of my
cards. Les would have been proud of me. I'd distributed more
in one night than I'd used in the previous year. Jameson slipped
the card into his notebook, bade us good night and headed
off.

Ghislaine watched him for a few seconds and then climbed
the steps to the door.

'I doubt they'll answer,' I said before she rang the bell.

'Why not?' she said.

'Because English hotels disapprove of their guests staying
out late.'

She shrugged and pressed the bell. There was a slight noise
within, like the fluttering of a pigeon's wings.

I snorted. 'They've put cardboard between the clapper and
the bell,' I said.

Ghislaine looked puzzled, then she angrily stabbed at the
button again. 'But my valise is there,' she said, 'and I have paid
for the night.' She frowned and looked up. Then she relaxed.
'So, I'll come back tomorrow. Tonight, I'll stay with you.'

'Yes,' I said. 'Let's find a taxi.' I didn't know if I was
pleased about this turn of events or not.

My history with Ghislaine was not an entirely happy one.

I was pleased to see her and flattered that she'd sought me
out, but I felt awkwardly adolescent, and the brandy roiled
around in my uneasy stomach. I was nervous.

She came slowly down the steps and slipped her arm into

mine. 'That man,' she said, indicating with a slight tip of her
head the direction that Jameson had walked. 'If he knows
Robert, he is not to be trusted.'

I laughed. 'Ghislaine, I know that Robert has upset you,
but that doesn't mean that anyone who knows him is
untrustworthy.'

'Yes,' she said darkly, 'it does if he met Robert at a
conference. The conferences Robert attends are not academic
discussions about the place of literature in modern life.'

I suddenly remembered that Ghislaine had a penchant for
melodrama and a tendency to hint at secrets, double-dealing
and little conspiracies. In the often febrile atmosphere of a
clandestine war, it hadn't seemed particularly inappropriate,
but I had learned that questioning such apparently resonant
statements rarely led to clarification. If there was anything
behind the comment, it would all come out in good time, so
I said nothing and looked down the street to see if there was
any chance of Jerry appearing with a cab. I didn't much want
to pay for two.

But the calm, elegant street was empty. We walked back to
New Oxford Street.

I had lost touch with everyone I had known in France during
the war. It hadn't been a conscious act. It had just happened.
And no one there would have found it easy to contact me.
Ghislaine, who had, she told me on the journey home, tried,
had her letters returned with something like 'unable to deliver'
written across them. Well, the postman couldn't be blamed:
it's difficult to put letters through a door that no longer exists.

It had been surprisingly easy to find a taxi and then persuade
the cabbie to go to Leyton. When he dropped us off and
continued up Lea Bridge Road towards Walthamstow I
suspected that the half-crown tip had been unnecessarily
extravagant, as he lived in the area and was just knocking off
for the night. I'd have to contact Les in the morning about
some expenses.

After talking a little about teaching and meeting up with
Robert again, Ghislaine had been quiet and thoughtful on the
journey back. I wasn't sure if she was just tired or if she was
as apprehensive as I was.

I fumbled the key into the lock and we squeezed into the

narrow passageway. If Ghislaine had been nervous she didn't show it. She pressed me against the wall before I had even closed the door, put her arms around my neck and rested her head on my chest.

'I have thought about you often, dear Antoine,' she whispered in French.

I leaned back against the wall in that dark, chilly passageway, feeling her warm, vibrant body against mine, and tried to think of something sophisticated to say. She smelled of cigarette smoke, perfumed soap and a little sweat, and her strong, elegant hands stroked the back of my head. All I managed was a pathetic echo of her words.

'Yes, I've thought a lot about you too,' I mumbled.

She lifted her head, and I felt her soft, moist lips on mine.

I reached out awkwardly and pushed the door to, then put my arms around her waist. It all felt curiously unreal, as if I wasn't really there, but looking on as someone else fidgeted uncomfortably in what should have been a passionate embrace. I didn't feel very passionate. After a few seconds I pulled my head away.

'Perhaps we should go upstairs,' I said.

She didn't move.

It was possible that she'd forgotten or recalled things differently but, silly though it was, I found myself waiting for Robert to walk in and laugh at us – or, rather, at me. He never laughed at Ghislaine. He may have treated her shabbily, but he did take her seriously. I was patronized and ridiculed because I couldn't do anything about it. I needed him. Ghislaine didn't.

I half disengaged myself from Ghislaine and manoeuvred us, her clinging tightly to me, up the narrow staircase.

But Robert's dismissive view of me as a rival was only half of the story. Callow though I was, I'd suspected that the attention that Ghislaine had shown to me was not because she found me irresistible, but had more to do with making a public statement to Robert. Ungallantly, I wondered if that was what she was doing again.

There was also Mrs Williams – Ann – and our Saturday night 'arrangement' to consider. It wasn't that there was the remotest chance of Ann discovering anything about Ghislaine. How could she? She lived on the other side of London in Hammersmith, and I couldn't imagine that she ever came further east than

Gray's Inn, where her late husband's solicitor had his chambers. It was really that, for all my flaws, and despite the oddity and curious formality of our relationship, I had been steadfastly faithful to her for the last six years. I suppose it must have been something like love. I'd even joined a football club over in Ealing so I could turn up at her house by six thirty, muddy boots in my army haversack, for a drink before dinner. And Mrs Williams was clearly fond of me too. Two years ago she'd finally accepted that I really didn't drink beer and had discovered that Berry Bros and Rudd sold very decent red wine.

Ghislaine had not asked about my domestic arrangements.

Jerry had obviously made it back. I could hear the faint, mellow sound of the cherished radiogram he kept in his room behind the shop. I couldn't quite make out what he was playing, but it sounded bluesy so it could have been Bird.

Ghislaine did not appear to be too fazed by the accommodation, not even when I explained about the steps that led down to the washing facilities in the scullery and the outside loo, which I shared with Jerry. She shrugged and said it was not so very different to the *appartement* in Paris she'd lived in before she married. She did, however, look askance at my single bed. I explained that I would haul my grandfather's old chair into the office and sleep there. She rolled her eyes at me and pouted, but seemed to accept the situation. Then she announced that she was hungry. I told her that I had some eggs.

'Ah,' she said, '*omelette aux fines herbes.*' Then she looked in my larder and amended that to, '*Omelette sans fines herbes.*' And then she curled her lip when she hesitantly sniffed and tasted the block of marge and saw what remained of the sliced white loaf I'd bought the day before and decided that perhaps she wasn't hungry after all.

I stripped the sheets off the bed, grateful that Fluffy was off prowling about somewhere else, and found some clean ones and an old shirt for Ghislaine to wear; then I went out into cool night air in the backyard. Jerry was still playing some jazzy blues, and I still didn't recognize it, but the faint sounds coming to me as I peed were very pleasant. I stood outside his window for a minute or two – partly to listen, partly to allow Ghislaine a little time to change – and then I went into the scullery and splashed water on my face, cleaned my teeth in a desultory fashion and emerged into the living room.

Ghislaine had somehow contrived to be completely naked when I appeared, and she made no great effort to pull on my old shirt, fiddling with it as if she couldn't quite work out how it went over her head. She was, I suppose, letting me see what I'd be missing.

She didn't have to remind me. It may have been ten years since I'd seen her without clothes, but my memory was not so bad and she hadn't changed much. Then I realized that she was trying to show me something else.

She was standing directly under the light in the centre of the room. It was harsh on her pale body and threw dark shadows across her belly and ribs. After a few seconds, I walked across to her and confirmed that they weren't all shadows.

'Ghislaine,' I said, putting a hand on her shoulder as gently as I could. 'Did Robert do this?' I said.

She nodded.

'What happened?' I said. I didn't like Robert much, but I had never thought of him as a wife-beater.

She put her arms around my neck again. 'Hold me, Antoine,' she said.

There was a terrible sadness in her voice, and I wrapped my arms around her.

'I told Robert that, unless he gave up his mistress, I was leaving him. At first he laughed and said that I couldn't, and then he grew angry and hit me. The next day I went to my mother in Rouen, but I knew he would follow me – or have some of his men follow me – so I borrowed money from her, caught a ferry in Le Havre, and here I am.'

'Ghislaine, I'm so sorry,' I whispered. 'Do you need to see a doctor?'

She shook her head against my chest.

We stood there for what seemed like a long time, then she started to shiver. I pulled away, picked up a blanket from the bed and wrapped it around her.

'Well, you're safe here,' I said.

She clutched the rough blanket tightly, but shook her head again. 'I'm not safe anywhere,' she said.

I grabbed the back of my old leather chair. 'I'll just take this through to the other room,' I said.

'I didn't mean to embarrass you or make you responsible for me,' she said.

I wasn't so sure about that, but I grunted that friends looked after each other, and I pushed the chair through the doorway.

I stood by the window. It had started to rain a little, and a few drops ran down the dirty pane. The street gleamed darkly in the light from the street lamps. There was a man standing under the Gaumont's awning, smoking a cigarette. As I watched, he pulled his hat down and turned the collar of his suit jacket up, and then stepped out into the rain and turned the corner. I fancied I could hear his footsteps slowly receding. A dark car swished slowly along Church Road, its headlamps throwing a yellowish beam on the slick road, and turned the same corner. It stopped a little way along Lea Bridge Road, just out of my sight, and then I heard the muffled whump of a car door closing. After that the idling engine was banged into gear with a screech like sheet metal tearing and the car roared off.

I hoped it was just a coincidence that the vehicle was a Humber Super Snipe.

I went back into the living room to collect a blanket. I could hear Ghislaine downstairs in the scullery splashing water around.

She was wearing my shirt when she came back. She looked at me sadly and then slipped quickly between the sheets. 'Stay with me for a few minutes,' she said.

I sat on the bed and stroked her head. She closed her eyes, and her steady breathing grew deeper. I looked at her unblemished face and thought bitterly that it was typical of Robert that he'd been careful to leave that unmarked.

As quietly as I could, I stood up, turned off the light and left the room.

My grandfather's chair, which survived the doodlebug that did for the house, is very comfortable, but I didn't fall asleep immediately. I was conscious of Ghislaine in the next room. I found myself hoping that Robert would find her with me, but I knew that the chances of him coming himself were slender. Robert had never been short of thugs.

There had always been something unsettling about Ghislaine. She was altogether too unpredictable and impulsive for me. What had seemed attractive when she was eighteen was less

so now. But I still liked her, and I knew that I'd protect her,
if I could.

I suddenly realized that I was getting set in my ways. A
little excitement might not be a bad thing. And Ghislaine was
guaranteed to provide that. But Mrs Williams had to be considered. I thought of her and fell into a shallow sleep, fractured
by fragmentary dreams involving the Imperial Club and, oddly,
Les Jackson.

FIVE

And it was Les Jackson I thought of first when I awoke. The hole in my finances must have been weighing on my mind. What I'd withdrawn from the bank on Monday had been earmarked for rent, food and the gas and electricity meters and had not been intended as walking about money. It was only Wednesday, but at the current rate of expenditure the money wouldn't last another day, let alone another week – and that was without force-feeding the electricity meter like a French goose.

I made a mental note to ask Jerry for any change from his taxi money.

Still, the Wardour Street office carried some petty cash. I'd try to pop in sometime in the morning. If Les was there, I might manage to prise out a little more information about Beverley Beaumont and her brother. A little more? Who was I kidding? I might be able to extract *some* information about them.

A few cars and a trolley bus splashed through the early morning rain as I lay there, uncomfortably hunched in the chair, staring at the scorch mark on the right arm. A lot of people on foot were scurrying along. In the distance, I heard the hooter from the Caribonum factory announcing that its workers only had ten minutes to get there.

I struggled into my clothes before the melancholy horn could boom out again at eight thirty.

Ghislaine was rummaging about downstairs in the scullery when I emerged.

'Antoine,' she called when she heard me, 'where is the coffee?'

'On the shelf above the gas stove,' I yelled, looking at the neat little mound of her clothes, carefully folded and piled on top of the wooden chair I'd borrowed from Jerry. Ghislaine's stockings hung down, empty, sad, wrinkled and baggy-kneed.

I heard her bare feet swishing across the stone floor.

'Well, I can't find it,' she shouted. She sounded a little petulant.

I grinned and ambled down to the scullery. She was wearing
my old shirt. Fluffy – back arched, tail erect – was rubbing
himself lasciviously against her leg. She reached down and
scratched the back of his head.

'It's in the bottle marked Camp,' I said.

'That is coffee?' she said, reaching up to take the bottle
down. She unscrewed the cap and took a doubtful little sniff.
'No, Antoine,' she said. 'You are mistaken. I don't know what
this is, but it most certainly isn't coffee.'

'Well, it's what passes for it over here,' I said.

She wrinkled her nose dismissively and screwed the cap
back on tightly.

'I can make you some tea,' I said.

'No, Antoine,' she said firmly, 'you can take me to a café
for proper coffee.'

'So young, so innocent,' I said in English. She looked
puzzled and pouted ominously so I added quickly, 'Did you
sleep well?'

'Thank you,' she said, 'I did. But, Antoine, I must have
coffee.' For a moment I thought that she was going to stamp
her slim, elegant foot, but, fortunately for Fluffy, who was
still weaving sensuously in and out between her ankles, she
didn't.

'Get dressed,' I said. 'Let's see what Enzo can manage.'

As it turned out, and unsurprisingly, Enzo didn't manage too
well, but he did produce a beverage that Ghislaine accepted
as coffee. Not very good coffee, but coffee. The burnt toast
smeared with marge met with less enthusiasm.

I drank my tea, ate my bacon sandwich and half-listened
to Ghislaine's entertaining recitation of dismay.

Enzo, standing behind the counter, was out of customers,
washing up and sorts, and so, having no *Daily Mirror* to flick
through and grunt at, he, irritatingly, fiddled with the dial of
the big, brown wireless, moving between the Light Programme
and the Home Service and back again, before finally deciding
on *Housewives' Choice*, as he always did at this time. I ignored
him, more or less, only grunting that I didn't know where
Jerry was, when he asked.

I was trying to plan the day ahead. So far I hadn't proceeded
further than: visit the address in Kennington that Jonathan

Harrison had been dossing at and then drop in at Hoxton's office. As plans go, it lacked a little something.

Ghislaine wondered if there was any chance of getting a refund from the boarding house. She pointed out very reasonably that she hadn't slept there or used any of the facilities and looked outraged when I said that, sadly, I doubted reason would come into it and suggested that if she wanted her suitcase back she might be advised not even to ask.

I then realized that what had seemed a woefully inadequate plan only seconds before did have the considerable advantage of flexibility. I could drop Ghislaine off at the boarding house, and so make sure that she didn't find out just how wonderful London policeman and hoteliers are, take the short stroll from Bloomsbury to Wardour Street, and then risk the uncharted territory south of the river *after* tapping Hoxton's coffers for money and Hoxton's boss for information.

I left Ghislaine, with her suitcase, a key to my flat, instructions on how to get there and fare for the journey, in a café in Greek Street that served decent coffee, and even something that resembled a croissant, and made my way to Hoxton's office.

We'd run into a dishevelled, yawning Jerry as we'd prepared to dash out into the light drizzle, and he'd promised to keep an eye on Ghislaine when she returned and – a little too reluctantly, I thought – found twelve bob change for me.

The rain had stopped, but the streets were still damp and the air was warm and moist. Soho smelt a bit like an old compost heap.

I passed the door to the Imperial Club, but it was firmly shut. The baker's was throbbing with customers, though, and the warm, yeasty smell of fresh bread lured me in. I bought a large slice of dark, moist and sugary bread pudding and munched it contentedly as I strolled along.

It was ten to eleven when I entered the cramped reception area of Hoxton Films and encountered the usual scene of noisy chaos. Canisters of film, boxes of posters and piles of brown envelopes, heavy with scripts and contracts, lay over the desk, the little mud-coloured sofa and much of the floor. And four messengers – two boys and two old men – stood about, talking in quick staccato bursts about the relative merits of West Ham and Spurs, drawing greedily on hand-rolled cigarettes, waiting to present themselves, when Daphne, the grey-haired harridan who ruled the front office, deigned to call them to her.

She saw me as I came in, took the cigarette from her mouth and waved with it. 'Go on through, Tony,' she said. 'His lordship was hoping to talk to you.'

'Thanks, Daff,' I said. 'I'll stop by for a chat when you've got a moment.'

'That'll be the day,' she said, beckoning to one particularly elderly messenger she'd decided to take pity on and see before he expired. He coughed thickly in response and shuffled over to the desk.

I peered through the little window next to the door to Les's office. He was leaning back in his chair, hands clasped behind his head, staring at the ceiling while dictating to his new, glamorous secretary.

I knew that she was new and glamorous without looking at her. Les's secretaries were always aspiring 'actresses', and they always moved on very quickly. Either they were amenable to his advances or they weren't – but, either way, they didn't stay long. The accommodating ones were found a bit part as a salt-of-the-earth barmaid in some cops and robbers production. One or two of them had even been able to act. The less obliging ones were lucky to last three weeks, and their acting abilities would remain a mystery.

Les leaned forward and saw me. He stood up and beckoned to me. 'Tony,' he said and beamed. 'This is Brenda, my new secretary. Isn't she lovely?'

And she was, in a cantilevered, blonde and vacuous kind of way.

'Good to meet you, Brenda,' I said. 'I'm Tony Gérard. I'm the odd-job man.'

She giggled.

'You'd better get on with those letters, dear,' Les said, and she swayed out of the office, her pad and pen clutched to her pneumatic bosom. Les watched her appreciatively. He didn't run his tongue over his lips, but he might as well have done. 'Wouldn't kick her out of bed, would you?' he said.

I shrugged in a non-committal way, and he gave me a fruity, condescending, no-point-in-lying-to-me laugh.

I shrugged again. 'You know, Les, you and your approach

to *amour* reminds me of a bloke who used to manage a football team I played for a few years ago. Before we'd go out on the pitch he always gave the same pep talk. What it boiled down to was: if it moves, kick it; if it doesn't, kick it till it does.'

'Meaning?' he said.

'Come on, Les, even you can work that out,' I said.

Les likes everyone to think that he's their mate, a no-nonsense, what-you-see-is-what-you-get sort of bloke. He even draws attention to the origins of his wealth by still wearing the thin, spiv's moustache that he cultivated during the war when he worked the black market. And the sharp, shiny suits and the loud ties say it in spades. 'While you were mug enough to be off overseas having your balls shot at, I was making my packet back home – and probably shagging your missus, as well,' he seems to shout. So it never hurts to behave as though you're taken in and have bought the Les he tries to project.

But he isn't as simple as that. He's a clever and hard-headed businessman, a shrewd deal-maker who's as devious as they come. Sometimes, I even wonder if he was a black market-eer during the war. But Daphne says he was, and she should know. She was married to him at the time.

'Pull up a pew,' he said. 'Plonk your arse down where the beautiful Brenda's was.'

He leaned back in his chair again and resumed staring at the ceiling. I sat and wondered what he saw up there. There were a few cobwebs in the corners and around the light fitting, and it could have done with a lick of whitewash. But it was just a ceiling.

'So,' he said. 'Found Miss Beaumont's brother yet?'

'I'm working on it, Les,' I said. 'I've got an address. I'm off there just as soon as I've picked up some exes.' He didn't say anything. He just kept staring at the ceiling. 'It's in Kennington. I'll have to take a cab.'

He sat up and shook his head dismissively. 'Don't worry about the expenses,' he said. 'Ask Daphne for what you need.' He looked at me. 'I'm a bit worried about Miss Beaumont, Tony. The sooner you can bring her some good news, the better. We're days behind schedule, and I don't want to lose any more time. You're the only man who can help me. Find him, Tony. I'm relying on you.'

I nodded slowly. At least he wasn't putting me under any pressure. 'I'll do what I can, Les. But if he doesn't want to be found . . .'

'Of course he wants to be found. Why else would he write to her?'

There was nothing to be gained by telling him it was unlikely to be that easy or by pointing out that young Jon had already legged it away from the only lead I had.

'Tell me about her, Les. Give me some background. What's she like?'

He sniffed. 'Fancy her, do you? Well, forget it. I'll tell you the truth, Tony. I've always thought she was a bit of a cold fish.'

I smiled.

'I know what you're thinking, but it's not that. She's not my type. You know I prefer 'em a bit more cuddly.' He held his hands in front of his chest as though holding two large grapefruit and gave a half-hearted leer. But his heart wasn't in it. 'I've never even tried it on with her.' He shook his head thoughtfully. 'You can always tell a game one. And she isn't.' He leaned forward. 'Don't get me wrong, though. She's not hoity-toity or anything. And she's good on the set. Very professional. And she comes across on the screen. Although sometimes it's the devil's own job to get a performance out of her. Jimmy says she's always asking about her motivation.' He shook his head again.

Jimmy Bolt is Les's favourite director. He has a well-deserved reputation for bringing films in on time and under budget. They aren't necessarily any good, but they don't lose money. He tends to go with the first take, so he's known by all the crew and some of the actors as the Lightning Bolt because he never strikes in the same place twice.

'You know the story about Madeleine Carroll and *The 39 Steps*?' Les said. I did because he'd told me before. But no more than three or four times. There was no point in mentioning it, as he'd tell me again anyway. 'Hitch couldn't get her to look as shocked as he wanted when the two blokes turn up on the moor so, at the crucial moment, he whips out the second half of his name. That got the reaction he was looking for. I always think about our Miss Beaumont when Hitch tells that story.' He grinned.

Yeah, I thought, Alfred Hitchcock was always getting off the *Queen Mary* and stopping at Les's gaff in Pimlico for a cup of tea and a custard cream. Probably on his way to see his old mum in Whipps Cross Road or wherever she lived these days.

'Anyway, she surprised me,' he said. 'She was really upset when she came to me and told me that her brother had disappeared. I didn't think she was that emotional.'

'What about the brother?' I said. 'Know anything?'

'Never even knew she had any family until yesterday.'

Something occurred to me. 'What's her real name?' I asked.

'Funnily enough, I think it's Beverley Beaumont. I don't think she changed it.'

'Is there a husband around?'

'There doesn't seem to be anyone close. Course, she's been around the block a bit. I mean, she must be close to twenty-five now. Could have been a husband at some time.' He looked thoughtful. 'Come to think of it, I should send a note down to publicity. See if we're missing a trick here. We could float a romance for her . . .'

He picked up a propelling pencil and jotted something down on a pad. He'd just finished writing when the telephone rang. He picked up the receiver, listened for a second, then put his hand over the mouthpiece. 'I've got to take this, Tony. Welsh distributor has got me by the Max Walls. Tell Daphne to give you what you need from petty cash. No questions asked.' He actually winked as he nodded at the door to dismiss me.

Daphne was drinking tea and smoking another cigarette when I stepped into reception again. The last of the messengers was just leaving, a bulky envelope under his arm, and there was relative calm. I knew from experience that it wouldn't last so I grabbed the moment.

In spite of what Les had said, she made me sign for the two five-pound notes she handed over. ('It's a lot of money, Tony. I don't care what his nibs says.')

Tricky financial negotiation out of the way, she relaxed and poured me a cup of tea.

'So,' she said as I took a slurp, 'found him yet?'

'Got an address,' I said, 'but he's flown the coop already.' The tea was stewed.

'Not surprised,' she said. 'If he's the little tart's brother,

I'm a Chinaman.' She looked around warily. 'She likes 'em
young.' Her eyes narrowed a little. 'And she likes 'em confused
an' all. If you know what I mean . . .'

I wasn't sure that I did, but I nodded sagely and drank some
more of the disgusting tea. I was thinking about the phrasing
of a question that might produce some clarification when the
switchboard started buzzing like a demented bluebottle and
another elderly messenger, breathless from the two flights of
stairs, coughed and spluttered his way in.

Daphne raised her eyebrows in resigned exasperation, shook
her head and mouthed, 'Here we go again,' and turned her
attention to the switchboard.

I nodded at her, put my unfinished cup of tea back on the
tray behind her and left.

Les and Daphne had been divorced for nine years now,
and I'd often wondered why they continued to work together.
I could see it from his point of view. She had always done
his accounts, so she knew where the bodies were buried.
I've always assumed that he rather took the view that it was,
as the saying goes, better to have her on the inside pissing
out, than on the outside pissing in. So he retained his book-
keeper and his secrets. It's possible that he liked having her
around as a reminder, a sort of conscience, but that's getting
into deep water and I'm not competent to swim there.
What she gets out of it, I don't know. Though, on reflection, she does slyly undercut his authority just by being
there. Maybe that's enough. And it's always possible that
she enjoys the job.

I pondered the mystery of Daphne and Les Jackson as I
wandered down Wardour Street. It was warm, and I started
to sweat a bit in my wool suit.

The cabbie muttered under his breath throughout the journey
and smoked Player's Weights constantly. I couldn't hear what
he said and so wasn't sure that his comments were directed
at me, but I decided to act as though they were and tip
accordingly.

He had a lugubrious, leathery face with moist brown eyes
and permanent five o'clock shadow, and he looked as hurt as
if I'd just sworn in front of his sainted mother when I handed
him the exact fare. He stared at the coins in his hand before

saying something very choice under his breath and driving off in a cloud of black exhaust.

I watched him go and then looked at my surroundings. It was a busy street and, if it had suffered during the war, all the damage had long since been tidied up. But there were no interruptions to the terraces, no grassy bomb-sites preparing to blossom in the London spring, so I guessed the road had escaped any direct hits.

The house I was outside was a big one. It was a bit run-down, and the woodwork was in need of a lick of paint, but the steps leading up to the front door and the downstairs windows all looked clean, and the small front yard was tidy enough.

The woman who opened the door could have stepped out of an Ealing Studios film. She probably wasn't any older than me, and she was still attractive in a worn, world-weary way. A long war and a hard life had obviously taken their toll, but she had a lean, trim figure and slim legs. She was wearing a white apron over a brown skirt and a short-sleeved green blouse, and she had covered the curlers in her hair with a flimsy scarf.

I said I was Jonathan Harrison's uncle and asked if he was there. She said nothing and didn't look as if she believed me. I added that his sister was worried about him.

'He owes me money,' she said and folded her arms across her ample bosom, a what-do-you-think-of-that expression on her face. I didn't think much of it.

'I'm sure we can sort something out.'

She looked as unimpressed with that as I'd been with her attempt to extort money.

'Can I see his room?' I said. 'He may have left some indication of where he's gone . . . The sooner I can find him, the sooner we can resolve any financial problems . . .'

We stood there in silence while she weighed up the pros and cons of being obdurate. I wasn't sure if I was prepared to force the issue. Her hands were big and red, and she had powerful forearms. She'd probably manage to slam the door before I could get a shoulder against it. Then inspiration struck, and I handed her one of my fancy cards. She looked at it sceptically for a few seconds and then it worked its magic. It was obviously rather more impressive than me because she opened the door a little wider and allowed me in. Perhaps she didn't notice the E10 address.

She took me up to the top floor and pointed at a door on the left. It wasn't locked.

She was standing outside, her impressive arms resolutely folded, when I came out.

'Do you have a telephone?' I said.

'No,' she said. 'There's one on the corner.'

'Well, perhaps you'd be kind enough to go along there and call the police,' I said. 'Tell them there's been a suspicious death.'

'Suspicious death?' she said.

I nodded. That was one way of putting it.

SIX

Garrotting someone isn't easy. It takes strength, technique and a ruthlessness most of us, thank God, lack. The victim fights back, desperately, and if he's stronger and better trained than the would-be murderer that can be a problem.

Richard Ellis, however, hadn't been particularly strong, and I rather doubted that he'd been trained in anything more lethal than pillow fighting in the school dorm. In any case, his murderer hadn't really given him a chance. He'd used a cruelly thin length of wire with sturdy wooden handles lashed to each end, rather like the implement a grocer uses to cut pieces from a slab of Cheddar, and had probably taken Richard completely by surprise.

Cheese, though, might crumble a bit and sweat, but it doesn't bleed.

Poor Richard hadn't been garrotted so much as almost decapitated. The wire had severed just about everything through to the spine, and the wire was still embedded in the purplish, torn and ragged flesh. The two wooden handles were dangling off each of his shoulders, bobbing slightly in a gentle draft, like fishing floats on a placid stream.

And, unlike a mature Cheddar, Richard had bled – a lot.

The room smelt like a slaughterhouse. The armchair Richard was slumped in and the carpet round about were sodden and dark with blood. Some had sprayed up one wall, presumably when one of his arteries was cut.

I managed to dissuade Mrs Elvin – Rosemary (we'd introduced ourselves properly on the way up the stairs) – from entering the room to see for herself, and she agreed that it was probably best if I stayed outside the room, to stop anyone else going in, while she telephoned the police. We then sat in the kitchen, drinking tea, while we waited for them.

While she'd been gone, I'd taken the opportunity to look around. But all I could do was look, as I didn't want to tread in blood or touch anything. So I stood just inside the door, handkerchief clutched to my face against the thick, cloying smell. I learnt very little, except that Jonathan Harrison wasn't there – and Richard Ellis had told me that the night before.

It was the kind of place far too many working men fell into after the pubs chucked out: a gloomy, depressing room with heavy brown curtains drawn across the one window. It was somewhere you slept. You didn't live there. There were two unmade beds along opposite walls, two battered armchairs, one occupied by Richard Ellis's body, a table and two wooden chairs. Apart from a small pile of books on the table, two white shirts, a striped tie and a jacket lying on one of the beds and a pair of brown shoes next to it, that was about it. The tie and the jacket looked like the ones Richard had been wearing in the club. Since he wasn't wearing any shoes, I guessed that they were his too.

It had been quite a while since I'd been this close to anyone who had died a violent death, and I noticed that the hand holding the handkerchief was trembling. I closed my eyes and imagined the wire biting into flesh.

Only, I didn't have to imagine it. I could remember it very clearly.

The victim then had been a boy too: a boy in a uniform.

The idea had been that it would be quick and silent: a loop of wire around the neck would stop him crying out. And it had. But it hadn't stopped him emptying his bowels or dropping his rifle on cobble stones or hammering and scuffing his boots on the ground and against the shins of the man behind him as he sawed through his throat. Nor had it stopped the heavy, rasping breaths and grunts of the assailant's exertions. Not silent at all. And not very quick either.

When I'd heard the front door bang, I'd opened my eyes and realized that Mrs Elvin had come back. I'd left the room and quietly shut the door behind me. The offer of tea had been very welcome. I had even sugared it liberally. I recognized that I was in mild shock.

New Scotland Yard isn't all it's cracked up to be. If you squinted out of the window in the office where Rosemary and I waited, you could just see the sun streak the slug-coloured Thames with some oily colour. But, apart from a brief glimpse as we'd driven over Westminster Bridge in the comfortable old police car, I hadn't seen the tower of Big Ben or the Houses of Parliament.

And the office itself looked as if it hadn't changed much in the sixty-odd years since it opened. The brown walls couldn't have been painted more than once since then, and the window hadn't been caressed by a shammy in a while. The wooden chairs reminded me of those I'd sat in at Sunday School when I was a kid. In those days, of course, my feet had dangled a long way from the floor. Now, they were firmly planted on the drab lino. The dark-brown seats of the chairs had all been worn to a dirty yellow by the countless bums that had rubbed across them. I wondered if any famous felons had ever sat on mine.

We were given more tea, sugary Nice biscuits and left to ourselves for an hour, which gave me a chance to discover everything Rosemary knew Jonathan.

She turned out to be nowhere near as hardbitten as I'd thought. She was rather sweet and more vulnerable than she appeared. Her big, work-hardened hands worried away at each other constantly, and she kept seeking my reassurance that she'd be allowed back into her home and continually asking me what her other tenant would do when he came home from work. I couldn't offer much, apart from bland platitudes about how sure I was that it would all be all right. Which I wasn't, not least because I was going to have a hard time explaining my own involvement.

Still, in between the pointless reassurance, I managed to keep her talking about Jonathan and Richard. But the big hands kept rubbing and scratching at each other, occasionally making forays upwards to pat at her hair. In fact, she couldn't tell me very much about the boys. They hadn't actually rented the place themselves, it seems. An older man had done that. He'd paid two weeks' rent in advance and a small deposit. He'd given his name as Jenkins and an address in Cambridge. He'd been 'ever so well spoken', a big man, conservatively dressed in black jacket and striped trousers and had worn a bowler hat. (A fleeting memory of Ghislaine when I'd first met her crossed my mind. Where, she'd asked, was my '*chapeau melon*'?) Rosemary had seen him again on the first day that 'the gentlemen' had been with her, but not since. And she hadn't seen or heard anything suspicious the previous night. But she had been in the snug bar at the Red Lion with her friend Florrie and had drunk three port and lemons and so had slept 'soundly'.

Well after three, a painfully thin inspector came in briefly to apologize for keeping us waiting. He said his name was Rose. He was wearing a blue bow-tie, the colour of speed-well. It matched his eyes and stood out from his sombre suit.

Ten minutes later Rosemary was summoned by a much chubbier man. I tried to imagine a police interview conducted by Laurel and Hardy, but my heart wasn't in it and, instead, I carefully considered what to tell them. I decided that it would be very risky to lie or mislead them. Les wouldn't be happy about my dragging Beverley Beaumont and the studio into it, but I didn't think I had any option. This was a murder, and if I wasn't already a suspect, I would be just as soon as they suspected me of telling fibs. The Imperial Club wouldn't be happy with me either, but I thought I could probably live with that. Anyway, the police would have made the connection sooner or later.

It seemed that I'd only been ruminating for a few minutes when I was called in.

I followed the portly detective sergeant – he'd introduced himself as Radcliffe – along a gloomy corridor to Inspector Rose's office. I was offered another worn, wooden seat and then the inspector asked why I'd chosen that day to seek out my nephew. I launched into a long explanation. And I told the truth.

There was just one thing I didn't volunteer. I felt no guilt about not saying anything because I didn't regard it as relevant. I said nothing about my knowledge of the use of the garrotte, learnt during the war. It would only have raised unfounded suspicions.

Consequently, the interview was all very sombre and rather dull. If Inspector Rose or Sergeant Radcliffe thought I'd murdered Richard Ellis they gave no indication of it. They seemed tired and bored rather than hostile. Radcliffe perked up and grinned at the mention of Beverley Beaumont but, apart from that and a few frowns when the Imperial Club came into things, neither of them betrayed any feelings at all. After twenty minutes of uninspired questions, I was asked to write out a statement. It was eighteen years since I'd written a school essay, and I was so out of practice that it took me another half hour. Inspector Rose read it, suggested a couple of changes and then I was free to go.

It had just gone five and Victoria Embankment was full of people hurrying to the Underground or rushing to catch buses. They were all very drab in their dark wool clothes, and a thin, low, very English sun glinted off the water and glanced off the grey concrete blocks and plate glass of the Royal Festival Hall on the opposite bank. The only flashes of colour came from the red buses. The river gave off a slightly unpleasant odour, a bit like an old, damp dog, and I turned away from it as soon as I could.

I knew that I was depressed and still mildly shocked from the discovery of the body, but London seemed unusually dull, ugly and unpleasantly noisy.

I marched up Whitehall, across Trafalgar Square and along Charing Cross Road, trying to dispel the dark mood that was threatening. As I approached Old Compton Street, it occurred to me that it would be a kindness to tell Roger the barman in the Imperial to expect a visit from the Old Bill. But, first, I thought I'd better tell Les Jackson the good news that I was off the case and the rozzers were on it. He'd probably sack me on the spot. I might just catch him, if he was still in the office and hadn't left early to go off somewhere to bang his new secretary, so I turned smartly left towards Wardour Street.

Daphne was still at her desk, still smoking and, judging by the colour and consistency of it, still drinking the same cup of tea.

'There's someone with him,' she said.

I shoved a pile of cheap, brown envelopes from one end of the mud-coloured sofa and slumped down into it.

'You look a bit rough,' she said. 'Want a cuppa?'

'No thanks, Daff,' I said, 'I've got tea coming out me ears. Any more and I could rent myself out as an urn.'

'Just so long as I don't have to fiddle with the spigot,' she said and turned back to the big Burroughs adding machine on her desk.

There was something oddly comforting about the banality of Daphne pecking away at her accounts, puffing on her fortieth

fag of the day, swilling her eleventh cup of tea while the faint
sounds of office life murmured all around us.

Most people – the secretaries and clerks – had already left,
so there was no pounding of typewriters, no tinkling of bells
as carriages returned, but the film industry isn't quite as nine
to five as a bank, and Hoxton's offices include an editing suite
where films are often worked on well into the early hours, so
there was still a certain amount of coming and going. I wasn't
sure that there was much point in the press office writing and
sending out releases, with the newspaper strike still going on,
but the *Manchester Guardian* was publishing and there were
probably some underemployed journalists around with time
on their hands and a thirst, literal and metaphorical, that needed
to be slaked. So I suppose there was still work to be done.

I sat for a few minutes just listening to the reassuring hum
of ordinary life.

Violent death was not something I'd ever got used to. I'd
seen my share during the war, and it always upset me. It was
messy and sudden. Everyone developed a different strategy
for dealing with it. There were even a few disturbing indi-
viduals who enjoyed it. Robert Rieux had been one of them.

I'd always become a little introverted after seeing action
and try to sit quietly for a while. Robert couldn't understand
this and went out of his way to disturb me, insisting on noisy
drinking bouts or more unnecessary but extremely tense
scouting activity.

Oddly, I always feel the same way after playing football. I
sit for a few minutes, listening to everyone else splashing about
in the bath. It means that the water is filthy by the time I
immerse myself, and I'm always the last one out of the dressing
room, but it gives me a chance to think through what's
happened. I've always consoled myself with the thought that
bathing in scummy water is probably no worse than sharing
the bath with twenty-odd men who think the height of sophisticated humour is releasing little bubbling farts. Not that I'm
that fastidious. If I were, I'd look for a football team with
changing facilities that include showers.

'How long's he going to be, Daff?' I said.

'God knows. It's a potential investor. Well, I assume it is.
He had me producing figures most of the afternoon. Production
costs, profit margins and all on a couple of pictures chosen

at random.' She snorted derisively. '"Chosen at random", my Aunt Fanny.' She swallowed tea. 'The two most successful films we've ever made.'

'Can I make a telephone call?'

'Sure you can, Tone. Here, use this one.'

She stabbed a plug into a socket and when I picked up the big, black receiver it purred in my ear like Fluffy after a fish tea. Fortunately, it didn't smell as bad.

I dialled very carefully, and Jerry picked up on the fifth ring. Louis Armstrong and Sidney Bechet were blending beautifully in the background.

'"Perdido Street Blues",' I said.

'Of course, Tony. I'm glad you phoned. There are a couple of messages for you. A Dr Jameson called this afternoon. And a Detective Inspector Rose about ten minutes ago. Would you be so kind as to call them? Tomorrow's fine for the policeman. What you been up to? I assume it can't be too bad as you don't appear to be in custody.'

'I'll tell you later, Jerry. Could you give Ghislaine a yell? I'd like a word.'

'Sorry, Tony. She went out about half an hour ago. A couple of people turned up for her, and she left with them.'

'What?' I said. 'Who?'

'How would I know?' he said. 'I just popped out for fifteen minutes, to pick up a pair of shoes from the mender, and I got back in time to see them leave in the car.'

'What car?' I said just as the door to the left of Daphne's reception area opened and Les appeared with a tall, silver-haired gent in standard City clothes of black jacket and striped trousers. He was carrying a tightly furled umbrella and a bowler hat.

'The car that was parked outside,' Jerry said. 'It was black and looked new. Well, it was quite shiny.' Jerry knew and cared less about cars than the average Girl Guide.

'OK,' I said, watching Les shake hands perfunctorily with the City gent as Charlie Lomax appeared and led him down the stairs. 'I'd better go.'

Les wasn't looking as pleased as he might be. Maybe the meeting hadn't gone well.

'Les,' I said, 'I really need a word.' Worrying about Ghislaine would just have to wait for a few minutes.

Les waved me through to his office.

'Who was that?' I asked as I sat opposite him.

'A potential business associate,' he said offhandedly.

'Not called Jenkins by any chance, is he?' The name just popped into my head.

'Of course it is,' he said, which puzzled me, but, before I could say anything, he changed the subject. 'So, what's so important that you turn up after hours? More exes?'

'No,' I said, 'the Beverley Beaumont thing – it's taken a very nasty turn.'

I told him everything, and this time he didn't show any surprise.

'I understand your position, Tony,' he said, 'what with a police murder enquiry and everything, but I'd appreciate you still looking. Discreetly. I wouldn't want you implicated. I know Miss Beaumont would be very grateful. So would I.' He rubbed his thumb against his fingers in a universal gesture.

'I don't know, Les. This is all a bit deep. The kid's involved in something.'

'Exactly, Tony, exactly. That means Miss Beaumont and the studio could be dragged into it too. Forewarned is fore-armed, Tony, and a man of your calyber is just the one to warn us.' He stood up to indicate that the discussion was at an end.

'All right,' I said. 'I'll do what I can, but I'm not going to stick my neck out.'

'No one expects you to, Tony.' He sniffed. 'And I really will be grateful. I'll arrange for a something special in this month's pay packet.' He held his hand out, and I shook it and turned to leave. When I reached the door, he called to me, 'Here, take this. There's a party tomorrow night. Bring someone. It'll be glitzy. We've just finished *Death in the Desert*, Jimmy Bolt's first war film. Right up your street – the Desert Rats and all that. We're having a screening tomorrow afternoon and then drinks in the evening. The stars'll be there.' He paused. 'Miss Beaumont isn't in this one, but I can persuade her to come . . .' He winked at me and held out a thick piece of card.

I took the printed invitation, glanced at it and smiled at him. 'Thanks, Les. Don't think I'll make it to the screening though. I'm going to be busy.'

I left the office and tapped the invitation against my chin. Les Jackson was by no means a parsimonious man, but the promise of 'something special' was unusual.

'A penny for 'em,' Daphne said.

'I think they may be worth more than that, Daff,' I said.

'Don't flatter yourself,' she said.

I slipped the invitation into my pocket and smiled at her. I'd just thought of something. 'Must go, Daff,' I said, moving to the door. 'I've got to see a man about a dog.' Well, not a dog exactly. More, see a man about a man. Ghislaine would have to wait.

And I desperately needed to force some pie and mash down me neck. I was starving.

SEVEN

Charlie Lomax usually parked the Roller in one of the grubby little side roads that ran between Wardour Street and Berwick Street. He said that he felt uncomfortable with the car on a main road where it could so easily be scratched. There was an element of truth in that but, since he tended to sit it just outside a quiet pub where he could keep an eye on it while he sipped a glass of Mackeson's, that wasn't all there was to it.

Charlie's little vice was an open secret but, as he invariably restricted himself to two glasses between twelve and two and another two a little after six, no one – and certainly not Les – felt compelled to mention the matter.

Well, that's not strictly true. Daphne had been known refer to it, but, because Charlie ferried Les to and from his various liaisons, she regarded him as complicit in her ex-husband's assorted peccadilloes, and that made him fair game.

It was just after six so the Rose and Crown had opened, though the interior was so dim that it was difficult to tell. The Roller wasn't to be seen, which meant that Charlie hadn't got back yet. I stood on the pavement, kicking at some litter, hoping that Charlie's posh passenger didn't live in Amersham or Harrow.

The market had closed a while before, but the earthy smell of decaying vegetables still drifted on the warm, evening wind and a few wooden crates had been tossed into a pile at the Berwick Street end of the road.

After a few minutes of waiting, I realized that I could use the time profitably and strolled off to the telephone box there. I trod carefully through the market debris piled around it – the slimy cabbage leaves, an orange with a delicate dusting of pale mould and a broken wooden crate – and rummaged in my pocket for some coppers, and then in my wallet for the sheet of paper David Jameson had written his telephone number on. The smell of ripe fruit in the box was very strong, which was just as well. Someone had mistaken it for a urinal in the recent past.

I dialled the operator and then waited patiently while she connected me. After ringing plaintively ten or more times, the college telephone was eventually answered by someone who sounded rather like the old drill sergeant who had yelled at me so ineffectively back in basic training.

Well, I thought, as I waited for Jameson, drill sergeants had to do something when they were too old to be useful to the army. And standing in the porter's lodge at some college barking at students seemed harmless compared to the damage they had done to the more vulnerable and less coordinated recruits. If it was the same vindictive old bastard, he'd probably be obsequious to all the senior members of the college. He'd certainly fawned over every officer in sight. (As my new-found mate at the time, Bernie Rosen, had said, 'So far up the CO's bum, all you can see are the hobnails in his boots.')

Eventually, David Jameson came on the line. 'Mr Gérard, thank you so much for calling.'

'That's all right,' I said. 'What can I do for you?'

'Well, it's more a matter of my having some information for you. According to one of the college servants, Jonathan Harrison came back to Cambridge yesterday. All he did was collect his post and leave: some letters and two small packages. A car delivered him and took him away. No details, except it was black and rather small.' He gave a little muffled cough, which could have been a half-hearted chuckle. 'College servants are snobbish about cars. If it's not a Bentley, they don't recognize it. I know that's not a lot of help, but it's all I have.'

'Thanks,' I said, 'it's more than I've come up with.' I decided not to tell him about Richard Ellis's murder. I don't know why. I guess I just didn't want to upset him. That was a job for the police. They're rather good at it.

'Oh,' he said, 'by the way, I'd take a little care with Madame Rieux. Monsieur Rieux is a powerful man with a long reach. I also have the impression that he wouldn't smile on his wife, erm, playing around.'

'Thanks,' I said, 'I appreciate the warning, but it isn't necessary. Robert and I have locked horns in the past. And Ghislaine and I are not, as you put it, playing around.'

'All the same,' he said. 'He's no respecter of borders, or facts, now that I think about it. He'll come after her.'

'I know,' I said.

'I just thought I'd mention it.'

'Thanks, again. I'm sorry. I don't mean to sound graceless. It's just that I know Robert and what he's capable of. Probably better than most.' He grunted something that sounded a bit dismissive. 'I'll be in touch if anything occurs and I find Jonathan.'

'Thanks,' he said abruptly and cut the connection.

I saw the Rolls-Royce turn into the street and glide almost silently to a halt outside the apparently deserted pub, still giving its world famous impression of the *Marie Céleste*. I caught up with Charlie before he opened the door to the public bar.

'Tone!' he said. 'Good to see you.'

'And you, Charlie. Listen, I need some information. That bloke you showed out a little while back, Mr Jenkins, the City gent with the silver hair and the bowler, did you take him somewhere?'

'Sure. The governor said he was very important and I was to look after him. And he is a gent. He slipped me five bob.'

'Where did you drop him off?'

'One of them St James's clubs.' He looked up at the ratty old pub sign, seeking inspiration. 'The Royal something.' He paused. 'The Royal Commonwealth Club.'

'Thanks, Charlie. Not a word to the governor, OK?'

'OK, Tone, if you say so.'

'Charlie, you're a wonder. I owe you. Now, where is this place?'

'I can't exactly give you the address, Tone. It's in one of them little roads that doesn't go anywhere, behind Piccadilly, just off St James's Street, by Green Park. He directed me there. I'll tell you what. The governor doesn't want me for an hour or so. I'll drop you off there, if you like.'

I was in the front passenger seat before Charlie had finished speaking. When he climbed behind the wheel I smiled at him. 'The Royal Commonwealth Club, James,' I said in my best BBC accent.

Charlie grinned and put his right index finger to his brow.

*   *   *

It's the only way to travel. And it's certainly the only way to arrive at a posh St James's club.

Even if the doorman was nonplussed by the fact that my suit and tie were more Montague Burton than Savile Row, he recognized a near-vintage Rolls-Royce when he saw one, and so was considerably more circumspect than he might have been if I had rolled up on an old green Raleigh bike. The fact that Charlie got out and opened the door to the Roller for me probably helped.

And, of course, it wasn't that long since Mr Jenkins had arrived in the same vehicle.

Charlie, ever helpful, gave me a big wink on the blindside of the doorman as he closed the car door. 'Would you like me to wait, Mr Gérard, sir?'

I nodded in a suitably imperious manner.

'Very good, sir. I'll be just round the corner in St James's Street,' he said, lifting his right index finger to his temple and then rolling smartly back behind the wheel.

The interior of the club wasn't quite as grand as I'd been expecting, but then I had no experience of St James's clubs to speak of and so had only the vaguest notion of what awaited me. It was all a bit obvious, really – lots of polished wood, a high ceiling built to echo back the quietest of whispers, the inevitable wide, sweeping staircase and an atmosphere of hushed deference – very much the clichéd gentleman's club of the films. There was even a brown sofa against the wall behind me, the hard leather cracked at the edges and comfortably worn. But the carpet that led along the hallway to the staircase was threadbare, and even in the dim light from the dusty chandelier I could see that the place needed a coat of paint nearly as much as my office.

I stood at the concierge's desk, sweating a little and feeling very self-conscious.

Eventually, a small, straight-shouldered man with a neatly trimmed grey moustache marched out of the little cupboard-sized room behind the desk, straightening his uniform.

'Can I help you, sir?' he said briskly, pulling at a frayed cuff.

It seemed that the officer class, even out of uniform and in peacetime, still found it useful to have NCOs around to keep the hoi polloi at bay. I cleared my throat and prepared to do battle with my second pensioned-off sergeant of the evening.

'I'd like to see Mr Jenkins, please,' I said. 'Could you tell him I'm here?'

'Who shall say is asking for him?' he said, picking up the receiver of his telephone.

'Tony Gérard,' I said.

'Is he expecting you?' he said.

'Er, no,' I said as nonchalantly as I could manage.

He firmly replaced the receiver. 'I'm afraid, sir, that Mr Jenkins left specific instructions that he is not to be disturbed.' I recognized the tone. There was firmness there, but with just the hint of regret, implying that it might be possible that those instructions could be forgotten.

'That's unfortunate,' I said, conscious that I was trying to sound much posher that I am and failing by a nautical mile. 'I've come a long way. Perhaps you could tell him that I'm here and I'd like to talk to him.' I slid two half crowns across the counter.

The expression on his face didn't change as he smoothly pocketed the coins and picked up the receiver again in one fluid and well-practised movement. 'Very well, sir. What is it regarding?'

'Tell him it's about a mutual acquaintance,' I said.

He spoke into the telephone with his back towards me. He apologized and explained that I'd said it was very urgent. Then he listened before ending the call with a decidedly servile, 'Very well, sir.' He turned back to me. 'Mr Jenkins will be down shortly, sir. Would you care to take a seat?' He indicated the old sofa by the wall.

I looked towards it and nodded at him as offhandedly as I could manage. Then I sauntered over and sat. Sweat was trickling from my armpits and the back of my neck was prickling uncomfortably. Either the place was seriously overheated or I was out of my depth and worried.

Jenkins didn't appear for some minutes. Then, suddenly and, it seemed, out of nowhere, he was looming over me, blocking out the light from the chandelier. He was wearing a dinner suit and black bow-tie and carrying a dark raincoat and a black hat.

'Mr Gérard,' he said, pronouncing my name correctly, with acute accent and all. He did not, however, offer his hand.

I stood up and didn't see any point in offering mine.

He was a tall, slim, good-looking man in the Anthony Eden vein, with slicked-back silver hair and strong, regular, patrician features. I wondered if he might be a Conservative politician. He must have been at least a major in the war.

He looked across at the concierge. 'Sergeant Metcalf,' he said, 'I wonder if you would be so good as to open up the snug bar for –' he glanced down at the wristwatch that slid out from beneath his snowy cuff – 'ten minutes.'

He didn't wait for a reply, but walked towards the staircase and turned sharply right, stopping at a big, dark-oak door.

I followed dutifully, and Sergeant Metcalf came scurrying along behind.

'Be so kind as to pour us two brandies and soda, Sergeant Metcalf,' Jenkins said as the good sergeant fussed with the key.

'Very good, sir,' Metcalf said, opening the door to a dark, wood-panelled, musty room that reeked of stale cigar smoke. He flicked a switch and a globe set in the centre of the ceiling gave off a sickly, yellowish light.

Jenkins sat at a small table in an uncomfortable-looking wooden chair, carefully folding his raincoat and placing it next him. He perched his hat – a rather natty homburg – on top. I plonked myself down opposite him. The chair was, indeed, as bone-jarringly unpleasant to sit on as I'd suspected. I heard the swish of soda as it gushed into a glass and then Metcalf appeared with a tray.

'I would be very grateful, Sergeant,' Jenkins said, without looking at him and absent-mindedly signing the chit on the tray, 'if you would make sure that I'm not disturbed.' He didn't add 'this time', but we all knew it wasn't necessary, and Metcalf, duly rebuked, left, only marginally comforted by the five bob clinking in his pocket. It would take a crisp ten-shilling note to get past him the next time.

'I was told that you are a resourceful man, Mr Gérard,' Jenkins said, picking up his brandy. 'But I didn't think you'd find me quite as quickly as you have.'

'It wasn't that difficult,' I said.

He raised his impressively unruly eyebrows.

'Anyway,' I said, 'who told you about me?'

He twitched the thin, insincere, politician's smile at me again. 'A mutual acquaintance,' he said, looking at his watch.

'I'm afraid that I don't have long,' he said, taking a packet of Dunhill cigarettes out of the inside pocket of his jacket and putting it on the table, 'but I will explain as much to you as I'm going to, and then I'm going to ask you, politely, to step away from the situation that we all seem to find ourselves in.' He paused and fiddled with the Dunhills without taking one out of the pack. 'And I should make it clear that when I say "ask", I don't really mean that.'

We both drank deeply.

'You clearly have no idea what's going on,' he said. 'Do you?'

I was tempted to lay claim to some knowledge just to dent his self-esteem briefly, but I shook my head lamely instead.

'Good,' he said, 'and I have no intention of enlightening you. I'm just going to tell you that the boy you've been asking about is mixed up in some pretty sticky business, involving all sorts of unsavoury people. I'm not saying that we've got everything under control, but we do know what we're doing, and you galumphing around is not going to help matters. You are muddying the waters in what is a very sensitive case for us. There's a lot of discreet surveillance involved, and we can't have you drawing attention to us. Do I make myself clear?'

I didn't see how I was drawing attention to whoever he represented, but I nodded my agreement. A certain tension left him, and he looked almost relieved. He nearly gave me a genuine smile.

'Good,' he said, leaning back in his chair and visibly relaxing. He finished his brandy and regarded me benignly. 'We won't be ungrateful for your cooperation, and we can always make use of someone like you. Let me know where we can contact you.'

And he'd been doing so well. I'd been completely convinced: the St James's club and the patrician manner had whispered Intelligence and Secret Service at me. But now I wasn't so sure.

'You can get hold of me via Hoxton Films,' I said. 'The Wardour Street office.'

'Good,' he purred again and stood up. 'Now, if you'll forgive me . . .'

I stood up too. 'Thank you for your time,' I said thoughtfully. 'I appreciate you taking the trouble.'

'Not at all,' he said and ushered me out of the room.

Charlie and the Rolls were just where he'd said they'd be – in St James's Street, outside Berry Bros and Rudd, facing the palace.

The wide, elegant street seemed eerily deserted and quiet, and I was conscience of my footfall echoing unnaturally loudly in the warm and slightly humid night air. It was just a lull in the traffic, of course, but the silence seemed vaguely threatening, and I turned around to see if there was anyone behind me. There wasn't, but, almost lost in the shadowy gloom of the corner of the little cul-de-sac I'd just left, the imposing, dark figure of Jenkins, now wearing his hat and coat, was watching me.

EIGHT

Charlie kept apologizing for only having the time to drive me to Tottenham Court Road Underground Station. He also told me why he'd wanted to see me on Friday. He was sure that Daphne wanted Les to sack him, and he asked me to put in a good word for him.

I was only half listening, but I promised I'd speak to Les. My mind was on other things.

When he dropped me off on the corner of Oxford Street and Charing Cross Road, I was a little relieved, especially when he said that he was glad we'd had a chance to talk as he couldn't make it on Friday for a pint after all. Les wanted him all day, Good Friday or not, and Charlie didn't think it was in his best interests to argue the toss.

As he pulled away and drove along Oxford Street, a twinge of guilt had me feeling a little wretched. I didn't know what Les was planning but, clearly, Charlie was worried, and I should have been more sympathetic. I was fond of the old bugger. He'd always done right by me. I decided to make good my promise to him at the first opportunity. He deserved better from me than casual indifference.

I suddenly remembered someone else who deserved better and abandoned my plans to head for home.

As I walked back down Charing Cross Road, bleak visions of Richard Ellis's body mingled uneasily with memories of the war.

My only two, official, encounters with Military Intelligence had not gone well. They hadn't ended in tears exactly, but that was only because soldiers don't cry in front of officers, even in frustration. Officers don't respond well to any hint of intelligence, free-will or passion, and even the newest of recruits knows better than to upset them.

The first occasion had degenerated into a straightforward shouting match with a pig-ignorant major with a clipped moustache, clipped accent and, as far as I could make out, a seriously clipped brain. He had briefed me on a new set of objectives. He had then told me exactly how my team was going to proceed. I told him, politely, that I didn't have a team, the team was Robert's, and Robert had his own set of objectives. He looked me up and down, told me that I was a disgrace to the uniform (which I wasn't wearing, and nor was he for that matter) and repeated his instructions. I told him what I'd told him before, enunciating it slowly and clearly. He accused me of being insolent, and I suggested that he didn't know his arse from his elbow. A short silence was followed by his announcement that he was putting me on a charge. I told him he could stick his charge up his elbow. For some reason, this failed to amuse him. He told me that orders were orders and I couldn't pick and choose. Then he put me on another charge and we started shouting.

The charges never materialized because he didn't make it back to London. I never did discover whether the Germans got him or if one of the other groups he had treated with the same arrogance and tactlessness he had shown to ours was a bit less forgiving than we'd been. When Big Luc, Robert's lieutenant, had told me that he would not be bothering us again, as he was drinking pink gins with all the other red-faced colonials in the afterlife, I didn't ask what had happened to him. I didn't want to be burdened with the knowledge.

Funnily enough, I still remember his name: Major Griffiths. I suppose that's because he taught me some important lessons. The first was that, when dealing with any branch of the military, dumb insolence is more effective than any other kind. And the second was that the intelligence in Military Intelligence is not always as apparent as the military. The final thing I learnt from the skirmish is that Military Intelligence tells you what to do: it doesn't try to bribe you with the prospect of future employment. And neither does Special Branch. If they want you to work for them, they tell you.

I would hope that the personnel are more suave these days than Griffiths, but the message that Jenkins, had he been in Military Intelligence or Special Branch, would have wished to impart would have been very simple. Stay out. Or else.

I was still brooding when I turned into Old Compton Street, and the gloomy, musty staircase and landing of the Imperial Club did nothing for my wilted *joie de vivre*.

The place had that quiet, expectant air of somewhere that

expected things to happen later when I stood at the entrance
and fumbled for my membership card. Connie yawned languidly
and asked after Jerry – at least I assumed it was Jerry, although
I suppose the description 'gorgeous little tart' could have fitted
Ghislaine. I told her I'd bring Jerry along next time. She didn't
look convinced. I wasn't sure if she thought there was unlikely
to be a next time or that I was keeping Jerry to myself.

Roger the barman wasn't quite in splendid isolation, but it
was close. There were two men knocking billiard balls about
in the further room. The satisfyingly restful click as one ball
kissed another hovered in the air. And there was one, slightly
seedy gent, almost lost in the shadows at the back of the room,
sipping gin, who looked up optimistically when I entered, but
resumed his slumped posture and air of disappointed resig-
nation as soon as he registered that I was as careworn and
nearly as old as he. Only his eyes showed any animation as
he glanced furtively at the door.

The place looked decidedly dusty and down-at-heel.

Roger bustled over as soon as I reached the bar. He leaned
over the counter, looked around as furtively as the old queer
in the shadows and pursed his lips. 'Got a message for you,'
he whispered in a stage whisper that could have been heard
in the Talk of the Town and pushed a card across the counter.

I read it quickly and then slipped it into my pocket. At least
one of the worries nagging at me was no longer a problem.

'I've got a message for you as well,' I said. 'Expect a visit
from Scotland Yard's finest.' And I told him about Richard
Ellis, as economically and with as little detail as possible. I
didn't describe how he'd died.

He looked thoughtful, but didn't ask any questions.

'The message,' I said, 'when was it left?'

'Oh,' he said, 'fifteen, twenty minutes ago. She was waiting
on the pavement outside when I popped out for a breath.'

'You can't point me at a decent fish and chip shop, can
you?' I said.

'Round here? The nearest decent one I know is in Notting
Hill. Geal's.'

'Missed my dinner,' I said.

He looked around again, making sure no one was taking
any interest.

'Tell you what,' he said, 'I've got a couple of pork pies in the back. For emergencies. You can have one of those, if you like. And some pickled onions.'

'Roger,' I said, 'you're a life-saver.'

'Here to serve,' he said and went off into his little store room.

'If you could find a halfway decent glass of Burgundy to go with it,' I called after him, 'I'd be in your debt for ever.'

'I said I was here to serve,' he said over his shoulder. 'I didn't say I could work bloody miracles.'

However, he reappeared a minute or two later, carrying a plate with a pie on it in one hand and a bottle in the other.

'Never let it be said that Roger disappoints,' he said. 'It's not Burgundy. Well, I don't think it is. But it is wine.'

Warm Riesling has never been my idea of heaven, but it did an adequate job of washing the dry, tasteless pie down and taking the sting out of the pickled onion.

I reached into my pocket after I'd wolfed the little meal down.

Roger shook his head. 'On the house,' he said dismissively.

After a couple of seconds, I realized I'd probably just eaten his supper.

'That's very decent of you,' I said awkwardly. 'I owe you.'

'No you don't,' he said, busying himself behind the bar and not looking at me. 'Thanks for the warning about our friends in blue. I appreciate it.' Then he did look up. 'A word to the wise,' he said. 'Steer clear of David Cavendish.'

'Oh, right,' I said. I'd forgotten all about him. 'What's his quarrel with me?'

'Who knows?' Roger said. 'But he's a vicious little so-and-so. I'd give him a wide berth.'

'Thanks,' I said. 'I will. Who is he, anyway?'

Roger shrugged. 'Works in the theatre, I think,' he said. 'Management or something.'

'Thanks for the advice,' I said.

Ghislaine, as she'd said in her note, was in the French, sat at the bar, talking to a young boy I immediately recognized.

He was nowhere near as solemn as he appeared in the photograph, and he was a lot more good-looking. Charming, too, if Ghislaine's response to him was anything to go by. She was leaning very close to him, and she touched his arm from time to time. I stood by the door and watched them through the crowd for a few seconds.

Ghislaine smiled when I bustled my way through and put my hand gently on her shoulder.

'Antoine, this is Jon. He came to your house this afternoon, looking for you. I didn't know where you were, so we came to find you,' she said. She was beaming and animated. There was something intoxicating about the company. She picked up her cigarette from the ashtray on the bar and drew on it languidly with her eyes half-closed against the thin curl of smoke that trickled out of her mouth and drifted slowly upwards to the yellowing ceiling. It irritated my eyes on the way.

'I got your note at the Imperial Club,' I said.

'I thought you would be here, or there,' she said with a smug, self-congratulatory look at Jon.

He stood up and offered his hand. I shook it. A scrupulously polite young man.

'Yes,' he said, 'Roger told a friend of mine you were looking for me. He said something about my sister . . .' And well spoken too.

'She's worried about you,' I said, looking towards Gaston behind the bar. He nodded that I was next in line.

'Nothing to worry about,' he said. 'Just a little holiday in the Smoke.' He indicated that I should take his bar stool and sit. A very courteous young man.

I sat just as Gaston came over. We exchanged a few pleasantries, and I introduced Ghislaine, then ordered a glass of the Beaujolais-Villages that he recommended. Ghislaine was drinking Sauvignon Blanc, and Jon thick, soupy, French *cidre*. I said nothing until our drinks had been delivered and paid for.

'So, Jon,' I said, raising my glass, 'which friend told you I was looking for you?'

'A college chum,' he said. 'Dick Ellis.'

'Oh,' I said, 'when did you see him?'

'This afternoon.'

I nodded. A scrupulously polite, well spoken, courteous young man who didn't always tell the truth.

I sipped my wine. Gaston was right. It was excellent.

'Anyway,' Jon said, 'you can tell my sister that I'm fine.'

I smiled. 'Tell you what: I'll pick you up tomorrow, and we'll visit her on the set. You can reassure her that you're all right. And everyone's happy.'

A little flicker of irritation crossed his pretty face, but he controlled it and smiled. 'I'm not sure that I can make it tomorrow,' he said. He clicked his fingers as if inspiration had just struck. 'I know. Perhaps you can do something for me. I'd be very grateful.' He favoured me with his most charming smile, reached into his pocket and took out a small package wrapped in brown paper and tied with string. He offered it to me. 'Take this to her, and she'll give you something for me. I'll meet you in here at seven tomorrow.' He paused. 'You can give it to me then.' His hand containing the little packet moved closer to me.

The bar was filling up, and I looked around carefully. Ghislaine was still smoking, but she was looking puzzled. She probably thought that she knew me well enough to recognize that I was not taken with this young man. She probably thought that I was jealous of his good looks and easy manner. She wasn't entirely wrong.

'What's in the package, Jon?' I said.

But he wasn't listening to me. He was looking over my shoulder. He quickly leaned down towards me and dropped the package in my lap. 'Tomorrow,' he said. 'Here. Seven.' And then he turned away, pushed his way through the untidy throng of drinkers and was out of the door before I could respond.

Ghislaine looked even more puzzled and a little angry. 'What did you say to him?' she said in French.

'I'm not sure,' I said, picking up the packet and slipping it into my pocket. I looked around again at the boisterous crowd in the pub and wondered who had frightened the boy. Then something occurred to me. 'Ghislaine,' I said, 'Jerry told me that you left with two people this afternoon. Who was the other one?'

'A woman,' she said.

'Does she have a name?' I said.

'Yes,' she said, 'I remember thinking that she is more *rouge* than *rosé*.' She giggled girlishly.

And then a large, meaty hand landed on my shoulder.

'Mr Gérard, fancy meeting you here. And just who is your charming companion?'

The accent was unmistakable, the pronunciation of my name impeccable, and a nasty little shiver rippled across my shoulders.

Jenkins towered over Ghislaine and was beaming at her like a lecherous old uncle about to try his luck with one of the bridesmaids at a family wedding. 'My dear, pray allow me to buy you a drink. And a beauty such as yours demands champagne.'

Ghislaine appeared bemused and looked at me for some explanation. I didn't have one.

'Mr Jenkins,' I said, 'Ghislaine Rieux.'

'Enchanted, my dear,' he said, taking her hand and pressing it to his lips.

Ghislaine gave him a faint, slightly sickly smile and reclaimed her hand as quickly as possible.

Jenkins rather grandly ordered a bottle of champagne – 'The widow, I think' – and four glasses, and I was suddenly aware of a small, tough-looking man at his side.

Actually, he wasn't that small. It was just that Jenkins managed to be very large, in that English-public-school way, and took up more space than was his by right.

They were both in evening clothes, but the smaller man didn't look all that comfortable. He accepted a glass of champagne, but he just held it in front of his chest. His limp, grey-blond hair hung greasily over his forehead, and his red, acne-pitted face looked as raw as if someone had taken a cheese-grater to it. The same someone had broken his nose at some time. But he stared at the world through thick-lensed glasses with remarkably clear blue eyes.

'I'm just showing my friend, Jan, the Soho sights,' Jenkins said. One of his big hands reached out and pulled Jan closer to us. 'Jan, this is Mr Tony Gérard, who I was telling you about.'

The man's face sharpened up with interest, and his thin lips tightened a little. It was a bit like seeing a fox sniff prey.

'Actually,' Jenkins said, 'I heard that a mutual friend was in here earlier.' He paused. 'Jonathan Harrison.' He was trying to sound casual, but he was much too studied about it. So, he wasn't here by chance, and he hadn't been following me.

'He's not a friend of mine,' I said.

'So you haven't seen him, then?'

I shook my head in a non-committal way and, mercifully, Ghislaine said nothing. With a little luck she hadn't followed the conversation.

He sniffed, took a sip of his champagne and looked around the bar. 'Excuse me,' he said, 'there's someone I must have a word with.'

He wove gracefully through the knots of drinkers and fell into conversation with a thin, sallow-complexioned man in a worn green tweed jacket who was standing opposite us at the other end of the horseshoe-shaped bar. The man looked quickly across at me and then nodded in reply to something Jenkins said. Jenkins pulled a large pigskin wallet out of his inside pocket, slid a ten-shilling note out and handed it to the man, who crumpled it up and thrust it into his trouser pocket.

'Sorry about that. Just a little business,' Jenkins said as he rejoined us.

The man he'd introduced as Jan was still staring into his glass of champagne, apparently fascinated by the bubbles trickling to the surface.

'Where are you from, Jan?' I said.

'Jan's come over from Belgium,' Jenkins said briskly, 'for a little holiday. Drink up, Jan. Plenty more to see in Soho before the night's out.' He turned to Ghislaine. 'Delighted to have met you, my dear,' he said, reaching out and taking her hand before she could hide it and pressing it to his lips again. Somewhat reluctantly, he released her hand and nodded curtly at me. 'And you, too, Mr Gérard.' He finished his champagne, plonked the glass on the bar next to the still half-full bottle and strode out.

The tough-looking Belgian put his glass down too and followed him out.

I watched them go, wondering what Jenkins thought Jan was about to give away. Belgium didn't mean much to me. I knew that Brussels was the capital, and I also knew that Adolphe Sax came from there.

I swallowed some Beaujolais and tried not to think what might be in the package Jonathan Harrison had pressed upon me. I looked around for the gaunt man with the sunken cheeks and worn tweed jacket, but he, too, had whispered away into the night. Just one of those fragile figures who flit from pub to pub in a fog of alcohol and cigarette smoke, cadging drinks, selling information for shillings.

NINE

We emerged from Leyton Underground station, which, as Ghislaine pointed out, isn't underground at all, into a cool evening breeze. It was something of a relief after the fetid, atmosphere of the train and, in spite of the sulphurous tang to the air, it was refreshing.

After clambering up the stairs and then ambling slowly along the High Road for a short while, we stopped at the chippie, and I introduced Ghislaine to the quaint old English tradition of eating scaldingly hot cod and chips, soused in vinegar and gritty with salt, out of the newspaper. She wore her severe, disapproving face and burnt her fingers and the inside of her mouth before abandoning the entire project in disgust, fastidiously rewrapping the soggy mess in its weeks' old wrapping. (I did point out that if food is too hot to touch it is probably inadvisable to put it in your mouth, but she just sniffed and grimaced rather unattractively.) It occurred to me that the chip shop owner must have been hoarding newspapers for ages.

I genially ignored Ghislaine's complaints and pointed out all the places of interest on our route – the library and town hall – and warned her that we would soon approach the local den of iniquity, the billiard hall.

I disposed of the grease-soaked newspaper wrapping, which still contained most of Ghislaine's fish and all of her chips, in a dustbin outside a featureless, terraced house. We licked our fingers thoughtfully and stared off into the dark interior of Coronation Gardens, the little park opposite. A large black and white cat, just an ominous, silent shadow on the darkened concrete pathway by the permanently dry and dirty fountain, padded sensuously towards a flower bed, stalking something.

I thought of Jenkins and his nasty-looking friend and looked bleakly back towards the town hall and library, but there was nothing out of the ordinary. An elderly drunk crossed the road with exaggerated care, a bus charged past, bright and

almost empty, and a boy on a bike, peddling furiously, tried
to keep up.

We walked on and, as we came abreast of Tyndall Road, I
pointed out the comforting solidity of the Midland Bank where
I liked to think that my money resides. I looked across at Osborne
Road and pointed out the stand of Leyton Orient Football Club
bulking darkly at the end. The Os were flattering to deceive
again.

I suddenly remembered I should have been at football
training. I'd have to try and get in touch with Reg, the manager,
to find out if he wanted me on Saturday.

I was suddenly struck by the absurdity of worrying about
the fate of a Third Division (S) football team and whether a
fourth-rate amateur team of spotty boys and clapped-out old
has-beens had a place for me when a boy had been brutally
murdered.

The door to the billiard hall opened, startling me and spilling
light and two men on to the pavement behind us. One of the
men nodded as they negotiated their way around us, apologizing to Ghislaine, touching a finger to his cap, and I nodded
back, realizing that I'd fallen into a strange, introverted state.

I walked more briskly, turning into Grange Park Road and
then Church Road. We passed the quiet, old graveyard of St
Mary's, which had always spooked me as a kid, and I didn't
show Ghislaine the bomb site where the house I'd grown up
in had stood, nor did I poke my head into the Antelope to see
if Jerry was there. I wasn't sure that Ghislaine would respond
favourably to being thrust into purdah in the Ladies Snug Bar.
The Antelope isn't as louche as the bohemian pubs in Soho.

I strode purposefully past Church Road Primary School and
the house of white-haired Mrs Wilson, my teacher there for
two years, barely pausing to remark on them, and then crossed
swiftly over the road.

It might have been guilt at missing football training and not
having been for a couple of weeks to the liniment-soaked
atmosphere of the sweaty Walthamstow gym where I jumped
rope and whacked the heavy bag, or it might have been just
a physical response to the prickle of anxiety I kept feeling
stab at my guts, but I was walking quite quickly as Lea Bridge
Road came into sight and Ghislaine was having trouble
keeping up.

I stopped though when I saw the dark-grey Humber Super Snipe parked outside Costello's by the bus stop. Carelessly, the driver had stopped too close to a lamp-post. There was enough light to see inside.

The engine wasn't running, but there was a man behind the steering wheel. I could see the outline of his trilby and, even as I watched, he revealed just how casual and unprofessional he was by flicking his cigarette butt out of the window.

I don't believe in coincidence, and I'd seen that car twice before. I knew that the driver was waiting for me.

I slipped as surreptitiously as I could into the shadows offered by a terrace of houses and drew Ghislaine with me. I explained to her what I suspected. She looked sceptical, but I had told her on the journey back a little about Jenkins and that Jon was in trouble and so, sceptical or not, she agreed to keep out of sight. I took out the little package and asked her to keep it for me. Just in case. She shrugged extravagantly and slipped it into her handbag.

Then I wondered how I was going to get across the road without being spotted.

The whine of an approaching bus gliding gaudily up the quiet, darkened road gave me an option. I waited until it was level with me and crossed in its wake. I was hidden from the driver of the Humber for a few crucial seconds and, with any luck, he was watching the bus to see if I got off.

He must have heard me open the rear door, but I was in the back seat and had my forearm pressed against his wind-pipe before he even moved. He struggled a bit, his hands pulling at my arm. I punched him once in the side of the head, and his hat fell off. Then I gripped my wrist with my other hand and applied more pressure to the stranglehold. He got the message and slumped down in the seat quiescently. The car had the smell of new upholstery overlaid with cigarette smoke. He smelt of Brylcreem and coal tar soap.

'What're you doing?' I said. 'Waiting for me?'

'Can't speak,' he croaked out.

'Sure you can,' I said. 'I'm going to count to ten and if I haven't heard anything, I'm going to apply some real pressure. One, two . . .'

'Waiting for a girl,' he wheezed. 'Taking her to the pictures. You're hurting me.'

'Not as much as I'm going to,' I said, tightening my grip.

He gave a pained, gurgling sound and started to choke. I relaxed my grip again, offering him another opportunity to talk. He didn't take it, but spent a few seconds coughing and spluttering.

I suppose I should have realized that they'd have the other man watching from somewhere else, but I guess there's something contagious about sloppy technique. I wasn't aware of him until he tapped on the window with the barrel of a Webley .38.

He beckoned me out of the car and had the good sense to step well back so I couldn't slam the door into him. I was too busy berating myself for my own lack of professionalism to have any appreciation for his.

We trooped across the road, with me in between them, like the cold beef in a sandwich. The driver led the way and kept coughing and feeling his bruised throat. He mumbled something about a crushed larynx, which clearly wasn't true, but I thought it best not to point out that he wouldn't be talking if I'd done him any serious damage.

The guy behind me kept just far enough back to cover any sudden moves in his direction and just close enough to forestall any I might make on the driver. Not that I had any intention of doing anything that might result in the discharge of the Webley. I'd seen two people gut-shot, and it hadn't been pretty. Big, affable Luc had been one of them, and he had wept bitterly with the pain. He'd survived though. Whether he recovered enough to ever drink his beloved Calvados again, I rather doubted.

It's funny the things you think about when you're walking up the stairs to your own flat with a man holding a gun a few steps behind you. *Le trou normand* had never figured much in my life, and yet there I was remembering Luc savouring his glass between courses, even when all we had to eat was a couple of hunks of bread.

Seeing Ghislaine again must have awoken memories I didn't know I had.

Ghislaine!

I hoped that she had the sense to stay out of the way.

We went into my office and the driver turned around, smiled evilly and hit me hard in the stomach. I sank to my knees, gasping for breath. He stood over me with a vicious look on his face. I thought I was about to get the savage beating before being asked the questions. But the other guy waved him away with the gun.

'Get up,' he said, 'and sit in that chair.' He was pure north London, Arsenal supporter, salt of the earth, good to his old mum. He wasn't a bad boy – he just happened to hurt people for a living.

I levered myself up and gulped in some air as I lurched to my grandfather's old chair. I wasn't suffering that much, but thought I'd overplay it and gain a little time.

I'm not a pub brawler and never have been, but I do try to keep in trim with the football, a bit of road-running and regular trips to the boxing gym. Not that I box. But I did, of course, at one time, receive intensive training in how to hurt people. Sadly, on a few occasions, I've had to resort to using some of what I was taught.

I had a feeling that this was going to add to the score.

I knew I could take the driver. He was slow and flabby and didn't punch that hard.

But the other guy was an unknown quantity. And he was holding the gun.

I slumped into the chair, held both hands to my stomach and groaned. It was a little theatrical, but I hoped to make them relax a little and come that crucial twelve inches too close.

The driver was behind me, slightly to the right. The gunman stood in front of me, five feet away. He had lowered the gun, which suggested that he wasn't used to handling it. A Webley is heavy and holding it at the ready for any protracted period can be tiring.

He was younger than I'd first thought. Still making his name as a hard man, then. Which made him dangerous. And he hadn't put a foot wrong so far. But he was sweating a little, which suggested he was nervous. It wasn't that warm in the flat.

'Just hand it over and that's the end of it,' he said.

'What?' I said very quietly.

He came a step closer and raised the gun again. The barrel trembled slightly.

'I'm not pissing about,' he said. 'Give me the package and we're on our way.'

'I don't know what you're talking about.' I expelled some

breath, hunched over and clutched my stomach again, as if I was still hurting.

And he made his first mistake. He moved towards me again, within grabbing range, and he lowered the gun, preparing to give me a clout.

I may not be as quick as I once was, but I'm still quick enough.

I pushed off from the balls of my feet and came out of the chair low, hard and fast. My left forearm hit him in the throat as I straightened up, with the full force of my body behind it. He gave a curious, phlegmy gurgle as my momentum carried him across the room and slammed his gun arm into the wall.

To his credit, he held on to the Webley as he dribbled slowly down to the floor, and I had to bring my heel sharply down on his wrist before he let go. I kept my foot pressed on him as I swooped down and picked up the gun. He was out of it. His mouth was open, drool trickled as slowly as molten lava down his chin and his eyes rolled up.

The driver was slow to move, and when he did it was just a half-hearted lunge. All I had to do to avoid him was lean back. He was nowhere near making contact, and I had to step closer to him in order to bring the gun barrel smartly down on the same side of his head as I'd punched him earlier. He went down like a sack of potatoes, more from self-protection than anything. I hadn't hit him that hard, but he was going to have a fair bit of bruising on that side of his bonce in the morning. When I turned the gun on him, he sat up quickly and put his hands in front of his chest, palms out. It was a fairly pathetic sight, but then all surrenders are.

'Pick him up,' I said, moving quickly away and pointing to the young guy slumped against the wall. He had started to cough and splutter as though he was choking.

'What,' said the driver as he stooped beside the sorry-looking hard man who was now seeing the world through teary eyes and gasping like a stickleback pulled from the Hollow Ponds, 'what are you going to do?'

'I'm going to let you go, of course,' I said. 'After you've told me everything.'

*   *   *

The Webley was a Mark IV with a five-inch barrel, very like the one I'd been issued in 1944. Well, issued is putting it a bit strong. The officer who sort of handed it to me no longer had any use for it. The heavy machine-gun in the concrete pillbox that he'd tried to take by marching straight at it, instead of sneakily sidling up to it and dropping a grenade through the letter-box, had made a bit of a mess of him. To cut a long story short, it was one of the few handguns that I knew my way around, and I think that Don, the driver, and Ray, the gunman, recognized that.

Well, I assumed they did, since they didn't offer any more resistance and we were on first-name terms within a couple of minutes of settling down for our little chat. In fact, we were getting on so well that when Ghislaine came tiptoeing up the stairs I yelled at her to put the kettle on for a cup of tea. I wanted her out of the way for as long as possible.

I'm exaggerating a little about how well we were getting on. Well, more than a little. In fact, I extracted no information from them. I had nothing to bargain with. I couldn't offer them money, and it was obvious that I wasn't going to smack them around or shoot them, and any threat to involve the police would have been a hollow one.

Don did start to mutter something about 'the foreign geezer' when I first asked them what this was all about, but he shut up when the recovering Ray gave him a very nasty look. Clearly, Don was more frightened of Ray than he was of me.

They had nice suits and ties, and they had access to a fancy motor, so they were definitely on wages. The Webley was in good condition too, recently cleaned and oiled. They saw no reason to jeopardize their employment and sullenly dared me to push them.

It did cross my mind to threaten them with Ghislaine's tea, but they'd probably never heard of a French *infusion* so it would have held no terrors for them.

I cut my losses and sent them on their way before Ghislaine had finished banging around in the scullery. They scuttled quickly down the stairs with me following. Seeing them off the premises was the least I could do.

I watched them climb into the car. I'd expected Don to screech away, leaving rubber on the road, but he pulled out from the kerb as gently as if he was taking his test. He even stopped at the junction and politely allowed a youngster leaving the Gaumont to cross the road.

I didn't expect them back soon. They'd be nursing their bruises for a day or two. But I knew they'd be back – Ray, in particular, looked like a grudge-bearer – and the next time they'd come mob-handed.

I stood there for a moment or two, wondering what to do. A lot depended on what was in the package Jon had dropped in my lap. Whatever it was, it looked like tomorrow was going to be busy.

Just when I thought an early night was in order, Jerry came tottering down the street and then up the stairs. He started talking nineteen to the dozen about some records he wanted me to hear. In particular, he'd tracked down a King Oliver recording, with the peerless Armstrong on trumpet. He'd even brought a small bottle of brandy back from the pub with him, in case I had returned.

An hour or two of cognac and jazz seemed like a good way to relax. If I was too distracted by recent events to be quite as enthusiastic as he probably expected me to be when I told him we'd be down in a few minutes, he was gracious enough not to show it. Although it might just have been that he'd had a beer or two too many to even notice that I was *un peu distrait*.

I thought guiltily of the effort that he must have put in to finding the record. After all, the great Satchmo was my weakness, not his.

Ghislaine was still in the scullery, fussing over a boiling kettle and staring at exotic kitchen utensils like teapots and tea-strainers. I asked her for the little package.

I was browned off with her for coming back before she could possibly know what the situation was, but I had to admire her courage and so kissed her gently on the cheek instead of taking her to task for putting herself in danger. She'd done it for me, after all.

I took the package from her and went into my office. She followed.

I sat in my chair, and she stood behind me, her hand on my shoulder, smoking, as I undid the string, tore open the brown envelope and carefully unwrapped the folded sheet of paper inside.

Oddly, she seemed unsurprised by the six little glittering shards of stone nestling in cotton wool.

'That guy,' she said – she used the word *type* – 'in the French pub, he is a gangster.'

I nodded my agreement. My few minutes alone with Don and Ray had not suggested to me that either of them knew how to handle a garrotte, or that they would be cold-hearted and grimly determined enough to do it. But Jan the Belgian holidaymaker . . .

We both stared at the diamonds for a few minutes. Then a thought occurred to me. Not a nice one. If I was right, Jonathan Harrison must have known that Richard Ellis, his great chum, was dead.

'I don't suppose,' I said, looking up at Ghislaine, 'that the name of the woman Jon was with was Rosemary, was it?'

'Perhaps,' she said, still apparently transfixed by the little faceted stones.

Jerry's shout broke the moment. 'Are you coming down? Your brandy's getting cold, and the jazz is getting hot.'

'On our way, Jerry,' I called back, carefully gathering up the diamonds and slipping them into the brown envelope. 'Not a word about these,' I said to Ghislaine. 'Not to anyone. It's important. I think that someone has already been killed for these.'

She looked at me quizzically.

I slid the envelope into my jacket pocket, put the Webley in the large, battered cardboard box that serves as my filing cabinet, under 'G' for gun, smiled at Ghislaine and, with an elaborate little bow, indicated that we should join Jerry downstairs. She smiled back, curtsied and took my arm.

We started walking to the door, but Ghislaine suddenly stopped.

'Antoine,' she said, 'I nearly forgot. I have something for you.'

She slipped off into the other room, and I heard her ferreting about in her suitcase. She came back with a smile on her face and a book in her hand. She presented it to me.

It was a book of poetry, *Les Fleurs du mal*. I thanked her and left it on my grandfather's chair.

I led her downstairs and into Jerry's back room and then asked him if I could put something else into his safe.

He was half-lying on the floor, his back against a big armchair.

He nodded languidly at me and waved his arm vaguely in the direction of the brandy and the two small tumblers. Ghislaine went over to the sideboard and poured herself a drink.

I nipped into the shop and opened the safe, intending to put the diamonds safely inside, with the lighter, envelope of money and cigarette holder. However, that would have been difficult: the lighter and money were no longer there.

TEN

There are some people who really are the salt of the earth – decent, hard-working people who'd share their last meal with you.

Bernie Rosen's family's like that. They are warm, hospitable people. The men of the family are always the first to the bar, and the women always have a pot of chicken soup on the stove.

Bernie is a bit more complicated.

'Well, well,' he said as he unbolted the door to his uncle's shop off Hatton Garden.

'Uncle Manny,' he yelled, 'look what the cat dragged in!'

'It's good to see you too, Bernie,' I said, shaking his hand. 'How's Rachel?'

'Good, Tony, good. And how are you, me old china?'

'As you see,' I said, '*en pleine forme, mon ami.*'

Bernie had never looked good in uniform – too tall and gawky – and here he was in the nearest thing that civilian life offered: shiny black suit, white shirt, black yarmulka and dark tie. Just like his Uncle Manny, who came out from behind the counter.

'Tony,' Manny said, grabbing my shoulders, 'you look good.' He stepped back, appraising me like I was a pearl necklace. 'A bit skinny, though. Come eat with us some time. My Ruthie will soon feed you up. Come Sunday.'

'I'd love to, Manny,' I said, 'but it might have to wait for a bit. How is Ruth?'

'A lot better now, thank you for asking. She has pills.' He raised his hands and looked up to heaven. 'So many pills.'

I stayed with Manny and the lovely Ruth in their house in Southgate for six months after I was eventually demobbed. Bernie had arranged it after we met for a drink and he discovered my parents had been killed and the house destroyed and that I was living in a flea-bitten boarding house. As we picked our way past the desperately sad and unruly piles of rubble that had once been a row of houses to find a decent pub, he said, 'Can't have you living like this, Tone. I'll sort something out.' And he did – the next day. The house was a palace – it even had a bathroom with hot running water. I spent that cruel winter in something approaching warmth and luxury.

Ruth's only son (I always thought of Manny junior as Ruth's – Manny never spoke of him) had died in Burma, and it was his room that I lived in. They were good to me, and I'm grateful to them. Funnily enough though, I couldn't wait to leave. Easy living didn't suit me. It was partly that I didn't fancy standing in for Manny junior, but it had more to do with me. I missed the tension, the anxiety, the raw excitement of being at war. Perversely, I missed being cold and hungry.

True to form, Manny forced tea on me, and we talked. After a few minutes, I took out one of the diamonds and asked Manny what he thought.

He looked at me quizzically, then took out his jeweller's loupe, sat behind the counter and studied the stone.

'What I think,' he said after perhaps five minutes of careful scrutiny, 'is that you didn't come by this legally.'

'Not exactly,' I said, 'but it wasn't illegal either. It dropped in my lap.'

Manny and Bernie both snorted derisively.

'Literally,' I said. 'It was dropped in my lap.'

'Well,' Manny said, 'unless this was one of your very rich lady friends doing the dropping, I'd hazard a guess that whoever dropped it didn't come by it too legally either.' He handed the loupe and the diamond to Bernie.

Bernie looked up and gave Manny a little nod of appreciation. 'What do you know about diamonds, Tony?' Bernie said.

'Next to nothing,' I said.

'What do you think makes them valuable?' he said, looking again at the diamond through the loupe.

'They're rare, aren't they?' I said.

'Not really,' Manny said. 'But the supply is carefully controlled. To give the appearance of rarity. Why else would chips of compressed carbon be that desirable?'

'When we look at a diamond, we look for colour, clarity, carats and cut,' Bernie said. 'This stone is as close to colourless as I've ever seen.'

'Is that bad?' I said.

'No, it's very good. And the cutting is excellent. Antwerp, I'd say, wouldn't you, Uncle Manny?'

'Sure,' said Manny, 'but most diamonds are cut in Antwerp.'

'So, what can you tell me about it?' I said.

'I can tell you that the sparkle and dispersion are uniform, that the table is centred and symmetrical,' he said, smiling mischievously.

'Thanks,' I said, 'but I don't have the foggiest idea what you're talking about.'

He chuckled throatily. 'It's a very good stone, Tony. Its value depends, of course, on what it weighs,' said Bernie. He paused and looked reflective. 'The Germans had access to Antwerp's diamonds during the war. Useful to the war effort and all that. Industrial diamonds, that is. But I bet they took the others as well. This could be one of those.'

'Yes, and it could be kosher,' Manny said. He paused and sniffed. 'Of course, there's the illegal trade. Millions of carats are smuggled out of West Africa every year, Tony. Most of those end up in Antwerp.'

I'd forgotten how much Manny and Bernie both liked to show off their knowledge. And how competitive they were about it.

'What you should do,' Manny said, 'is take it to Scotland Yard and explain.'

'That's complicated,' I said. 'I'm not sure I can do that.' Finding a body was one thing; finding six diamonds was another. I was sure the murder and the diamonds were connected, and I didn't much fancy being the only link between the two that the police had. 'I couldn't leave it with you, could I?' I paused. 'And the five others.'

'Five others!' Manny and Bernie both shouted at the same time.

Manny wiped his hand across his mouth and shook his head. 'I can't afford to take the risk, Tony. Receiving stolen goods is a serious offence.'

Manny is a fundamentally decent man. And an honest one.

'We don't know that they're stolen. And it wouldn't be receiving them. Just storing them for a day or two,' I said.

'A nice distinction,' Manny said, 'but not one a judge is likely to make.'

I knew Manny well enough not to force the issue. 'I

understand, Manny. It's not a problem. I thought they would be safe here.'

'Take my advice,' he said. 'Go to Scotland Yard.' He paused and smiled, relieved that I wasn't pressing the point. 'And come eat with us some time soon.'

I was sweating in the warm sunshine as I dawdled along Hatton Garden. Les Jackson wasn't expecting me at Hoxton Films for nearly an hour, so there was no need to hurry and get even sweatier. I'd called him at home first thing and told him I'd seen Jon. He said he'd take me to see Miss Beaumont, to tell her.

I passed three youngish women, elegant in their narrow-waisted cotton frocks, loitering on the pavement, peering into a shop window. I thought of Mrs Williams.

And then I thought of Ghislaine. It was early closing day, and Jerry had promised to take her to see the sights – the Tower, Buck House, the greasy old Thames – and to Tubby Isaacs' whelk stall in Petticoat Lane and for a pint in Dirty Dick's. If the weather stayed fine, she might enjoy herself. She might even forget about Robert for a few hours. And Jerry's a simple soul. Squiring a beautiful, older (well, she was a few years older than him), sophisticated *French* woman around London is about as close to Paradise as he'd been for a while. The only thing that could have made him happier would have been if she'd been American, a jazz lover and rich. OK, that's three things, but no one – and certainly not Ghislaine – is perfect.

I had lain awake for a while the night before, after we'd finally left Jerry's room, 'Canal Street Blues' and 'Tears' still resounding in my brain, reading some of the poems in the book she'd given me. I didn't really understand them – I'm not much of a one for poetry – but they made you think. There was this bloke writing about a big city and trying to turn the squalor, the crime, the tarts and all that into something beautiful. It made me look at London a bit differently. I still couldn't see it as beautiful though.

I was almost at Holborn Circus when Bernie caught up with me. He was out of breath and very sweaty.

'Glad I caught you, Tone,' he panted. 'Let's grab a cup of coffee and talk.'

I didn't need to look at my watch, but I did anyway.

'Ten minutes tops,' he said.

We retraced out steps and then turned off into Leather Lane. The market was just opening up, and there were no shoppers about, just the stallholders. Most of them knew Bernie and nodded at us.

We went into a nasty little caff that was half full of cheeky cockney chappies, all drinking mugs of tea, smoking roll-ups and coughing up phlegm when they laughed at off-colour jokes. It was the sort of place that made Costello's look like the Savoy Grill. The window was steamed up, and the atmosphere was heavy with the smell of fried meat, cigarette smoke and cabbage water.

The coffee was filthy – grey and scummy – but not as filthy as the tea-stained spoon chained to the counter that Bernie used to shovel sugar into his cup.

'Bloody hell, Bernie,' grumbled the greasy little weasel who'd served us. 'You trying to put me out of bleeding business? I'll have to bloody charge you double for all that bleeding sugar.'

'You kidding?' said Bernie, stirring the cup vigorously and then replacing the spoon on the counter. 'This stuff is undrinkable without sugar. You start making proper coffee, I'll stop using all your sugar.'

'You don't like my coffee, you can piss off,' the weasel said and turned back to the cigarette he was smoking and the bacon he was frying.

Well, everything was in order: the worn scraps of colourless lino that covered the floor were just as dirty as his mouth.

We took our coffees to a rickety old wooden table, stained and scarred from too many culinary skirmishes.

Bernie took a sip and looked at me thoughtfully. 'You really got six diamonds like that one?' he said quietly.

I nodded.

'I'll take them off your hands,' he said. 'There's a market for stones like those.'

'I don't think I can sell them, Bernie,' I said. 'I may have to do what Manny says and take them to the police.'

Bernie made a face. 'Uncle Manny's going to be sixty-eight next month,' he said. 'He's got his comfortable house; he's

got Auntie Ruth to worry about. He doesn't want to take risks.
You and me, we're the war generation. We take chances.'

'Manny did his bit in the first lot,' I said.

'Sure he did, but that was a long time ago. He's an old man
now. Me and you? We see an opportunity and we take it.
Right?'

To be honest, I wasn't sure that was right, but I had nothing
to gain by disagreeing with him. Except a lecture. 'Maybe,'
I said. 'I'm not sure I can see any opportunity yet. I don't
know enough.'

'But you intend to find out, don't you?'

'I thought I'd have a go,' I said. 'Ask a few questions . . .'

Bernie snorted into his coffee. 'Who do you think you are?
Dick Barton?'

I laughed. 'Not unless you're Snowy,' I said.

'You and me,' he said, snorting again, 'we're more like that
Sid James and Tony Hancock!' He paused and looked at me
thoughtfully. 'Tell you what. I'll keep them safe for you and
do a proper valuation. You can let me know what's what in
due course.'

I sipped a little coffee. It tasted as bad as it looked.

'I said it was undrinkable,' Bernie said. He must have read
the expression on my face. It wouldn't have been difficult.

'Do you know something about these diamonds, Bernie?'
I said.

'Course not,' he said. 'No one recognizes a diamond. Unless
it's big and famous. The one you showed me is just a very
nice stone.' He paused. 'What do you say?'

I looked around the shabby little caff and sighed. I really
wanted to be out of there.

'All right,' I said, 'I'll be in touch next Tuesday or Wednesday.
After Easter.'

I had no intention of letting him sell them, but I reckoned
they'd be safer somewhere with a bit of security, like a
jeweller's safe, rather than at my flat where anyone could
walk in, or in Jerry's safe, which, again, anyone, apparently,
had access to.

I really didn't want to carry the diamonds about any longer,
and I handed Bernie the little brown package. He slipped it
into his jacket pocket without a glance.

I figured I could trust Bernie a bit. He knew me well enough to know I didn't care for people lying to me or trying to take me for a ride. But, like I said, Bernie's complicated.

'You know,' he said, looking around and waving his arm at the people inside the caff, 'everyone reckons that this street is named after a tanner or a leather merchant.' He shook his head. 'Not true. The name's a corruption. Back in medieval times, it was called Le Vrunelane, which was probably someone's name, and that became Loverone Lane, and that became something else, and now it's Leather Lane.'

'I didn't know that,' I said, remembering why I was so fond of him.

'Not many people do,' he said, leaning back in his chair and smiling smugly.

Daphne looked at me sourly as I poked my nose into reception at Hoxton Films. Although it could just have been the cigarette smoke making her squint.

'Hi, Daff,' I said, squeezing past the waiting couriers.

'Hi, yourself,' she said.

Not the cigarette smoke then.

'What's up, Daff?'

'What's up? You and that Charlie taking his nibs off gallivanting when I've got all these cheques for him to sign.' She indicated a bulky-looking folder. 'I'm not happy.'

'Come off it, Daff. I don't want him to come with me to see Miss Beaumont. I'll see if I can talk him out of it.'

She gave me a 'some hopes' look, but then smiled. 'Go on then,' she said. 'If you can, I owe you a dance at the Christmas party.'

'I'll give it my best shot,' I said. 'I'll get out the old silver tongue.'

'No,' she said, 'save the silver tongue for the Christmas party.' And then she actually winked at me.

That was frightening. I was still shuddering when I knocked on Les's door.

Still, it was nice to feel that something approaching normality still existed in my life. Jerry, Bernie and now Daphne had reminded me that, usually, I didn't find bodies or diamonds or young toughs waiting to ambush me. Usually, I listened to jazz, cooked tradesmen's books, ate potato latkes with Bernie's family and flirted with Daphne.

Les eased himself out of his chair and glided elegantly round the desk. 'Great,' he said. 'Charlie's waiting downstairs.' He rubbed his hands together.

'If you're busy, Les,' I said, 'there's no real need for you to come.'

'Of course there is,' he said. 'Beverley's one of my stars.' He looked towards the door guiltily and lowered his voice. 'To tell the truth, Tony, I think Daphne's got something lined up for me. She's got that look about her. You know: her mouth set in a straight line, a file under her arm. I'd rather make meself scarce.'

I followed him out and gave Daphne a 'nothing I could do' shrug, and she mouthed, 'I still want that dance,' and winked again.

I decided to give the office party a miss.

Les and I made our way to Noel Street where the stately Rolls graced the seedy little road. We clambered into the back and Charlie swept us away.

Les stared gloomily out of the window at the drab city. The bright sunshine emphasized the smoke-blackened dreariness of the big buildings. He slid a silver flask out of his hip pocket and took a swig. He offered it to me.

'Bit early for me,' I said, shaking my head.

'That's because you haven't got toothache,' he said, pouring more brandy down his throat and screwing the cap back on the flask and slipping it back into his pocket.

'So,' I said, 'where we going?'

'I don't know. Somewhere in Kent,' he said. 'Charlie knows where. People hire these places and tell me afterwards. I'm just the poor sod who signs the cheques.'

Or doesn't, I thought.

'All I know is it's on the way to Folkestone. That's by the seaside.'

The seaside meant Southend or Walton-on-the-Naze on the annual Sunday School outing to me. Little tubs of whelks, candy floss, sticky rocks, painfully stony beaches, sunburn, cinders in the eyes when you poked your head out of the train window . . . The list of seaside delights was endless.

After a few minutes of silence, I thought I might as well use my time with Les. 'So, Les,' I said, 'what's the story with this bloke Jenkins?'

He looked at me blankly.

'Jenkins,' I said, 'the City gent you met yesterday.'

'Oh, him,' he said. 'Interested in putting some money into the company. Maybe he will. Incidentally, thanks. If it comes to anything, I owe you.'

'Me?' I said.

'Yeah. He mentioned you. Had your card as well.' He paused. 'Come to think of it, it was a bit odd. Him not recognizing you in reception.'

'Nothing odd about it. I'd never seen him before,' I said.

'Wonder where he got your card then.'

Good question. Richard? Rosemary? The Imperial Club? Dr Jameson? 'Who knows?' I said. 'I do hand them out.' Just not as much as Les would have liked.

'Good investment those cards,' he said thoughtfully. He winced. 'Must get Daphne to fix up a visit to the tooth doctor.'

We were out in the country now, winding our way along narrow roads and through picturesque little villages. It reminded me of France. Well, it was green and it had trees. These didn't seem to have any Germans hiding behind them though.

I peered out of the window and squinted at the signs. One was for Folkestone and one for somewhere called Hawkinge, which rang a bell. Since we were in Battle of Britain country, I assumed there'd been an airfield there or something.

It was funny. I felt relaxed and alive. After my usual post-violence period of reflection, last night's rumble had put me on my toes. I hadn't thumped anything, apart from the heavy bag in the gym, in a long time.

'What are you smirking at?' Les said, holding his jaw.

'Nothing,' I said. Mrs Williams once said that her late husband had only been truly, physically vibrant during the war. Oh, he'd been frightened, like everyone else, but there'd been something about him then and, when it was over, that fire inside him had flickered and died. She was talking about me as well.

'You will be discreet, won't you? Murders and all. Wouldn't want Beverley upset,' Les said. A distraught star can play merry hell with a filming schedule.

Charlie turned off the road, into a big, flat field. In the distance, I could see a row of Nissen huts and one big hangar. We'd arrived.

ELEVEN

Miss Beaumont had been misled about the nature of the film she was making. Unless it was a romantic comedy set before the French Revolution.

Although I'd been working for Les and Hoxton Films for a couple of years, this was only the second time I'd ever been on set or in a studio when they were actually filming.

Or not filming.

The reason that I knew the film was an historical drama and not a romantic comedy was that all the actors were wearing wigs and, depending on sex, frock coats and sashes or impressive gowns with ribbons and shiny costume jewellery.

And the reason that I knew they weren't filming was because they were all milling about outside the hangar in the bright sunshine, drinking mugs of tea, smoking and talking. And the soundmen and cameramen, in shirtsleeves and braces, were clumped together in a little knot, looking bored.

Oh, and Les was furious.

He'd taken one look at his watch, and his mouth had set in a thin line, the frown lines on his forehead had become deep furrows, and his complexion had darkened.

As soon as Charlie parked, Les flung open the rear door and, without a word to us, strode off towards the technicians mooching around the refreshment van. They all huddled together in a rough circle, like a rugby scrum, and stared into their drinks or discovered some fascinating spot on the ground. They were working on the theory that if they pretended they hadn't seen him then he would pretend he hadn't seen them.

It didn't work.

'George,' he bellowed at the senior soundman. 'George, come and talk to me.'

The unfortunate George shrugged at his companions, swallowed some tea, carefully placed his mug on the nearest flat surface, a large cardboard box with 'Props' stencilled on the side, and shuffled towards Les.

Les put a hand on the man's shoulder and pushed him towards the hangar.

Charlie hauled himself out of the Rolls and nodded towards the crowd of actors. 'They'll be laughing on the other side of their faces in a minute,' he said.

I wasn't as familiar with the film-making process as Les or, apparently, Charlie, but it didn't look all that unusual to me. The studio in Walthamstow where Grand-père had worked had long closed by the time I was born. So, I'd only ever set foot in a studio once before, and I don't think they shot any film in the two hours I was there. They'd drunk a lot of tea, though. There'd been a technical problem. Something to do with the lights.

'It'll be a technical problem,' I said.

'Nah,' Charlie said confidently, shaking his head. 'All the chippies and sparks are over there. No, it'll be an *artistic* problem.' He put a heavy emphasis on what Mrs Wilson had explained was the describing word. He scraped his foot in the dust and looked down. 'Have you,' he mumbled, 'had a chance to say anything to the guv'nor?'

'Not yet, Charlie,' I said. 'I could hardly talk to him in the car with you there. And this morning was not a good time to speak to Daff.'

'When is it ever?' he said morosely.

I couldn't argue with that.

'Yeah, well, I might give Daff a miss, but I will talk to Les,' I said. I suddenly remembered that there someone else I was supposed to talk to. 'I don't suppose there's a telephone around here,' I said.

'If there's an office,' he said, 'there might be one.'

'Bugger! I haven't got the number anyway.'

'Who you got to call?'

'A police inspector at Scotland Yard.'

'Whitehall one two, one two,' he said. 'Just like they say on the wireless.'

'Of course,' I said lamely.

Charlie looked around and poked the toe of his shoe into one of the many wide cracks in the crumbling surface. Tough-looking dandelions and clumps of coarse grass trembled in the light wind. They were in the vanguard. Nature was reclaiming this place. I looked at the rusting Nissen huts and tried to imagine the place as it would have been fifteen years ago, fizzing with young men fuelled by beer and fags.

'What you been up to that Scotland Yard is after you?' Charlie said.

'Nothing, Charlie. You know me: clean in thought, word and deed. He's probably got me mixed up with someone else.'

'Yeah, some other Boy Scout,' he said. 'If there's an office, it'll be in there.' He pointed to the hangar.

I nodded and headed off in that direction.

I was about to go in when one of the carpenters I vaguely knew shook his head.

'I wouldn't, Tony,' he said.

'Hello, Fred,' I said. 'Good to see you. What's going on then?'

He rubbed his hand over his sweating bald head and sighed. 'Beverley, the ice princess, is having one of her moments,' he said. He put the back of his hand to his forehead and spoke in a ridiculous falsetto. 'I just can't today, Jimmy, I just can't.' As an impression of Beverley Beaumont's husky delivery, it didn't cut the mustard, but it was pretty funny, especially as Fred bore more than a passing resemblance to Kenneth Horne.

'I thought she was usually very professional,' I said.

'Not on this film. Been complaining about everything all morning.'

'Is there a telephone inside?' I said.

'I think so,' he said, cocking a thumb to the left. 'Just inside. If you sneak in, they may not spot you. On your own head be it if they do. It was all delicate diplomacy half an hour ago. Mind you, the gaffer's entrance has probably put paid to that already. Not always known for his diplomacy when money's a-wasting, the gaffer.'

I nodded at him and slipped inside the big hangar, between the two huge, heavy doors. One of them hadn't been fully shut.

It was dark inside, after the sunshine, but there was one big spot shining at the far end of the hangar. It lit up part of what looked like a ballroom complete with a balcony and a wide staircase. I knew it was all canvas and wood really, but it was impressive from this distance.

On the bottom step of the staircase was a little group of people.

I could see Les in the thick of it, and there was George,

standing apart from the main group, looking shifty. Jimmy the Lightning Bolt had to be there somewhere, and so, of course, did Beverley Beaumont. I couldn't think who the others would be. An assistant director or two, I supposed, and maybe the leading man. And they'd all be trying to persuade her back to work. I felt a bit sorry for her. Being harangued by Les is bad enough at the best of times but, having suffered Jimmy threatening and imploring for half an hour, this wouldn't qualify as the best of times.

I looked around and saw a door marked 'Office' in the gloom to my left and was just starting towards it when Les broke away from the rolling maul that had formed around the leading lady and strode towards me.

'Cometh the hour, cometh the man,' he said, stopping me before I could slip into the little prefabricated room that had been plonked down in the great hangar. 'I mentioned to her majesty that you had news for her, and she can't wait to see you.' He looked me up and down, a sceptical smile on his face. 'Can't see the attraction myself.'

'There's no accounting for taste, Les,' I said. 'After all, not everyone falls for your boyish good looks.'

He ran his hand over his jowls and recovered some of his usual good humour. 'You know what Raymond what's his name, the fellow who wrote *The Blue Dahlia*, called Veronica Lake?' He paused while I dutifully shook my head. 'Moronica! I bet that's nothing to what he would call some of our so-called stars.' He put his hand on my shoulder. 'Sort this out and I'll owe you a day's filming. She's costing me hundreds.'

'I'll try,' I said, 'but what I've got to tell her isn't all good news.'

'Can't you leave the bad out? I'm serious, Tony. She's in a right old state.'

'Message understood, Les. I'll be as tactful as I can.'

'Good man,' he said. 'I'll introduce you to Dolores Hart at the party tonight.' He ran his hand over his five o'clock shadow again. It made a noise like sandpaper scraping across a freshly sawed plank. 'Then we'll see whether my boyish good looks can win against your sophisticated wit and charm.'

'That's no contest, Les,' I said. 'You're so much taller than me when you stand on your wallet.'

He slapped me on the back and laughed. 'You'll want some privacy,' he said. 'You can talk to her in the office.'

He strolled back to the little tableau harshly lit by the spot. A few seconds after he entered the bright pool of almost-white light, Beverley Beaumont stood up, looked around in a slightly bewildered way, saw me and, painfully slowly, headed my way.

She was wearing a sumptuous heavy gown and a ridiculous coiffed wig. Her natural pallor had been emphasized by thick black eye make-up and crimson lipstick. The small mole under her left ear had been obscured by foundation and powder, and replaced by a silly beauty spot on her left cheek.

I held the door to the office open while she slipped inside. I followed, fumbling for a light switch and shutting the door at the same time.

She had slumped into the rickety old chair and so I perched on the edge of the old desk that was the only other piece of furniture the spartan room boasted.

'Mr Gérard,' she said listlessly, 'Mr Jackson says that you have news. About Jon.'

'Yes, Miss Beaumont,' I said, considering how and what to tell her.

'Have you found him?' she said. There was a hint of animation in her voice, and she raised her head and stared directly at me. There was something embarrassing about the frankness of her gaze, something too naked and too revealing about it.

'Not exactly,' I said. Her eyes misted over a little and became unfocused and so I added quickly, 'But he found me. I saw him last night.'

'And?' she said, turning that longing gaze on me again.

'He seemed well,' I said lamely.

She looked down at her hands in her lap.

I remembered the shrewd look Daphne had given me and what she'd said. 'He's not your brother, is he?' I said.

She didn't say anything for a few seconds, then she looked up at me again. 'What makes you say that?' she said.

I shrugged and shook my head in an 'I don't know really' kind of way. 'He gave me something for you,' I said thoughtfully.

'What?' she said. There was an eagerness in her sultry voice that hadn't been there before.

'It was a package,' I said. 'I don't have it any more. Some men wanted it and came to my house for it last night. Do you know what was in it?'

Well, I might not have told her the whole truth and nothing but the truth, but this was an old aircraft hangar, not a court of law, I hadn't sworn on a stack of Bibles and, anyway, I hadn't actually lied to her. It *was* a package, I *didn't* have it any more and two men *had* come for it the previous night.

She looked around hesitantly. It was artfully done, which didn't mean the hesitation wasn't genuine. It was just that I could never forget that she was an actress.

'It's my . . .' She paused for a beat or two, then said firmly, 'It's my medicine.'

I looked the question at her.

'I get the blues,' she explained. 'Jon gives me something that helps.'

I didn't say anything. I could see how a few diamonds might cheer you up if you were broke and miserable about it, but I couldn't see anyone describing them as medicine.

'I've got the blues now,' she said vaguely. She started tapping her fingers nervously on her thighs. She looked up. 'Do you have a cigarette?'

'I'm sorry,' I said, 'I don't smoke.'

We sat in an uneasy silence for a few seconds. Her fingers fidgeted with a thread on the skirt of her dress. She picked at it assiduously.

'I didn't get the impression,' I said carefully, 'that the men who visited me last night were after "medicine".'

She looked puzzled. Again, I couldn't help feeling that she was performing.

'It's a special medicine,' she said. 'Not entirely legal.'

The penny dropped. She thought I'd brought her cocaine.

I don't think of myself as particularly innocent, but I can be very slow on the uptake. I just didn't have her down as someone who consumed dangerous drugs. A washed-up American has-been might well, sure. But why would a fresh-faced English rose, making a career for herself?

'I see,' I said, although I didn't. 'Jon obviously leads a very interesting life – for a student.' I remembered something Dr Jameson has said on the telephone the previous night. He'd picked up two packages on his brief trip to the college.

'He's . . . resourceful,' she said.

'He's trouble,' I said.

'Perhaps,' she said quietly. And then she looked straight out defiantly. 'And perhaps that's what attracts me to him.'

'I think he's *in* trouble,' I said.

'I think so too,' she said, leaning across and putting her hand on my knee. There was nothing sexual about the gesture, but it was intimate and disturbing. I wasn't sure if she understood the impact she had on men. 'Will you help him?'

I thought about it. There was no reason for me to help Jonathan Harrison. And he really was trouble. 'Will you go back to work on the film?' I said.

'I would be happier if I knew that someone like you was looking out for Jon,' she said. 'That would make it easier for me to work.'

In the films, a beautiful woman looks to the tall, good-looking hero for help and you know that he'll sort things out and they'll be in a clinch before the credits roll.

The thing is that I'm not tall or good looking and I'm certainly not a hero. I also knew that Beverley Beaumont and I were not going to end up together. Even if she offered, which she was not going to, I wasn't sure that was what I would want, anyway. Like Jonathan Harrison, she was trouble. Not the same kind of trouble. His came with thugs and guns, and you knew where you stood with them. Hers came with messy emotional stuff, which was much more difficult to cope with.

I thought of all the reasons not to agree to help.

'It's a deal,' I said.

She stood, reached up, put her arms around my neck and gently brushed her lips against my cheek.

That was as close to the loving clinch as I was going to get, and we were a long way from the final credits. Clearly, I'd been auditioning for the part of the expendable boy next door, the one who gets shot in the second reel.

'Never had you down as a miracle worker,' Les said.

Les, Charlie and I were eating bacon sandwiches and drinking tea in the sunshine. Everyone else – except the catering staff, who were busily slapping margarine on bread, frying sausages and peeling and chipping potatoes – was back inside and making movie magic. Jimmy the Lightning Bolt would have it all in the can in no time.

'The only thing is, Les,' I said, 'I've agreed to do something for her. And I'll need Charlie and the car. For the afternoon.'

Les looked doubtful. 'You haven't agreed to anything that would get the company into trouble?'

'You know me better than that, Les,' I said.

He looked even more doubtful, then he brightened up. 'All right, you can have Charlie,' he said, 'but not the Rolls.'

'There's always the Wolseley, Mr Jackson,' Charlie said helpfully.

'That's right,' Les said. 'Yeah, you can have the Wolseley. You'll have to drop me off at the office first though.'

I looked at Charlie, who nodded enthusiastically.

'I'll need Charlie for this evening,' Les said. 'At eight. Sharp.'

We chewed our sandwiches and swilled our tea for a few minutes in silence.

'I don't suppose,' I said, 'that Jenkins gave you a card or anything?'

'You seem to be very interested in this Jenkins bloke,' Les said.

'I thought I might look him up,' I said. 'It's personal.'

'He left a telephone number and an address. It'll be back at the office.' He looked up at the sky while his tongue worked at a piece of bacon rind stuck in one of his back teeth. He winced as he hit a sore spot. He gently massaged his jaw and looked thoughtful. 'A word to the wise,' he said. 'I don't think Jenkins is someone who should be taken at face value.'

He looked up at the sky again, a little wistfully, and poked a finger inside his mouth, waggled it about and then extracted it. He studied one of his fingernails for a few seconds. 'I met blokes like him during the war. They'd come along in their Savile Row suits, with their posh accents, and they'd never say they came from this ministry or that ministry, but it was understood. Not true, but understood.' He paused. He was, I think, remembering some of the scrapes he'd got into. 'Of course, some of them really did come from a ministry, and they'd be the worst. It'd be the Ministry for Turning Spoons into Bombers, and you'd hand over your spoons. But I never heard of a bomber made out of silver spoons.' He sniffed. 'All

I'm saying is, tread carefully. The upper-class bastards are the most ruthless. Your East End thug may be nasty, but he has a soft spot for his mother. Guys like Jenkins never had mothers.'

'Thanks for the advice,' I said. 'I appreciate it.'

'But you'll ignore it,' he said. 'Anyway, don't misunderstand me. If he offers me money, I'll take it. But, for what it's worth, I don't trust him.'

'I mean it, Les,' I said. 'I'll walk on eggs.'

'Just see that you do. And if you tell him I said any of that, I'll feed your bollocks to Daphne's cats. With you still attached.'

'Wouldn't dream of saying a word to him about you, Les,' I said. 'In fact, I probably won't go anywhere near him.'

'Sure, Tony,' he said cynically. He turned to Charlie. 'Look after him, Charlie. Keep the silly bugger out of trouble. I'm relying on you, mind.'

Charlie smiled his sweetest smile. He was back in favour.

I smiled too, but I had an uneasy feeling deep in my stomach.

TWELVE

Daphne arched a meticulously plucked and painted eyebrow when I deposited Les back in the surprisingly quiet Wardour Street office at just after one thirty. The eyebrow rose like a sliver of dark moon above the glassy horizon of her plain National Health spectacles.

I decided that if there was any credit going, I might as well grab it and shrugged in a self-deprecating way, smiled sweetly and mouthed, 'He's all yours,' at her behind his back. She put down her egg and tomato sandwich and smiled wickedly back.

Les didn't get past her desk. A rampaging, fourteen-stone England winger would have been stopped dead by such a body-check.

'You,' she said, 'have to sign these.' And the bulky brown file that she had swept up when she had risen majestically from her seat was thrust into his arms.

To his credit, Les, who might just weigh in at eleven and a half stone after a good lunch and who has never rampaged down the wing at Twickenham, knew when he was beaten, and he offered no argument, just slunk off to his office, murmuring meekly, 'No calls for the next hour, please.'

Charlie had told me he'd be back with the Wolseley in twenty minutes, and so I asked Daphne for a telephone line and if she could dig out that address for Jenkins.

While she grumbled away, looking for the number, I rang Inspector Rose at New Scotland Yard. He was in a meeting, but the genial Oliver Hardy of a sergeant took my call. All they wanted was my fingerprints – 'For the purposes of elimination only, sir, I assure you. Your dabs are on the door knob somewhere, aren't they?' – and so I arranged to be there in forty minutes.

Daphne handed me a slip of paper. 'Rum sort of address, that,' she said, picking up her sandwich, 'for a gentleman in the City.'

It was. Mainly because it wasn't a London address at all. Mr Jenkins, it seemed, was based in Cambridge.

Daphne chewed her sandwich, said nothing and concentrated on looking inscrutable.

I sat on the sagging sofa.

'He's not an investor,' she said eventually, when she'd finished eating.

It was my turn to raise my eyebrows.

'You can always tell,' she said. 'Investors come in with their financial advisers or their accountants.' She paused and looked at me. 'Blokes like Jenkins are usually looking for introductions to the starlets. Sure, they put a few bob into a film, but it is only a few bob, and they expect to make a handsome profit and get to marry the star.' She laughed. 'You should hear them whinge when they lose their money and the girl.' She paused and looked thoughtful. 'You know, sometimes I even feel a bit sorry for poor old Les having to put up with them. Not that that lasts, mind you. He always manages to do something that reminds me why I divorced him.'

'You love him really, Daff,' I said. 'You know you do.'

She couldn't even be bothered to reply, and the look on her face as she turned back to what remained of her lunch suggested that if I really believed that then I was a bigger fool than even she took me for.

The comfortable, old, pre-war, black Wolseley 25 looked completely at home parked on the Embankment outside New Scotland Yard. It wasn't so much older than those that ferried the senior policemen about. In fact, there was one of a similar vintage pulling away from the kerb with a uniform in the back as I, with inky fingers and a guilty look, scuttled nervously along the pavement.

'They let you out, then,' Charlie said when I opened the passenger door.

I slid into my seat, took a slightly grubby handkerchief out of my pocket and rubbed at my fingers, and gave Charlie the address down in Kennington.

'But that's south of the river,' he said.

'Not that far south,' I said, 'and there aren't any dragons down there these days. St George dealt with them all.'

'Well, if you know how to get there,' he said doubtfully and, apparently relying on the oncoming traffic to mistake us

for a police vehicle, pulled across the road without even
pretending to look.

As we glided over Westminster Bridge, the afternoon sun
sparkling on the murky water and the grubby government
buildings, he started to look anxious but, surprisingly, we
didn't get lost, and we drew up opposite Rosemary Elvin's
house only ten or so minutes later.

I had a moment of apprehension as I remembered the scene
in the upstairs bedroom the last time I'd been there.

A police constable, standing four-square on the doorstep,
looked uncomfortably hot in his heavy uniform. He gave me
a worried look as I approached. He may have been moment-
arily thrown by the car. When I didn't produce a warrant card,
he relaxed.

'Afternoon, Officer,' I said. 'I just came to see Mrs Elvin.'

'Sorry, sir, but she's not here.'

He was a big man in his fifties, red-faced and sweating.

'What's going on?' I said. 'Has something happened to Mrs
Elvin?'

'No, the lady's all right,' he said. He looked around, pulled
a big handkerchief out of a trouser pocket and wiped his
forehead. 'She's staying with a friend round the corner.' He
indicated the next street along with his thumb. 'Number
twenty-seven.'

'Thanks,' I said. I nodded at the house. 'Must have been
serious.'

'I can't say.'

I smiled at him. 'Something really juicy, was it?'

'Hop it,' he said.

I looked around and smilcd at him again. Teasing a policeman
is always harmless fun and, you never know, he might let something slip.

'Thanks for your help, Officer,' I said. I peered up at the
sky. 'You might get some shade in an hour or so.'

'Hop it,' he repeated as I strolled away. I didn't quite catch
what he muttered under his breath.

I waved to Charlie and indicated that I was going around
the corner. He acknowledged the wave with a little hand
motion of his own and followed me.

Number twenty-seven had a well-cared-for air and the black
door looked as if it had been painted more recently that most

of its shabby neighbours. The step had been scrubbed, and the brass lion's-paw knocker and the letter-box had both been polished. All in all, it had that respectable look, which you didn't see that often these days.

I waited until Charlie had slid to a halt on the other side of the little street and then raised the knocker.

The woman who answered my knock had the same look. From the carefully knotted floral scarf that covered her hair, down to the sensible flat-heeled black shoes, she radiated respectability. Which, judging by the narrow-eyed, suspicious look she gave me, was more than I did. I should have borrowed one of Jerry's hats. Going bareheaded into the wilds of south London was clearly not done.

I gave her my most charming smile, told her who I was and explained that I'd found the body the previous day and that I'd just come to see how Mrs Elvin was. She pursed her lips and sniffed. She was clearly immune to whatever charm I could muster. Then, although you could hardly say she relaxed, she unstiffened slightly, gave me a tight smile and said she'd ask if Rosemary was prepared to see me, and firmly closed the door.

I stood on the step, hoping that I wasn't making it too dirty and wondering if I should use my handkerchief to wipe away any marks that I might have made on the knocker by using it. I decided against that when I remembered the state of the handkerchief. Fingerprinting ink makes a terrible mess, especially to an article already in need of a trip to the bagwash in Capworth Street. After a minute or two, the door reopened and I was invited into the front room.

It was one of those rooms that you could easily imagine playing host to a coffin on a set of trestles. There was something funereal about the muted colours of the drawn curtains and the rug, and about the smell of furniture polish. This was obviously a room kept for 'best', where one gave the vicar tea (or the priest cream sherry) and made awkward conversation. The dark sideboard no doubt housed the good china and a bottle of cooking brandy.

Rosemary Elvin was perched on a high-backed chair just in front of the window, her big, red hands working nervously at each other as they lay on her thighs.

A little patch of silver on the sideboard caught my eye.

'Mrs Elvin. Rosemary,' I said.

'Thanks for coming, Mr Gérard,' she said, 'but I'm fine really.'

'I'm glad to hear that. And it's Tony,' I said.

'This is my friend Florence,' she said. 'Florrie.'

I turned and smiled at the neat and tidy householder. She gave me a suitably neat and tidy smile in return. I didn't fool myself into believing there was any warmth in it.

'To tell you the truth, Rosemary,' I said, 'apart from wanting to know that you were all right, I was wondering if you happened to know where I might find Jon.'

She glanced quickly at her friend and then shook her head firmly.

'Only, I thought you met up with him late yesterday,' I said.

She shook her head again. 'No, I'm sorry, I can't help.'

I nodded and smiled, wondering why she was lying. It seemed that she'd wanted my help the day before when she'd taken him to my flat. I was fairly sure about that. Beverley Beaumont's slim cigarette case on the sideboard indicated that someone she knew had been into Jerry's safe, and I rather doubted it was her.

'Well, if you do see him,' I said, 'you know how to find me. And I'm glad you're all right, Rosemary.' I nodded at the other woman. 'Florence. I can let myself out.'

Their relief as I stepped out of the room and into the hall was palpable. I stood at the foot of the stairs for a few seconds and listened, but I heard nothing beyond a few creaks, the steady ticking of a grandmother clock just along the hall and a dripping tap. There may have been a few creaks more than were to be expected in a house that had long since settled, but nothing too far out of the ordinary.

I waited for as long as I reasonably could without arousing suspicion, even kneeling down and pretending to tie my shoelaces, but if there was anyone else in the house, they didn't betray themselves, and I slipped quickly through the front door.

There was a black Ford Popular parked a couple of doors down. I wondered if that was the vehicle that had carried Jonathan Harrison to Cambridge and to Leyton. And, at the far end of the street, sat the only other car in sight, apart from the Wolseley.

It was the big Humber Super Snipe that I'd had dealings with before. It *was* parked a long way away, but it was still careless of them. I decided not to make a meal of it, just in case someone was watching, and walked briskly over to Charlie and the Wolseley.

'Charlie,' I said as I closed the heavy door with a clunk, 'see the Humber down at the end of the road?' He nodded. 'Can you drive past it slowly? Though not so slowly that it's obvious.'

He started the engine, checked his mirrors, pulled out into the middle of the road and we moved sedately, at something not much above the pace of a funeral procession.

Well before we drew alongside, it was apparent there was no one in it.

Charlie took a left into another quiet street, and I asked him to pull over.

If I turned around, I could just see the front bumper of the Humber. I glanced at my watch. A quarter past three.

'Why don't you take the car a hundred yards or so further on? I'll just loiter around this corner for a bit.'

I climbed out, into the warm sunshine, watched Charlie drive off and then looked for somewhere I could see both the house and the Humber, without being too obvious myself. It wasn't easy. Apart from a lamp-post, there wasn't much to hide behind. The only car in this little street, another black Ford Popular, was parked too far from the corner for me to see anything from behind it. I decided that all I could do was stand and wait in plain sight, unless anything happened and then I'd have to move quickly for the cover of the car. I thought I'd give it half an hour: anything less and it wasn't worth waiting, any longer and I'd probably find myself moved on.

In the event, I didn't even have time to develop too much of a thirst.

I'd only been pacing up and down for five minutes, sweating like the policeman in his blue serge, when the brakes of a muddy-brown Morris Oxford squealed alarmingly as it drew up outside number twenty-seven. I recognized the man who clambered out of the passenger side. It was Jan the Belgian. The driver stayed put with the engine still running, so it didn't look like I was in for too long a wait. Within a minute Jan the Belgian reappeared, accompanied by two other men. One of

them was the young tough who had waved the Webley at
me. The other one was no bigger than a grizzly bear. He wasn't
much smaller than one either. I wondered how he'd managed
to keep his presence in the house hidden. If he'd just stood up,
the place would have leaned over like a ship whose cargo had
shifted. Jan was collecting muscle.

The three of them climbed into the Morris Oxford and the
driver pulled away, smoothly and neatly, and swept towards me.

I retreated to the safety of the Ford, ducked down and
watched as the driver changed his mind about the direction
he wanted to go in, turned around laboriously and slowly,
wrestling with the heavy steering, and then headed back the
way he'd come.

I was sweating heavily by the time I'd trotted briskly down
to the Wolseley.

Charlie was standing on the pavement, smoking and looking
at me like I was a candidate for the loony bin.

'You'll need a bath before the party,' he said, 'haring around
in this weather.'

'We have to follow a car,' I said, pulling open the passenger
door and jumping in.

Infuriatingly, he took another drag on his cigarette before
ambling round to the driver's side.

I told Charlie what we were looking for and which direction it had taken.

We turned even more slowly than the Morris and had to
wait for a coal lorry to trundle past. The Morris was nowhere
in sight when we came to the end of the street.

'Left or right?' Charlie said.

'Left,' I said, 'towards town.'

My face felt flushed and sweat was running down my back.
I wrestled my suit jacket off and opened the window. A mercifully cooling breeze blew in, ruffling my hair and plastering
my damp shirt against my arms and chest.

There wasn't that much traffic, so we made good speed to
Waterloo Bridge, and there, nine or ten cars ahead, at the far
end of the bridge, caught up in the chaos of the Strand, was
the Morris.

'Well done, Charlie,' I said, trying not to sound patronizing
or unduly ironic. 'Just follow him now. Without being too
obvious about it.'

He must have taken offence at the idea that he didn't know
how to follow someone unobtrusively. He looked hurt and
sulky.

We turned right at the Strand and followed the car into
Kingsway. When it hung another right at High Holborn, I
started to have a sneaking suspicion about where we were
heading. As the big car nudged and wriggled its way along,
amongst the clutter of taxis, buses and delivery vans, past
Gray's Inn Road, that sneaking suspicion turned to a very
nasty, sick feeling.

Bloody Bernie, I thought as I watched the Morris Oxford
approach Holborn Circus and bully a taxi, amid squealing
brakes and an angry horn, into allowing it to slide into the
left-hand lane for a turn into Hatton Garden, why couldn't he
ever do what you asked him to?

THIRTEEN

Exasperatingly, we were marooned behind a couple of buses. They lurched slowly – oh, so slowly – forward, and I knew we weren't going to get to Manny's shop in time. I wasn't sure what we'd be in time to do, I just knew we wouldn't be there in time to do it. And, even with the windows wide open, it was getting hotter in the car. My damp shirt was sticking to the seat. I hoped that the Morris Oxford was similarly trapped between buses and, somewhat malevolently, that the occupants were suffering as much as I was.

'Charlie,' I said, 'you got any coppers?' He nodded. 'Let me have 'em. I've a telephone call to make. Just go around the corner, into Hatton Garden. Wait for me there.'

He fumbled in his pocket, then handed over a fistful of pennies, and I leapt out.

There was a telephone box close to Chancery Lane Underground station, and, thankfully, it was unoccupied.

I didn't know what kind of security Manny and Bernie had, but I seemed to remember that they had some impressive bolts and shutters. Unfortunately, they wouldn't be much good if they weren't in use.

The telephone only rang two or three times, but it seemed like for ever. I was muttering between clenched teeth and my right leg was twitching nervously when, finally, Manny's calm, slow voice recited the number back at me and I rammed my thumb against the button that dropped the coins into the cash box with a rattle and a clunk.

'Manny,' I said, 'say nothing. There isn't much time. Armed men are on their way to the shop. They'll be there in minutes. Just lock up and close early.'

'Tony, I can't just shut up because you think—'

'Manny, I don't think. I know. Now, don't argue, please. Just do it. If necessary, call the police. Just lock up. Please, Manny. Trust me.'

'You send armed men to my shop. Why wouldn't I trust you? What can I say?'

'Just say "yes", Manny, please.'

'All right already. Yes,' he said. 'Happy?' And he put the receiver down.

It was oppressively hot in the box, and I reached into my pocket for my handkerchief to wipe sweat from my forehead. Then I remembered the ink and left it where it was.

The traffic had miraculously cleared, and it was now moving freely. I walked briskly to Holborn Circus and turned into Hatton Garden.

The Wolseley was pulled up at the side of the road, near-side wheels almost brushing the kerb, just twenty or so yards along.

I leaned down and spoke through the window. 'Leave the car, Charlie. We'll walk from here.'

He nodded and lumbered out. He waited for a taxi to drive past and then walked behind the car and joined me on the pavement.

I must have been looking as grim as I felt.

'Trouble, Tone?' he said, flexing the fingers on his right hand.

'Could be, Charlie,' I said, grabbing my jacket and putting it on.

We marched silently up Hatton Garden.

The brown Morris Oxford was parked outside Manny's shop, and three men were standing on the pavement, looking unhappy and aimless.

It was clear that Manny had done exactly as I'd asked and had locked the shop up. He'd even turned out the lights. It looked authentically closed to me.

Jan the Belgian was peering up at the upper storey of the building, muttering angrily to himself, when I strolled up, and Ray the tough was banging on the door. The big brown bear wasn't doing much of anything.

I stood next to Jan and looked up at the sky. 'Taking in the sights?' I said.

He started, looked at me and called me a son of a whore in French.

I tutted at him and said, '*Ta gueule*,' which was the most offensive way I could think of of telling him to watch his mouth. My French had never leaned towards the racier slang. Big Luc's thick Normandy accent had kept most of his more colourful expressions a mystery to me.

However, Jan the Belgian looked gratifyingly nonplussed. 'I was just going to my favourite café to buy a coffee,' I said amiably. 'Can I interest you in a cup?'

He looked even more confused, and I wasn't sure if it was because he'd been to the café in Leather Lane and couldn't believe it was anybody's favourite or if he just hadn't understood my English. To be on the safe side I repeated it in French.

He snarled something that I didn't quite catch, as it was, I assumed, in some Belgian *argot*, but I was sure that it compared me to a piece of ordure. He also reached angrily into his jacket pocket. But before he could pull out whatever it was he had in there, Charlie, who had been standing just behind me, took one step forward and clipped him neatly on the jaw.

If you learn how to hit someone properly, I guess you never forget the secret. It was a classic jab and only travelled about six or seven inches, but it had all of Charlie's considerable bulk and expertise behind it. Blink and you missed it. It was a punch for the connoisseur. The hard-looking Belgian simply collapsed like a Niger tent with a broken ridge pole. I'd never seen Charlie hit anyone before, and I looked at him in open admiration. He shrugged self-deprecatingly.

After a second or two of blank confusion, Ray the tough came racing over, but stopped short and took a step back, hands held up in surrender, when Charlie assumed his fighting stance, left arm covering his face, right arm cocked.

I turned to face the big brown bear, who should have been lumbering over to join the fray. But he wasn't. In fact, he was laughing.

'Charlie,' he boomed. 'Charlie Lomax as I live and breathe. I'd recognize that right hand anywhere.'

Charlie looked across. 'Blimey,' he said. 'Herbert Longhurst, the Bermondsey Battler. Didn't see you there, Herbert.'

I was puzzled by that, as Herbert Longhurst was about as unobtrusive as Mount Everest.

'It's got to be twenty years,' Charlie was saying to the Battler as I turned to Ray. If the two of them were going to reminisce about heroics in the ring then I reckoned my problems might be over, for the time being. Certainly, the driver demonstrated no inclination to even get out of the car, Jan the

Belgian was out cold and Ray was looking very unsure of himself.

'You,' I said to Ray, 'had better have a look at him.' I indicated the prone Belgian, who was started to groan and move. 'And then I want a word with you about what you took from the shop last night.'

He looked the very picture of injured innocence. 'I never went in no shop,' he said.

'So you didn't find a silver cigarette case there?'

'Cigarette case?' he said. Then he smiled. 'No, the boy had that.'

'The boy?' I said.

'No . . . I mean . . . I'd better look after the frog,' he said, bending down and holding a handkerchief out to the recovering Jan.

We were attracting some attention now, and a little crowd had grown around us. A middle-aged woman nudged me in the ribs.

'Is he all right?' she said, pointing at Jan, who was now sitting up and dabbing with Ray's handkerchief at the blood coming from his mouth.

'He's fine,' I said. 'Just an accident. Nasty fall. But no bones broken.'

And then it all went wrong.

Instead of staying down as he was supposed to, Jan adjusted his glasses, which had fallen askew, lurched to his feet, shrugged off Ray's attentions, snarled something in incomprehensible and very ugly French, took a German Luger out of his pocket, pointed it in Charlie's general direction and, without taking aim, fired.

The crowd gasped and shouted warnings, one or two of the men ducked and the woman who'd poked me put her hands to her ears and started to sob hysterically. Then, two of the men moved uncertainly towards Jan, but they were too late. I dived at him and smashed my shoulder into his chest.

He didn't go down, but I'd knocked the wind out of him and he wasn't about to fire again in the immediate future. I reached out to grab his gun hand when, unfortunately, Ray decided now was the time to show his stuff, and he hit me hard in the right kidney, and then again in the back of the head.

I did go down, and I hit the pavement hard. I wasn't unconscious, just a bit dazed, and I was aware of Ray bundling the gesticulating Jan into the Morris Oxford, which then roared off towards Leather Lane.

It suddenly occurred to me that twice in the last few days I'd charged at a man who was holding a gun. I'd gone through the entire war without doing it once. That was something only mad majors did. I made a mental note not to make a habit of it. Being acquainted with Jonathan Harrison wasn't good for my health, or my sanity.

By the time I'd stumbled to my feet, surrounded by solicitous people asking inane questions, the car had disappeared and Manny and Bernie were standing in front of me.

'Well,' said Manny, 'what's going on?'

I looked around. 'Is anyone hurt?'

'Apart from you?' Bernie said.

'Yeah,' I said. 'He got a shot off. At Charlie . . .' I forced my way through the little knot of well-wishers and there was Charlie. 'Charlie, are you all right?'

'Sure I am, Tone,' he said, 'but Bert here took a hit.'

'I'm all right,' the big man rumbled. 'It missed me, really. Just scraped me arm.'

There was a tear in the left-hand sleeve of his jacket, just about at the biceps. It looked as if he was right and had only been nicked. All the same, he was very pale.

'That frog owes me a new suit,' he said, rubbing at the rip. A little blood seeped out. 'I don't like working with foreigners. Remember that Eyetie heavyweight, Charlie? Dirtiest fighter I ever come across. All black curly hair and smelly breath.'

I rubbed at the sore spot on the back of my head. My own suit was the worse for wear. I could see the graze on my knee through the ragged cloth. 'A cup of tea might be a good idea,' I said. 'I'm sure Manny can organize it.'

'I wouldn't mind a sit-down,' the Bermondsey Battler said. 'Me legs are feeling a bit weak.'

We shuffled off, Bert and I giving a good impression of the halt and the lame, into the shop, and the crowd slowly dispersed.

I wondered how long it would be before someone came back with a policeman. At least one of the onlookers would have gone in pursuit of one. Manny may well have called them.

I hadn't a clue what to say to them. I supposed that the truth was an option.

The Bermondsey Battler and I sat quietly on the two chairs that were supplied for customers while Manny heaped sugar into the tea – 'Good for shock,' We'd managed to wrestle Herbert's coat off and cut his shirt sleeve away, and we had a shufti at his arm. It was a nasty-looking wound and needed professional attention.

I heard the clanging of an emergency vehicle's bell in the distance. It grew louder and stopped. Then the bell started up again and slowly faded back into the distance. That was a relief. The police had, presumably, been sent off after the Morris Oxford. They'd be back to bang on Manny's door later, but I'd be long gone.

Charlie and I decided to run the Bermondsey Battler down to Bart's and see if we could find a doctor to clean his wound and put a decent dressing on it. (Bernie casually told us that Bart's had been founded in 1123 by one of Henry I's courtiers. 'Rahere,' Manny said. 'That was his name. He caught malaria on a pilgrimage to Rome, and he had a vision of St Bartholomew.' Charlie and Herbert attempted, very successfully, not to look impressed. I didn't have to try.)

Then I embarked on the difficult task of quietly apologizing to Manny for the trouble. He didn't ask any questions, just listened as I told him what I knew about the diamonds, which wasn't very much. When I'd said my piece, he looked at me shrewdly.

'So what made them think the diamonds were here?' he said.

'You might have to ask Bernie about that,' I said.

'And what do I tell the police when they come knocking?' he said.

'That you closed up early – Easter and all that – and that it was just as well?'

'I could tell them that,' he said. 'And no doubt they'll take me for a pious Christian.' He indicated to Bernie that he wanted a word in the other room.

After Bernie and Manny left the main shop area, I took the opportunity to ask Herbert, as he gulped down sweet tea, what he'd been doing down in Kennington.

'Minding job,' he said. 'Some young boy the boss wanted

to lean on. I just had to make sure he stayed put. He's a bit slippy, you know.' He paused and glugged some tea. 'You ain't got a fag, have you?'

I shook my head, but Charlie nodded and found a couple. Charlie fumbled with a box of matches, and they both started to smoke.

'So, who's the boss?' I said.

Herbert blew smoke at the ceiling. 'Mr Jenkins,' he said. 'He's completely legit, but he sometimes has to deal with some dodgy characters and then he calls on me to give 'em a slap or two. Nothing too serious. This lad nicked something, and Mr Jenkins wants it back.'

I suspected that Herbert Longhurst really was a simple soul who didn't know very much. His battered, old fighter's face and misshapen hands suggested that, unlike Charlie, he'd stayed in the ring for a few years longer than had been wise, and now he made a living as best he could. I didn't think there was much to be gained from questioning him more closely, and I left Charlie to reminisce with his old friend and went into the back room of the shop for a word with Bernie.

Manny looked up. 'I'll go see about some more tea for the others,' he said and left us to it.

Bernie was sitting at a desk cluttered with little packages and piles of paper, pretending to peer at a diamond ring through his loupe and write some notes on the back of an old invoice.

'So,' I said, 'sold those diamonds yet?'

'Course not,' he said without looking up. 'You only gave them to me this morning.'

'You put the word out though.'

He did look up at me now. 'What makes you think that?' he said.

'Just the fact that one of the guys who thinks he's the owner came visiting,' I said.

'All right,' Bernie said, 'so I put the word out. I didn't know you'd stolen them from some bad guys, did I?'

'*I* didn't,' I said. 'But I thought I made it clear I hadn't come by them entirely legitimately.' I paused. 'I also seem to remember that you were just going to hold on to them for me.'

Bernie shrugged sheepishly. 'You know me, Tony,' he said.

'Yeah,' I said. 'I know you, Bernie.'

The small back room had a very peaceful atmosphere. It was

dark and cool, with only one, high, small window. The only light came from the one lamp on Bernie's desk. It was golden and restful.

Bernie sniffed and took a brown envelope out of his jacket pocket. He waved it absent-mindedly in front of me for a few seconds. 'You know, Tony,' he said, 'sometimes you're a real pain in the backside.'

'I imagine that's why we get on so well, Bernie,' I said. 'I'm acute agony in the rectum, you're a savage wrench to the neck.'

'Here,' he said, handing the envelope over. 'You owe me a pint.'

I looked at the envelope carefully for a few seconds. 'Hang on to them for me,' I said, putting it down on the desk.

'You sure you trust me?' he said.

'No, Bernie,' I said, 'but I can't think of anyone I'd rather see make money out of this. I'll have to tell some fibs to mislead the bad boys, but that can be managed. In the meantime, do me a favour – well, two favours.'

'If I can, Tony,' he said, slipping the envelope back into his pocket.

'Be a bit more discreet about selling them. And when the rozzers come round about this afternoon's little ruckus, spin them a yarn and keep me out of it. If you have to mention me, make me a concerned passer-by or something. A good Samaritan.'

'I'll give it a go,' he said. He looked thoughtful. 'I've already spun Uncle Manny a yarn. About putting out some feelers on your behalf. He was right browned off, but I'm sure he'll keep his mouth shut.' He paused. 'The police'll be easy. After all, why would robbers turn up at a jeweller's?' He gave a little laugh.

A policeman was talking to a couple of people on the street when we emerged from the shop. A certain amount of hand waving accompanied a, doubtless, chaotic account of what had taken place, and one man was pointing emphatically towards Leather Lane.

The policeman was absorbed in the taxing task of spelling 'proceeding' correctly and writing with a pencil blunt enough to require constant attention from his tongue. The others were staring off into the distance, presumably looking for the phantom car.

None of them noticed us as we slipped – well, lumbered and limped – past.

'Try not to bleed on the seat,' Charlie said to Herbert. 'The gaffer'll give me hell.'

'I'll be fine. I never was much of a bleeder,' Herbert said.

'Just a silly one,' Charlie muttered under his breath.

'How many people back at the house in Kennington?' I asked casually.

The Battler looked puzzled for a minute, then he realized what I was asking. 'Just the one left,' he said. 'Don. Soft as butter. Good job the boy doesn't know that or he'd have legged it by now.'

It was worth a go. I could take Don. And, after all, I had promised Beverley Beaumont that I'd look out for Jon. He didn't deserve it. He was a slimy little toe-rag. I wasn't sure that she deserved it either, but a promise is a promise.

'Look after your man here,' I said to Charlie, 'and don't forget that Les wants you at his place later. I might see you at the party. I'll get a cab from here.'

'All right, Tone,' Charlie said. He pointed at my torn trouser leg. 'You'd best be off and change your suit.'

I nodded and saw a taxi letting off a fare back on High Holborn and dashed for it.

FOURTEEN

The cabbie was decent sort who made no bones about making a brief recce south of the river, into enemy territory. He talked a lot though.

And he threw question after question at me, over his left shoulder: What did I make of Sir Winston resigning? What about the dock strikes? What was up with the weather? What did I make of all these West Indians coming into the country?

Fortunately, he wasn't interested in what I had to say on any of these weighty matters. Which was just as well, as I had no worthwhile opinion about them. 'The 'undreds of darkies' crossing the Atlantic, apparently making the long journey for the sole purpose of taking the bread out of the mouths of poor cab drivers, seemed to have completely passed me by. Although, come to think of it, there was one rather well-spoken, well-dressed black man who'd moved into one of the streets close to Leyton Underground station. But he was from Africa.

I asked the cabbie to drop me on the main road, just short of the turning to Florrie's neat little house. I was perhaps a little too scrupulous about his tip, counting it out very carefully, but that was likely to prove less memorable than being either too stingy or flamboyantly generous. As I waited for him to turn around and drift back towards the centre of town on a cloud of filthy exhaust before making my way to the street corner, I reflected that a touch more *insouciance* wouldn't have come amiss.

The truth was that I didn't feel very *insouciant*. My knee, my back and my head hurt; my best suit was ruined; I was hot and sweaty; I was tired from travelling all over London on pointless journeys; and, most of all, I was seriously hacked off with Jonathan bloody Harrison for heaping all this suffering on me.

I made a conscious effort to calm down. I closed my eyes briefly and went where I often went when I needed something to cheer me up. I started with Sidney Bechet's haunting 1938 recording of 'Summertime'. By the time I was outside Florrie's black front door, I was buoyed up by Sidney's miraculous soprano sax on the New Orleans Feetwarmers' 1932 record of 'Shag'. Memory is a marvellous thing. And so is music.

The Humber was still parked down the road, but there was no sign of the Morris Oxford. I rat-tatted on the door in time to Ernest Meyers' blissful scat singing, reckoning that luck was on my side and that, if it wasn't, I couldn't think of a more joyous tune to be listening to when I found out.

I didn't mess about. When Florrie opened the door, still resplendent in her headscarf, her lips pursed in disapproval, I held the wagging finger of authority up and whispered, 'Which room are they in? Front or back?'

She looked perplexed.

'Which room, Florrie?' I repeated.

'Back,' she hissed. 'Back bedroom.'

I pushed my way past and, ignoring my various aches and pains, took the stairs two at a time.

The door to what had to be the back bedroom was ajar, and I just charged in.

Don was, unfortunately for him but happily for me, standing right behind it, listening, and it hit him very hard. He was staggering and a little dazed. I didn't give him a chance to recover and just hit him once in the face. I didn't catch him properly and felt a knuckle pop. Oh, well, what was another bruise among friends? Don was down and out of the action, though, lying beside the single bed. The New Orleans Feetwarmers had worked their magic yet again and brought me luck.

Jonathan Harrison was not looking quite as urbane as he had the previous night. In fact, he was looking a little sorry for himself. He was loosely tied to a high-backed chair. He was unshaven, and there was some bruising on one of his cheeks and some dried blood around his mouth and nose.

'Cheer up,' I said. 'It's the Seventh Cavalry.'

'Mr Gérard,' he said, ever polite, 'thank goodness.'

'Goodness,' I said as I untied the women's nylon stockings that held him to the chair, 'has nothing to do with it.' I think that my Mae West impression wasn't as good as I liked to imagine. It didn't even raise a hint of a smile.

I nursed my hand while he stamped some circulation back into his legs.

The curtains were drawn in the neat little room, and it was dark and airless, stuffy and quiet in a drowsy July sort of way. The only sound was a large bluebottle buzzing against the window, which added to the illusion that summer had come early.

Don stirred and tried to sit up. I knelt down and grabbed him roughly by his tie, tightening it against his throat.

'I don't want any trouble from you,' I said. 'Just sit here quietly. Understand?'

He nodded meekly, and I let him go. He leaned back against the bed.

I turned to Jonathan Harrison. I'd decided I was fed up with forking out for taxis and travelling by underground, especially when there was a nice, comfortable Humber just a short walk away.

'Can you drive?' I said.

He shook his head.

'So who drove you to Cambridge and to my place?'

'Rose,' he said. 'She was a driver during the war.'

I thought about it for a minute and decided I didn't want anyone else involved.

'You,' I said to Don, 'are going to drive us back into town in the Humber, and then, if you know what's good for you, you'll forget all about where you took us.'

I had Don drive us to Liverpool Street station. He could make what he would of that. I rather hoped that he (or Jenkins) would reckon that Jon had headed back to Cambridge.

In fact, of course, Liverpool Street is not just a British Railways station; it is also on the Central Line, only a handful of stops from Leyton.

The Humber was not as nice a ride as Les's Rolls. But beggars can't be choosers and all that, and it was every bit as comfortable as the Wolseley. For someone who can't drive and who wouldn't be able to afford a car even if he could, I'd been in some very classy motors in the course of the one day.

I did think about disabling the car by yanking out some crucial wires, if I could find any, but one look at Don's reproachful face and I just didn't have the heart for it.

Instead, I told him to be a good boy and forget he'd ever

seen me or I'd be back to haunt him. He didn't quite raise a
sneer, but he did manage a degree of sullen resentment that
implied he didn't think I could make good on the threat. On
reflection, though, he might just have been worrying about
how he was going to explain the loss of his captive to his
employer. That wasn't going to be an easy conversation for
him. My heart strings remained untugged.

I waited until he'd driven away before turning my attention to Jonathan Harrison. In my haste to get away from
Florrie's little house – I'd decided that, as I didn't know when
anyone was likely to be back to check on Jon, it would be
wise to get away quickly – I hadn't done more than tell Rose
and Florrie that we were leaving. I hadn't even given him a
chance to clean himself up. In the glare of daylight he was
looking decidedly the worse for wear, bruised and bloodied.

I negotiated our way through the crowds waiting to board
trains and took him into the cool quiet of the men's toilet. It
smelt strongly of disinfectant, but I suppose that was better
than the alternative.

The attendant looked askance at us. Conscious that my torn
suit and Jon's bashed face suggested we were a couple of
street brawlers, I smiled at him warmly. He didn't appear
noticeably reassured and just turned away, back to cleaning
one of the cubicles with his mop and dented, grey bucket of
filthy water.

I left Jon at one of the basins to wash and went to the urinal
to pee.

The great, long, stained trough gurgled into life as I stood
there and water sluiced down, swirling the soggy fag-ends,
used matches, Spangles wrappers and other assorted debris
along to the clogged drain at the far end. I hoped it wasn't
too clogged. I really didn't fancy seeing my own – even much
diluted – pee washing over my shoes. Fortunately, the water
stopped flowing just before it reached that point, though
shredded tobacco and a green sweet wrapper I recognized did
float past again, on the backwash.

I heard the attendant banging about as he moved into the
next cubicle and two people strode across the damp, stone floor,
their footsteps echoing in the cathedral-like acoustic, to join me
at the urinal before I finished.

Of course, when I'd rebuttoned my fly and turned back to

the basins, Jonathan Harrison, ungrateful little toe-rag of this and every other parish, had scarpered.

I knew it was pointless, but I raced out into the station anyway. There were a couple of trains fired up and waiting to leave, steam gushing out from their wheels and billowing gently up to join the smut-laden black smoke roiling from their chimneys. And there were people everywhere – it was, after all, edging towards six – but not one of them was Jonathan Harrison.

Somehow, I didn't think that I was likely to see him in the French at seven either, in spite of the arrangement he'd made the previous evening. A more pressing engagement must have come up.

I stood there, among the hundreds of people milling about, waiting for their trains to Seven Kings, Chadwell Heath and Shenfield, bereft without their evening papers, and decided that enough was enough. Even if he hadn't quite reached the age of majority and couldn't vote, he was certainly old enough to steal, lie and seduce his way through life. From now on, he could do it all without me. I'd fulfilled my promise to Beverley Beaumont. I'd tried to look out for him. My conscience was clear.

Don was probably right. I almost certainly wouldn't be back to haunt him. But I couldn't help the nagging suspicion, gnawing away at me like a mouse in the wainscoting, that Jonathan Harrison would be back to haunt me.

Jerry was looking incredibly fresh-faced and cheerful when I dropped in to ask him if he wanted to come to the party. I didn't come straight out with it and ask him, as he, disconcertingly, adopted some odd postures. He kept jutting his chin out and grinning at me. It slowly dawned on me that he was posing. Then I realized why.

'You've shaved off the goatee,' I said.

'Yeah,' he said, going for a self-deprecating nonchalance and missing by a considerable distance. He did manage to look embarrassed and self-conscious though. 'Ghislaine thought I'd look better without it.'

'Ah,' I said. 'How is she? And where is she?'

'She's getting ready. And she's fine. Great, actually,' he said.

'Getting ready for what?' I said.

'Maurice Chevalier is on at the Palace Theatre.' He went for nonchalance again. 'We thought we'd go.'

'Maurice Chevalier?' I said and raised a sceptical eyebrow. Jerry and Maurice Chevalier are not natural bedfellows. But then, he probably wasn't looking to share his bed with the sophisticated *boulevardier* and *chanteur*.

'Yes,' he said. 'There's not much else on.'

'No,' I said, 'I guess not.'

'In fact,' he said, 'we'd better get our skates on, if we're going to make it on time. Hurry her up, would you?'

I clumped up the stairs.

Ghislaine was looking as cheerful as Jerry and had dressed in an elegant blue cotton dress.

'So,' I said, 'Maurice Chevalier and Jerry?'

'He is very sweet and good looking. He is what I need at the moment, Antoine.'

'Maurice Chevalier?' I said.

She hit me on the shoulder.

'Have fun,' I said as she danced down to the corridor.

Well, if a light-hearted dalliance was what she needed, I'd rather she had it with Jerry than me. Or Maurice Chevalier.

The ungallant, but welcome, thought that I might be able to reclaim my bed cheered my aching bones. I remembered that I hadn't called Reg, the football manager. Well, I didn't much feel like playing on Saturday, but I did want to see Mrs Williams.

The Fray Bentos steak pie that I'd found lurking in the larder and the tin of peas I'd warmed up to accompany it were sitting a bit heavily on my stomach as I walked towards the function room at the Savoy that Les had hired for his party.

I didn't know why Les had chosen the Savoy. As soon as I walked into the foyer, I felt out of place in my tired old grey suit. Les was fighting well above his weight here. It was way too posh for me, and for Hoxton Films. I wondered why he was going ahead with the party. What with Fleet Street being out on strike, he wasn't going to benefit from widespread press coverage.

The muted hubbub became considerably less muted as I walked along the dowdy corridor that led to the room I'd been directed to by the offhand and supercilious doorman when he'd finally agreed to recognize my existence. I nearly asked him what he'd done to earn all that braid, but decided to restrict myself to a jaunty, 'Thank you, my good man,' instead. It was just that touch more insulting and all the better for being subtle. I thought that the corridor was nowhere near opulent enough to justify the doorman's sniffy attitude. But then I was feeling slightly aggrieved and looking for fault. The faded carpet and the dingy wallpaper made me feel better. So did the peerless Louis Armstrong leading the Hot Five in 'Muskrat Ramble', which resounded jauntily in my head and insisted on a brisk, springy stride.

From the sound coming from the room I guessed that there was a good turnout.

Charlie, looking considerably smarter than me in his dark suit, white shirt and tie, was at the door, carefully inspecting invitations and it was good to see a friendly face after the annoying bonehead at the front entrance.

'Hello, Tone,' he said. 'You've probably missed the champagne. The boss didn't order that much.'

'That's all right, Charlie,' I said. 'I'm not much of a one for champagne. How's your mate? Herbert.'

Charlie broke off to greet another couple of latecomers – a large, florid, self-important man, who pushed past me impatiently, and his four-square wife, resplendent in her double string of pearls, who waited, rather graciously, for me to step aside and then acknowledged me with a friendly nod of her extravagant perm and a pencilled eyebrow raised in apology for her oafish husband. I smiled at her.

'He's all right,' Charlie said after ushering the couple inside. 'He had a lot worse in the ring. He wasn't much of a fighter. Too big and slow.' He paused. 'Mind you, he was sweating and bleeding like a good 'un and the quack was suspicious. I don't think he believed me when I told him that Herbert had caught his arm on some barbed wire.' He sniffed. 'Still, he didn't call the rozzers,' he said cheerfully. 'You'd better get in before they run out of those horses doovers. The boss didn't order too many of those either.'

'I'll probably survive,' I said, feeling a meaty burp build up somewhere behind my sternum and choking it back. 'I'm not sure I'm dressed smart enough for this though.'

He looked me up and down. 'You'll do,' he said. 'Everyone'll think you're a chippy or a soundman.'

'Thanks,' I said, feeling even shabbier than I had before. The grey suit really was a bit long in the tooth. I wondered if Maurie, the elderly tailor next door but one to Jerry's record shop, might be able to repair the tear in my blue suit. I didn't have high hopes and suspected that a trip to Foster Bros was very much on the cards. 'And thanks for all your help this afternoon. I really appreciate it, Charlie.'

I slipped quickly away before he could smack me on the shoulder – what is it with my friends and my shoulder? – with the punch that he was shaping up to deliver. I'd seen the damage he could do when he put his mind to it.

There were a lot of dark-suited backs and a surprising number of elaborate-looking hairdos, all enveloped in a thick fug of blue-grey smoke. And there was braying laughter and high-pitched giggling rising above the general noise level. The crowd was like a single entity, rippling fluidly across the floor, giving off heat, noise and, it has to be admitted, smell.

I snaffled a glass of red wine from a passing waiter and sipped. It was nasty – oily and cheap. I looked around for a friendly face.

I saw Les on the other side of the room, surrounded by four or five large, beefy men, all smoking cigars. His pneumatic secretary was by his side, looking at him adoringly. And Jimmy Bolt stood on the other side of the room, at the centre of a group of young men and women, sounding off about something. Pompous little prat.

Daphne saw me, broke away from the group she was with and sauntered over.

'You're looking very glamorous, Daff,' I said. And she was. A black cocktail dress showed off her legs to good advantage, and she'd had her hair done since I'd last seen her. The rope of pearls coiled around her neck rested on a very impressive *embonpoint*. I could see what had attracted Les twenty years ago. Pity he hadn't realized that it all came wrapped around a very astute brain and an acerbic tongue.

'Enjoying yourself?' she said. She had that slightly glazed look that suggested she'd been drinking solidly for the past hour and a half.

'Only just got here, Daff,' I said.

'Well,' she said, 'don't drink too much of the champagne. It does funny things to your eyesight. I keep thinking there's more than one Les here. And that's an awful thought.'

'I can think of worse,' I said.

'I can't,' she said firmly. She tried to take a sip from her empty glass. 'Bugger,' she said. 'Excuse me, I have to go see a man about a horse. Or a dog.' She tapped her nose and looked meaningfully at her glass.

'Let me get you a refill, Daff,' I said and extended my hand.

'No chance,' she said. 'You don't know where the secret bottles of champagne are.' She tapped her nose again and drifted unsteadily away.

I risked another taste of the filthy wine and wondered how soon I could leave.

I looked around and saw a couple of actors I recognized, including an oily creep I'd failed to find in a basement club in Soho once. The yellow electric light gleamed on his brilliantined hair, which shone as brightly as his patent-leather shoes. A few young women were hanging on his every word. Not that that would get them anywhere. He was a creep with a taste for the exotic. I thought about warning them, but I was distracted.

I recognized her perfume before she spoke, and I didn't need to turn to know who it was when I felt her light touch on my arm.

'Miss Beaumont,' I said.

She left her hand on my arm. 'I just wanted to thank you, Mr Gérard,' she said. 'For rescuing Jon.'

So that was where the little piece of ordure had fled.

'It was nothing,' I said.

She was looking more animated than I had ever seen her, almost glowing.

Maybe she was a woman in love, the better half of me thought. And maybe Jonathan Harrison had cured her blues with some of his 'special' medicine, the less attractive half of me suggested.

'Tell me about him,' I said. 'He, er, slipped away before we got a chance to become acquainted. But he seems a rum sort of English student.'

'He is,' she said. 'I met him at a party in Cambridge. Well, just outside. He didn't know who I was, which was refreshing. So I knew he was just attracted to me, not the film star. You don't know how unusual that is. And he was young, of course. And good looking. And, in spite of everything, very innocent.'

'In spite of everything?' I said. 'What?'

'In spite of the way he pays his way through university,' she said.

I looked the question at her.

She laughed. It was a pleasant sound, rich and deep, and it flowed over you like warm honey. Even though she was laughing at me, it was very seductive.

'I didn't have you down as naive, Mr Gérard.'

'I thought you liked innocence,' I said.

'Only the real thing,' she said, 'and I do believe you're flirting with me.'

'No, no,' I said, and I felt my face reddening.

She smiled and put her hand to my cheek and tapped it lightly. 'And now I've made you blush,' she said. 'I am sorry.' And she laughed her warm-honey laugh and left her hand against my cheek for a teasing second or two. 'Anyway, I wanted to say thank you, because I don't suppose Jon remembered. So, thank you.' And she stepped forward again and brushed her lips against my cheek. Then she looked behind me and the smile and the animation left her face. 'Excuse me,' she said. 'My agent just came in. I'd better say hello.'

She walked towards a lean, well-dressed man I recognized from our brief encounter in the Imperial Club. From the vicious look he gave me, I suspected that David Cavendish recognized me too. I decided to melt into the crowd. I turned and bumped into someone. Before I could apologize, he spoke.

'Well, well, well,' said a familiar voice. 'You've obviously made a hit with the beautiful Beverley Beaumont, Mr Gérard.' It was the use of the acute e that gave him away. 'I wonder if you'd mind stepping outside for a moment. We have much to discuss.'

I shrugged, looked around for a surface to put my glass on, relinquishing the remaining wine with little regret, and followed Jenkins out of the sweaty, stuffy room.

FIFTEEN

I f it was warm back in the function room, the atmosphere was positively icy out in the dim, musty corridor.

Jan the Belgian stared through the thick lenses of his spectacles bleakly and unremittingly at Charlie, who glared back. Charlie looked tense and uncomfortable, and he pulled and tugged at the collar of his shirt as though it was chafing his neck. Next to the Belgian was a compact, hard-looking man of about my age. He was wearing a blue suit and what looked like a regimental tie with red and yellow stripes. He was holding a black trilby. Over his arm was a neatly folded fawn mack. In contrast to Charlie, he looked confident and relaxed. In contrast to Jan the Belgian, he looked amused.

Jenkins lit a cigarette – one of his Dunhills – and blew smoke at the ceiling. 'What am I to do with you, Mr Gérard?' he said amiably. 'You just won't be told.' He nodded at Jan the Belgian, presumably to indicate the impeccable source of his information. The Belgian favoured me with a contemptuous glance.

Suddenly, I vividly recalled standing in Mr Barraclough's office, with the sun gliding in through the grimy window, dust motes floating in the still air, the gentle early-summer breeze carrying the boisterous shrieks of schoolchildren from the playground. 'I remember my old headmaster saying much the same thing,' I said.

'You should have listened to him,' Jenkins said. He shuffled a few steps along the corridor. 'Walk with me, and I'll endeavour to explain some of the more essential and pressing facts of life.' He reached towards me with one of his big hands and beckoned.

I fell into step beside him. He looked down with sad, rheumy eyes. I assumed it was the smoke from his cigarette that was making him a little tearful, rather than any compassion for my situation. He put his arm around my shoulders, as though we were the best of friends. I could smell his cologne and the sharp, acrid smoke on his breath.

'I'm guessing that you think that Jan is not a nice man,'

he said, 'and I'm not going to disagree with you and sing his praises. He isn't a particularly pleasant fellow.' He paused and sucked on his cigarette. 'But he does love his diamonds.' A thin streak of smoke rose up into the air. 'Well, they're mine really, but that doesn't make him love them any less. We've shared them ever since 1947, and we hope to share them for years to come. They enable us to live rather well, although not too ostentatiously. I wouldn't want to attract the attention of my former employers.'

We had reached the foyer. Jenkins' hand slipped down to the middle of my back, and he firmly eased me out of the door, which was held open by the same functionary who I'd seen on the way in. He was as fawning and unctuous to Jenkins as he had been graceless to me. I chalked that up against him as well.

'I'll be honest,' Jenkins said as we emerged into the grey night and the little crowd that milled around outside the hotel, waiting for taxis. 'I came by the diamonds in unusual circumstances after the war, in Berlin. You don't need to know the details. All you need to know is that Jan facilitates their passage to this fair and sceptred land, via my little team of penniless students.' He sighed. 'You are probably wondering why I trust him when he is so obviously untrustworthy. Well, the short answer is that I don't. And that is where Alfred, the gentleman with Jan, comes in. If you think that Jan is not pleasant, I can assure you that he is as jovial and good-natured as Father Christmas when compared to Alfred.'

I noticed that he was steering me towards a car – the Humber Super Snipe, no less – parked on the Strand. I glanced back and saw Jan the Belgian and the apparently not very nice Alfred following us very closely.

'So,' I said, 'what's all this got to do with me?'

'Ah,' he said. 'This is all just by way of a preamble to let you know what's what. You and I, and Jan and Alfred, are going back to your grubby little flat over in Leyton and you are going to let me have those diamonds that naughty little Jonathan handed to you and then we're all going to forget this ever happened.'

I felt slightly aggrieved at his description of my flat but there were more pressing concerns. Like the fact that I didn't have the diamonds. And doubts that he was going to forget it had all happened.

I contemplated telling him about my lack of diamonds but then he'd ask me where they were and I couldn't drop Bernie in it. So I said nothing.

I thought about making a break for it and haring off down the Strand, like Roger Bannister with his shorts on fire, but I couldn't see what I'd gain. Even if I got away, which was by no means certain – Jan and the redoubtable Alfred really were following us very closely – they'd find me in a day or two. I might gain a few hours, but we'd still end up in my crib confronting the essential issues. And, in the meantime, I'd be watching my back all the time. That wasn't how I liked to lead my life.

The Germans took me in for questioning once. It had just been a routine round-up in some small town in Normandy – Pontorson, where I had foolishly ventured by bicycle, some way from our stomping ground, to see Mont St Michel – but they hadn't liked my papers. They took me off to Caen, held me for three days and then, inexplicably, let me go. Robert hadn't said anything, but he watched me closely for ten days and reined in our operations so I knew he'd assumed that I'd sold them out and only gradually came to accept that I hadn't. In fact, I'm not sure that he ever did trust me completely again.

My time in that cell and in the little office used for interrogation hadn't been pleasant, and I still don't know how I got away with it, but I did. Ghislaine, to snorts from the hard-line atheist Robert, talked about me having a guardian angel, but I don't really believe that there's someone up there looking out for me. Like my father, I tend to think that you face up to what life throws at you and it'll either sort itself out or it won't. So far, it had always sorted itself out. My father's fatalism, always expressed with a shrug and an amiable grunt, had a surprisingly optimistic side, and so does mine.

Since I had no intention of racing off to Bernie, reclaiming the diamonds and handing them over to Jenkins, I climbed meekly into the Humber, noting that Don wasn't driving, and settled down in the back seat, reckoning that I might as well face up to things now.

I did vaguely wonder if Charlie might alert someone to my predicament, but that was asking a lot of him and I rather doubted it. He had a party to police.

Alfred and Jan the Belgian sat down on either side of me. Both of them looked depressingly determined and competent.

My thinking, in not charging off to Bernie and reclaiming the stones, was that, oddly, I stood more chance of staying alive by not giving Jenkins what he wanted, although I recognized that, either way, my chances of survival were slim.

I looked from Jan's red, pitted face to Alfred's unremarkable, even features and wondered which one would pull the trigger, or tighten the cord. Then I slumped down in the seat and used the silent journey to consider what Jenkins had told me.

Jerry had been stationed in Germany, although not in Berlin, for part of his National Service, and I'd been there briefly, sat incongruously behind a desk, trying to keep track of NAAFI supplies. My pre-war experience in accountancy coming back to bite me through my coarse battledress in the backside. Rumour constantly bubbled away about corruption and theft. There were even a few arrests. Jerry was of the opinion that everyone was at it, to a greater or lesser extent. I wasn't so cynical, but I'd certainly heard of fortunes being made in the chaos. Jenkins' reference to his former employers suggested that he had been in some branch of Intelligence, which meant he had access to former Nazis. It wasn't a big step to guess at a middle-ranking member of the party bribing his way to freedom.

Quite how Jan and Alfred fitted in I wasn't sure, but Alfred had the slightly mad look of some of my former colleagues in Special Operations. He'd make an excellent enforcer. For those in the know, the threat of someone like Alfred was more than enough. And Jan was probably, as Ghislaine had suggested, a racketeer. And that was about as much as I would ever deduce or learn. Not one of the three of them was likely to risk their operation out of any misguided sentiments for my well-being. And Jenkins had already told me more than was good for him, or, more pertinently, for me. I hadn't exactly made my bed, but I was still going to have to lie in it.

Such were my gloomy thoughts as we drew up outside Jerry's shop. It was quiet and dark, although it was only nine thirty.

At least Jerry and Ghislaine wouldn't be back for a couple of hours.

We sat quietly for a few seconds, listening to the rumble of the big, idling engine.

I can't speak for the others, but I was preparing myself for what was to come.

A match rasped harshly against the abrasive edge of its box and flared into flame as Jenkins lit another cigarette. We all automatically looked at the burning match, and I could almost see why moths might be so fatally attracted to the light. There was something faintly hypnotic about it. Soon, wispy curlicues of smoke drifted over Jenkins' right shoulder, slowly forming delicate, insubstantial question marks in the stale air before settling languorously into a thin, bluish-grey fug.

I stared straight ahead, looking through the windscreen at the balmy spring night. I thought about telling them that I didn't have the diamonds, but then the smoke tickled my throat and I gave a rough, ragged cough instead and completely broke the moment.

The driver turned off the engine, all four doors were flung open, and they all clambered out and started stretching, coughing and yawning. I slid across the seat and edged out myself. The only advantage I had was that I knew the area. If I was going to make a run for it, now was the time.

But I didn't, partly because I couldn't see the point and partly because I'd just remembered something.

I ambled slowly to my door and stood in the gentle light of the ornate old lamp-post while I ferreted about in my trouser pocket for my key. It was cool and damp after the closeness of the car, but the gentle wind carried the sulphurous taint of coal smoke from a million fires and gritty particles of industrial effluvium.

I stabbed the key at the door. The lock was very loose in its mounting and moved an eighth of an inch or so before the key engaged. I assumed that had something to do with Don and Ray breaking in the other day. It was odd that I hadn't noticed it before.

The four of them gathered together around me, like a rugby maul forming, as I opened the door. I led them along the dark corridor and up the stairs. I turned the light on in my office. The element fizzed like an R. White's lemonade bottle opening, and then the bare bulb cast a dim light into the room, throwing soft-edged shadows on the walls.

'Tea, anyone?' I asked politely.

Alfred barked out a humourless laugh. It wasn't a comforting sound.

'This isn't really a social occasion,' Jenkins said, and he looked meaningfully at Alfred and nodded.

Alfred shifted his weight forward on to the balls of his feet. I'd seen that slightly mad grin before, on the faces of others, just before they launched themselves at the enemy. There was something about him of the mad, naked berserker that had caught my imagination in a history lesson once. The idea wasn't as appealing somehow as it had been back then in the dusty old classroom smelling of sweat and bad feet.

Talking my way out of this had always been unlikely, but at that moment it looked about as possible as Orient winning the cup, when they'd been knocked out back in January. If I was going to make any kind of move, however pointless, now was the time to make it – before Alfred exploded into imaginatively violent and, for me, painful action.

'No,' I said, 'I suppose it isn't. More of a business meeting, really.' I moved swiftly across the room and bent down to rummage in the battered old cardboard box where what I humorously called 'my filing' lurked, gathering a patina of dust, spiders and that curious mystique that ancient, worthless artefacts attract. 'I imagine you'd like to collect the diamonds and be on your way.'

Jenkins exchanged an uncertain look with Alfred, who took a step towards me. But he was too late. I already had the Webley in my hand. He stopped and stood still, his right hand hovering in front of his chest.

'You could,' I said, standing up and looking him straight in the eye, 'reach for the gun you've probably got in your pocket, but I'll shoot you before you can get it out.'

Alfred inclined his head in a gesture of acceptance, moved his hand down to his side and stepped back. Jan rather theatrically raised his hands in the universal gesture of surrender. He had a sour look on his face. Alfred's expression gave nothing away. He might even have been smiling. Neither look suggested that either of them was defeated. They were both just recognizing the immediate reality and waiting for an opening.

They didn't have too long to wait.

I hadn't really weighed the driver up before, and now I regretted that. He was a barrel-chested, thick-necked bruiser, and he stepped in front of Jenkins and walked towards me. I guess he had me down as what my old sergeant used to call 'a useless jessie'. To be fair, lack of resistance on the journey may have misled him. But I'm not quite as useless a jessie as Sergeant Bartlett imagined me to be, and I lowered the gun and fired. Because of the weapon's double action, the driver managed a step more than I'd allowed for and, instead of the bullet going through the floor in front of him, he anticipated its trajectory perfectly and placed a foot in its path.

I'd forgotten just how much noise a Webley made in a confined space, and the roar of this one deafened me slightly. Which was just as well, as it meant I couldn't really hear the driver's squeals as he fell over, clutching at his left boot. Even through my deafness, he sounded like a stuck pig. The recoil was a bit more than I'd remembered as well.

The ringing in my ears, the sharp stink of gunpowder, the slight pain in my right wrist from the recoil and all the other sensations associated with shooting someone – in this case, the guilt, remorse, the fear of reprisals and consequences – meant that I was distracted, and Alfred was on me before I could react.

He bundled me to the floor and pressed my face against the mouldy-smelling, dusty boards. Then I was aware of his warm breath on the back of my neck, camphor from the moth-balls his suit had been locked up with, stale cigarette smoke, sweat, the hard weight of him sprawled across my back and his strong hand gripping my wrist, and I relaxed. Futile strug-gling wasn't going to get me anything, except hit very hard in the kidneys.

'Drop the gun,' he said, just like in all the best Westerns.

He let go of my wrist to reach for it, and I heaved up as hard as I could and smacked my elbow into his throat. He gave a very satisfying gurgle and fell backwards.

And I might have got away with it if Jan the Belgian hadn't chosen that moment to kick me painfully in the shoulder and then again in the ribs. I didn't think he'd broken anything, but I was seriously winded and collapsed back to the floor, drag-ging air into my lungs in ragged gulps. He kicked me again, but his heart wasn't in it and he didn't do any more than add to the bruise he'd already given me. Alfred, though, had recovered enough to pick up the gun, and he lashed out at the back of my head with it and that did sting.

As I sank into semi-consciousness, it crossed my mind that I'd managed to get through his mask of wry amusement.

I lay there panting, my head throbbing alarmingly. Ah, well, I'd given it my best shot, and I'd hurt one of them. Pity it hadn't been Jan or Alfred.

I was aware of Alfred getting to his feet and then of someone grabbing the collar of my jacket and hauling me upright. Then I heard a voice I hadn't heard for some time.

'Anthony, forgive me for disturbing you, but I just wondered where you keep your coffee. I can't seem to find any in your kitchen.' There was a pause. 'And it looks as though you are involved in an altercation. I had hoped to find that you had changed your ways after all these years.' There was a sigh and a cloud of pungent cigarette smoke.

Only, of course, he didn't say exactly that, because he was speaking French.

SIXTEEN

Robert Rieux has always made me feel uncomfortable. It is, I suppose, a combination of his dangerous ideological certainty, his glib and cruel tongue, his sheer ruthlessness and the fact that he has never even tried to conceal his contempt for me and my wishy-washy politics. He has always managed to keep me off balance as well because he is frighteningly, sometimes whimsically, unpredictable. The word capricious could have been invented to describe him. Consequently, there have been few occasions when I've been happy to see him, but this was one of those rare moments.

It wasn't an unmitigated pleasure, of course, because I knew why he was there. Nevertheless, the sight of him and his three companions crowding into my already packed office was a temporarily uplifting one.

For a few seconds the only sounds were the shuffling feet of the Frenchmen and the soft sobs of the wounded driver. He had quietened considerably, but he wasn't demonstrating any Spartan spirit in his response to pain. I was starting to feel real guilt.

Robert looked at me, smiled and then spoke in Spanish. 'What's going on, man?' he asked. He had fought in Catalonia as a young man, and it was a phrase he had often used as a greeting. This time he really wanted an answer.

'I think,' I said carefully, in French, 'that these men are planning to kill me.'

He smiled again. The years had been as kind to him as they had been to Ghislaine. A little too much soft living had added some bulk, but he still looked fit and sleek. He was certainly expensively dressed in a dark, double-breasted suit, blue shirt and blue tie. He was carrying a black fedora, not unlike Jerry's, which he placed on the old kitchen table.

'I can't allow that, can I?' he said. 'You're an old comrade in arms.' He paused and looked thoughtful. 'Besides,' he continued, 'I may want to reserve that pleasure for myself.'

He paused again and looked at the driver. 'And that man there?' he said.

'Unfortunately,' I said, 'he placed his foot in the way of a bullet that was intended for the floor.'

Robert raised his eyebrows.

'It was a bullet of warning,' I explained. 'Not one of lethal intent.'

Robert nodded and pursed his lips, then straightened up and looked around. He rattled something off to the young man standing to his right. I didn't catch what he said, but Jan did and his hand dropped to his coat pocket. However, Robert's companions already had guns in their hands, and Jan sensibly froze and didn't reach further.

I recognized the compact, durable, black Mle 1935s as the young man moved towards Alfred and took the Webley from him. The Mle 1935s wasn't the most powerful of weapons, but it would be very effective from four feet and Alfred was wise not to make a fuss.

An older man, a fat, damp, yellow cigarette dangling from his lips, nonchalantly relieved Jan of his revolver.

'OK,' Robert said briskly, switching to heavily accented English, 'we must now negotiate a peace.' He beamed and looked around. 'What is the – as our American friends say – the beef here?'

Jan and Alfred both glanced towards Jenkins, who looked uncomfortable and cleared his throat loudly. Robert smiled at him and, with a little open-handed gesture, invited him to speak.

'This gentleman,' Jenkins finally said, 'your friend, has something of mine.' The ironic emphasis he put on 'friend' suggested that he was sceptical about our relationship. He didn't know how right he was.

'Well then, Antoine, you must return this man's something, his property,' Robert said. He was enjoying himself.

'But I don't have it,' I said.

'There you are, then,' Robert said, turning back to Jenkins. 'An honest mistake.'

'You don't understand,' Jenkins started, but Robert cut him off sharply.

'No,' he said, 'it is you who does not understand. This is finished. Over. My friend says that he does not have your property, and I know him to be an honourable man. Therefore it is so. You must look elsewhere for your thing.'

There was a long silence broken only by the mechanical weeping of the driver who was hunched over now, clutching his foot, evidently in a great deal of pain. A certain amount of blood was seeping out from his sodden boot on to the floor. Jerry was going to have an unsightly stain on the shop's ceiling in the morning. Ah, well, it was nothing a few coats of paint wouldn't deal with. Although there might be something of a hole as well. The driver might not be so easily sorted out, depending on what tissue the heavy bullet had smacked into on its way down into Jerry's record emporium. As I looked at him, it occurred to me that, with the right shoes, suit, hat and raincoat, Roger the barman could have taken him for Special Branch. Maybe he had been.

'But I am facing a very substantial loss.' Jenkins was blustering now and standing on his dignity. He was losing face.

'Perhaps,' Robert said, 'but I think you are an affluent man. I also think that you are a robber. That man –' he pointed at Jan – 'is known to me. He is older now, but I do not forget faces.' Jan looked shifty. 'Leave now and talk to him. He will explain why you would be advised to forget all about this. My friend Antoine is very dear to me.'

'But—' Jenkins said.

Robert cut across him and addressed his young lieutenant in French. 'Emile, it seems that Voltaire was right and that the English need to be "encouraged" from time to time.' He looked at Jan and then at Jenkins. 'As there is no admiral available, shoot that one –' he indicated Alfred – 'in the arm.'

The young man, whose handsome, broken-nosed profile made him look quite like a gangster from a thirties film, nodded. The little Mle 1935s whispered in comparison to the big Webley, but it still gave a substantial bark and the bullet tore an impressive path across Alfred's biceps before embedding itself in the wall. Either Emile was a great shot who had intended to do Alfred only minimal damage or he couldn't shoot for toffee. Either way, it was only a superficial wound – a graze, really – and probably no more than had been inflicted on Charlie's friend Herbert, but it had the desired effect. Alfred grimaced and clutched his arm, but made no sound. It must have hurt, but there was more of the little Spartan boy my teacher Mrs Wilson had been so fond of about Alfred than there was about the driver.

Jenkins looked a little shocked, but he hid it well. 'I thought we were talking,' he said. His voice was firm and calm, but a glistening snail trail ran from his hairline to his jaw, showing the path of a translucent bead of sweat that hung to his chin for a second before falling gently on to his tie.

'That was before,' Robert said. 'Then we were negotiating the peace. Now I am enforcing it.'

There was a long, tense pause, but Robert knew he had made his point. Jenkins would leave. Apart from anything else, Robert's men held all the guns. It was time for some magnanimity, even some compassion.

'I think you must go,' Robert said. 'Two of your men have need of medical attention. For this one here –' he indicated the driver – 'I think it is a matter of urgency. He is in considerable discomfort. I think you must know a doctor who will show discretion. And, please, do speak with this gentleman here –' he clicked his fingers impatiently – 'Jean, Jean, yes, Rotfus. You see, I have remembered his name.' Jan the Belgian looked even shiftier than he had before. Jenkins' eyebrows moved slightly closer together as his forehead furrowed briefly in a little frown. This was news to him. 'And consider what he has to say carefully before you make a decision about how to pursue this matter.'

'But how can I leave? I have no driver,' Jenkins said.

'I can drive. I'm all right. I've had worse,' Alfred said, moving towards the door, his left hand pressed against the ragged tear in his right sleeve. His back teeth were grinding together. 'You,' he growled at me, 'owe me a suit. I'll be back to collect.'

I thought ruefully about my own ruined trousers.

Jenkins turned to Jan and indicated the driver before marching out. Jan glanced at Alfred, who winced and shrugged, and then the pair of them helped the man up and supported him as he hopped slowly out, dribbling blood all the way. There were thirteen heavy muffled explosions as he was helped slowly down the stairs.

I felt bad about him, I really did.

         *   *   *

I stood by the window and watched the car pull slowly away from the kerb – the big tyres whispering quietly against the damp, black road – and vanish into the night.

I wondered when Alfred would be back. Sooner rather than later, I imagined.

I turned back to face Robert. 'Would you,' I said, 'let me have the big handgun back? I may need to defend myself in the future.' My French was flowing surprisingly well, particularly when I considered that, Ghislaine apart, I hadn't used it all that much in nearly ten years.

Robert laughed. 'I think you will,' he said. 'And perhaps I will let you have the gun.' He sat down behind my desk. 'We have one or two things to discuss first. And, by the way, I was serious about the coffee. Do you have any?'

I shook my head.

'A pity,' he said, 'but I will survive. A little cognac, perhaps?'

I shook my head again.

He sighed. I was living down to his expectations. 'Well then, perhaps you could offer me a wife?'

'Not at the moment,' I said. 'She's out. With Maurice Chevalier.'

One of his men coughed loudly. I glanced at him, and he coughed again. He was a large man in a dark-brown suit. His face had a number of old shiny scars around the eyes. I realized that he was coughing to disguise the fact that he was laughing. Ghislaine and Maurice Chevalier seemed to amuse him.

'With Maurice Chevalier?' Robert said.

'Not exactly "with",' I said, 'but they are in the same building. He's performing tonight.' I paused. 'How did you know she was here?' I asked.

'An English comrade saw her with you,' he said.

Perfidious Cambridge, of course. It had to be Jameson.

'And the Belgian, Jan, how do you know him?' I asked. I wasn't really playing for time. There was no point. I was genuinely interested.

Robert shrugged and laughed. 'Is that what he's calling himself now?' he said. 'I don't recall all the details, but it was in Paris just after the liberation. You remember? We all travelled there together.'

I remembered. How could I forget one of the most exhilarating weeks of my life?

'It was after we lost contact with you. He was a cheap crook
I came across. From down south somewhere – Marseilles,
probably. Anyway, he'd been running contraband and stealing
from the proletariat. We chastised him a little, and some of his
gang – there may have been a broken bone or two, but it was
no more than parasites and *collabos* deserved. Maybe I should
have killed him when I had the chance.' Robert looked a little
rueful. 'Sometimes I am too tender-hearted.'

The large ex-boxer (I'd decided he must have been in the
ring) started to cough uncontrollably.

'Henri,' Robert said sharply, 'that's enough.'

The man straightened up.

Robert ran his tongue along his top lip and then sucked his
teeth. 'I really never do forget a face. My memory has served
me well over the years.' He sounded reflective for a moment,
but then he was his old brisk, ironic self. 'So,' he said, 'what
should I do about you and my wife?'

'Nothing?' I said.

Robert smiled and leaned forward. He looked amused, which
was worrying. 'Explain,' he said and fell back into the chair.

I cleared my throat and then I told him the truth. 'Well,' I
said, 'I haven't seen Ghislaine in nearly ten years. Not since
Paris. And then I am in a pub and there she is. She says she
is having a little holiday and asks if I can let her stay with
me. I can't turn down an old friend, and she sleeps in there –'
I pointed to the living room – 'and I sleep here. She sees the
sights of London, and I work. There is nothing for you to do
about your wife and me because there is nothing to worry
about.'

I couldn't see any point in telling him that I knew about the
bruises and the mistresses. It would only have complicated
matters unnecessarily.

'And you just . . . met. Quite by chance,' he said.

'Well, not by chance on Ghislaine's part,' I said. 'Obviously,
she went to the French pub to find me. It was chance on my
part that I happened to be there that evening.'

'Indeed,' he said. He sounded sceptical. And I couldn't
blame him. It didn't sound like the truth. Also, he was French
and an accomplished adulterer, and Robert had always lacked
a capacity for empathy. He could only judge others by himself.
Oddly enough, it was a trait that had served him well in the

war. His guesses about the Germans' reactions and intentions had often been surprisingly accurate.

He looked thoughtful and then, a little theatrically, he raised his right forefinger and tapped it against his lips. 'I will think about this for a while,' he said. 'I would not wish to, as the English say, jump to a conclusion.' He had always been proud of his grasp of a few English idioms and, I remembered, had often thrown them in to his conversation, to the consternation of those of his comrades who only spoke French. But, of course, he hadn't done it for their benefit. It was aimed at me. Just because I was reasonably fluent in French didn't make me smarter than him.

I touched the sticky patch on the back of my head and winced. Still, there wasn't too much blood.

I wandered over to the window and looked moodily out. There was a crowd of people leaving the Gaumont, milling about, talking loudly, smoking, waiting for buses or setting off for home. Their footsteps and their voices carried clearly across the road. A couple of young men were bantering with a group of girls and not getting very far.

I wondered if anyone had heard the shots. It wasn't all that likely. No one, except Jerry and me, lived in this row of shops, or those opposite, come to that, which had no living accommodation above them because they were part of the cinema. Someone passing might have heard, but they would probably have shrugged them off.

A feeling of deep weariness threatened to overwhelm me. I hadn't slept much since Ghislaine had appeared, and the back of my head hurt. I wanted to lie in my own bed and sleep for eight hours. My grazed knee and bruised shoulder both decided to throb in sympathy with my head. I really was tired of all this. Perhaps I should ask Les if he could find something else for me to do. I could help Daphne with the accounts.

Maybe I should get a job in the Caribonum factory or at the London Electrical Wire Company. Regular, steady work, just a short walk from home, checking invoices, stuffing little brown wage packets with a few pounds and a couple of shillings, week in, week out, with a fortnight every summer in a B&B in Ramsgate or Canvey Island. And maybe I should get myself a proper home. And maybe Mrs Williams could be persuaded to make an honest man of me. And there were so many pigs flying past the window that it looked like they were setting out on a thousand-bomber raid.

I stared out into the night and watched the crowd outside the Gaumont dwindle as a bus came and took most of them away. Then the cinema's lights dimmed and the two middle-aged usherettes limped out, their varicose veins and corns troubling them, calling out their farewells to the portly manager as he locked up.

All I was really seeing was my own morose reflection in the glass. I was fed up with my life and had been since I'd returned from the war. I turned back into the room.

Robert was leaning back in my chair, staring at the ceiling. His men were spread about the room, their backs against the walls, smoking.

'All right, Robert,' I said. 'I'm tired, and my head hurts. You've had more than enough time to think. If you're going to shoot me, shoot me. If you're not, it's time to go.'

He looked at me for a few seconds and then smiled. 'You are quite right,' he said. 'I have done my thinking. Now I am waiting.'

'For what?' I said.

'For my wife, of course,' he said, standing up. 'I imagine that, after her liaison with Maurice Chevalier, she will return here and be overjoyed to see me. Don't you think so?'

'How could anyone not be overjoyed to see you?' I said. 'I know that I am.'

Robert beamed and spread his hands wide. 'Emile, Henri, Patrice, what did I tell you about my old friend? I told you he is without fear; I told you he is honourable. But I didn't tell that he is a humorist.' He turned towards the door. He paused to pick up his hat and said, 'Shoot him.'

SEVENTEEN

'Dead, comrade?' Henri, the boxer, said. 'You want us to shoot him dead?' He sounded puzzled rather than bothered.

Robert waited a beat and then turned back into the room. His timing was impeccable. It was a long enough pause to have me dripping with sweat and shaking with panic, but not quite long enough for things to go wrong.

'Absolutely not,' he said, barking it out exactly like the actor who played the murderer and thief in *Les Enfants du paradis*. 'I am joking. I'm just showing Antoine that I, too, am still capable of joking.'

But I wasn't sweating. Or panicking. I'd seen him do this before. So, I rather think, had Emile and Patrice. Neither of whom had moved a muscle. Of course, the last time I'd seen him do it there had been no Marcel Herrand impersonation, it had been during the war, and the hapless victim had done rather more than sweat.

'It's still a good joke, Robert,' I said. 'You'll have to excuse me. I must go and change my underpants.'

As I should have expected, he completely – probably deliberately – missed the icy undertone I tried to inject into the comment and chose to recognize only a wry irony. He burst into a great peal of laughter. His was a baritone, manly laugh. 'Ah, Antoine,' he said, 'you remember.'

'I remember,' I said, wondering if he was alluding to something else because Robert rarely did or said anything casually, and I also remembered sitting next to Ghislaine in a grand old cinema in Boulevard de la Madeleine for three hours almost exactly ten years before. It had been the last time I had seen her until her appearance in the French pub.

Which may be why I remembered *Les Enfants du paradis* so well. Although the fact that it was the best film I've ever seen might have had something to do with it. I suspected that Robert was telling me that he knew about that rendezvous in the early summer of 1945 when I was on leave. As I recalled that day, I also vividly remembered the thin faces, the yellow, crooked teeth of the people milling about outside, the sharp bitter smell of tobacco and the harsh clump and clatter of the women's wooden shoes on the boulevard as Ghislaine and I shook hands, kissed cheeks and said our goodbyes, and that had nothing to do with the quality of the film.

Robert strode back into the centre of the room, tossing his hat back on to the table, and put his arm around my shoulders. 'I have missed you, my old friend,' he said, steering me towards the window. 'And so has Ghislaine.'

I couldn't say that I'd missed her and not mention him, so I said nothing and stared out at the empty street.

'And I miss the times we had,' he continued, 'fighting for a cause.' He paused and his hand lifted and fell heavily on my shoulder. 'I still do fight for a cause, of course, but it is not the same. Then, everything was so vivid. I think that perhaps the prospect of capture, imprisonment and death made me more aware of the sheer physical pleasure of being alive. Was it like that for you?' I nodded, and he smiled and continued. 'I relished every day. Now it's dull meetings and shabby compromises, and I feel as if I am dying a slow death. If I didn't have Ghislaine, I don't think I could continue.' He looked at me meaningfully.

'Robert,' I said, 'I don't become entangled with other men's wives.' Unless the man in question is dead.

'How can I believe that?' he said. 'You and Ghislaine were "entangled" once.'

'We were much younger then.' I paused. 'And she was no one's wife.'

He sighed deeply and stared into the gloomy room. After a long silence he spoke again, reflectively, quietly, almost as though he were speaking just for himself. 'Strange times indeed. We were too late, you know. Even before we "found" that old truck and then "liberated" the necessary gasoline from the Americans, de Gaulle had outmanoeuvred Colonel Rol and the moment was lost. You know, de Gaulle's *fifis* didn't do much of the fighting in Paris. That was nearly all down to us. ' He paused, smiled ruefully and then his voice took on its usual resonance. 'Even though we were too late, Paris was the place to be then, don't you think?' He paused again.

I vaguely remembered that the Force Francaise Intérieure

had been affectionately, or disparagingly, I wasn't sure which, known as *les fifis*, but I'd never heard of Colonel Rol. It must have been a *nom de guerre*.

'I wouldn't have been anywhere else,' Robert said. 'There was the *épuration*, after all: the *collabos*, like your friend Jean, to be dealt with.'

'Did you really meet him?' I said.

'Who knows?' he said and shrugged. 'I certainly met someone like him, and he didn't deny it. Perhaps it was him.'

I thought of the unfortunate *collabos horizontales* and an image of the beautiful Arletty as Garance, smiling serenely and telling the most irritating of the young men who was in love with her, the mime, that he was a little boy. I liked to think of her like that, serene and lovely, when she'd been making the film, rather than later, without her *Luftwaffe* lover and her suite at the Ritz, arrested and facing the icy and implacable ferocity of men like Robert. That September I'd even heard a hideous rumour that she'd had her breasts cut off, but it was probably only her hair. I hadn't known who she was then. It wasn't until the following year that I fell in love with her in the warm fug of the Madeleine Cinema.

'I thought we were planning to celebrate the liberation,' I said, 'not join the revolution.'

He shrugged. 'You weren't one of us. You were useful to us, but we couldn't trust you.'

I stared out of the window again, but I wasn't really looking at the quiet street. All I could see was my reflection, shadowed and unreal, hovering against an impenetrable and disconcerting black background that seemed on the verge of swirling and sweeping inexorably forward and enveloping me completely. It was as if I were slowly drowning in a thick, peaty bog. I turned away from the window and leaned against the wall.

Robert lit a cigarette and absent-mindedly offered the pack to me. I shook my head slowly, and he slipped it back into his jacket pocket. Of course, he was still smoking Gauloises, the cigarette of *les poilus* in the Great War, the cigarette of *les maquis*, *la cigarette de l'homme fort*. The strong, sharp, distinctive smell stung my nostrils as he breathed out. Drains, coffee, hot bread and burning tobacco – the delicious mix of olfactory delights that said Paris to me.

The other men were all smoking too, and the atmosphere in my drab office was like the Embankment on a fog-engulfed November night. They were murmuring quietly together, a reassuring, male rumble.

'You know what I remember most about Paris?' I said.

Robert gave me one of those expressive Gallic looks, inviting me to tell him without in any way suggesting interest. He was a remarkably good-looking man still. The deep creases that the last ten years had carved into his cheeks only emphasized the sharp planes of his face, and the lines around his eyes and mouth suggested that he was laughing all the time. The streaks of grey at his temples caught the light and suited him. If he carried a little more weight than he had in his prime – and the generous cut of his suit suggested that he did – it just meant that he now had more *gravitas*, even more presence.

'It was the sound of the wooden shoes,' I said, 'clattering on the cobbles. Everyone seemed to be wearing wooden shoes. I thought for a while that it was something that Maman and Grand-père had neglected to tell me. That it was something so commonplace that it wasn't worth mentioning. I'd been there five days before I understood that there was just no leather.'

I paused, and Robert made no comment. He just shrugged very slightly, and his mouth turned down at the corners. It was a dismissive gesture. Whether he was dismissing the shortages and privations of war as unremarkable or commenting on my words I couldn't be sure.

'I must have been,' I continued, 'a very ignorant young man.'

'Inexperienced, perhaps,' he said, 'and insular. But don't underestimate your importance. You may not have been one of us, but you held us together, kept us all focused. You were brave and organized and certain. We needed that. Your –' he thought for a few seconds, trying to find *le mot juste* – 'toughness.' He looked up at the ceiling.

The word he had used was *dureté*, which surprised me a little. I'd never thought of myself in that way – hard, unyielding, cold-hearted even. I'd certainly been alone and nervous, and I knew I couldn't reveal that. My attempts to disguise it may have led to me appearing to be aloof. But brave, organized, certain and tough? It sounded to me as if Robert were describing himself.

He went on. 'You English always surprise us, you know. What happens after the war? France, the nation of revolution, falters, but not the British! They elect a Socialist government. They sweep away much of the old régime bloodlessly in a very pragmatic English way.' He sighed. 'We French just procrastinate.'

I wasn't convinced that he understood as much as he thought he did about the English. 'I think,' I said, 'that we all just remembered what happened to our fathers after the last lot – the homes for heroes that never materialized – and we voted for change. I know that's what I did. I didn't become a Socialist. And nor did anyone else I knew.'

'Perhaps not,' he said, 'but it looked a little like it from the other side of *la Manche*.' He paused and then beamed. 'But perhaps now we have another little war to get our teeth into. You must have heard about our problems in North Africa.'

I hadn't and, in truth, I had little interest in listening to him lecture me on the post-war world, and I touched the swelling on the back of my head. The blood had dried, but it was very tender, and I decided I'd better do something about it.

'Robert,' I said, 'I'm just going to clean up a little, see if I can't take the sting out of this bump.'

'Sure,' he said. 'Emile can help you.'

Emile looked up and nodded.

'It's not necessary,' I said. 'I'm not going to try to run away. I have no reason to.'

He laughed. 'My suspicious friend,' he said and patted me on the arm. 'I meant what I said. Emile has a little medical training, and he can help you.'

And keep an eye on me at the same time, I thought as I walked through my bedroom to the scullery with Emile carefully shadowing me. I noticed three ex-army, khaki knapsacks standing neatly at ease by the bed, a worn but expensive brown-leather suitcase looking on impassively.

It suddenly occurred to me that I had no idea how Robert and his little unit – I was sure that was how he thought of them – had travelled to Leyton.

I winced as I pressed a grubby flannel, soaked in cold water, to the lump on the back of my head, and then sighed, recognizing that it rather looked as if I'd be playing host to an extra four guests for at least one night.

As I'd suspected, the application of the cold compress and then witch hazel to my various bruises was a spectator sport as far as a bored Emile was concerned. He did, though, grunt his approval when I swallowed a couple of aspirin, so perhaps his medical training was not a complete fiction.

It was late when Ghislaine and Jerry arrived back.

I heard them when they were more than a hundred yards away. Church Road was enjoying its quiet midnight, and the sound of their soft conversation and the solid crunch of shoe on pavement carried. I guessed that they'd swayed swiftly through the black tunnels on the last, bright, sweaty train from the West End and had walked from the station.

They whispered an excited and conspiratorial good night, and then Ghislaine clattered up the stairs and into the solid fug that filled my office.

Her happy little smile froze when she saw Robert and then curdled into a sour, narrow-eyed scowl. Suddenly, I could see what she would look like as an old woman. The network of fine lines and wrinkles was already in place, waiting for the chance to turn her into a pinched-faced, bad-tempered harridan, the scourge of rambunctious boys. Thankfully, she relaxed, the lines faded, and she gave me a wan, apologetic nod.

'Robert,' she said, turning back to face him, 'what a surprise. I didn't know if you would even notice that I'd gone. You've been so busy lately.' She looked around, smiling brightly again. 'And you've brought some of your little friends along. How pleasant.'

'One moment, Ghislaine,' Robert said abruptly and turned to me. 'Antoine, I don't think that it's necessary for you to remain here. Perhaps you have somewhere to go? To allow a husband and wife some privacy.'

Ghislaine gave me an anxious look.

'Of course, Robert,' I said, 'but I'd like your assurance that this privacy is for you to talk. I wouldn't like to think of any accidents taking place.'

He looked puzzled and then understanding washed across his face. He glanced questioningly at Ghislaine, but she refused to meet his eyes. He held his hands out expansively, palms up, and smiled his most sincere smile. 'Antoine,' he said, 'I love my wife. I wouldn't hurt her.'

We stood in silence for a few seconds, then he took a step towards me.

'I promise you,' he said, 'that Ghislaine is safe here with me.'

I looked into his eyes and decided that he was telling the truth, and I nodded to him, smiled a little 'chin up' smile at Ghislaine and moved towards the door.

Robert followed me. When we were on the landing he spoke. 'It occurs to me that whatever you are involved in with those men earlier is not just going to disappear. I think they will be back.'

'You're right, Robert,' I said. There was not enough light escaping from my office for me to see his face clearly, but he gripped my forearm in a reassuringly friendly way.

'You may need some help with them,' he said. 'We will talk tomorrow.'

'Thank you,' I said, but he had already let go of my arm. He turned back into my office and closed the door behind him.

I stood on the landing. It was cool and refreshing after the closeness of my office. The stairway reeked of damp earth, old cooking and rotting wood, and there was always the faint, musty smell of small, scurrying rodents, but that was still better than the smoky air inside. I breathed deeply and felt my lungs respond with a phlegmy cough. I rubbed the smoke from my eyes and, perversely, now they had less reason, they started to water.

I was afraid that Robert was looking for another war, and even a small one that wasn't his would suit him. I knew I'd be grateful for his assistance, but I also knew him to be uncontrollable.

The low, deep rumble of his voice leaked out from around the edges of the ill-fitting, damp-warped door in the same frustrating way that the dim, yellow light seeped through. There was not enough light to see by, and I couldn't hear what was said. I could only hope that he was in a conciliatory mood, because I couldn't see any way in which I could help Ghislaine if he wasn't. But I knew I'd have no choice but to try. That was, after all, why she'd come to me. She had always assumed that I wasn't afraid of him. I was no longer completely sure, but I'd always thought she was wrong about that.

I walked slowly down the stairs, feeling my way in the

darkness, listening intently but in vain for the slightest sound of a raised voice or a cry of pain. I owed Jerry an explanation or two. There was the damage to his ceiling. And there was Robert.

I stood in the corridor for a few seconds, listening, and then knocked on the door to the shop.

It took Jerry more than a minute to open it.

I didn't sleep well.

Jerry's old, lumpy *chaise longue* – a family heirloom, he said – was stiff and unyielding. Perhaps there's something about inherited furniture that militates against comfort. Or perhaps it was just that my head was buzzing.

Bernie always tells me that I worry a lot. That's probably true but, sometimes, that's because there's a lot to worry about.

I guess I must have dozed off a little before dawn, because I came to suddenly, disorientated and slightly alarmed, to the sound of Peggy Lee singing about it being a good day and Jerry thrusting a cup of tea under my nose.

I couldn't decide whether the choice of Peggy Lee was an ironic statement or not. Jerry looked so cheerful and full of beans that he probably meant it. And it was, after all, Good Friday.

He really hadn't taken on board what I'd told him about Robert and was far more concerned about his ceiling, which I'd promised to make good. To Grand-père's dismay, my father hadn't followed him into the Walthamstow film studio as a cinematographer, but had instead set himself up as a painter/decorator. I'd picked up enough from him to know how to replaster a small patch of ceiling. Although the patch wasn't actually that small. It looked like I'd used a small mortar rather than a large handgun.

Peggy Lee stopped singing, and I sipped my tea while Jerry lovingly extracted a recording from its brown cardboard sleeve with his fingertips, blew dust from the surface, carefully positioned the shining black disc on the turntable and then delicately lowered the needle into the run-in grooves. There was a hiss and then the haunting, achingly melancholic sound of Sidney Bechet's 'Petite Fleur' filled the room.

Jerry nodded approvingly, smiled and went to his little kitchen area. The gas ignited with a pop and then bacon started to sizzle.

This was more like it: Bechet and bacon for breakfast.

I dressed, visited the WC and then splashed water on my face and rinsed out my mouth at Jerry's kitchen sink.

We sat down to eat, listening to some early Armstrong recordings, and I tried to explain to Jerry that Robert was not someone who took kindly to another man taking his wife to Maurice Chevalier concerts. And that Ghislaine, although a very nice woman, was not quite as innocent as she liked to appear. He didn't listen to me.

Even so, awash with gallons of strong, brown tea, full of salty bacon and crisp toast, basking in the sounds of good jazz, I felt like I was ready for whatever the day could throw at me.

There were still no sounds from my flat so I assumed that they were all still sleeping after talking long into the night.

I went into the shop to survey the damage in the light of day. In fact, it wasn't so bad. A sizeable piece of plaster had fallen down, but it hadn't landed on any records. There was dust and debris to clear up, but that wouldn't take very long.

I'd just finished sweeping when there was a loud banging at the front door and I discovered that I was less prepared for what the day had to offer than I'd thought.

I opened the door to two burly, uniformed policemen. One of them, a battle-weary sergeant with heavy features and sad, rheumy eyes, ascertained that I was Tony Gérard and then asked if I would be so kind as to accompany them to the station in order to help them out with their enquiries.

When I asked, he reluctantly admitted that I didn't have a lot of choice.

EIGHTEEN

Good Friday is always odd: a Bank Holiday that doesn't feel quite right. Respectable people treat the day a bit like Christmas, so there were no more than half a dozen kids rioting outside the cinema and only a couple of them boisterously, and noisily, smacking a rubber ball against the low brick wall that separated one side of the London Electrical Wire Company from the street. They quietened down when they saw the policemen.

The Caribonum workers were still safely tucked up in bed, and there weren't any shoppers about, as the only shop that was open was the baker's. Costello's was shut, and there was no sign of the lugubrious Enzo. There were so few buses about that, although there was probably a Sunday service operating, there might not have been.

Of course, walking along the streets as the meat in a particularly hefty bobby sandwich made this a stranger than usual Good Friday.

We strolled at the leisurely regulation pace, past the firmly locked library and the empty windows of the Co-op, up Lea Bridge Road in the direction of the Bakers' Alms, before turning sharp right. The coppers had presumably decided to walk a part of their beat on the way as this wasn't the most direct route to any local nick that I could think of.

I tried to chat amiably to my two large companions, in the hope that anyone seeing us would not automatically assume that I was under arrest, but they were having none of it and were monosyllabic at best. At worst, they were downright rude.

It's not a long walk to the police station in Francis Road, in spite of the slightly circuitous route that we took, and we were there by a quarter to ten. I had a sense of real foreboding as we climbed up the four steps that led to the big door.

I had the uneasy feeling that I should have told Jerry where I was going, but it hadn't seemed like a good idea to hang around, just in case the policemen got nosey and discovered bloodstains on the stairs, a couple of bullet holes and a houseful of armed Frenchmen. That might have aroused their suspicions. However, as we crossed the threshold of the cop shop and the duty sergeant booked me in, I realized that I would have felt more comfortable knowing that someone had an inkling of where I was.

I was told to sit on an almost black wooden bench, which had been polished to a dull gleam by the worn trouser seats of a couple of generations of felons, tearaways and drunks, until 'they' were ready to see me, and then left with only one of my new-found policeman friends for company – the other headed off to the canteen for a 'cuppa'. Apart from a few throat-clearing sounds and a gurgling stomach, my policeman companion was as uncommunicative as ever. He sprawled back against the bench, his arms and legs spread wide, looking bored and tired. I examined the scuffed and scratched oak floor, feeling decidedly uneasy.

Very respectable people may not have gone out much on Good Friday, except to buy hot cross buns from the baker, but policemen and the more disreputable elements of Leyton society seemed just as busy as usual.

A couple of unsavoury-looking types, dishevelled, unshaven and rumpled, emerged from somewhere in the building, each accompanied by his own policeman, and were duly signed out. One of them had a couple of bruises on his forehead and some dried, flaking blood around his mouth. A couple of drunks disturbing the peace, I assumed. A night in the cells seemed to have done the trick. They didn't look like they were up to disturbing anyone's peace for another hour or two.

Nobby Clarke, the street bookie, was brought in, wearing his regulation shiny bronze-coloured suit with the worn pigskin money bag still around his waist, his aromatic cigar held delicately between his thumb and forefinger. The overhead light glinted on his shiny, pink, hairless scalp and on the thick gold ring on his pinky.

'You know the form, Nobby,' the sergeant behind the desk said as he slid something across the counter.

'I do,' Nobby said, taking an expensive-looking pen out of his inside pocket. 'How's the missus?'

'She's well, Nobby, thanks. I'll tell her you was asking. Just stick your moniker on that and we'll skip the formalities.'

'Thank you, I appreciate that,' Nobby said, signing the prof-fered paper with a flourish. He then took a crisp ten-bob note out of his satchel, snapped it a couple of times and slapped it down on the counter. 'Here,' he said, 'buy some sweeties for the nippers.'

He turned, nodded at me and winked and then left, presumably to return to his pitch down by the Osborne Arms on the corner of Crescent Road and be arrested again later, in the afternoon, when everyone had had time to drink a beer or two, study form, discuss it with their mates and put their bets on.

Nobby and his distant relationship to the gee-gees reminded me of sporting matters, and I suddenly realized that this was the make or break weekend for Orient's hopes of promotion. Three matches in four days usually decided things one way or another.

I wondered what the police wanted. Images of the nearly decapitated corpse came and went. And the reek of that room filled my nostrils again. I felt mildly sick. I had the feeling I was missing something.

Then it nearly came to me. Jenkins had absolutely no reason to want poor Richard dead, and if Jan or Alfred were responsible then it couldn't even be a case of mistaken identity because they wouldn't kill Jonathan until they had their diamonds back.

Unfortunately, I didn't have time to pursue the thought. The Laurel and Hardy double act from Scotland Yard marched into the reception area and peremptorily summoned me.

We walked in single file, me in the middle, along a little corridor, turned right along another one and then entered a shabby little room at the back of the building. Its only claim to being an office was a battered desk with a wonky leg. It really seemed to be a storeroom for chairs. There were at least a dozen of them pushed up against the walls. They were all cheap dark-brown wood, with round backs. And every one of them was broken. I didn't care to speculate how they had come to be in that state, but I reassured myself by reflecting that Inspector Rose didn't look like a violent man.

We stood around while the inspector, who was today sporting an emerald-green bow-tie, took an old briar pipe and a tobacco pouch from his baggy jacket pocket and proceeded to fill the bowl of the pipe with shreds of golden-brown tobacco, the colour and consistency of soggy shredded wheat, tamping them down carefully with his finger. He then returned the tobacco pouch to the pocket of his brown jacket and pulled out a box of Swan Vestas matches. He gripped the stem of the pipe firmly between his teeth and then struck a match. When the tobacco was burning to his satisfaction and the elaborate ritual was at an end, he nodded at the large police constable who had accompanied us.

The constable looked at Sergeant Radcliffe, who jerked a thumb towards the door. 'Outside,' Radcliffe said, and the constable lumbered off.

Rose took the pipe out of his mouth and pointed the stem, shiny with saliva, at me. 'You been cautioned?' he said.

'I don't think so,' I said, shaking my head.

'Well, consider yourself duly cautioned,' he said.

'All right,' I said. 'What's that mean?'

'It means,' said the sergeant, moving in very close to me and whispering in what I took to be a menacing manner, 'that you tell us the truth. Or else.'

'As if I'd do anything else, Sergeant,' I said innocently.

'Don't get clever,' he said. 'It doesn't suit you.' He then took a step away, so that he was standing just behind me.

Rose looked weary. He closed his eyes and squeezed the bridge of his nose between his thumb and his forefinger. 'You told us the other day,' he said patiently, his eyes still shut, 'that you were looking for Jonathan Harrison.'

'That's right,' I said.

'Well,' he said, 'we have it on good authority that you found him.'

'I did come across him, briefly, yesterday,' I said.

'That's what we understand,' Rose said.

Sergeant Radcliffe moved in close again. I could smell something unpleasant on his breath. 'So, where is he?' he said.

'I don't know,' I said. It wasn't really a lie. I didn't actually know where he was. I knew who he'd been with the day before, but I had no idea where she lived.

'That's a pity,' Sergeant Radcliffe said, 'because that would have solved a few problems.'

'What problems?' I said.

'Well,' Inspector Rose said mildly, sucking on his pipe, 'if you'd been able to tell us where he is, and he turned out to be there, happy and content, then we could drop any enquiries we have relating to you abducting and falsely imprisoning him.'

'What?' I said. I was genuinely outraged. 'Is that ungrateful little toe-rag going around saying that I kidnapped him? I haven't seen him since I got him out of a tricky situation and he legged it at Liverpool Street Station. He was certainly healthy enough and free enough then.'

'What tricky situation was that?' Rose said quietly.

'Oh, nothing much,' I said, deciding to lie again. 'He just owes someone some money, and they were getting a bit heavy-handed with him.'

Rose nodded and sucked hard on his pipe. It had gone out, and a flicker of ill humour passed across his face before he struck another match. He puffed again and, when a cloud of sweet-smelling smoke drifted up towards the ceiling, he smiled at me. 'Who is this someone?' he said.

'I don't really know,' I said.

'You don't know very much, do you?' Sergeant Radcliffe said.

'I guess not,' I said. Though I did know that Jonathan Harrison had given me nothing but grief since I first heard of him. 'Listen, what I told you yesterday is true. Beverley Beaumont claimed to be worried about her brother, and the studio asked me to see if I could find him. I went to the room he was renting and found the body of his friend. You know all that. Then it turns out that he was driven to my flat, looking for me. I looked into who had driven him there, and it turns out it was his landlady. I found out where she was and went to see what she could tell me about where he was. As it happens, by a stroke of luck, I found him there. I got him out, but before I could ask him what was going on, he'd done a runner. So that's why I don't know anything. As for where he is now . . . That's anyone's guess.'

That was easily the longest speech I'd made since I'd nervously introduced myself to Robert in France all those years ago. It left me breathless. Something about it seemed to amuse Rose. Either that or his pipe was giving him more pleasure than usual, because he was definitely smiling.

'Mr Gérard,' he said, favouring the usual English pronunciation. His lips made a little popping sound as he puffed out some smoke without removing the chewed stem of his pipe from his mouth. 'Tony, I must say that if that outrage was faked then you ought to be on the stage, and I hope you won't think that I'm casting aspersions on your reliability as a witness if I say that it would be nice if I could speak to young Mr Harrison so that he can confirm your account of things.' He paused and drew contentedly on his pipe. The studied smoking ritual was beginning to annoy me. But then I imagined it was supposed to. 'So,' he finally said, 'you found him yesterday, so perhaps you could find him again today and bring him in to see me.'

'How am I supposed to do that?' I said. 'If you can't find him, how can I?'

'Well,' he said, 'I don't know the answer to that. But we couldn't find him yesterday either, and you did. Maybe you were just born lucky.'

'Yes,' I said, 'that would explain why I'm standing in a police station on Good Friday being accused of something I haven't done.'

'There's no call for sarcasm, Tony,' he said mildly. 'I just thought you might prefer to go looking for the young man rather than being arrested on suspicion of something. After all, we have a very good set of your fingerprints on a piece of silver that doesn't belong to you and does have some connection to Jonathan Harrison. And we have two very respectable witnesses who say that you abducted Jonathan Harrison from a house yesterday afternoon, and, as far as we can tell, he hasn't been seen since.'

I knew when I was beaten – and, I realized, in his own way, he was giving me the benefit of the doubt. I nodded. 'All right,' I said, 'I'll try, but I'm not going to promise anything.'

'Just as long as you bring him in by close of business today, you don't have to promise me a thing,' he said.

'And if I fail?'

A little flicker of amusement lifted the corners of his mouth and emphasized the network of wrinkles around his eyes. 'Do you know the old Eddie Cantor song?' he said. '"Budge, right into jail."'

I nodded. Actually, I was of the opinion that Eddie Cantor sang 'Bud' rather than 'Budge', but I wasn't going to argue the toss. The meaning was ominously clear.

'Good,' he said. 'Now, I imagine you're anxious to start, so don't let me detain you.'

I stood there for a moment.

Rose smiled at his fat sergeant. 'Sergeant Radcliffe,' he said, 'I wonder if you'd be kind enough to escort Tony to the front desk and sign him out.'

'Wait a minute,' I said. 'Jonathan Harrison could be a witness in a murder enquiry. He might even be a suspect for all I know. And you aren't out scouring the city for him?'

'What gives you that impression?' he said. 'Of course we're looking for him. But, for your information, while he is someone we're anxious to interview about the murder of his friend, he isn't, at the moment, a suspect. He has been given a watertight alibi. He was in Cambridge at the time of the murder. With Mrs Elvin, who left him there.'

'Oh,' I said.

'Oh, indeed. Now, run along with the nice sergeant.'

Sergeant Radcliffe guided me along the corridors back to the grim reception area where I was duly signed out. He then walked me to the door.

'He's winding me up, isn't he?' I said.

Radcliffe's heavy, dark jowls shuddered a little as he shook his head in a non-committal gesture.

'The inspector,' I said, 'he's playing games with me. He wouldn't really arrest me.'

'I would,' he said. 'Like the inspector says: we've got two very respectable and credible witnesses who say you abducted the lad, we've got a very nice set of your dabs on an expensive silver cigarette case found at the scene and we've got no lad.' He paused and looked up at the smoke-stained ceiling. 'I'd lock you up.'

'Oh, come on,' I said. 'As soon as Jonathan Harrison turns up, I'm in the clear.'

'Exactly,' he said. 'I'd be grateful, if I were you, that the inspector's giving you the chance to produce the body.'

'What?' I said.

'*Habeus corpus*,' he said. 'Show us the body. Or something like that.'

'*Ars gratia artis*,' I said, which was the only phrase of Latin that I knew.

'What's that mean?' he said.

'You're talking out of your backside,' I said.

'No need to be offensive,' he said. 'Now, on your way and

bring little Jonny in to see us sometime this afternoon.' He beamed at me cherubically. It was odd. There was this heavy-set, sweating man, his breath smelling of onions, with a five o'clock shadow at ten in the morning, showing his crooked, yellow teeth in a big, wide, childlike smile, and it came across as charming and winsome.

It was infectious and I couldn't resist smiling back.

'I'll do my best,' I said. 'In fact, succeed or fail, I'll be there by six.'

'Succeed would be best,' he said and turned away to walk back to his boss.

I stood on the step outside. It was half past ten in the morning. It was warm and sunny. I was free to go about my business. There was quite a lot about what the inspector had said that hadn't sounded right, but there was something specific in there that was nagging at me.

I closed my eyes, relishing the heat of the sun on my face, and tried not to think about the unresolved problems that were steadily piling up, concentrating instead on one salient fact. I was at liberty, which meant I could do something about them.

My roomful of armed French Commies was no longer quite as pressing a problem as it had been. In fact, my study boasted only one. Emile had evidently drawn the short straw, and while the others, including Ghislaine, had set off on the heroic quest to find the café of London legend selling good coffee and fresh croissants, he sat at my desk unhappily nursing a luke-warm cup of Typhoo tea.

The room stank of cigarettes and unwashed men.

But that was easily dealt with. I opened the window.

I then told Emile – for no other reason than he had been left behind to keep an eye on me and he had a gun – what I had to do and promised him a cup of coffee. He brightened up and accompanied me down to Jerry's shop and the phone.

Jerry was morose and uncommunicative, but I decided to ignore that. Anyway, every Englishman ought to have his heart broken by a sophisticated Frenchwoman at least once in his life.

It took only fifteen minutes and two telephone calls to track down Les and discover that Beverley Beaumont wasn't filming today and was resting at home. Something to do with union agreements and some technical problem. He gave me her address without any hesitation. He offered to ring and let her know I was coming. I told him not to bother, that I'd ring myself. I had no intention of doing so, of course. I rather hoped to find the elusive Master Harrison at home.

Les was monumentally hung-over. I could almost hear his head throbbing down the line. It cheered me up no end.

'Good party, Les?' I said.

'Yes,' he said. 'Sorry I didn't get a chance to talk to you.'

'I had to leave early,' I said.

'You missed Dolores then,' he said.

'I think she can probably live with the disappointment.'

'By the way,' he said, 'that Jenkins bloke was on the blower this morning. Wants me to sack you. Says he won't put money into one of my films while I still employ you.'

'What did you say?' I said.

'I told him I didn't employ you.'

'But that's a lie, Les,' I said.

'Yeah, but Daphne says he's not a genuine investor. So, who gives a toss? We'll worry about that if he comes up with any dosh.'

'You'll sack me then?'

'No. God knows why, but Daphne has a soft spot for you.'

'All right, Les, I'll try to repay your loyalty and confidence in me.'

'You do that, son,' he said and hung up, presumably to take another Alka-Seltzer.

I turned to Emile. 'Well,' I said, 'let's go and find you some coffee, my friend.'

He almost smiled and headed towards the door. I followed.

Jerry stopped fiddling with a large pile of sheet music. 'Where're you going?' he said.

'Out,' I said. 'Emile needs coffee, and I have to see someone.'

'What about my ceiling?' he said, pointing at the ragged hole.

'It'll have to wait, Jerry. This is really important.'

'So's my ceiling,' he said.

He sounded and looked so miserable that I stopped by the door and decided to give him what little advice I could on affairs of the heart.

'Jerry,' I said, in as kindly a tone as I could manage, 'don't brood about Ghislaine. She makes her own decisions, whatever Robert may think, but I wouldn't make too many plans that include her, if I were you. She has a tendency to use the female prerogative.'

He looked puzzled.

'She used to change her mind a lot,' I said, 'and she probably still does.'

He nodded sadly and turned back to his sheet music. I watched him as he listlessly shuffled the pile. It didn't look as if my words of comfort had had the desired effect.

NINETEEN

I left Emile in a little café close to St John's Wood Underground station. A shiny coffee machine chuckled to itself on a shelf behind the counter and a few cakes and pastries sat uninvitingly under a round glass container next to the till. A pretty young waitress had smiled warmly at Emile – well, he was a good-looking boy – and called him 'luv'. He looked happy enough, sat at a Formica-topped table, staring dreamily at the seams on her stockings as she coaxed the machine into hissing and dribbling coffee into a cup.

I'd explained to him that my visit to Beverley Beaumont was a delicate matter and involved an affair of the heart, and so, after a little shrugging and head scratching, his Gallic sense of propriety overcame his orders from Robert and he allowed me to go alone. I'd given him the address, explained how to get there and agreed to be back in half an hour.

And I was completely sincere about this. I felt I was going to need all the help I could get in order to manhandle Jonathan Harrison to New Scotland Yard. Emile, and his ugly little black pistol, would figure prominently in any argument I had with the boy.

I strolled along, the opening bars of Bessie Smith belting out 'Careless Love' resounding in my head, on the opposite side of the street to the long, featureless brick wall that encircled Lord's Cricket ground until I came to the brand spanking new block where Les Jackson's second or third most important asset lived.

The glass front door was open, and there was no one in the little lobby. There was a calm about the place that whispered quiet money at me.

I ignored the lift and ran up the stairs to the second floor. Evidently, Miss Beaumont hadn't taken up residence to watch Test matches for free. Maybe the flats in the lower floors came at a discount.

I stood outside her door and listened for a few seconds, acutely conscious that I was wearing the same, shabby suit and soiled shirt I had been wearing the previous night, aware that they were in an even worse state after my run-in with Alfred and Jan than they had been when I'd seen her at Les's party. I sniffed, but couldn't detect more of a pong about me than usual. That didn't, of course, mean that Beverley Beaumont wouldn't.

There was someone in. I could hear the wireless playing a light orchestral piece. I rang the bell, and the music stopped immediately, but no one came to the door. I waited for a few seconds and then crouched down and opened the letter box. There wasn't much to see beyond a dark little hallway with a few firmly closed doors leading off it.

'Miss Beaumont,' I called quietly, 'it's Tony Gérard. We need to talk.'

I was about to call again when one of the doors opened and she came into the hall. I stood up straight while she fiddled with the locks. She opened the door a few inches and peered through the gap.

She wasn't wearing any make-up, her dark hair was tousled and she looked very young, vulnerable and naked. In fact, she more or less was. A thin, satiny, pink dressing gown clung to her and suggested strongly that she wasn't wearing anything underneath. Her feet and legs were bare.

'I wasn't expecting anyone,' she said. 'I'm sorry, I'm not dressed yet.' She hesitated. 'I'm not really myself this morning.'

She was very pale in the half-light of the hall and seemed distracted. Her eyes shone.

'Don't worry,' I said, smiling as reassuringly as I could. 'I won't take long.'

She nodded and opened the door a little wider to allow me to enter, closing it carefully when I was inside.

I followed her into the small living room. The solid, dark old-fashioned furniture wasn't altogether right for the modern space, which would have been full of light from the French doors that led out to a tiny balcony had the heavy brown curtain not been partially pulled across, but, in the dimness, it didn't jar too much. She sat on a big, solid-looking green sofa, curling her legs up under her, and indicated that I should sit on a matching armchair.

'Actually,' I said, 'I was hoping to speak to Jon. Is he around?'

She shook her head.

'Do you know where I can reach him?' I asked, leaning forward.

She shook her head again and turned away slightly. A small tear leaked out from her right eye and she brushed at it. 'He left about an hour ago,' she said. 'Someone came to the door, and he left.'

'Willingly?'

She shook her head slowly. 'I'm not sure,' she said. 'But there wasn't any noise. No raised voices, no scuffle or anything.'

'Do you know who it was?'

'I didn't see anyone,' she said. 'Or hear anything, really. He just went to the door when the bell rang and then he left.'

She was crying properly now, emitting raw little gasps, her chest heaving, her nose running.

I stood up, unsure what to do.

'Please find him,' she sobbed out, 'I'm worried about him.'

With good reason, I thought.

'I'll try,' I said, 'I really will.'

I imagined him turning up at New Scotland Yard without me, floating past with the other flotsam, his head just above the scummy water of the Thames. That wouldn't play too well with Rose and Radcliffe.

'I'll find him,' I said firmly, leaning down and patting her shoulder. She didn't look noticeably reassured, but, oddly, I felt better. 'Where's the kitchen? I'll make tea.'

She pointed across to another door, and I went through it into a narrow, neat and shiny little kitchen area. I filled the kettle, put it on the stove and then fussed around with a teapot, a packet of tea and some cups.

I didn't hear her come in and was only aware of her when she put her arms around me and pressed herself against my back.

'Thank you,' she said quietly, her soft warmth, the touch of her fingers on my chest and the overwhelmingly heady smell of her perfume making me more awkward and uncomfortable than I'd been before. We stood there in silence for a few seconds, her moulded to my back, me helplessly holding a cup in each hand, staring out of the window at the cricket ground's drab wall and the dreary buildings beyond. Yes, these lower flats would not be as expensive as the upper floors with their clear view of the playing area. A coalman's cart clopped slowly past, the huge blinkered horse labouring in the morning sun, hooves and hide gleaming, black dust shimmering on the sacks and on the leather neck-piece of the coalman's hat.

I wondered at the intense pressure and the impossibly long period of time it took to turn coal into diamonds. But really I was just trying not to think about Beverley Beaumont's unrestrained breasts nestling against my cheap suit. Then, just before the moment stretched out too embarrassingly, the kettle started to whistle.

'Tea,' I said, and she released her grip and stepped away.

'Yes,' she said, 'I think I need some. And a cigarette.'

She padded back into the living room as silently as she'd come.

When I carried the tea through, she was curled up on the sofa again, a cigarette held fastidiously at arm's length. Guiltily, I remembered that her holder was still nestling, in splendid isolation, in Jerry's far from impregnable safe.

I put the cups down on a small side table. 'I put two sugars in,' I said. 'I thought you might need it.'

'I don't usually,' she said, patting her stomach. 'My figure, you know.'

I picked up my own cup and sipped. 'So,' I said, 'who knew that Jonathan was here?'

'No one,' she said.

'Well,' I said, 'I did.'

She nodded, but said nothing.

'Was there anyone else?' I said. 'Did you or Jonathan mention it?'

She put her cigarette in a large glass ash tray, picked up her tea and frowned. 'Oh, Jon did call his college right after getting here,' she said.

'Who did he speak to?'

'His tutor, I think,' she said.

We sat in silence for a while.

'Anyone else know he was here?' I finally said.

'David,' she said. 'My agent. David Cavendish. Well, he's my manager, really, I suppose. I mentioned it to him last night. At the party.'

The intemperate Mr Cavendish.

'Anyone else?' I said.

She shook her head firmly.

'Could Jonathan have called anyone else?'

'I don't think so,' she said.

Well, I hadn't told anyone where he was, so that cut the possibilities by a third – if we really were the only three people who knew that he was holed up with her.

And assuming that she had nothing to do with his disappearance.

That such a thought could even cross my mind was mildly dismaying. I put it down to the company I'd been keeping recently.

I knew that I ought to be asking her searching questions about Cavendish and Jameson, but I couldn't think of any. I was just framing an inconsequential enquiry about how Cavendish had got on with Jonathan when the doorbell rang.

Beverley Beaumont looked startled.

I was reminded of something Jerry had once said about someone starting like a guilty thing upon a fearful summons. Well, it went a bit like that. Except that I didn't think she was guilty. Just frightened.

'Would you like me to answer that?' I said.

'Please,' she said very quietly.

By the time I'd walked the few yards to the door, the letter box was open and our visitor was peering through, rather as I'd done twenty or so minutes before. It was too late to pretend there was no one in. He must have seen me.

'Who is it?' I said.

'Tony? Is that you? Open the door, you daft bugger,' a familiar voice growled.

'Les?' I said as I fiddled with the lock. 'What are you doing here?'

He looked around and leaned towards me conspiratorially. 'Daphne got a tearful call about half an hour ago, and she thought I ought to come round and find out what's what. Then I remembered you were coming here, and I thought you might have upset her nibs. Then I thought, no, not my Tony. Too much the gentleman. So what's the story?' he said *sotto voce* as he slipped into the hall.

He didn't look too bad, considering how hung-over he'd sounded on the phone.

'Boyfriend's gone AWOL,' I whispered. 'With persons unknown and without so much as a peck on the cheek.'

'Boyfriend? Oh, Jonathan. You found him then?' he said.

'Yeah, the other day, and he came running here.'

Les shook his head and then walked into the living room. 'Beverley, love,' he said. 'Daphne said you were upset so I come straight round.'

'Thanks, Les,' she said. She lit another cigarette. She was using a box of matches, which looked wrong. 'But Tony's here and he's going to find Jonathan.' She tilted her head up and blew smoke towards the ceiling.

'Yeah,' Les said, 'you can trust Tony. Solid as the Rock of Gibraltar he is.' He favoured me with a sly look and a smile that I chose to interpret as sceptical.

He sat down next to her on the sofa and, with his big, meaty right paw, grasped her pale, slender hand, patting the back of it gently with his other palm. I suddenly realized that Les had come because he was concerned about her, not about the film or business. For all his philandering and Max Miller vulgarity, Les was that rarest of men – one who actually liked women and enjoyed their company. I wondered if I did.

'Well,' I said, squinting at the big alarm clock perched incongruously and at an odd angle on the mantelpiece, 'I'd better get started, if I'm going to find him today.'

'Yes,' Les said, letting go of her hand and leaning back. 'If you're all right, Beverley love, I might totter off with him.'

'I'll be fine, Les,' she said. 'Thanks again for coming.'

A little cynically, I thought that Jonathan Harrison had probably left her enough 'medicine' to alleviate her blues for a few hours and that she was looking forward to being alone to administer some.

Les insisted on taking the lift down, and I overcame my mild fear of them and entered it with him.

'So, what's the plan?' he said.

I shrugged. 'Well, she says only two people, apart from me, knew he was here, so I thought I'd start with them.'

'Who?' he said as, mercifully, the doors to the little lift opened and we stepped out into the hallway.

'Jonathan's tutor in Cambridge, and Miss Beaumont's agent.'

'Cavendish?' he said.

I nodded.

'Well, Charlie and I can drop you off at his office if you like,' he said. 'The Roller's just outside.'

'Thanks,' I said as we emerged on to St John's Wood Road, realizing that I'd completely forgotten to ask Beverley Beaumont for an address for him.

'Will he be there?' I said.

Les looked puzzled.

'It's Good Friday, Les,' I said.

'Of course it is,' he said. 'Yeah, he'll be there. Theatrical agents aren't human. They don't take Bank Holidays.'

Seeing Emile standing on the pavement, gazing dreamily at the old black Rolls, reminded me that I'd forgotten something else as well. He was a strange Communist, going weak-kneed and dewy-eyed at the sight of such a piece of capitalist opulence.

Evidently, Charlie, who was standing, arms folded, flint-eyed, between Emile and the car, didn't much like the look of the lascivious way the young man was ogling the elegant old lady.

I decided I'd better introduce them before Charlie called Emile out to defend her honour. As soon as I'd explained that Emile was a friend, and he, through me, had told Charlie how much he loved and admired the beauty of such machines, they were all smiles. Charlie, unprompted, perhaps feeling guilty for his earlier hostility, even raised the bonnet so Emile could fully appreciate the finer aspects of the engine.

Les raised his eyebrows and climbed into the back. I joined him. We waited for a few minutes until Charlie remembered his chauffeuring duties. A beaming Emile sat next to Charlie, telling me that this was his first time in a Rolls-Royce. I told him that I wouldn't tell Robert if he didn't. His smile faded only slightly.

Les gave Charlie an address in Regent Street, and we glided off, Charlie sitting just a little straighter than usual.

Les nodded towards Emile. 'What's the story there?' he said.

'It's a little complicated,' I said, 'and involves some old friends from the war. They turned up the other day. Emile here is a sort of watchdog.'

'Watching you or watching out for you?' Les said.

'A bit of both,' I said. 'But he's a nice enough lad.'

'Tony,' he said, 'why is that I always have the impression that your life is a lot more interesting than mine?'

'If it is, then yours must be particularly boring,' I said.

'That would explain it,' he said. 'By the way, you look like someone's been using your head as a cricket ball.'

I put my hand up to the lump on the back of my skull.

'You don't have to tell me what's been going on,' he said, 'but I might be able to help, you know.'

'If I thought you could, Les,' I said, 'I wouldn't hesitate to ask but, believe me, you're better off not knowing. The Old Bill has an interest, and you may prefer to remain in a state of blissful ignorance.'

'Fair enough,' he said. 'In the meantime, if you need Charlie and a motor, they're yours.'

'Thanks,' I said. It occurred to me that a trip to Cambridge would be more pleasurable in the Rolls than in a train.

The Rolls pulled in to the kerb next to a long colonnade of shops opposite the Café Royale. Les pointed to a door between two swish clothes shops. Even from the car, without being able to read the price tags, I knew that buying a suit here was out of the question. 'Fourth floor,' he said, 'for the charming Mr Cavendish.'

The door opened when I pushed it, and Emile and I entered a dim and smelly corridor. There was a board on the right-hand wall with a directory of the offices in the building. Sure enough, The Cavendish Theatrical Agency was listed between Brampton's Fine Tea Importers and Frasier's Tweed and could be found on the fourth floor.

There was an old lift with a cage door that you pulled across, but I'd had enough of lifts for the day and made for the dingy brown staircase next to it. Emile didn't demur, and we trotted up at a respectable pace.

The smell of the stairwell wasn't evil or disgusting, just musty and old. It was the smell of generations of scampering rodents and elderly dust. It was the smell of damp, water gone bad. And it stuck in your chest and slowed you down.

As we climbed, the lift whirred into action and started to rise very slowly, creaking, grinding and lurching alarmingly. The cable hauling it up looked far too insubstantial to hold it, and I shuddered slightly at the thought.

The lift groaned to a halt on the fourth floor, just as we came to the door that led into the corridor. I was in the lead, and I was able to see through the window in the door. And I saw Alfred, his left arm in a sling, pulling open the cage door of the lift and ushering another man into it. The other man was Jenkins.

I held my arm up to stop Emile bursting through the door and pointed. He looked out and then grinned at me, pointing at his arm with boyish enthusiasm for the damage he'd inflicted.

Then we stood and waited, breathing in that ancient air, until the lift had started moving unsteadily downwards with a dismaying lurch. Once it was in motion I reckoned it would take a while for it to change course and thought it was safe to venture out into the corridor and find David Cavendish. I wasn't sure what I was going to say to him. The connection between him and Jenkins was probably Miss Beaumont and that worried me.

Cavendish's office was directly opposite the lift and had his name painted on the glass. And Les had been right. David Cavendish was not enjoying the luxury of a day off.

He was in his little reception area, talking casually to his secretary, sat on the edge of her desk. The walls were covered with photographs of Cavendish with the rich and famous. There was even a small picture of him beaming, with his arm draped around Beverley Beaumont. She didn't look as happy.

He and his secretary both glanced up when we entered: the secretary, a middle-aged lady wearing large spectacles and a solid-looking perm, with a professional smile, Cavendish with a puzzled frown.

'Mr Cavendish,' I said, 'we haven't actually met, but we have encountered each other a couple of times. I'm Tony Gérard. I work for Hoxton Films, and I wondered if I might have a few words about one of your clients – Miss Beaumont.'

His handsome features took on what I recognized as their accustomed look, poised halfway between disdain and anger.

'I don't know that I have anything to say to you about Miss Beaumont,' he said.

'Perhaps not,' I said, going for conciliatory, 'but she is rather upset and has asked me to assist with a personal problem. I thought you might like to help.'

He looked thoughtful and stood up. He stroked his chin

with his thumb and forefinger. In the still, quiet air they rasped against his beard growth. He was older than I'd first thought, in his late thirties or early forties.

'Of course,' he finally said. 'Let's go into my office.'

TWENTY

D avid Cavendish waved airily, and more than a touch imperiously, at an elderly, straight-backed wooden chair in front of his small, cluttered desk. I sat down in it stiffly, imagining that he perhaps thought that it did something for his clients' postures. Or maybe it was his way of suggesting to aspiring acts that austerity and sacrifice were still the order of the day in the theatrical world.

He relaxed into his leather chair and started fiddling with a couple of files. Through the smudged panes of the window behind him I could see a jumble of rooftops and chimney pots in higgledy-piggledy contrast to the elegant if grubby facade that I'd entered through. It was a bit like a film set: the palaces, castles and elegant homes that you saw on the screen were just an illusion, a lie constructed of canvas, paint and plywood. Behind the backdrop was an unsightly clutter of paint-spattered newspapers, dirty brushes, empty pots, rags and sawdust.

I thought of the ruined London I'd returned to after the war. The pinched-faced, dispirited people hadn't looked like victors, and I certainly hadn't felt like a conquering hero. Things were better now. Definitely. All the same, the city still looked grim and shabby, in spite of the new concrete buildings that had been put up by the Thames for the Festival. Even when, like today, a clear, blue sky showed them at their best, the people still looked down at heel and a little bit mean.

I suddenly ached to see Paris again, just once, even if only for a couple of days.

David Cavendish coughed nervously. I smiled at him, wondering what he'd done in the war. Probably been active in essential work, like entertaining the troops, a tireless administrator for ENSA, selflessly and assiduously booking acts he had an interest in.

'So,' he said, 'what's this all about?'

'Well,' I said, deciding on a degree of formality and a flatness of tone learned in the bureaucratic limbo I'd found myself in while still in uniform after the war, 'Miss Beaumont asked me to help track down a young man she had an interest in. I was able to do so, but he has subsequently disappeared. I was hoping that you might be able to shed some light on that.'

He sniffed, picked up a yellow pencil and started sharpening it with a small penknife with a tortoiseshell pattern on its handle. 'How much do you know about Beverley Beaumont, Mr Gérard?'

'Not very much,' I said.

'I've known her for eight years. Ever since she was a gawky sixteen-year-old playing the maid in provincial productions of JB Priestley. In all that time there's always been a young man that she has "an interest in" and it's never been the same young man for longer than a few months. Beverley Beaumont likes young men, Mr Gérard. Pretty young men.' The last phrase came out with a little sneer and a vicious stroke of the penknife. I seemed to recall Daphne saying much the same thing, only without the violence and the sneer. She'd just been spreading malicious gossip. 'I can think of at least nine and, without exception, they have all been spongers and wastrels who have threatened her career in one way or another, either through scandal or bad advice. Some of them stole from her, all of them leeched off her. I don't imagine that this latest one is any different, and if he really has disappeared I will breathe a huge sigh of relief. I wish they'd all disappear. Permanently. Nothing could make me happier.' He paused. 'Even if I knew what had happened to him, I wouldn't give you any information that would help to find him.' He inspected the pencil and then placed it on his desk, folded the blade away and slipped the penknife into the pocket of his dove-grey waistcoat. He stood up and looked at his watch. 'Now, if you don't mind, I have another appointment.'

Much as I wanted to get off the instrument of torture that was numbing my backside, I remained seated. 'Thanks for your time and your, er, candour,' I said.

He sighed. Clearly, I was an exasperatingly stupid nuisance.

'Just one more thing,' I said, deciding that I could bear to annoy him for a few more minutes. 'Those men who left before I arrived. What did they want?'

'What the hell's that got to do with you?' he said.

No question I'd managed to annoy him with that one.

'It's just that I've come across them before, and I wondered

what business they had with you.' I paused. 'If you don't want
to tell me, I can always ask them . . .'

He had coloured up considerably and looked as if he was
about to explode, but he evidently thought better of it and
sank slowly back into his seat. I could almost see his thought
processes. Was I bluffing? Would I jeopardize whatever he
was up to if I wasn't? He picked up the pencil and tapped it
against the desktop, breaking the lead. He gave it a venomous
look and hurled it into a waste-paper bin. It landed with a
dull thunk.

'If you must know,' he said after a few seconds, 'I met them
at a club I go to. We got talking, and it turns out that they're
interested in becoming angels.'

'Angels?'

He sighed again. This time it was, presumably, at my
ignorance. 'They're looking to put money into a show. And
they'd like Beverley to star.'

'I thought Miss Beaumont had an exclusive contract with
Hoxton,' I said.

He looked at me viciously, and I had the impression that
he'd like to hurl me into the bin too. 'This is only a possi-
bility at the moment. Exclusivity clauses are always open to
negotiation,' he said very carefully. 'Anyway, they would like
a meeting with Beverley, and I was just arranging for them
to go to her flat.'

'Now?' I said. The worry I'd felt earlier turned into a full-
blooded anxiety. They must be looking for Jon. Since he wasn't
there, she'd probably be all right, but . . .

'Why not? I'd appreciate it if you'd keep all this under your
hat. There's absolutely no reason for Hoxton Films to be
involved yet. I'll talk to Les Jackson in good time.' He stood
up again. 'Now, I'm afraid that I really must ask you to go.
I have an important client waiting.'

With some relief, I stood up and attempted to stamp some
life into my right leg. I offered him my hand, but he chose
to ignore it, instead sitting back down at his desk and opening
a dark-brown folder which contained a single sheet of paper
and a large glossy photograph.

I nodded at him and left. Only Emile and the secretary
were waiting in the reception area. There was no sign of his
important client. He must have gone to the lavatory. Or

Cavendish had lied to get rid of me. I wondered what else he'd lied about.

I led the way slowly out of the office and down the stairs. Once outside, Emile and I stood by the shops in the long arcade in Regent Street. He was staring in at the window of one. I had the feeling that he was admiring his reflection rather than looking at the expensive tailoring on display, but I might have been wrong. I was watching the traffic and wondering what to do.

It seemed to me that there were two courses of action. I could follow Alfred and his boss to Beverley Beaumont's flat. If Cavendish didn't call to alert them to our conversation, I would have a slight advantage. Or I could contact Jameson in Cambridge.

A couple of buses and a taxi roared past, and two well-dressed men, wearing bowlers and brandishing tightly furled umbrellas, gave me a wide berth and some filthy looks. I guess I must have appeared to them as unappetizing and disreputable as I felt.

Well, when caught on the horns of a dilemma, it's always best to act decisively. I chose a third option.

'Emile,' I said, 'let's go and have a drink.'

Connie was fussing with her battered Oxo tin when we clumped up the musty staircase to the dingy landing outside the Imperial Club. She turned around when she heard us and scowled impressively. Emile's handsome face expressed surprise.

Well, perhaps shock would be a better description.

'Afternoon, Connie,' I said amiably. 'Are you open yet?'

She nodded.

'Roger in?'

She nodded again. Somehow, she managed to impart a certain amount of suspicion into her nods.

I was moving towards the door when she spoke.

'She's not a member,' she said, pointing an accusing finger at Emile, who was showing some reluctance to follow me in and still registering some level of astonishment at Connie's appearance.

I suppose she was a slightly disturbing sight at that time of day. She was wearing one of her wispy, ethereal white gowns and was extravagantly coiffed in a ringletted blonde wig. Unfortunately, she didn't appear to have shaved that morning and, in spite of a thick layer of orangey-brown make-up, the general effect was a little undercut by her luxuriant beard growth, which thrust its way through in a dark, surly and decidedly menacing way. There was also a large, rainbow-coloured bruise on her left temple.

'I thought maybe you'd let us in for a few minutes,' I said. 'I need a word with Roger.'

Connie sucked in her cheeks and thought about it for a moment. 'All right,' she finally said, 'since she's so pretty.'

'Thanks, Connie,' I said, wondering what Emile would have done if he'd understood her. 'I owe you.'

'Just bring that sweet-looking one you were with the other night back,' she said, 'you faithless little tart.'

I was nearly through the door when she called me back.

'Here,' she said, thrusting a small rectangle of cardboard at me. 'Just in case the law drops by. Temporary membership.'

I looked at her big, calloused hand for a moment. 'But you don't have temporary memberships,' I said.

'Sometimes we do,' she said and handed the card to Emile, who looked at me helplessly, baffled by what was going on.

I smiled at him and told him that he needed membership, as this was a club, a special club. He looked at Connie and said something that I think would probably best translate as 'no kidding', with an expletive used as what Mrs Wilson back at Church Road Primary would, I'm sure, have called an intensifier.

I smiled at Connie. 'He's French,' I said.

'I know, dear,' she said. 'And I very nearly understood what he just said.' Then she laughed heartily.

Roger was, of course, standing behind the bar, surveying his badly lit domain, which was, of course, almost empty.

'The wanderer returns,' he said. 'What can I get you? And your charming friend?'

'I'll have a brandy, Roger, please. And so will Emile.' I put a pound note down on the counter. 'And have one yourself. And keep the change.'

He raised his eyebrows. 'I'll just have a little half,' he said, picking up the quid delicately, between thumb and forefinger, as though it were a rare and exotic flower, and carrying it carefully to the till as if he were adding it to his valuable collection.

He poured the drinks and brought them over. Then, looking at me thoughtfully, he leaned across the bar conspiratorially. 'I'm guessing – and this is only a guess, mind – that you'd like a chat,' he said.

'You must be clairvoyant,' I said.

'That's me,' he said. 'Madame Roger. Cross my palm with silver and I'll tell your fortune.' He took a delicate sip of his beer. 'So, what can I tell you?'

'I don't really know,' I said.

'Well, let me guess again,' he said. I shrugged my agreement. 'You'd probably like to know what your friend David Cavendish said to that nice man from Special Branch who came in yesterday.'

'I don't think he's with Special Branch,' I said. 'Big man? Silver hair? Looks a bit like Anthony Eden? Calls himself Jenkins?'

'That's him,' he said. 'He and Mr Cavendish got quite friendly. I missed what was said, but there was an exchange of business cards and the distinguished-looking gent left.' He sipped some more beer. 'Incidentally, thanks for the warning about the boys in blue. They turned up, and we helped with their enquiries, but not, I'm afraid, very much.'

I sipped cognac. That was disappointing. He'd confirmed what Cavendish had said. That didn't suit me. I really wanted Cavendish to be guilty of something. Besides being an insufferable and arrogant ass, that is.

Emile was perched uneasily on one of the tall stools next to the bar. The place seemed to bother him as much as it had Jerry. He peered into the semi-gloom of the billiards room as if he expected something awful to come lungeing out. Funny, I would have had them both down as being more broad-minded than that.

Richard Ellis had seemed comfortable enough in the place.

'Richard's mate,' I said, choosing my words as carefully as I was able, 'Jonathan. How did he fit in? Here.'

Roger shrugged. 'The life and soul of,' he said. 'Very popular. Everyone liked him.' He gave a particular emphasis to 'liked'.

I finished my cognac and pushed the glass towards Roger and nodded at it.

'On the house,' he said as he plonked the refill down in front of me.

That was just as well as, after lavishly handing over the quid, I didn't have much cash left and the bank wouldn't be open again until Tuesday. Maybe Jerry could lend me a few bob to tide me over.

I stared at the drink gloomily, hunched over the bar. Maybe I should do a correspondence course and become a proper accountant. I was definitely not cut out for what Jerry saw as this detective lark. Minding drunk actors, putting things right with bookies, keeping things out of the papers: I could manage all that, just. But this was another barrel of apples altogether.

I sipped a little more cognac and then asked Roger if there was a telephone around that I could use. He directed me outside to Connie's domain. Emile looked at me anxiously as I got up and explained that I would be back in a minute or two, and I asked Roger to fill his glass. This one was on the house as well. Emile did not look reassured and sniffed his new drink suspiciously as if he thought he was about to be drugged and sold into the male equivalent of the white slave trade.

Connie showed me into her tiny little office as coyly as if she were leading me into her boudoir. She sat me down solicitously at her desk and even lifted the receiver off its cradle and handed it to me before leaving. I looked at the big ugly black thing for a while, realizing that I was just calling Jerry for something to do, then dialled.

He answered very quickly, so he must have been in the shop. There was something playing in the background, but I didn't know what it was and Jerry didn't ask me. He must have been feeling very gloomy.

Ghislaine and Robert had returned briefly and collected their things. Robert had booked all of them into a hotel near Marble Arch. He'd left the address for Emile.

There were two messages for me. Dr Jameson had called in the morning soon after I'd left and asked that I telephone him, and Les had just been on the line.

I went back out on to the landing and asked if I could make another call and Connie nodded amiably. That is, she didn't actually snarl or bite.

I didn't call Jameson. I had nothing to tell him and, as he

appeared to have been in Cambridge that morning, he could hardly have been the mysterious caller at Miss Beaumont's flat.

Daphne answered when I called Hoxton Films. She didn't bother with any banter, just put me straight through.

'Thanks for calling, Tony,' Les said. 'I've been ringing Bev for half an hour, and she isn't answering. I'm worried. She can be a silly girl. Even Daphne thinks there might be something up. Would you drop round and make sure she's all right? I'll send Charlie.'

I told him where I was and said I'd be outside in five minutes.

I left Connie's broom cupboard office and gave her a tanner for the phone. Her big hand swallowed up the coin.

TWENTY-ONE

C harlie swept us back up to St John's Wood as smoothly and as swiftly as the Rolls could manage, which was very smoothly and very swiftly. Emile sat in the front again, and Charlie was definitely showing off as we glided along Shaftesbury Avenue far too fast.

I sank uneasily into the comfort of the back seat and tried not to think about anything as we whispered our way majestically through the traffic.

It was difficult.

All manner of possibilities buzzed in my head. Beverley Beaumont just wasn't answering her telephone. Beverley Beaumont simply had a lunch engagement. However, lurking at the back of my mind was the one thing that I definitely knew: David Cavendish had sent Jenkins over to see her.

We pulled up outside the block of flats and walked up to the second floor.

I rang the bell, stepped well back, indicating to the others that they should do the same, and waited. Then I rang the bell again. I was about to press the button a third time when Charlie put his hand on my arm and waved a key in front of my face.

'Mr Jackson give it to me,' he said.

'What's Les doing with a key to Beverley Beaumont's flat?' I said.

Charlie shrugged and shook his head. 'I think she left this with him for safe keeping when she bought the place. Just so someone had a spare. I don't think there's any more to it than that,' he said and slid the key into the lock.

Maybe there wasn't. I'd have to ask Daphne. She usually had a reason for disliking someone, and she certainly disliked Miss Beaumont. And no one had ever said that Miss Beaumont favoured young, pretty boys *exclusively*.

The door swung open, and I walked into the little hallway. It was nowhere near as dim as it had been when I'd come before because all the doors that led off it were wide open and the rooms all had their lights on.

Charlie peered into the bedroom. 'Someone's had a right go at this place,' he said.

He was right. The bed had been turned over and most of Miss Beaumont's clothes taken from her wardrobe and dumped on the floor. There were a couple of men's shirts, a blue tie and a tweed jacket lying there as well.

The second bedroom had fared a little better, mainly because there wasn't much in it. A chair was resting on its back, its thin legs sticking out pathetically in front of it, and a couple of books had been knocked off the desk. A children's dictionary and a copy of *Cupid Rides Pillion* by Barbara Cartland.

The living room was pretty much untouched, although one of the cups I'd set out earlier was in pieces, adrift in a little puddle of cold, brown tea on the wooden floor, and the sofa had been pushed back at an odd angle.

I poked my head into the bathroom – just in case – but she wasn't reclining in a rapidly cooling bath, Roman-style, her wrists slit.

I joined Charlie back in the hall and started to think about Jenkins and Alfred. I wondered if they'd given Miss Beaumont time to get dressed. I hoped so and that they'd given her some privacy as well. If they'd showed her any discourtesy, it was probably just as well for them that Robert hadn't given me back the Webley.

Charlie sniffed. 'What we gonna do, Tone?' he said. 'I'll give Mr Jackson a bell, if you like.' He pointed to the telephone on its little table in the hall.

'No,' I said. 'He'll just tell us to find her. So, let's do it.'

He sniffed again and this time there was no mistaking a hint of scepticism in it. 'And how are we gonna do that?' he said.

'Your mate Herbert,' I said. 'Do you know where he lives?'

'No,' he said.

I cursed softly. 'Not a clue?' I said.

'No,' he said. 'Why?'

'Because I'd like to have a word with him,' I said.

'Oh, that's easy enough to arrange. I know where he'll be about now,' he said.

'Well, why the hell didn't you say so?'

'You asked me where he lived,' he said, sounding aggrieved at my exasperation. 'You never asked me if I knew where to find him.'

I took a deep breath and then smiled at him. 'No more I did,' I said. 'Sorry, Charlie.'

I looked around for Emile. He was in Miss Beaumont's bedroom, examining her underwear a bit too assiduously for my taste.

I called to him that we were leaving and then told him to take the black suspender belt out of his pocket and put it back where he'd found it. I admit that I couldn't remember the French for suspender belt and said something about 'intimate garments', but that was no excuse for his obvious reluctance to comply. My meaning was clear.

There was a strong whiff of horse liniment, bad feet, stale sweat and uncorked fart as we walked up the creaking wooden staircase and entered the gym where Charlie was convinced his mate Herbert would be.

The gym sat above a church hall on the Whitechapel Road, not far from the Royal London Hospital and the shop that was supposed to have exhibited the Elephant Man, and the smell was appropriate, I suppose, for a part of London that had developed around the more malodorous industries that the gentry hadn't wanted near their fashionable residences – the breweries and the tanneries and so on. I remember some character in a Dickens book I read as a nipper saying that Whitechapel wasn't 'a wery nice neighbourhood', but it had never seemed that bad to me.

Of course, these days Whitechapel still looked the worse for wear because of the bashing the Luftwaffe had given it during the war. They'd missed that rundown church hall, though. But not by too much. There was an old, overgrown bomb site just behind it that I could see through the windows at the back.

Herbert Longhurst, the Bermondsey Battler, a long way from the manor of his moniker, was standing by the ring, watching a couple of scrawny boys in ragged vests thrashing away at each other. Neither of them looked to have anything other than raw aggression going for them, but they were only ten or eleven and painfully undernourished. About half a dozen other youngsters, all around the same age, were leaning on the edge of the ring, watching proceedings intently. They were in the same gym uniform of grubby vests, big brother's baggy shorts and black plimsolls. Their thin, white, bony limbs were as grubby as their vests, but none of them seemed to be suffering from rickets.

The Bermondsey Battler gave us a big, soppy grin when he saw us and told the lads to take a break. They looked at us without interest and started talking to each other.

'How's the arm?' I said, pointing at Herbert Longhurst's sling.

'Itches like buggery,' he said. 'Apart from that, it's all right.' He poked a thumb towards the boys. 'What do you think of them?'

'Keen,' I said, 'very keen.'

'What do you think, Charlie?' the Battler said.

Charlie made a little non-committal movement with his mouth, thrusting his lower lip out. 'I've seen better,' he said. 'A lot better. But they're young and they've got no meat on them. No weight behind any of the punches.'

'That's right,' Herbert said. 'But they are keen. The gentleman here's right.' He indicated that they should continue, and we watched them for a minute or two as they flailed ineffectually at each other.

'So,' Herbert eventually said, his eye on the boys, 'what can I do for you gents?'

'Well,' I said, 'I just wondered if you could tell me if your boss, Mr Jenkins, has a lock-up somewhere. A place where he keeps his valuables.'

'Why do you want to know that?' he said, looking a little uneasy.

'I'm pretty sure he has something he shouldn't have, and I want it back,' I said.

'No,' he said, shaking his head firmly, 'Mr Jenkins is straight as a dye. He wouldn't have nothing of yours.'

I considered my options. Herbert Longhurst was a decent sort, commendably brave and loyal. A physical threat was obviously pointless. Not that I'd even consider one. On the other hand, I reckoned he was probably kind to old ladies and dumb animals.

I leaned forward and put my hand on his uninjured arm. 'It's not really Mr Jenkins I'm after, Mr Longhurst,' I said.

'Call me Bert,' he said amiably.

'OK, Bert. The thing is that I'm worried about that Belgian bloke. I think he's taken a young lady friend of mine, against her will, and I'm really concerned. I'm sick with worry, really, and so's her mother.'

Charlie raised his eyebrows at me, but I didn't care if I was laying it on thick.

'Belgian bloke?' Bert said.

'Yeah,' I said. 'Jan. The bloke who shot you.'

'Oh, him,' he said, his hand moving to his sling and rubbing it. 'The frog.'

I looked at Emile, but he was watching the lads working themselves into a lather and hadn't heard him. Not that he'd have understood anyway, I told myself.

'Yeah,' I said. 'If you could give us any idea where she might be, I'd be really grateful. And so would her mother.' I ignored Charlie.

Bert looked troubled. He thought about it for a few seconds, then turned back to the ring and told the boys to take another break.

'I wouldn't trust that frog as far as I could throw him,' he said.

I thought that that might be a considerable distance, but didn't say anything. Apart from anything else, I didn't want to interrupt Bert's laboured thinking process.

'All right,' he said (actually, he pronounced it in the good old London way, with a 'w' replacing the 'r'), 'there is a place.'

'Where is it, Bert?' I said, looking at my watch. Jerry was always talking about hearing time's wingèd chariot at his back, and I was beginning to understand what he meant. I wasn't going to find Jonathan Harrison and get him to Inspector Rose before close of business.

'It's just down the road,' he said. 'Mile End. I can't remember the address, so I'll have to come with you.'

My heart didn't exactly rise, but it certainly didn't sink any further. Bert accompanying us was fine by me. It was his not very devious way of ensuring that he could keep an eye on us. It didn't fill me with joy because I couldn't be entirely sure which way he'd jump, but I thought he was a decent sort and he might prove useful, even if it was just in getting us through the door. The lock-up being just around the corner did offer a glimmer of hope.

I was wondering whether or not I had time to call Les, to give him the bad news, when one of those coincidences occurred that suggests there is meaning in life. Ray, the young thug who had pulled the Webley on me the other night, sauntered into the gym. He obviously didn't see me at first, masked as I was by Charlie, and he just yelled at the Bermondsey Battler from the doorway. 'Bert, get your skates on. The gaffer's got a minding job. You'll like this one.' Then he did clock me. It took him another couple of seconds to realize who I was, but then he turned and raced back to the stairs, his jacket flapping. He skidded on the landing and pelted down the staircase, taking the stairs three or four at a time.

I'm not as fast as I once was, but I can still chase and catch an out-of-condition toe-rag over a short distance, and I was only a few yards behind him.

We hared down the stairs at much the same speed – something to do with gravity being constant, I suspect, since we both spent a certain amount of time at its mercy, half-flying, half-jumping down – and hit the ground floor still separated by those few yards.

Ray then surprised me, and lost a few feet of his advantage, by turning sharply and, instead of heading out of the front door, making for the rear of the building.

I followed him slowly and carefully along the dim, narrow corridor. It smelled strongly of furniture polish and old Bibles. There was a small table covered with little piles of garish bookmarks with biblical texts and flowers printed on them and some neat stacks of religious tracts.

I stopped running and trod warily because I was sure that Ray intended to hide in some handy, darkened alcove and ambush me. I hadn't heard him open a door and leave.

A sprung floorboard groaned as I put my weight on it before taking the left turn under the staircase. I instinctively pulled back slightly and so, when Ray came charging out of his predictable hiding place under the stairs, he didn't hit me with his shoulder nearly as hard as he'd intended, since I wasn't quite where he expected me to be. Instead of smacking into me hard in the midriff, he caught me in the chest.

But the blow was hard enough to force the breath out of me and to ruin his plans completely. He bounced off me and caromed into the wall opposite, banging into the table. The bookmarks fluttered to the floor like so many exotic butterflies.

Unfortunately for Ray, the edge of the table came into violent and painful contact with his groin, and he fell to his knees clutching himself.

I was spun around and slightly winded but, not having been hit in a particularly tender part, recovered first. I grabbed him by the lapel of his jacket and hauled him to his feet. He made a fist as if he was about to resist, but then saw Emile, who had followed me down the stairs, pointing his ugly gun at him and wisely thought better of it.

I slammed him against the wall, and we stared at each other for a few seconds, breathing heavily. I then straightened up and leaned on him with my right hand pressing him against the wall and my left cocked as though I intended to punch him.

'So,' I said, 'where's this minding job?'

His head was hanging down and he was still carefully cradling his balls.

I gripped the lapel of his jacket – grabbing some of his shirt, and possibly some of his flesh as well, judging by the authentic-sounding yelp – more tightly, pulled him forward and then hammered him back against the wall.

'I'd like an answer,' I said.

He lifted his head sullenly. 'I dunno,' he said, 'I really don't.'

'Sure you do,' I said. 'I wouldn't want my friend here to get the wrong idea and assume you aren't cooperating.'

He looked at Emile in some alarm and started thinking about it. 'Well,' he said, 'all I can tell you is where Bert is supposed to show up.'

'That'll do for a start,' I said.

Ray looked down at his well-polished black Oxfords and sniffed. 'He's to go to the gaffer's club, wait outside and he'll be picked up and taken somewhere,' he said.

'Where?' I said.

'I dunno,' he said, trying to paste an open expression of innocence on his face, eyes wide, mouth slightly agape. He only succeeded in looking sly and deceitful.

'Have a guess,' I said.

He shrugged, in as far as he was able with me pinning him

to the wall. I felt it, rather than saw it. 'Out of town somewhere?' he said. 'Minding someone.'

'Who?' I said.

He tried to shrug again.

I relaxed my grip a little. 'When you came in, you said he
was going to like it. Why?'

'I dunno,' he said again and looked down at the bookmarks
strewn across the floor. He resembled nothing so much as an
errant twelve-year-old schoolboy, an expression somewhere
between sullen and guilty plastered across his mug.

We stood there in silence, apart from our still laboured
breathing and Emile tapping the barrel of his ugly black gun
against his leg.

I heard traffic on the Whitechapel Road and then the sound
of people leaving the gym and coming down the stairs. I
thought it would be Charlie and Bert.

'All right,' I said, 'I'm going to make it easy for you. You
don't have to say a thing, and you can honestly say that we got
nothing out of you.' I paused and he looked up at me, genuine
puzzlement on his face. 'I'll tell you who it is. If I'm right,
don't make a sound. If I'm wrong, cough. Understand?'

He nodded.

'It's a young and attractive woman called Beverley
Beaumont. She's a film actress and your boss is taking her
somewhere safe because he has some idea that Jonathan
Harrison will return the diamonds he, er, mislaid in return for
Miss Beaumont.'

Ray didn't make a sound.

Of course, the flaw in my reasoning was that I had to assume
that he knew what was going on and that his silence meant
that I'd guessed correctly. Neither assumption could be relied
on. Unfortunately, I didn't have much else going for me.

Charlie and Bert had appeared in the corridor while I'd
been talking.

'What's the score, Tone?' Charlie said.

'I'm not sure,' I said. 'Things are not quite as simple as
they were ten minutes ago, and they weren't simple then.' I
looked at Ray. 'Where's the club? Is it the one in St James's?'

He nodded.

'When is Bert going to be picked up?'

'The boss said to get him there for half four,' Ray said.

I released my grip and looked at my watch. It was five and twenty past three. How time flew when you were having fun. My stomach rumbled.

Ray smoothed out the creases and rumples in his jacket and brushed it down. Then he slumped against the wall.

'Were you supposed to call in, saying if you'd found him or anything?'

'Leave a message with the club doorman.'

I looked at Bert. 'Is there a telephone here we can use?' I said.

'There's one in the office,' he said, looking unhappy.

I grabbed Ray again and marched him up the stairs to the gym, with Charlie, Bert and Emile following on. Everyone except Emile looked glum. But then Emile didn't know what was going on.

The boys had disappeared, presumably into the changing room.

The office was surprisingly tidy. The big old telephone sat on it solidly, its thick brown cord hanging down off the edge like a schoolgirl's lank and dull plait. Apart from that and an empty wire tray, there were only a few pencils and a pad.

I asked Ray for the number of the club and dialled. I left a message with the same curt doorman I'd met a few nights before. I just said that the message was from Ray for Mr Jenkins and that Bert couldn't make it by half four. Could he call the gym and tell Bert where to meet him?

I then yelled to Charlie, who was waiting outside the door, and told him to keep an eye on Ray, who I sent out to him.

I sat on the desk, staring at the big, wooden filing cabinet, wondering how many boys' dreams of fame and fortune in the ring were turning yellow with age inside.

I waited for ten minutes for a call and then went out into the gym.

Ray was looking worried. Charlie was holding his arm tightly, and Emile was standing by the door, his hand in his jacket pocket, a grim smile on his face.

I stood there for a minute, considering the sense of what I was about to do. Since the alternative would lead either to an appearance in court or to digging a hole in Epping Forest and stuffing him in it – and possibly both – I decided that I didn't have a lot of choice. After all, I was supposed to be the good guy here.

'All right,' I said to Ray, 'you'd better be off. I'd stick to a simple story if I were you. You saw Bert, he couldn't get away immediately and leave it at that.' I paused to let it sink in that he could go. 'If you don't stick to that you'll find yourself in big trouble with your boss. Worse, you'll be in even bigger trouble with me.' I took Charlie's hand from his arm and pushed him towards the door.

I called to Emile in French. 'Escort our friend down to the street. See if there's anyone waiting for him in a car. If there is, don't do anything. Just come back up and tell me.'

He nodded. He was used to doing what Robert told him.

As Ray left the gym and we heard the two of them clatter down the stairs, I turned to Charlie. 'Do you know how to get to Cambridge?' I said.

'Yeah,' he said. 'Why?'

'I've decided against Mile End,' I said. 'I thought we could all do with some country air.'

TWENTY-TWO

I'm not much of a one for the country. I'm a Londoner, and Londoners don't go there.

Not even on holiday. We go to the seaside: Southend, Clacton, Ramsgate or, sometimes, the most intrepid of us venture as far as Lowestoft and Great Yarmouth. You don't get cockles and whelks in the country.

During the war, youngsters, and sometimes their mothers, were evacuated to places like Bicester (which isn't pronounced how it looks, apparently, and rhymes with sister – but that's the country for you) and treated like skivvies on cold, wet, mucky, smelly farms. It was, for some, a scarring experience. For a few, it was so bad they hopped on the first bus back, preferring to take their chances with Goering's Luftwaffe.

I can sympathize with that. My mother took me to a place called Wickford when I was a nipper. I suppose she thought it would be a nice day out. It was market day, and I saw my first pig. It was black and enormous, had long, vicious-looking bristles on its backside and emitted the appalling noise that Grand-père made when he fell asleep after Sunday dinner and too much beer. I've never forgotten that pig's backside.

Going to the Hollow Ponds to fish for sticklebacks with a length of twine and a safety pin or to High Beech (where Dick Turpin is supposed to have had his hideout) to pick blackberries doesn't count. That's Epping Forest and is always full of Londoners.

I know that it's a bit of a joke, but it's true all the same. The country scares Londoners. The noises are unfamiliar and unpredictable. The rain is constant, and city shoes aren't built to cope with bogs. Anyway, I had a bellyful of cows, pigs, wet fields and small-minded country people during the war. There was commando training out in somewhere remote, cold, very damp and in Scotland. And then there was France.

All the same, I have to admit that the drive up through the Essex countryside that balmy April evening touched something and gave me that odd, joy-mixed-with-sadness feeling that I suppose translates as cheap sentiment.

As the sun went down on our left and smeared the big sky a deep red, for some reason a jaunty record that my mother had had sent over from France before the war kept buzzing around my head. I couldn't remember many of the words, just something about when our hearts go *boum!* it is love that is waking up. I think there was a lot of stuff about turkeys and birds on a lake and deer as well, all making pleasant noises. Clearly, the song had been written by a *Parisien* who had, with the unerring ability of the most popular of lyric writers, homed in on every city dweller's misty-eyed view of the countryside, seeing it as a larger version of the Bois de Boulogne, without *les putains* and *les pédés*, of course. Still, the chirpy melody cheered me up.

Emile had taken what had become his usual seat, riding shotgun, sitting in the front, next to Charlie, so Bert slumped next to me, snoring energetically. Evidently, the country had no appeal for him. It was something best slept through. The steady rhythm of his breathing reminded me a little of that pig in Wickford.

Emile suddenly turned and asked me if there was a *chalet de nécessité* near. I laughed, partly because we were in the middle of nowhere and partly because I'd always thought that my mother had invented the term to protect our modesties. Emile, however, obviously thought that I was mocking him and looked hurt. I told Charlie to pull over and explained to Emile that we could all probably do with going and that there were enough trees around for us all to have our own personal *pissoir*. He looked at the field that Charlie had stopped by and a little frown of worry creased his forehead. Which made me laugh again. A *Parisien* who wouldn't think twice about pissing against a wall not far from a bustling boulevard was concerned about urinating in an empty field.

As we hauled ourselves out of the car, Charlie jerked a thumb up the road. 'Not far now, Tone,' he said, yawning and rolling his shoulders.

I nodded and strolled through the old gate that Emile had opened, down the little rise and into the field.

The low sun was warm on my back as I stood and peed against a giant conker tree, and it threw a long, dark, distorted shadow across the grass. The conker tree is one of the only two or three I can recognize. There's the oak, of course; the copper beech, when it's in leaf; and the sycamore because of the strange whirling seeds that drop from it. Oh, and the monkey puzzler. That's five, so maybe I've soaked up more country lore than I'd imagined. I could probably have a stab at spotting a silver birch. On the other hand, apart from pigeons, sparrows, starlings and seagulls, birds are a mystery to me.

The back of my head was still sore and so was my knee, but the sun felt good. And the air smelt clean, although it hinted at compost and cow pats. I felt like lying down and snoozing for half an hour.

I looked across at the others. We'd all discreetly chosen our very own tree. The field was fringed with nine or ten. On my left, Bert was fiddling with his fly with one hand, rummaging around as though unpacking a large trout, and holding his brown trilby in the other. Beyond him I could see a few black and white cows eyeing us balefully.

A dowdy, brown-coloured butterfly with glossy black spots on its wings fluttered around, and a small cloud of gnats gathered under the branches just above me. A couple of nondescript, black, shadowy birds drifted across the blue sky. It was very peaceful and pleasant. It's amazing what a little sun – and a complete absence of pigs – can do for the countryside. I turned my attention back to the gnarly old bark of the tree and concentrated on emptying my bladder.

I didn't even miss the sound of the traffic. But, then, there was a car passing at that very moment.

It can't have been the first vehicle to have rumbled past, but I noticed this one – and as it roared by, just out of sight on the other side of the trees and the thick hedge, it re-awoke the sense of urgency that the balmy evening had so effectively dissipated.

I didn't have much of a plan, and most of it – well, all of it, really – consisted of beating Jenkins and his boys to our destination and surprising them. Always assuming I'd guessed right, of course.

Charlie was leaning contentedly on the gate, and Emile had just finished lighting a cigarette and was sucking the smoke deep into his lungs. He flicked the match casually to the ground. Bert was still peeing in little fits and starts.

I rebuttoned my fly and was starting to amble back towards the gate when I was suddenly aware that the car that had just passed us had stopped a little way up the road and the engine note had changed to the higher-pitched whine of a vehicle reversing.

Of course! It was the bloody Roller! Instantly recognizable! I remembered Jenkins taking a long, hard look at us when we'd been parked in St James's Street.

I yelled a quick and incoherent warning to Charlie and Emile and started to run. Even if Emile hadn't understood, he was a bright boy. He'd get the gist.

Bert looked puzzled as I dashed past him, but I didn't bother to explain. He was one of them, really. He could look after himself.

The rutted ground was treacherous in my thin-soled city shoes, and I risked a turned ankle with every step, but it was no worse than most football pitches after a January freeze and at least the recent spell of fine weather meant that no mud sucked at my feet.

I heard a commotion behind me and thought there may have been a shot. I risked a quick look back and saw Charlie and Emile running off in the opposite direction – Emile way out in front – with a bloke following in a half-hearted sort of way. One man, unmistakably Jenkins, was standing, arms folded, by the gate, waiting for Bert to amble across to him. Alfred, again unmistakable in his white sling, stood slightly in front of him, levelling a pistol with his uninjured arm. They must have quite some armoury somewhere because Robert had disarmed everyone the night before and I didn't recall him handing the weapons back when they'd said their good nights and slunk away. Given how far Emile was away, Alfred would have to be a first-class shot – or very, very lucky – to hit anyone at that distance. It rather looked as if he was neither. Unfortunately, I couldn't stick around to find out. The would-be tough who I'd tangled with earlier in the day was coming after me, and he was moving fast. Perhaps he thought he had something to prove. Just because I'd dealt with him twice before didn't mean I'd manage it successfully this time.

Still, one against one was promising.

I was aiming for a small copse about sixty or yards further on. I had some idea of circling around and outflanking our attackers but, first, I'd have to deal with young Ray. And he, too, was armed. I became aware of that because he fired two shots at me in quick succession. One howled harmlessly past, hopelessly wide, but the other was much too close for comfort. He was probably a lousy marksman who had got a bit lucky, but even so I pumped my arms faster and zigged and zagged.

I pounded on, breathing hard, wishing I hadn't missed quite so many football training sessions, but I made the cover of the little wood easily and without the searing pain of either a bullet or a stitch. I stopped to regain my breath and then I bent over and peered through the delicately trembling little trees, which were certainly how I imagined silver birches to be. Ray was only a few seconds behind me, and so I quickly plunged into a thicker part of the wood and ducked behind a large old oak, pressing my back against the rough, furrowed bark.

I heard him enter the wood. Only a deaf man wouldn't have. He was wheezing badly, and dry sticks were cracking under his feet. To be fair, I already knew he was chasing me, so even complete silence wouldn't have helped him.

I hunkered down at the base of the tree and waited. I was grinning, and I realized that I was looking forward to this. It wasn't the violence, I told myself. It was the excitement, the awareness of everything around me, the feeling of being really alive and relishing it. I sniffed the air and fancied I could smell the stale cigarette smoke on his clothes, the brilliantine in his hair, the Lifebuoy soap on his skin. I grinned again and listened.

He was treading more cautiously now, warily, and he was very close.

As he came abreast of the tree, to my right, I moved slowly, carefully and, above all, silently, to my left, keeping the tree between us. When I was sure that I was behind him, I stood up and risked a look.

He was standing about four yards away, the gun in his right hand, extended in front of him. His hand was shaking noticeably.

Two strides took me right up to him, and I punched him twice in the small of the back. He grunted and sprawled forward on to the damp earth with a soft oof as the air left him, and I didn't muck about. I kicked him in the side and then leaned down and hit him once behind the ear. He lay there, moaning.

Not third time lucky then, Ray, I thought. If I felt any guilt at all, it left me when I saw the sleek, black pistol that he'd dropped. I had no doubt that he would have used it if I'd given him the chance.

Quickly, while he was still more or less out of it, I pulled his jacket down over his arms, took off his braces and used them to tie his wrists to his ankles. It wouldn't incapacitate him for ever, but it would keep him occupied long enough. I rummaged in his pocket and found an old snot rag and forced it into his mouth. Then I retrieved his gun and pocketed it. It was a Luger – a memento from the war, I imagined. I'd come across them often enough, but I'd never used one – and so I wasn't sure I'd be able to start now – but it might come in handy as a frightener.

Leaving Ray there, coming to and struggling already, his coughing and spluttering muted by the handkerchief, I turned sharp right, back towards the road, carefully walking through the dense undergrowth, which threatened the legs of my trousers, my last decent pair, until I came to the fence.

I peered out of the trees and along the shadowed road.

There wasn't all that much to see. The Humber that I'd become quite familiar with was parked about thirty or forty yards in front of the Roller, which was just visible beyond it. But standing next to the Humber, his back to me, watching the fence and the field, was Jan. I'd wondered if he was around. It must have been 'intime' in the Humber.

As I climbed over the fence, the bellowed instructions of one of the Special Ops instructors up in 'arry's egg, as the Poles and the French on the same commando course called the place, came to me: 'Use the available cover, you tosser!' I doubt that he had a grey Humber in mind when he offered that advice – he leaned more towards wet, muddy depressions in the landscape and viciously barbed brambles – but that was what I had.

I crossed the road, putting the car between me and the Belgian and, stooping, I closed the gap between us as swiftly and quietly as I could.

Jan must have heard something as I reached the car because he started to turn to his right, away from me and looked back towards the wood.

My old instructor would have been proud of me. It was straight out of the manual. I stopped, hunkered down for a few seconds and then, still crouching, I awkwardly waddled along the few feet of road to the car door.

Then I lifted my head enough to look at Jan through the driver's window.

He peered towards the little wood for a few seconds and then sniffed, spat on the grass verge and turned back towards the gate.

I worked my way back around the bonnet of the car and stepped out behind him.

One of the other things that tough, old instructor used to bark at us was, 'Don't piss about. Just do it.'

It was sound advice and, as with Ray a few minutes before, I followed it.

Jan wasn't wearing a hat, and I hit him hard enough with the butt of the gun to crack his skull. Certainly, it was hard enough to dislodge his spectacles, and they hit the ground before he did. He went down with no more than a gentle sigh, and he stayed down. He twitched once or twice, but he was out.

I opened the back door of the car, and there was Miss Beaumont, sitting in the space behind the front passenger seat. Her hands were tied in front of her, and she was gagged, but she'd managed to loosen the rope around her ankles. I noted that at least they'd had the decency to allow her to dress in the same chic suit that I'd first seen her in. It was more crumpled and less chic than it had been then.

I decided not to waste time and picked her up and draped her across my shoulder. She was surprisingly light.

I crossed the road quickly to the field that invitingly offered itself there. It looked like the mirror image of the one I'd just been in, but I suppose there must have been differences. I lowered Miss Beaumont over the fence as carefully as I could and then climbed over myself. Crouched there, I managed to untie her and pull the gag, which was a man's tie, out of her mouth.

She threw her arms around my neck and leaned her soft cheek against mine. 'Thank you,' she breathed into my ear.

Her intoxicating perfume was absent, but she was, if anything, even more fragrant.

'Don't thank me yet,' I whispered. 'We're not out of the woods yet.'

She lifted her head, looked up at the tree we were sat under and laughed quietly. 'Yes, we are,' she said. 'If one swallow doesn't make a summer, then I'm fairly sure that one tree doesn't make a wood.'

I smiled at her. I don't think I'd heard her crack a joke – even a laboured one – before. Perhaps she wasn't made of porcelain after all. And I'd been expecting her to be all sobs.

'I think you know what I mean,' I said.

I risked lifting my head for a quick shufti over the hedge. Amazingly, there was still no one by the car. Charlie and Emile must have been doing a great job, but I couldn't see Charlie lasting much longer. On the other hand, if all they were up against was Don the driver then they might well come charging back over the hills at any minute. He wasn't a match for either of them. Then I heard a thin wail, a wan call for help. It was coming from the wood on the opposite side of the road. Ray must have managed to spit out his disgusting snot rag.

'Come on,' I said, 'let's find some cover before they notice you're missing.'

She nodded.

'Incidentally,' I said, 'when we're mentioning people in despatches and handing out the gongs, don't forget Charlie. He's risking heart failure, leading them off in the wrong direction.'

'Charlie?' she said.

'Charlie Lomax,' I said. 'Les's driver.'

Clearly, she didn't know who I was talking about. 'Anyway,' I said, 'let's go.'

'Wait a minute,' she said. 'I can't run in these.'

She slipped off her white, high-heeled sandals and then hitched up her skirt, unfastened her stockings and slipped them off. As the soft fabric slid slowly down her smooth, white skin, I couldn't help noticing that she had a great pair of pins, slim and shapely. She caught me looking and gave me a narrow-eyed look.

'Sorry,' I said and turned away in embarrassment.

She patted me affectionately on the shoulder, like I was a pet dog who'd just done something naughty but endearing. 'Ready,' she said. 'And were you?'

'Was I what?' I said.

'Mentioned in despatches?'

'Yes,' I said.

'What does it mean?' she said.

'They give you a chunk of bronze cast as an oak leaf,' I said.

'No, what does it mean? What did you do?'

'Nothing that hundreds of others didn't do better and more often.'

It suddenly occurred to me that when Jenkins and Alfred noticed that she was missing, which must be any minute, they'd probably reckon that she would have run away from them, down the road in the direction they'd been travelling, and not risk passing them at the gate. I decided that we'd do just what they thought we wouldn't.

TWENTY-THREE

I t was just like old times.
   Except that Beverley Beaumont wasn't Ghislaine; this
wasn't a French apple orchard, damp with morning dew;
Big Luc wasn't running a fuse from explosives packed under
a railway line; Jenkins and Alfred weren't enemy soldiers in
Feldgrau; and I wasn't twenty-one any more. You can't have
everything.

The immortal Bix Beiderbecke was building up a head of
steam with 'Tiger Rag' in my head as, hugging the hedge, we
swiftly – well, as swiftly as you can when walking in a crouch
and one of you is barefoot, carrying her stockings and shoes
– headed in the direction of the Rolls, the gate and the men
we were trying to elude.

If I'd had a cigar in one hand and if Beverley Beaumont
had been much larger and in front of me and if I'd painted a
black moustache on my upper lip I would have been a dead
spit of Groucho Marx stalking Margaret Dumont.

I could still just about hear Ray plaintively seeking help.
His thin, reedy pleas carried on the warm, evening breeze. If
I could hear him, it was a racing certainty that Jenkins could.
With a bit of luck, Alfred would have gone to his aid. With
a bit more luck, both of them would be ministering to him
even now, gently rubbing his wrists to encourage the circulation of blood back into his hands. Not that I'd tied him that
tightly.

The Rolls was visible through the hedge, the last rays of the
setting sun gleaming on its flanks. I couldn't see beyond it into
the field, so I didn't know what was going on, but an absence
of shouting, shooting or scuffling suggested nothing much.

Waiting around to find out didn't seem like the best plan,
but I wanted to know. I moved five yards to my left and stood
up, but I couldn't see around the Rolls. Still, the dear old
thing protected us from any prying eyes in the field. However,
while I watched, animated voices drifted across the road, and
I crouched down next to Beverley Beaumont.

'You know, this is just like *The 39 Steps*,' she whispered.

I suddenly remembered the story that Les had told me about Hitchcock and Madeleine Carroll and smiled. I had a sneaking suspicion that Beverley Beaumont's eyes wouldn't register even mild surprise if the great man gave her an organ recital. She'd probably yawn, peer at him short-sightedly for a few seconds before rummaging in her handbag for her spectacles.

'Just a bit,' I whispered back.

The lively conversation of just a few seconds before had turned into something else, and angry raised voices drifted across the road. I couldn't hear what was being said, but the sound grew steadily louder. I heard what sounded like Bert's bass rumble and Jenkins' imperious, aristocratic bark. It seemed that Jenkins' party was leaving the field. In a minute or so they'd probably discover Jan and then that Miss Beaumont was missing.

I hoped that Charlie and Emile had got away.

I looked around for some cover. There wasn't much. The field sloped very gently down for about two hundred yards to what looked like a small stream – although it could just have been a drainage ditch – and then rose again to a slight rise where, more than a quarter of a mile away, a few trees straggled. Further on, there was a church spire thrusting up towards the darkening sky. However, as the sun set and colour leached slowly out of the landscape, if we stayed where we were, hunched up against the hedge, we might pass as a large bump in the ground, or the stump of a felled tree.

I took the unfamiliar gun out of my pocket and examined it cursorily. Not that I had any real intention of using it. Accidentally shooting one man in the foot and seeing two others wounded was more than enough gun action for one week.

Big Luc had always used a Luger. He'd taken it as a trophy off some German staff officer whose fate I'd never asked about. He'd tried to explain the toggle mechanism to me one quiet evening and just how the recoil worked but my grasp of technical French hadn't been up to it. Or perhaps it had been his that had been deficient.

As I thought of Big Luc, I remembered the oak leaf that lay, not quite forgotten, with other, more mundane, service medals – my Africa Star, the one I received for managing to wear a uniform for twenty-eight days, and another star just for setting foot in France – under my few shirts and socks. It was a guilty reminder.

It should, of course, have been Luc's, and Robert's, and Ghislaine's, and the others'. But I was the British soldier – the junior officer (promoted way beyond his competence) – who tagged along as they knocked out fortified cottages and German machine-gun emplacements during the bitter fighting south of Caen, around Tilly and May-sur-Orne in July 1944. And mine was the only name the battered Canadian and British troops we came across remembered and passed on. But it was Big Luc who was shot in the gut. And it was the two young brothers barely out of school, Maurice and Albert, who caught the shell the Panzer tank lobbed at them.

Suddenly, there was some spirited shouting, an unpleasant oath or two and the sound of running feet from the other side of the road. I assumed that Miss Beaumont's absence had been noted. Then the sound of running receded. The runner was heading away from us. So far the ploy of doubling back seemed to have worked.

A car drove past, the daffodil-coloured light from its head-lamps penetrating the hedge and sweeping over us as it drifted around the bend in the road. Miss Beaumont's pale, intense face peered at me briefly out of the gloom.

'Shouldn't we be trying to find a policeman?' she whispered.

'Probably,' I said.

'What are we waiting for, then?' she said, sounding just a little impatient and much more than a little imperious.

I made allowances for her. After all, a number of men had tied her up and abducted her from her flat. She'd spent an uncomfortable hour or two in a car. She must have been worried sick. Of course she was anxious and afraid. All the same, her manner rubbed me up the wrong way. I couldn't help feeling that maybe she wasn't sufficiently grateful for being rescued.

'Well,' I said as patiently and as patronizingly as I could manage, just to put her in her place, 'if you see one cycle past, be sure to let me know. Anyway, I'm not altogether sure that it's in your interests to go to the police. Or that Hoxton Films would be overjoyed about the publicity that resulted.'

There was a short silence.

'Don't be daft,' she said. 'Hoxton would love it. A real kidnapping! It's better than anything the publicity department could dream up.'

'I don't know,' I said. 'Why do you think they kidnapped you?'

'Money,' she said. 'A ransom, of course.'

'Well, they are after something. But it's something they think Jon has. Although I suppose it's possible they might just have settled for a ransom demand to cut their losses. But Jon's involvement makes it a bit more complicated. And I'm not sure that "Film star's drug-dealer boyfriend" is the kind of headline Hoxton wants.'

There was another silence.

Well, it wasn't a *silent* silence. There were plenty of strange noises – rustlings in the trees and the hedge, scufflings, creakings, coughs and barks – and some not so strange – another vehicle rumbled noisily past, and there were sharp exclamations, low murmurs and the raw sound of someone retching – probably Jan – coming from across the road. No, it wasn't silent at all. All I mean is that Beverley Beaumont didn't speak for a while.

'He isn't a drug-dealer,' she finally said. 'He runs errands for people. That's all.' She paused. I looked at her. Her delicate little chin was pointed out defiantly. 'Anyway, if *they* are drug-dealers, they're not going to incriminate themselves, are they?'

She had a point.

It was my turn to reflect in silence for a few seconds.

She definitely had a point. Jenkins was hardly going to cough to smuggling in his little cache of illicit diamonds. In fact, I rather doubted that he'd cough to anything, and I was willing to put ready money on him having a devious, assiduous and probably bent brief who'd ensure that he walked away without, as they say in all the best newspapers, a stain on his character.

Eventually, I nodded. 'You're right,' I said. 'Let's go find a cop shop, or a telephone to call one.'

She put her hand on my arm. 'He isn't a drug dealer,' she said. 'He really isn't.'

I said nothing, but handed her the gun, hoping that she wouldn't use it on me.

'Here,' I said, 'hang on to this. Just in case.'

She held it at arm's length and looked at it for a few seconds.

'What am I supposed to do with it?' she said.

'Keep it hidden,' I said. 'Hand it to me if we get into trouble.'

'Why don't you hold on to it?' she said, not unreasonably.

'No one's going to search you,' I said.

She sniffed dismissively, thought about debating the point, but then seemed to accept that there was some merit in my argument and slipped the gun under her jacket and tucked it into the waistband of her skirt.

I lifted myself up on my haunches, turned, cautiously raised my head above the hedge and peered over.

I was expecting to see a little knot of men milling around by the Rolls, smoking, talking quietly together and managing to look bored and alert at the same time. I was wrong, and it seemed that I would have lost any money I'd been prepared to put on them outwaiting us.

In the huge, black shadows thrown by the giant conker trees, I could just about make out the bulky figure of Bert supporting what looked like Jan the Belgian and half carrying him towards the Humber. Ahead of them, a couple of other figures were already climbing into the car. In the increasing darkness, it was difficult to be sure of the exact number, but it certainly looked as if they were beating a strategic retreat. It occurred to me that Jan might have been as badly injured as I suspected. It was possible that Ray could do with some treatment as well. I couldn't resist a slight sense of smug satisfaction at the thought that they were heading off to lick their wounds.

I sank back down behind the hedge again.

Beverley Beaumont leaned towards me. For some reason she ran her hand down my cheek. My stubble rasped under the light touch of her soft fingers. I felt again the strange intimacy of shared danger.

'You need a shave,' she whispered.

'Sorry,' I said.

'It suits you,' she said. 'The rugged, tousled hero. Dirk Bogarde in *The Sea Shall Not Have Them*.'

I hoped it was too dark for her to notice the blush spreading up from my neck.

Then there was the distant sound of a powerful engine

sparking into life, slipping into gear and pulling smoothly away, the tyres spitting gravel.

I sat up a little, and Beverley Beaumont's hand slipped from my face and rested on my shoulder.

And I experienced once more the feeling of shared relief when danger passed.

We sat quietly for a few seconds, listening to that country silence.

'Do you think they've gone?' she said. Her voice had an eager edge to it, and I caught again that deep, sensual, Joan Greenwood timbre I'd heard in my office.

'Stay here,' I said. 'I'll go and see.' I stood up and then added, 'If there's any kind of problem, wait here quietly for a few minutes and then head off to the nearest house. There must be one back along the road.'

She nodded, and I leaned down, smiled and awkwardly patted her shoulder.

Night was coming in surprisingly quickly. The big, old Rolls Phantom must have been named for times like these. It was a silent, sleek shadow, eerily insubstantial and other-worldly, and the field beyond it was lost in darkness. I could just about make out the white-painted gate, but it was as if a thick blackout curtain hung behind it, with one single, thin line of fiery orange-red glaring through where the very last of the sun just touched the horizon.

Ten quick, quiet strides took me across the road to the side of the ghostly Rolls. My eyes had long since adjusted to the darkness, but I couldn't see any movement in the field, and I couldn't hear any unnatural sounds, apart from some distant farm vehicle coughing and hiccuping its noisy way back to the barn. Even the squabbling and brawling birds were quiet now.

I relaxed a little and walked to the gate. There was the faint smell of cigarettes hanging there, but that was explained by the half-dozen fag-ends littering the ground.

I imagined a crouching figure in every shadow, but no one leapt out at me and no one worked the mechanism on an automatic pistol and slid a bullet into the chamber.

The opening clarinet *glissando*, as Jerry had once told me it was called, from 'Rhapsody in Blue' wailed into my head.

Then there was the slightest sound behind me, and I briefly

thought that Miss Beaumont had ignored my instruction to stay put until something like the shoulder of a prop forward smashed into the small of my back and knocked me to the ground.

Before I even registered what had happened, a foot pinned my left arm to the cool, dry grass, a knee savagely hit the small of my back and my right arm was forced up my back in a half-nelson. Then someone growled softly in my ear.

'My, my, isn't it amazing what crawls out of the woodwork if you're patient enough?'

He'd been in the Rolls, of course. And, yes, of course, I should have checked.

I lay there and remembered the tale that Mrs Wilson had read to us when I was eight: a wily Greek, a false retreat and a wooden horse stuffed with soldiers. Les would have been mortified to think of his beloved Rolls compared to a wooden horse, but there were a few obvious resonances.

'Beware of Greeks bearing gifts,' I managed to force out in a pathetic and rather absurd attempt to sound relaxed and comfortable.

His knee ground into my back painfully. 'You're a smart Alec,' he said. 'And I don't like smart Alecs.' He wrenched my arm up my back. Any further and something would tear or break. He growled into my face again, breathing stale cigarette smoke and sour beer all over me, 'I told you I'd be back and that you owed me a new suit.'

He leaned back slightly, slackening his grip on my arm. For a moment, I was able to breathe more freely and I thought he was going to let me up. Then I felt cold metal against the left side of my head and he tapped me, very hard, with the barrel of his gun.

I've come across a few American, tough-guy novels that talk about the lights going out, or the curtain coming down, or seeing stars, but none of those phrases really does justice to the explosion of intense white light and pain that briefly follows an expertly applied blow to the head with a blunt instrument.

TWENTY-FOUR

I don't recall any of the American tough-guy novels I've read mentioning just how much your bonce hurts when you finally struggle back to consciousness after being comprehensively beaned. That seemed to me at that moment to be an important omission.

I didn't want to open my eyes or even move. After a moment's disorientation, I knew where I was and what had happened, but I was incapable of thinking beyond that. Alfred could do what he wanted with me. And he probably would.

Except when I did open my right eye – my left eye didn't make it more than halfway, and I had a feeling that it might be like that for quite some time – it wasn't Alfred's bland features and crazed eyes looking down at me, cradling my head in his lap.

The eyes were not crazed at all. The features were anything but bland. And the lap was much more inviting than Alfred's. They all belonged to Beverley Beaumont.

None of that made my head hurt any less, of course, and it did puzzle me, so I closed my eyes, lay very still and tried to put some coherent thoughts together.

I remembered lying with Ghislaine like this, but all we'd had to worry about had been whether Robert or the German army would find us first.

I opened my right eye again. 'Where's Alfred?' I said.

'I don't know. Who's Alfred?' she said.

'The *type* with the gun,' I said. 'The bloke who hit me.'

'He ran away,' she said.

I sat up and that hurt and I groaned. She gently pulled my head to her soft breast.

'Ran away?' I said. 'Why?'

'Because I shot him, I suppose,' she said.

I groaned again.

Fortunately, she thought it was the pain in my head that had caused the groan, rather than the thought that she could find herself facing a charge of attempted murder. And me with her. After all, I'd supplied the weapon.

I took a deep breath and concentrated on ignoring the pounding in my head. 'Where did you hit him?' I asked.

'I don't know,' she said.

I took another deep breath. '*Did* you hit him?' I said.

'I don't know. But I must have done,' she said. 'Why else would he run off?'

'Well,' I said, 'he wouldn't have been running at all if you'd hit him anywhere important, so I suppose that's something to be grateful for.'

She sent a stabbing pain through my head by pushing it away from the comfort of her bosom. 'I thought that you might be a bit grateful for me saving your life,' she said.

'I am,' I said. 'Really. But I'm just worried about things. Like whether or not he's coming back. Where did he run to? Which direction?'

'I don't know,' she said again, irritatingly. 'I just pointed the gun at him, closed my eyes and pulled the trigger. I didn't open them again until no bullets came out when I squeezed. And then he wasn't anywhere to be seen.'

I would have laughed if I hadn't known how much it would hurt. Alfred must have thought he was under attack from Rommel's entire Deutsches Afrikakorps when four or five bullets – or however many had still been in the Luger's magazine – came flying out of the dark, more or less in his direction. Though quite how she'd managed to fire the gun was something of a mystery.

'You're wonderful,' I said. 'Thank you for saving my life. My avenging angel.'

'You're welcome,' she said, a little acidly. She obviously didn't take kindly to being teased, even gently.

'I don't suppose you have any aspirin on you?' I said. 'Then you can add ministering angel to your list of accomplishments'

She shook her head.

I thanked heaven that it hadn't been Ghislaine's lap I'd woken up in. If it had been, there would have been a body lying next to me waiting to be disposed of. As it was, there wasn't a chance that Beverley Beaumont had hit anything.

Unfortunately, I was soon to discover that not to be true.

With a little assistance I struggled to my feet and, fighting an
almost overwhelming need to vomit, walked unsteadily to the
driver's side of the Rolls. I was about to ask her if she could
drive when I noticed that the rear tyre was completely flat.
Even a cursory investigation indicated that a bullet had hit it.
I wondered what other damage it had done on its way through.
I had thought that she would have aimed high, but it seemed
that at least one bullet kept very low indeed.

I could hear Les already: 'I don't care that it wasn't you,
Tony. What were you doing giving her a gun in the first
place?'

Still, it would probably give Daphne quite a laugh.

It suddenly occurred to me that the fact that the Rolls' tyre
had been holed meant it wasn't completely impossible that
Alfred had taken a bullet. If he hadn't been hit, where was
he? It was possible that he wasn't quite as icily fearless as he
pretended. More likely, he had gone for reinforcements.

I was mulling this over when I heard the sounds of laboured
breathing and soft footsteps muffled by thick grass. Alfred
must have found his comrades more quickly than I would
have liked.

I grabbed Miss Beaumont's arm and pulled her down beside
me in the road behind the car, putting my hand over her mouth
as I did so.

And I waited to be discovered. It was all I could do.

Pretty soon they'd be outwith the field.

Outwith? Where had I got that from?

Then I remembered: one of the Scots at Arisaig on the
commando training course used the term. It reminded me of
my proudest moment at Church Road Primary.

There was silence, apart from something hooting and the
breeze disturbing the leaves of the trees.

I once won a bet for Mrs Wilson.

The gate creaked open and then clunked shut. They were
definitely outwith the field now.

She had been so certain that her class would know what
'without a city wall' in the old 'Green hill' hymn meant that
she had bet the martinet Mr Thompson from the class next
door a shilling. It hadn't looked good for her when the pret-
tily bovine Christine Milne, her top pupil, had leapt straight
in with 'there's no wall around the city' and the unpleasant

Thompson had grinned evilly. After a protracted silence, during which Mrs Wilson's lips had pursed and she had looked increasingly uncomfortable, I put my hand up. She took a second or two to recognize me. I then tentatively suggested that it just meant outside the city walls, and she smiled triumphantly. It was no great thing – I think I must have seen a French translation of the hymn that Maman had lying around somewhere. Old Tommo never forgave me and would give me a hard time afterwards whenever he could. I remember thinking that the shilling must have meant a lot to him.

Someone shuffled on the dry, packed earth by the gate, then stepped lightly into the road. Three or four others scuffed the ground nearby.

I braced myself.

'Do you see anyone, John?' said a dry, cracked voice I recognized.

'No one here, David,' was the crisp reply from the other side of the car.

I wasn't sure that I was entirely relieved, but I stood up slowly, speaking as I rose. 'That's not quite true, Dr Jameson. It's Tony Gérard.'

John, the man by the car, was already aiming a gun at me in the correct and approved two-handed stance.

'What's happened to this country?' I said, holding my hands up, palms out. 'Why does everyone suddenly have a gun?'

'It's all right, John,' Jameson said. 'I know this man.'

John lowered his gun and nodded at me. But I noted that he made no effort to reholster the thing.

'Anyone would think this was the Wild West,' I said.

'John's just doing his job,' Jameson said very quietly.

There was another man with him and, behind them, standing by the gate, were Charlie and Emile.

'It's good to see you again, Mr Gérard,' Jameson wheezed out. 'And well, too. Your colleagues –' he turned slightly and indicated Charlie and Emile – 'were worried about you. They said they heard some shots.' He took a step towards me. 'What's this all about?'

'You mean you don't know?' I said.

'Well –' he turned towards Charlie and Emile again – 'your colleagues said something about a kidnapping . . .'

I was conscious of Beverley Beaumont rising to her feet.

'Actually, he isn't at all well,' she said. 'He's taken a very nasty bang to the head.'

Jameson looked at me.

'Miss Beverley Beaumont, the kidnap victim,' I said. 'This is Dr Jameson.' I paused. 'Miss Beaumont is an actress. In films.'

Jameson stepped forward and inclined his head towards her. 'Miss Beaumont,' he said, 'I'm afraid that I'm not familiar with your work. I hope you'll forgive a dusty old scholar who spends too much time with his books.'

In the darkness and under his hat, it was difficult to detect the full extent of his disfigurement, but Beverley Beaumont still stared at him a little too hard.

'Films are not everyone's cup of tea,' she said eventually. 'Mine are not very distinguished.'

'I have to ask,' he said, 'but have you been abducted? And was this gentleman involved?' He extended his mittened hand towards me.

'I was taken from my flat by force,' she said. I noticed she was speaking very formally. 'But this gentleman was on hand to rescue me.'

'Miss Beaumont's right,' I said. 'I'm not feeling too good.' I leaned against the Rolls. The legs had just lodged a complaint, indicating a disinclination to support my weight. 'But I don't understand,' I said. 'What are you doing here, Dr Jameson?'

'I just happened to be passing,' he said.

I shook my head and instantly regretted it. 'No,' I said, 'no one just passes this place.'

'I do,' he said. 'Frequently. It's a nice walk, and I have friends nearby.'

Yeah, I thought, and you always go for a walk with an armed companion.

He walked around the car and stood next to me, peering at my head. 'My goodness,' he said, 'that's quite a bump you've got coming up. We'd better get that some attention. We'll drop in on my friends. A cold compress, a cup of tea and a little sit-down, and you'll be as right as ninepence.'

He made an awkward gesture with his hand, as if he intended to pat me on the shoulder reassuringly but then thought better of it.

I was starting to feel very groggy. I sank down and sat on the ground, my eyes closed, my head between my knees.

I wandered in and out of consciousness for the next few minutes.

I was half-aware of a little kerfuffle when Charlie saw the Rolls' flat tyre and then of another car arriving and being helped into the back of it, while Charlie and Emile banged and clanged with tyre levers and spanners. And there was me thinking that Rolls-Royces came with a mechanic strapped underneath.

Then, in the comfort of the back seat, I drifted away as the car purred along the road.

We stopped, and I struggled to sit up.

Beverley Beaumont leaned across from my right and, ineffectually but pleasantly, attempted to help me by placing one hand on my shoulder and the other on my thigh. Jameson, on my left, inclined his head towards me.

'It's a short walk from here,' he said solicitously. 'Will you be able to make it, do you think?'

I nodded and instantly regretted it as the now familiar wave of nausea swept over me. All I wanted to do was curl up and sleep for a week.

We left the car, its driver and John, the passenger in the front, and, very slowly, walked about a hundred yards along a frighteningly dark road towards a large, bleak-looking house skulking behind a high hedge and some tall, elegant trees.

I wondered why we were walking when then was a perfectly serviceable motor car to hand, but I was in that strange, concussed state where a curiously reckless euphoria battled with a permanent and intense headache and the thought didn't go anywhere.

The sky, bright with stars, stretched above me, immense and breathtaking. I stopped, awestruck, to look up at it. I didn't think I'd ever seen anything quite as impressive.

Beverley Beaumont – wearing her shoes again, I noted – waited with Dr Jameson by a narrow gap in the hedge.

The dove-grey skirt and jacket and her pale face and legs were a strong contrast to the black hedge and road and brought her forward into the foreground. Grand-père would have liked the shot. Jameson was visible only as a shadowy dark outline. And the hulking house brooded in the background.

I caught up with them, and we then made our way – me still a little unsteadily – to the big front door, which nestled at the back of a little porch.

Jameson looked at me apologetically and nodded at the black knocker. It took me a second or two to understand that he wanted me to use it.

I lifted it and tapped lightly. The bright, brittle, metallic sound hung in the air. At first, nothing happened, and I reached up to the knocker again just as a light flicked on in the hall.

The stained glass in the panels on either side of the door came to life. Deep reds and bright greens leapt out at me and spilled little lozenges of flickering colour on my drab suit. I looked down and realized that the step I was standing on was an intricate mosaic. Pieces of faded blue and yellow tile covered the centre of the step, apparently set into the yellow-brown stone surround. Everything was surprisingly fresh and clear. If my head hadn't hurt quite as much, I would have been fascinated.

The door opened, and an elderly lady peered out suspiciously. She was thin and frail with pure-white hair and a sallow complexion. Her face was deeply wrinkled and the puffy bags under her eyes were violet.

'Yes?' she said, staring at me.

'It's me, Miss Hardiman,' Jameson said quickly, removing his hat. 'I said I might drop by.'

The old lady's head turned slightly towards him, but almost immediately snapped back to fix me with a wary stare. 'So you did, Dr Jameson,' she said. 'And who is this?' Her voice was high, crisp and querulous.

'This gentleman has been in an accident,' Jameson said. 'I know him.' His voice cracked. He waved his left hand at Beverley Beaumont. 'This lady is his companion.' I noticed that those parts of his fingers that extended beyond the mitten seemed to be fused into a lump of angry, red flesh. 'The gentleman needs some attention,' Jameson continued. 'I thought perhaps . . .' He looked into the hall.

'Of course, Dr Jameson,' Miss Hardiman said. She stared at me for a moment longer and then stepped back. 'Come in,' she said uninvitingly, daring us to enter.

I shuffled to one side, allowing Miss Beaumont and Dr Jameson to precede me. I wasn't sure if I was showing courtesy or cowardice.

The hall was wide and lit by a single, shaded bulb. A tall wicker basket by the door held two umbrellas. A narrow table against a wall supported a tall vase full of late daffodils and a telephone. A large painting hung on the opposite wall, between two doors. It was a wild and woolly landscape, a steep mountain pass. I guessed it was a romanticized view of Scotland. Certainly, it bristled with trees and foamed with cascades of white water. But there wasn't a stag in sight.

Under Miss Hardiman's unwavering scrutiny, I self-consciously wiped my feet on the coconut mat. And then, after she had firmly closed the door, I followed her along the hall and into the big, old-fashioned kitchen.

By the kitchen door, Jameson stopped. 'I'll leave you to it for the time being,' he said, 'and pay my respects. Is himself in the study?'

'In the front parlour,' Miss Hardiman said. 'We have company.'

'Jolly good,' Jameson said. 'The more the merrier.' And he retraced his steps back towards the front door.

Beverley Beaumont, who had been trying very hard not to stare at Jameson's face and hands, and I followed Miss Hardiman into the kitchen, in my case dutifully, recognizing that my natural place in a resolutely middle-class house like this was below stairs, even if only in a manner of speaking.

'Below stairs' was, in fact, very comfortable, if more than a little warm because of the big, black range that ran along one wall. A battered kettle sat on it, puffing steam.

Miss Hardiman pointed me at a wooden chair by a long table. She then indicated a chipped enamel bowl with a blue rim to Beverley Beaumont, who eventually picked it up and went to the huge sink. She stood hesitantly by it before turning on the tap with some difficulty and filling the bowl. She brought it back to the table and dipped a flannel that had been lying next to it into the icy water. She wrung out the excess and then leaned towards me. The cool flannel felt good against my head, and I closed my eyes.

I opened them after a few seconds when Miss Beaumont took the compress back to the bowl. Miss Hardiman placed a small glass of water and a couple of aspirin on the table in front of me. I swallowed them with a gulp of water.

Miss Hardiman busied herself making tea in a large brown teapot, and Miss Beaumont did what she could to reduce the swelling above my left eye with cold water, a sodden flannel and a certain gentleness. Perhaps she really was an angel of mercy.

After a few minutes, Miss Hardiman left us with a pot of tea, two teacups with a blue floral design, a blue and white striped milk jug and a plain white sugar bowl. Miss Beaumont played mother to perfection and insisted on two heaped teaspoons of sugar in my cup, 'for the shock'.

We sat in silence, sipping tea and listening to the creaks and ticks of the big, old house. Halfway down my second cup of tea I was starting to feel a little better. I lay back against the hard chair and closed my eyes again. I must have dozed for a while because when I opened my eyes again, and reached for my cup, the tea was stone cold.

'The swelling has gone down just a little,' Miss Beaumont said, smiling at me.

I smiled back. 'I feel a little better,' I said. 'The aspirin must have helped.'

She looked tired. Which wasn't surprising. She'd had a hard day. She also seemed to have lost most of the perkiness and resilience she'd shown earlier. She was back to the distant, fragile creature she usually showed the world.

Some noise came from the front of the house – a door opening, and some people shuffling and stomping along the hall towards the kitchen – and I lost what perkiness and resilience I'd regained in the last fifteen or twenty minutes too when Jenkins entered.

'Don't bother to get up. We'd only have to force you back down,' he said.

I don't think I've ever seen anyone grin wolfishly before, but I swear he did, showing big, yellow teeth, as Ray and Don the driver came into the room, followed by Alfred. Alfred didn't grin, and neither did a pale, sick-looking Jan. Then the bulk of the Bermondsey Battler filled the doorway before he shuffled sheepishly into the kitchen. His amiable mug offered a little respite from the narrow-eyed and mean looks of the others. Dr Jameson – perfidious Cambridge in person – brought up the rear and gave a dismissive little shrug when he saw me staring the proverbial daggers at him.

Beverley Beaumont sobbed quietly.

TWENTY-FIVE

I n spite of Jenkins' instruction to stay put, I did get up. Well, I attempted to. The chair legs rasped against the wooden floor as I struggled to move away from the table. But my legs wobbled and the sudden movement left me dizzy and seeing the little pinpoints of bright, white light that are so often described as stars. The room started to spin alarmingly, and I swayed and staggered back.

For all his bulk, Bert moved surprisingly quickly and, for all his strength, he forced me back into the chair very gently.

'Sorry, Tone,' he said, 'but you was told to stay put.' He leaned on me, a big hand on each shoulder, to emphasize the point.

'It's all right, Bert,' I said, recovering a little. 'I'm not going anywhere.'

A wireless was playing somewhere in the house. The warm, soft sound drifted into the kitchen. I imagined Miss Hardiman sitting in an old, comfortable armchair, her knitting to hand, the gentle yellow glow from the illuminated panel of the dark-wood wireless spilling on to her already sallow face. After all, *Friday Night Is Music Night*, I thought. The pleasant, distant sound of normality was unsettling.

Miss Beaumont had stopped blubbing and was now staring miserably at the table-top, although I doubted her thoughts were on the whorls and scars of the old wood. Bert's hands were heavy on my shoulders and became heavier as I leaned across to place my hand reassuringly on hers. I patted the back of one pale, slender finger and then sat up, in spite of Bert, and looked at the men arranged aggressively around the doorway.

Confidence is everything, Robert whispered to me once.

I thought I'd give it a go.

'So,' I said brightly, 'anyone heard the football scores? How did Orient get on?'

'No one's heard the football scores, Mr Gérard,' Jenkins said softly. 'We've been chasing you over half of Cambridgeshire. Remember?'

'Funnily enough,' I said, 'I do. You tend not to forget people shooting at you. Or cracking your skull.' I paused. 'Do you, Jan?'

Jenkins coughed and looked up at the ceiling.

'Mr Gérard,' he said slowly, 'there is nothing, absolutely nothing, stopping Alfred from taking you into the garden and –' he paused – 'disposing of you for good.' He paused again. 'Except my good nature. Please don't take advantage of that.'

I took the hint and shut up. Robert had also told me that sometimes confidence isn't confidence at all, but foolhardiness, and that most men can recognize the difference.

Bert took his hands off my shoulders, moved away from the table and joined the others by the door.

Surprisingly, it was Jameson who took a step forward and started to speak. The quiet, dry rasp of his voice carried a certain authority but no reassurance. 'All Jenkins wants to know is where to find Jonathan, and he thinks that Miss Beaumont can tell him where he is.'

She shook her head.

'That's a pity,' Alfred said. 'Now we'll have to hurt Mr Gérard.'

There wasn't any hint of reluctance or regret in his voice and, as he took a couple of steps towards me, I braced myself. But he stopped and snapped his fingers.

'Although, come to think of it, hurting Tony here might well give me some pleasure, but it isn't going to get us anywhere, is it?' he said. Still looking at her, he reached out his uninjured arm and patted me on the head. 'I ought to warn you,' he said, 'I wouldn't ordinarily hurt a woman, but I'm willing to make an exception in your case, and I am very, very good at hurting people.'

To prove the point, he moved his hand from the back of my head and punched me sharply on the bruising on my head. It wasn't a hard blow, just a vicious one, and the pain was excruciating. The swelling split and blood trickled down my face. He patted the back of my head again.

'So,' he said, 'what have you got to say, Beverley? Where's little Jon?'

Her reply was so soft even I didn't hear it.

'What was that, Beverley? Speak up,' Alfred said, leaning towards her and cupping his hand theatrically to his ear.

She looked up at him, her chin defiantly thrust forward.

'I don't know,' she said very slowly and clearly.

I was ready for the blow this time, but it didn't hurt any less and the trickle of blood became a torrent. I reached for the flannel that still lay in the little enamel bowl and held it to my head, to staunch the flow.

There was icy anger flowing now too. I wasn't about to allow him another free hit. And I certainly wasn't going to let him start on Beverley Beaumont. 'You ought to step back a little, Alfred,' I said. 'I wouldn't want to bleed on you.'

He patted my head again. 'Still the smart Alec, eh?'

'Yes,' I said, 'still the smart Alec.'

I leaned forward and slumped on the kitchen table, and his arm slipped from my head on to the back of the chair. I sniffed and then took a deep breath. No matter how bad I felt, it was now or never.

I threw my full weight back against his hand, trapping it between my shoulder and the chair. My momentum meant that all three of us – me, Alfred and the chair – went flying backwards in a great jumble and landed on the kitchen floor. A sharp, sickening snap suggested that a bone in Alfred's arm had broken, and his shrill scream confirmed it.

I was on top of the heap and rolled off as quickly as I could and stood up. 'I told you stand back,' I said, panting slightly, feeling decidedly wobbly and giddy again but all the better for having taken him out. 'Now you've got blood all over you.'

His face was twisted and deeply lined with pain, his lips pulled back from his uneven teeth, his eyes tightly shut, and he clutched his arm, but, to his credit, he wasn't whimpering. It must have hurt like a bastard, as Bernie would have said. My head hurt like a bastard too so I wasn't about to waste any sympathy on him.

Ray and Don the driver were looking around uneasily, each of them waiting for the other one to make a move. Without a lead from Alfred, they really weren't very professional – actually, they weren't very professional even with a lead from Alfred – but I remembered that Don had been waving a gun around in the field. He probably still had it.

Jan looked as if the bash on the head had rendered him incapable of thought, let alone action. He even took step backwards and then stood still, looking pale and wan.

Jenkins also took a step back – a big one – and looked as if he was about to run for it. Jameson must have been standing behind him because I couldn't see him.

Bert sniffed and shuffled around with a puzzled smile on his phizog. He was the only one of them who looked ready for a ruck.

In fact, the least likely person made the first move. Beverley Beaumont suddenly stood up, holding the Luger in her trembling hand. She was a little bundle of contradictions: crying one minute, quicker on the draw than Audie Murphy the next. Admittedly, the gun waved like the branch of a tree in a gale, but it looked lethal enough.

And only two of us in the room knew that the magazine was empty.

'Give me the gun, Miss Beaumont,' I said. '*I* know you know how to use it. *They* don't. But they know I shoot straight.'

I slid over to her, crab-style, and held out my hand. The gun was warm, and I remembered that she'd tucked it into her skirt, next to her body. It was another odd intimacy that had meaning for me but probably none for her.

An old Afghan proverb says that two men are frightened of an empty rifle – the man facing it and the man holding it. I can certainly vouch for the truth of the last part and dearly hoped that the wisdom of the Afghans held good for the other bit as well.

We stood there in relative silence for a few seconds, me covering them with the gun, feeling like I was slightly less than half in control. Then it went wrong.

It was, of course, Bert who came towards me. He knew I wouldn't shoot him. And he was right. I wasn't about to damage the amiable old boy.

'Stand back, Bert,' I said. 'I mean it.' But he knew I didn't and kept on coming.

As soon as he was close enough that his big body was shielding them, Ray and Don both rushed at me.

I didn't have much of a chance and went down by the sink under a swirl of weak and ineffectual blows. I managed to land a few of my own though and, remembering at least one rule of unarmed combat, fought dirty.

Don gasped and pulled back when he realized he was going to have bruised goolies for a few weeks.

Fortunately, Bert remembered that we'd broken bread together – well, I'd bought him a bacon butty when we'd stopped on the road – and so he didn't hit me. But he did reach down and pin my arms to my side. He was strong and I wasn't and, after a futile struggle, I just gave up and faded into semi-consciousness again.

Ray continued to pummel me for a few more seconds until Bert told him to lay off.

We were all panting, Don was groaning, Jenkins was talking loudly and Beverley Beaumont was inhabiting her less decisive self, emitting little high-pitched shrieks.

I was dazed, my head ached badly and all I wanted to do was close my eyes.

I did and must have half slipped out of consciousness for a while because I was only dimly aware of something else going on as well.

Four or five burly policemen, under the guidance of two blokes I knew I'd seen somewhere before, were feeling collars and fastening handcuffs, but they weren't feeling *my* collar or measuring me for the bracelets. For which small mercy, much relief.

I was so out of it that I didn't even feel confused. The hubbub in the kitchen was considerable as Bert, in particular, added 'resisting arrest' to whatever charges he was already facing but, somehow, I lay there and no one trod on me and all seemed right with the world. Except for the headache, of course.

Then Miss Beaumont was kneeling next to me asking if I was all right. And so was one of the blokes I recognized. The name John floated to the surface of my groggy mind.

I gave them my most beatific smile. 'Aren't English policemen wonderful?' I said.

The low murmur of quiet conversation wafted around the stuffy interior of the car. My body was aching as much as my head as we drove slowly along a straight road in the centre of a town I assumed was Cambridge. Someone said something about Downing College. Neoclassical, they added, whatever that meant. I turned my head slightly and saw, very briefly, a gracious group of white buildings set back from the road.

Beverley Beaumont was sitting on my left, occasionally

offering a comment to someone in the front. Moving hurt, so I remained slumped down and didn't strain to see who it was.

John had force-fed me more aspirin back in Jenkins' kitchen and then had bathed my face and bandaged my head.

Miss Hardiman hadn't reappeared, and I assumed she'd stayed in her room, listening to the wireless, her knitting needles clacking away, while her boss and his associates were invited to enjoy the hospitality of the local nick.

One of the policemen had taken a brief statement from Miss Beaumont but, for some inexplicable reason, hadn't insisted that we both accompany him to the station to lay charges. Instead, he'd left us with John, who was now driving us through Cambridge.

But it wasn't John Miss Beaumont was talking to.

The front-seat passenger turned a little to his right and the lights of a car coming towards us lit up his shadowed face for a split second.

I considered opening the door and jumping out, but thought better of it. I was in no shape for daring and damaging escapes from moving cars. The body was bruised enough.

I tried to make sense of it. Jameson had dropped me in it twice – first with Robert and now with Jenkins – and yet here he was, playing the good guy. Surely he wasn't planning to drop me in it again. There weren't that many wolves left for him to throw me to. Unless Les was on the warpath about his Rolls.

There was Inspector Rose, of course, but I was already in enough trouble with him. Jameson couldn't make that situation any worse. Size ten boots were probably already beating a path to my (well, Jerry's) door. Oh well, in the words of the old song, what can't be cured, has to be endured. I'd worry about the size tens tomorrow.

The car stopped outside an unprepossessing little house in the middle of a terrace. We all climbed out, John gallantly racing around to open the door for Miss Beaumont. I had to stumble out unaided.

John took a key from Jameson, unlocked the door and then ushered us inside.

I stood outside for a moment, staring at the open door and the rest of the unremarkable exterior. Newish sash-windows on the right-hand side of the door, two more above those, just like the houses on either side. Did Nazi bombs blow out windows in Cambridge? I didn't have a clue.

The night air was fresh and reviving after the warmth of the day and the stuffiness of the car – another elderly Wolseley, I couldn't help but notice.

I realized that I didn't feel quite as groggy as I had every right to expect. Either the aspirin were working or the bash on the head wasn't as serious as it might have been.

For a moment, I wondered whether there was any chance of making a break for it.

John looked young and fit, and I knew he carried a firearm, and he still stood by the door, waiting patiently for me to follow the others. I decided that his courtesy and patience merited a degree of trust and, anyway, he could probably outrun me, so I entered the little house, smiling at him as I passed.

A breathy baritone sax floated around a mellow trumpet that lingered lovingly on 'My Funny Valentine' – the first music I'd heard in my head since the thump. I was rapidly returning to normal. The bitter-sweet melancholy was more Jerry's taste than mine, but I liked it. Jerry had beamed delightedly when I'd asked him to play it again. There was something of the evangelical about him when it came to modern jazz.

There was an open door to my right, and Jameson stood just inside it. I could hear Beverley Beaumont talking about pictures to him. He didn't respond as she gushed over *Rear Window* and told him that he really had to see it. John closed the front door and waited, ever patient, for me to join Jameson and Miss Beaumont.

Jameson seemed to have only the one hat. I remembered the battered trilby from our encounter on Tuesday night. He took it off and threw it on to an uncomfortable-looking couch that was covered with books and papers.

'Sorry about the mess,' he said, 'but I was working in here last night.'

Another, much more inviting, couch was already adorned by Miss Beaumont, her elegant legs crossed and her hands resting primly in her lap. She had that distant, cool look about her that suggested our earlier intimacy was over. I also thought I recognized the beginnings of what she called 'the blues'.

The excitement was over, and she was reverting to type. I wasn't so sure that the excitement was completely over, and I remained standing.

'So, Dr Jameson,' I said, 'what's going on?'

He turned to look at me, and the electric light from the lamps in the room shone on his red and scarred face.

The room was comfortable and expensively scruffy, all old dark furniture, worn rugs and books. I'd never seen so many books outside Leyton library. Mrs Williams sometimes had a woman's magazine or two lying about, and Jerry had a small bookcase of Penguins, but there must have been hundreds in here, and they all looked old.

'Ah, Mr Gérard,' Jameson said, '"A brave man struggling in the storms of fate." First of all, I must apologize to you for earlier. It was not my intention to add to your discomfort. And, secondly, I must offer you and Miss Beaumont a little supper. It will only be cold cuts in the kitchen, I'm afraid, but I hope it will restore some of your *joie de vivre*. A drink? Miss Beaumont?'

'Perhaps a small sherry,' she said in her best Joan Greenwood voice.

John moved quickly to a side table by the window where a tray with four decanters and some glasses shimmered and shone.

'A whisky for me, John, please,' Jameson said. 'Mr Gérard?'

I shook my head. 'Some answers first,' I said.

If he could have, I'm sure he would have smiled, but his face remained expressionless, mask-like. 'A man after Dean Swift's heart,' he said. 'He was of the opinion that business should be done before dinner too. Ask away.'

John did smile, and he poured the drinks, including one for himself.

'Well,' I said, 'how is it that you're not under arrest?'

Jameson took his whisky from John, clutching it in both hands and raising it to his lips to sip a little. Then he sighed. 'I thought it expedient to slip away during the fracas,' he said. 'In fact, I opened the door to the noble boys in blue, whom John and Andrew had summoned, and then I decided to absent myself in Miss Hardiman's room. It didn't seem to me that my presence in the kitchen would serve any useful purpose, and Miss Hardiman is an elderly lady who needed reassurance. I

was able to give her that and keep out of the way.' He looked
at John, who nodded. 'The thing is, Mr Gérard, and I know
that we can rely on your discretion here – and, of course, on
Miss Beaumont's – but there is a cloud hanging over Cambridge
in the light of recent . . .' Jameson paused and considered what
word to use. He finally decided on one. 'Events. And the powers
that be have taken a keen interest in any suspicious goings-on.
They asked me to keep an eye open. The truth is that I have
been keeping an eye open for some years. I move in academic
and left-wing circles without attracting too much attention, in
spite of . . .' He made a clumsy gesture, the glass still in his
hands, and indicated his face. 'That's how I know your friend,
Monsieur Rieux . . .'

'Yes,' I said, 'and that's another bone I'd like to pick with
you.'

'Again, I apologize, but it seemed like too good an opportunity to let slip. A simple telegram ensures some goodwill
with a well-known French Communist trade union leader and
further establishes my *bona fides* without doing too much
harm.'

'If you think that'll put Robert in your debt, I'm afraid you
don't know him all that well. And you really don't know what
harm it could have caused.' I laughed and shook my head.
'But what's all this got to do with Jenkins and Jonathan
Harrison anyway? And why use Miss Beaumont as a tethered
goat? There are no cloaks and daggers in Jenkins' wardrobe.'

John spoke for the first time. 'Oh?' he said. 'So, what is it
all about,' he said, 'if we've got it so wrong?'

I sighed. 'Perhaps I will have that drink, after all,' I said.
'Is there any red wine?'

Jameson nodded. 'Yes, and I'm told it's good, but I wouldn't
know. No sense of smell or taste,' he said, raising his hands
to his face again in the same clumsy gesture. 'A source of
regret.'

John poured me a glass of something almost purple from
one of the decanters, and I sat next to Miss Beaumont. Jameson
had not been misled. It was good wine.

'Sometimes,' I said, inclining my head towards John, 'you
intelligence types are too clever for your own good. But how
come you found us this evening?'

'I was in Cambridge, visiting old tutors and so on,' John

said, indicating Jameson, 'with my boss, Andrew, who's down at the station, and it really was a coincidence that we were out for a walk and bumped into your two friends. A kidnapping offered a pretty good excuse for some arrests. We've been looking to question Jenkins for a while. We'll let him stew in custody for a day or two and talk to him in due course.' He sipped his whisky and then looked at me with a wry smile. 'So, tell me how we've got it so wrong.'

I did, and I asked them to put in a word for Bert, who wasn't involved in the abduction. They didn't promise. They also didn't reassure Miss Beaumont about Jonathan.

I carefully avoided being too explicit about a couple of things, but I must have come across as evasive because John asked the really awkward questions. Where was Jon? And where were the diamonds? I gave the only answer I could. I didn't know. John didn't believe me. And I don't think he was convinced that there wasn't more to the whole affair either. But that's clever-clogs intelligence men for you.

Jameson shook his head and quoted, he said, from Dean Swift again. '"I never wonder to see men wicked, but I often wonder to see them not ashamed."'

I wondered if this Dean Swift was any relation to the Jonathan Swift I'd heard of, the one who wrote about an island of little people.

TWENTY-SIX

I awoke suddenly with a crick in my neck from sleeping on the sofa and the certainty that there was someone else in the room. An insipid, watery light from a street lamp outside seeped into the room through a gap in the heavy curtains, and I saw a pale movement by the door.

I knew instantly that I was in the room we'd talked in before the supper of ham, cheese, home-baked bread and pickles. The heavy aroma of John's cigar lingered in the stale air. I sat up and coughed. My head still ached, and my neck was stiff.

Miss Beaumont, a ghostly figure in a man's white shirt, slid through the semi-darkness and sat on the sofa next to me. 'You do know where Jon is, don't you?' she said.

'I've an idea,' I said.

'Find him,' she said, 'please. And warn him about what's going on.'

'I'll try,' I said. But I was thinking that warning him wasn't going to help at all.

She laid her head on my shoulder. 'You're a nice man, Tony,' she said. 'Reliable, loyal, decent.'

All those things that Jonathan Harrison was not, I thought. She might as well have said dull, unexciting, unattractive, boring. I was conscious that neither of us was wearing very much and that the light from the window was backlighting her shirt and rendering it almost transparent.

I closed my eyes and thought of Mrs Williams, Ann.

'We should leave now,' she said. 'Before anyone gets up. We could catch the first train to London and go to Jon. Warn him.'

I didn't say anything. I couldn't see the point.

'I don't trust those men,' she said. 'I think they want to go with us to find Jon.' That didn't sound like such a bad idea to me. 'If we can get a start on them . . .'

'If we leave now,' I said, 'that really will raise their suspicions. They'll think we know something, and they'll track us down. They'll have someone waiting for the train.'

'We'll go by taxi.'

'To London! How much money do you have on you?'

'None,' she said.

'Well, I don't know if I have enough for train tickets. And I certainly don't have enough for a taxi.'

She took her head from my shoulder and folded her arms.

'Why don't we lull them into a false sense of security?' I said. 'Continue with our story that we don't know where Jonathan is. They can feed us breakfast, find me a clean shirt and take us back to London. Then, when they're not watching, I'll look for Jonathan.'

'It may be too late by then,' she said.

'It may be too late now,' I said.

'You promise you'll find him?' she said, laying her head back on my shoulder.

'I promise I'll try,' I said, wondering again why I didn't just tell Jameson and his friends where I thought he was and leave it to them to pick him up. But I knew, really. One of the reasons was leaning softly against me. The other sat – solid, hard and gleaming – in Bernie's safe.

I sloshed about in a hot bath for fifteen or twenty minutes and that felt good. I shaved and that felt better. I dressed in clean underwear, shirt, socks and a good quality grey suit that Jameson had found that all more or less fitted me, and that felt wonderful. My shoes lacked polish and looked as though they'd been used to daub a hut with more than its fair share of mud, but apart from that I felt dapper enough.

I let John take the bandage off my head, bathe the wound and then dab it with TCP. I wasn't so keen on the last bit, but he seemed to know what he was doing.

I'd acquired a few bumps, scrapes and bruises in the last few days, but this one took the biscuit. Technicolor couldn't have done it justice. Still, I wasn't seeing double and the swelling had gone down. Anyway, everyone I knew loved me for my personality, not my matinée idol looks.

Surprisingly, John's boss, Andrew, had not turned up to interrogate us, so I assumed that they were planning to turn us loose and see what transpired.

I tucked in to the bacon, eggs, toast and tea that Mrs Atkinson, the amiable, lean woman of forty or so who 'did' for Dr Jameson, placed in front of me. If she was surprised or put out in any way by my and Miss Beaumont's presence, she didn't show it.

Miss Beaumont nibbled at a slice of toast and sipped at a cup of tea while I made an attempt on the world record for number of slices of toast munched and cups of tea consumed in one ten-minute period.

By a quarter past nine we were ready to be whisked away to the Smoke.

I asked if Harrison had turned up at his rooms yet, but Jameson just shook his head. The enquiry didn't go unnoticed by John. His eyes brightened, and a little smile tugged at his lips. About as subtle as a brick through a window, then.

I tried to lessen the impact of that by smoothly moving on and asking how I should return the clothes to Jameson. He dismissed it by just saying, 'As and when . . .'

Mrs Atkinson had wrapped my own crumpled and soiled garments in a neat brown-paper parcel tied with string. I thanked her and tucked it under my arm.

The resolutely male nature of Dr Jameson's home meant that Miss Beaumont was dressed in the same clothes as the day before, but she didn't complain. In fact, she didn't even seem to notice. And if she was a little less than her delightfully fragrant self, I wasn't going to comment.

The Wolseley was outside, and John's boss was behind the wheel.

It was another lovely day. The only clouds were white and lonely.

Miss Beaumont sat as far from me as possible on the back seat and stared out of the window. John and Andrew talked quietly together, traffic buzzed past us and stretched out in front like a slow-moving military convoy. I reminded myself that Easter Saturday was upon us. I dozed off. Once you've seen one field, you've seen them all.

I awoke when John asked for directions to my humble abode. (Actually, he didn't use that phrase, but, since we were gliding along a drab and rundown Leytonstone High Road, I thought I detected a slight sneer in his voice.) I suggested turning right at the Thatched House into Crownfield Road and following that to Leyton High Road. Not the most direct route, but we eventually pulled up outside the Gaumont.

Enzo was standing at the door to his café smoking, passing

the time by glaring fiercely at two small boys who were kicking a ragged, grey tennis ball perilously close to his steamed-up window. He occasionally glanced glumly up at the still clear sky, probably anticipating rain. I nodded to him as I hauled myself and my brown-paper parcel out of the car. He raised a hand in a half-hearted greeting and retreated back inside. Clearly, he thought the danger to his window had passed and drizzle was imminent.

I thanked John and Andrew and said a stiff farewell to Beverley Beaumont. I asked her if she would be all right on her own, but she waved away my concern. John reassured me that he would see her safely in her flat. I told him quietly that it was in a little disarray and then asked him how he would get in as I didn't think she had her keys. He said he'd manage. Then he smiled knowingly and told me to take care.

I watched the car turn into Lea Bridge Road and then, adjusting my parcel under my arm, waited for a bus and an old lorry to lumber past before marching smartly across the sunlit road and setting the bell jangling on the door to the shop.

Artie Shaw's big hit from before the war, 'Begin the Beguine', rippled pleasantly and welcomingly around the untidy little room. The hole in the ceiling didn't look out of place in the general chaos of half-empty boxes of records, sheet music and Hohner mouth organs. In fact, it looked right at home.

Jerry greeted me as warmly as the music. He looked up at the intrusion, put down the descant recorder he was examining, beamed and came out from behind the counter. He peered at me and then stepped back to admire the new contours of my face.

'Wow,' he said, 'that's some bruise.'

'You should see the other guy,' I said automatically and laughed at the thought of Alfred with both arms in slings. Well, it would save on handcuffs. And it would make wiping his bum with the old San Izal an interesting experience.

'I don't think I care to meet the man who could do that to you,' he said. He patted my back. 'Nice suit. I don't think I've seen that one before.'

'A recent acquisition,' I said.

'Listen, there's someone upstairs. It's a bit awkward,' he said.

'Who?' I said.

He shrugged, and I thought it best to just trudge up the stairs and find out.

Ghislaine was sitting on my grandfather's old chair, smoking. The fug in the room suggested she'd been there for some time. I dropped my package on the old kitchen table and smiled at her. 'Where's Robert?' I said.

'He's a pig,' she said.

'Does he know where you are?' I said.

'Of course. I told him I was going to someone who cared about me.'

I heard Jerry clumping up the stairs.

'He'll come for you, Ghislaine,' I said. 'And probably for me.'

She shook her head firmly, and her hair tumbled over her eyes. She brushed it away with a careless sweep of the hand holding her cigarette. 'No. He told me to do what I must.'

That didn't mean that he would let her.

'He even gave me money,' she said. She picked up her handbag, balanced it on her lap, rummaged in it and then triumphantly waved a handful of notes. There must have been twenty-five or thirty pounds there. 'And –' she patted the bag affectionately – 'I have brought some protection.'

Jerry was standing in the doorway. He put his hand on my shoulder. 'I'll put the kettle on,' he said and scuttled off to the scullery.

Ghislaine thrust the money back into her bag and stood up. 'But, Antoine,' she said, looking at me for the first time, 'your head. What happened?'

Nothing, I thought, compared to what will happen if Robert decides to turn up and take offence.

'It's a long story,' I said and looked around rather theatrically. 'Where's Emile?'

Ghislaine gave an exaggerated shrug. 'Someone delivered him to the hotel late last night. He was still sleeping this morning when I left. Robert laughed, saying that one day with you has exhausted him. He should have suffered one year, as we did. It's taken us nearly ten years to recover.'

I sighed and sat down behind my desk and stared at the dust motes spiralling slowly in the rays of sun that slanted through the window. It reminded me of smoke swirling in the light from the projector in a cinema. At least Robert was cracking jokes at my expense. That probably meant that he wasn't planning to cut my throat in the immediate future.

I've never asked that my life be uncomplicated, but I would like it to be less of a mess than it is. Neat, elegant solutions to simple problems is all I ask. But the people I know seem to be messier and less predictable than most. One problem takes a step back, fades into the background and then another steps forward, hogging the spotlight, upstaging the others, mugging away at me.

Ghislaine looked at me anxiously. Her eyes were red-rimmed. They might have been irritated by the smoke from her cigarettes, but it looked to me as if she'd been crying.

I smiled at her. 'Did Robert really beat you?' I said. 'Before you came, I mean.'

'It's not that,' she said. 'It's everything. I'm angry at him, but it's not his fault.'

I looked askance at her. She sounded like Beverley Beaumont. What is it with women and good-looking and feckless, brutal men?

'He is a passionate man, and he loves me,' she said defensively. 'But, Antoine, I'm so weary of everything. I have to get away. You know, winter in Paris can be so cold – in January last year *les clochards* were dying in the streets. And then, in the summer, they were dying again, but of the heat. And there's the politics: one government after another. Robert loves it, and I hate it. He still looks forward to the triumph of the workers. I dread it. I think I want to be somewhere stable for a little while: a city where people don't die of the cold in winter and of the heat in summer.'

'London isn't paradise, Ghislaine. People die here of the cold,' I said.

'*Tant pis*,' she said sadly as Jerry came in carrying a tray with a teapot, a milk bottle and some cups on it.

'What's that mean?' he said.

'So much piss,' I said.

'Really?' he said, raising an eyebrow and lowering the tray on to the table at the same time.

'No,' I said, 'not really, but that sums up my life. And Ghislaine's.'

He busied himself at the table, clinking cups, and said nothing.

We waited in gloomy silence for the tea to brew, then Jerry looked up and smiled grimly. 'Well,' he said, 'at the risk of making your life even pissier . . .'

'Go on,' I said bleakly.

'I don't quite know how to put this . . .'

'Come on, Jerry, out with it,' I said.

'Orient lost two nil to Brentford yesterday.'

Ghislaine, if not at all bewitched or bothered, certainly looked bewildered as Jerry and I laughed like drains.

The musty landing outside the Imperial Club smelled faintly of sour beer, urine and vomit, although Connie's powerful scent and perfumed talcum powder masked most of it. I sneezed hugely when I arrived at the top stair.

'That's a nasty case of hay fever,' the lady herself, resplendently draped in one of her voluminous flowing gowns and perched on her little chair, murmured. 'At least, I hope it is. Can't let you in with a cold, can I?' She looked around, beyond Ghislaine, who had followed me up the stairs. 'And where's the good-looking one with the little beard? You never bring her.'

'Jerry's minding the shop,' I said, and it was true. He had declined Ghislaine's offer of a meal, saying that he had a living to make and Saturday was his big day. 'And he's shaved his beard off,' I added.

'I'll bet she looks even prettier,' Connie said and waved us in.

Ghislaine giggled. I imagined she found Connie amusing. I doubted that she'd followed the conversation.

After eating chips, peas and tough, salty gammon topped with a slice of fibrous tinned pineapple at Enzo's, we'd made our way into town. I didn't really want Ghislaine with me, but she was keen to come and so leave Jerry on his own. I think that, in spite of what she'd said, she worried that Robert would turn up, and she didn't want him to find her with Jerry.

I wanted to ask Roger if he'd seen Jonathan Harrison in the last day or so, but that was just an excuse. I told myself it was about leaving Ghislaine somewhere safe (because I intended leaving her with Roger), but I could have done that by telling her I'd meet her in a couple of hours at the V and A. No, I knew that I was delaying the inevitable.

I'd already done a fair bit of that. I'd phoned Les to tell him that Beverley Beaumont was safe, but that it might be a good idea for him to check up on her. He hadn't mentioned any damage to the Rolls. I'd phoned Inspector Rose and left a message to the effect that I was on the case. I'd even phoned Reg to apologize for not making football practice or the match. He'd harrumphed and told me they'd miss my experience, which I took to mean that he'd replaced me with someone younger and faster. I'd phoned Mrs Williams and told her to expect me later. She'd said that she looked forward to it. She'd used a term of endearment. Bernie had answered, but told me that he couldn't talk business on the Sabbath, and so my instructions about the diamonds went unsaid.

And now here I was, at my last port of call. No more excuses after this.

Roger glided over to our end of the bar. I wondered if he'd ever been a dancer.

'My goodness, but you've been in the wars,' he said, studying the bruise.

'It's not so bad,' I said. 'Anyway, it'll remind me to duck when the sign on the door tells me to mind my head,' I said. 'Two cognacs, and whatever you're having.'

'Too early for me, dear,' he said. 'Hang on to your money.'

'Anyone been in?' I said to his back as he busied himself with glasses.

'If you mean young Jonathan,' he said, 'the answer's no. If you mean the boys in blue asking about him, the answer's yes.'

'Oh,' I said as he slid two glasses on to the counter and took my ten-bob note.

'Came in not long after you yesterday. Poor Connie's been interrogated within an inch of her life,' he said.

'I'm sorry to hear that,' I said.

'She'll get over it. She loves it, really. All those big men with large, flat feet . . .'

His eyes moistened and, for a moment, he went AWOL. The sound of billiard balls clacking together and a little groan of dismay from the farther room reminded him of where he was, and he grinned at me boyishly.

I smiled wanly and took the drinks over to Ghislaine, who

had chosen the same table we had sat at on our first visit. I plonked myself down next to her.

I sipped at the brandy and wondered if Jenkins had disappeared from my life. I had the feeling that John and Andrew would encourage the police to oppose bail so – temporarily, at least – I was probably free of them. In the long run . . . But then, as someone much cleverer than me said a while back, the long run is a misleading guide in current affairs. I don't suppose he'd had my situation in mind, but it was a thought that held good.

Maybe I *could* forget about them.

John's interest in the diamonds might possibly prove more problematic. Especially if he prised anything out of Jenkins. Still, he probably wouldn't. He must have bigger fish than me to fry. One or two of them might even *be* spies for the Russkies. I remembered all that baptized wine in Paris and the intelligence officer. He would have been amused at the idea of setting a Cambridge man to catch a Cambridge man.

Perhaps I could forget about John as well.

Which left the problem I was sitting next to and the one I was about to confront.

Ghislaine sighed and lit another cigarette. She hadn't touched her brandy and was staring off at the bar through a fug of blue-grey smoke.

I followed her gaze and saw Emile and one of his companions standing uneasily at the bar. As soon as he noticed I'd clocked them, Emile nudged his mate, whose name I could not recall – Henri, perhaps – and they made a beeline for us. I wondered how they'd talked their way in and immediately realized that Connie would have remembered Emile and let him through, thinking he was with me.

Henri just stood around, looking large, imposing and awkward, while Emile started talking rapidly to Ghislaine.

The gist of it was that Robert had changed his mind. He was intending to head back to France that night and had decided that Ghislaine would accompany him. He would expect to see her at Victoria Station at six o'clock.

I asked him what would happen if she chose not to turn up. He appeared to be amused and merely said that she would be there. Then I asked him how he'd known where to find us. He shrugged and said that Robert had telephoned Jerry and he had suggested that they try looking here. I must have looked surprised because he said, almost apologetically, that Robert could be very persuasive. I said that I remembered.

He shook my hand and said that he'd see me soon, although I didn't see how, and then he and Henri left.

Ghislaine looked pale and tight-lipped, and I knew I couldn't leave her in the bar.

TWENTY-SEVEN

I told Ghislaine to stay in the taxi while I went inside for a minute or two. I didn't want her with me, and I figured that the driver might actually wait if I left her as a hostage. And, of course, there'd be less chance of young Jon doing a runner if I could bundle him straight into a cab.

Predictably, the driver objected. He couldn't possibly park on a busy street like that, mate, could he? It didn't look all that busy to me, but I suggested that he pull around the next corner, telling him that I'd be out in less than five minutes, and I didn't wait for a reply, but marched smartly up the steps to the big, old door and rapped on it.

The cab rumbled slowly off. Fortunately, although I could see the driver grumbling away, he was wasting his breath. I couldn't hear him, and I doubted that Ghislaine could understand him. Besides, she was too lost in her own worries to concern herself with his.

The road was warm-Saturday-afternoon quiet, the blokes all in shirtsleeves and braces digging up their allotments or snoozing in the armchair while the missus sat at the kitchen table, dunking sugary Nice biscuits in a well-earned cuppa between washing up after dinner and opening the tinned salmon for tea. A newish black Ford Popular was parked five doors along, and a few kids, a hundred yards away, squatted down on the pavement, playing marbles. Somewhere a wireless hummed a subdued melody.

I turned back to the door and rattled the knocker again. I waited for a few seconds, but I heard nothing so I looked furtively around and, since there was no one watching me, reached into the letterbox and found the piece of string I'd seen dangling there the other day and pulled it through. It was the work of a few seconds to open the door with the key tied to the end and enter. I closed the door quietly behind me and stood in the hallway.

It was cool, musty, dark and quiet. The house creaked and groaned a little, and somewhere a tap dripped – the steady splash,

splash, splash quietly comforting – but anyone in residence remained silent and hidden.

I stood there, tasting and smelling blood, but I knew that was just my imagination. I should be smelling bleach and other cleaning agents. The police had probably been gone for a day or two. Mrs Elvin should already have started making the room habitable again. Maybe I was wrong and there was no one here.

But then I caught the faint smell of fried bacon and walked along the hall towards the kitchen. The sound of the dripping tap grew louder and the smell grew stronger. There was the frying pan, the bacon grease glistening and congealing, still on the gas stove. Two plates, smeared with deep-yellow egg yolk and strewn with fatty rind, and two tea cups cluttered the blue-Formica-topped table.

I walked noisily back down the hall, opened the front door and then banged it shut, with me still on the inside, and stood quietly.

After a few seconds, a door on the floor above me opened and bare feet pattered on the lino. Then a pair of lean, athletic legs appeared on the staircase, and there was Jonathan Harrison in grubby vest and pants.

'Ah,' he said and ran a hand through his already dishevelled hair. He yawned.

'Just wanted a word,' I said.

'Didn't hear you knock. Been asleep.' He yawned again. 'Do you mind if I throw some bags and a shirt on?'

'Where are you sleeping these days?' I said.

He looked puzzled.

'You're surely not sleeping in your old room,' I said.

'Oh,' he said. 'No. Rose let me use, er, another room.' He looked over his shoulder. 'I'll be back in a minute.'

'It's all right,' I said, 'I'm not overly bothered by the sight of men's hairy legs. I see them on a football pitch every Saturday. Come on down. We'll talk now.'

'I'd rather get dressed,' he said.

'This is a come-as-you-are party. I'm sure you have them in Cambridge.'

He didn't move and looked uncomfortable, turning to look behind him.

'I can help you come down, if you like,' I said amiably.

'No, no,' he said quickly, looking over his shoulder again. 'Let's talk in the parlour. On your left.'

He started down the stairs very slowly.

I held the door open and ushered him into a neat, clean, little room with some comfortable, green armchairs and a light-oak sideboard with a dark wireless on it. Three green and white ducks flew across busy, floral-patterned wallpaper towards a liver-spotted mirror on the chimney breast. I pointed Jon to a chair by the fireplace, and he slumped into it. I pulled the other armchair into the middle of the room, to cut off any attempt at escape and sat in it.

'What do you want to know?' he said, staring down at his pale, muscular thighs, and spreading them a little to better reveal the impressive bulge in his underpants.

'How did you fall in with Jenkins?' I said.

A car backfired noisily outside.

'Oh,' he said, 'met him at a lecture on art at Trinity. Some chap who used to teach there. He's now something to do with the Queen's pictures. Very interesting.' He paused. 'We got chatting. That's all.'

'And he asked you to run some errands for him?'

'Eventually,' he said. 'It was fun. The odd weekend in Belgium all paid for. Trips to London.'

'But you found out what you were smuggling in and decided to take a piece of it.'

'I always knew what I was carrying,' he said. 'Which is why I didn't carry it. I used to post it to myself. I don't know why Jenkins didn't think of it. Would have saved him a lot of money,' he said.

'Possibly,' I said, 'he did think of it, but knew there's a risk that such parcels will be examined by Customs and Excise.'

'Really?' he said. 'I guess I must have been lucky. Thanks for warning me. Tell you what, old thing, I'd like that package back. I gave you the wrong one for Beverley. As you probably know.'

I had to admire his self-assurance.

'Don't know what you're talking about,' I said.

He shook his head and smiled sourly. 'What do you really want to know?' he said.

'Where you were on Tuesday night when your friend, Richard Ellis, managed to get himself killed.'

'I was in Cambridge with Rose. Just like she told the nice policeman,' he said.

'I know what Rose told the police,' I said. 'But she told me something else. She told me she went out to the pub with her friend, Florrie. I'm inclined to believe that. So, where were you?'

The clock on the mantelpiece ticked away the seconds of a brief silence. Then Jonathan Harrison sighed. 'Actually, I was in Cambridge. Just not with good old Rose.'

'So you didn't kill Richard and don't know who did?'

Again, he didn't answer for a while and then looked up and smiled at me insolently. 'Funny, I didn't take you for a dickfer,' he said.

'A what?'

'Someone with a dick for brains,' he said. 'Of course I didn't kill Richard. He was my friend. I liked him. I didn't like him quite how he liked me, but I liked him.'

'And how did he like you?' I said.

'Oh, come on,' he said, and sighed theatrically, 'even you must have heard of the love that dare not speak its name. Of men who are not as other men.'

'I've heard rumours,' I said.

'Well . . .' He spread his hands, palms upwards.

I looked up at the chipped plaster ducks. They reminded me of Maman. Not because she had any. On the contrary. She was caustic about anyone who possessed such ornaments. 'She has no taste,' she would say, her pretty face soured and lined by an unbecoming disdain. Grand-père would chuckle. 'Not at all, Mireille,' he would say, teasingly, 'she has plenty of taste. All of it bad.'

The car backfired again.

I heard a creak on the stairs.

'So,' I said, 'what you're saying is that Richard had feelings for you.'

'You could say that,' he said and smiled again.

It was my turn to sigh. 'So, was he jealous?' I said.

He shook his head. 'More moonstruck,' he said. 'Others might have been jealous of him . . .'

'Like?'

'Bev, for a start.'

'I don't see Miss Beaumont as the garrotting kind,' I said.

He shrugged. What do you know? he seemed to be saying.
And he was right. I didn't know anything about her really.

'What about Mrs Elvin?' I said. 'Rose.'

He giggled. It wasn't a girlish, coquettish sound, just a
childish one.

'She's certainly passionate enough,' he said. 'And very
strong. She was a Land Girl in the war for a bit, as well as
a driver. And then she worked in the laundry straight after.
Working those mangles must give you muscles.'

I saw in the mirror the door behind me swinging open. I
couldn't make out who stood in the gloom of the passageway
outside, but he started to speak and I recognized the voice. I'd
been expecting Mrs Elvin, and the male voice was something
of a surprise.

'You really are a little tart, aren't you? Is there anyone
you've come across who you haven't slept with?' he said.

Jonathan Harrison giggled again as David Cavendish came
into the room and stood behind my chair. In the mirror, I
could see that his shirt was unbuttoned, and he hastily tucked
it into his trousers. He wasn't wearing braces, and his belt
was in his hand.

'Well,' Jon said, 'I haven't slept with this gentleman. Mind
you, he hasn't asked.' He looked at me enquiringly.

'I don't like you,' I said, 'and I make a point of only sleeping
with people I like.'

'Your loss,' he said.

'I don't think so,' I said. 'You have all the charm and appeal
of rancid lard. And I think you know who killed poor harmless Richard and why.' I looked up and back at Cavendish.
'And now I think I do too.'

Harrison laughed and stood up. 'Are you going to let him
talk to me like that, David?' he said. 'More to the point, can
you safely let him leave?'

Cavendish looked a warning at Jon and then he looked
down at me. 'What do you mean?' he said. 'I don't know
what you mean.'

'Oh, come on, David,' Jon said. 'I know. And so does he.
Now.'

Cavendish ran a hand through his blond hair and then wiped
it down his handsome, boyish face. The hand trembled a little.
Suddenly, he lifted the belt, looped it around my neck and

pulled on it viciously. The stiff leather bit into my throat. I managed to slip my right index finger between it and my Adam's apple, but that wasn't going to do me much good unless I could get some purchase on the belt and pull it away. As things stood, I'd just have a finger crushed in addition to my larynx.

I tried to stand up to change Cavendish's angle of attack, but he yelled at Jonathan Harrison to stop me and Jon was only too willing to oblige. He dived on me, grabbed me around the waist and his weight forced me back into the chair. I hit him twice with a couple of short lefts in the face, but he held on to me. It was no consolation to know that he wouldn't be quite as pretty for a few days.

I clawed at the belt, but I could feel the veins standing out on my forehead and I thought my head was going to explode. I was running out of breath and knew I only had one more effort in me before they'd have it all their own way.

I heaved upwards and dislodged Jon. He fell to the floor and dragged me with him. Our combined weight hauled Cavendish after us, and the heavy armchair moved sideways, the feet catching on the carpet and rucking it up.

I lay on my back, on top of Jon, with Cavendish off balance. I reached up and tugged on the belt, pulling Cavendish over the armchair. He fell awkwardly, but still kept hold of the garrotte. My throat felt as though it was on fire, but I managed a gulp of air as the improvised noose loosened just a little. I flailed at Cavendish desperately. There wasn't much fight left in me.

We thrashed about a little more as Harrison struggled to get out from under me; I strove to get a grip on the belt around my neck and pull it away, and Cavendish manoeuvred himself behind me, sat me up and put his knee in my back and started to pull. Harrison panted like an old hound in hot weather, and there was a sharp animal stink coming off us all.

And that was how Ghislaine found us.

She stood in the doorway for a couple of seconds and then reached into her bag and took out one of the little black guns I had seen Emile use to shoot Alfred.

She yelled at Cavendish to stop, but either he didn't speak French or he wasn't going to stop until I was dead. The edges of my vision were turning from red to black, the pounding in my head became a deafening drum solo and I could feel myself slipping into unconsciousness. I wanted to tell him that she would shoot him, but I couldn't speak.

I don't remember hearing the gun fire, but I was aware of Cavendish slumping down behind me and the excruciating pain in my throat easing. Then, through a haze, I saw Jonathan Harrison get up and walk towards her. Quite what he intended to do, I don't know but it hardly mattered. The only important thing was what Ghislaine thought he was going to do.

I made a sort of hoarse gurgling noise, but it made no difference. And this time I did hear the gunshots – both of them – as she shot Jonathan Harrison in the chest.

His hands didn't move to clutch at the dark stains that appeared on his vest, but he did take a step backwards and a faint look of surprise, the 'this can't be happening to me' expression that I'd seen during the war, flickered across his face before it went blank and he collapsed in an untidy heap, like dirty sheets in a laundry. Though this particular pile was leaking bright-red blood.

Ghislaine stood there for a moment, with what the Americans call the thousand-yard stare in her eyes. Then she knelt beside me, put her hand to my face and asked if I was all right.

I croaked something out and put my hand on hers. We sat like that for a long time before she spoke again.

'Do you remember,' she said, and I saw some tears in her eyes, 'when you strangled that German sentry in the goods yard just outside Caen?'

I managed a slight, painful nod. I remembered all right. It was the worst thing I have ever done in my life. We sat in silence as the clock ticked away minutes of my life that I would never have again, and so very nearly never had at all.

'I hated you then, and I hated the war that turned us into monsters. Afterwards, I saw your eyes. They didn't gleam like Robert's or Luc's after a kill. They were sad, and your hands were trembling. You are not a monster, but you did a monstrous thing.' She paused. 'I thought all that was in the past, and now I have killed again.' She started to sob quietly, then she sniffed and rubbed her hand across her eyes, pulling herself together. 'Why was this man strangling you?' she said.

'Because,' I croaked out, 'I knew something he didn't wish anyone else to know.'

She nodded and stood up. 'What do I do now?' she said.

'You meet Robert and go back to France,' I said. I stopped to cough harshly. I needed water, but I couldn't ask Ghislaine to fetch any. Fingerprints on glasses could hang someone. 'You drop the gun in the Channel, and you forget you ever came here.' Suddenly, I remembered something. 'The taxi,' I said. 'Is it still out there?'

'No, the driver insisted I pay him, and he left. So I came to find you. I could hear the sounds of a struggle, and the key was in the lock, so here I am.'

'Thank you,' I said.

She bent down and kissed the top of my head.

'All right,' I said. 'Now you have to go. Walk a little way and then take a taxi, when you can find one, back to the hotel. Leave with Robert and the others. I'll rest here and call the police in an hour or so. By the time they start investigating you should be on the boat. I'll tell them I was unconscious and don't know what happened. They probably won't believe me but, with luck and a closed mouth, I'll get away with it.'

I wasn't kidding about the resting. I was feeling awful. I lay back and closed my eyes.

When I opened them again, another half hour of precious life had ticked away and she was gone.

TWENTY-EIGHT

They kept me in hospital overnight, 'for observation'. I think the police may have suggested it so that they knew where to find me, but I wasn't complaining. The bruising on my throat was considerable, and I had trouble swallowing. The young doctor was more bothered about the bump on my head, but finally satisfied himself that I wasn't keeping a fractured skull from him.

I'd remembered to tidy up a little, smudging any finger-prints Ghislaine might have left on the key and any door handles, before staggering down to the nearest call box to phone the police. I hadn't had to exaggerate my weakness, and they'd sympathetically booked me on the first ambulance to Bart's and had only taken the briefest of statements. At first, they assumed that I'd had an accomplice who'd done the shooting, but then worked out that he would have taken me with him. Then they wondered why I hadn't been shot as well. I hoarsely pointed out (admittedly, untruthfully) that I'd been unconscious at the time and maybe whoever it was had thought I was already dead. And they left it at that.

Inspector Rose and his plump sergeant came to see me in the morning, just before I was due to be released, as I was finishing dressing. The inspector was carrying a paper bag with two Easter eggs in it. He put it down on the bed.

I had the distinct impression that he didn't believe much of what I told him, but that may have been because I knew that some of it was untrue and felt guilty. And I did have a lot to feel guilty about. As he said, I may have helped clear up one murder, but I'd left him with two unsolved killings. 'Doubled my workload,' he said.

All I could do was apologize and claim, again, to have been unconscious when the killings took place. He took out his pipe, but didn't light it. I noticed that he was wearing a spotted blue cravat and a double-breasted blue blazer, instead of bow-tie and suit. It was Sunday and he was in mufti.

'We can't even be sure about the time of the shooting,'

Inspector Rose said. 'Apparently, there'd been a car backfiring all over the place, and the locals must have taken the shots for backfires.'

I shook my head sadly on his behalf as I folded my tie up and slipped it into my pocket. My neck wouldn't take kindly to such sartorial flourishes for a few more days.

'The only thing that is clear is that no one thinks you fired a gun. No powder marks or anything.' He paused for a long, lugubrious sigh. 'Worst of all, no gun.'

I shook my head sadly again. His sergeant glowered at me.

'We'll find him, though,' Rose said. 'Rest assured, we'll find him and hang him. We always do.'

I nodded sagely, but this didn't satisfy the sergeant. He still glowered at me.

'Are you sure that this, er, Cavendish killed the other boy?'

'Well,' I croaked, 'he did say so before he put the belt around my neck.'

Inspector Rose nodded and clenched his pipe between his teeth. 'Did he happen to say why?'

'No,' I said, 'funnily enough he didn't. But I think he was jealous. He was in love or something with Jonathan Harrison. And saw Richard Ellis as a rival, I suppose.'

Rose tched-tched, and his sergeant looked uncomfortable and even sourer.

'A crime of passion then, as the French say,' Rose said.

'I suppose so,' I said, worried at the reference to the French, wondering if he knew something.

He took the pipe out of his mouth and smacked his lips. 'Dear, dear,' he said, 'what are we coming to?'

He sniffed and looked at the quiet corridor outside my little alcove. It had four beds in it, but mine was the only one occupied.

'Well, Sergeant,' Rose said, 'we'd better be on our way. Tony probably wants to get on home, and I've my grandchildren to see.' He picked up his paper bag. 'Oh, by the way, Tony, you must have some important friends. My chief had a call from one of them. He was told to play it softly softly with you. It seems there are others with an interest in you, and they have some kind of priority.'

'Others?' I said.

He tapped his nose. 'The people you do a little work for.'

'Oh,' I said, completely baffled. I couldn't really see Enzo carrying any weight with Scotland Yard, and certainly not Les.

'I was told to tell you that Andrew sends his regards,' he said.

'Oh,' I said again, this time with a sinking feeling in my stomach.

'Bye,' he said. 'And if you could spare the time to pop in later in the week and give us a proper statement, I would appreciate it.'

'Of course,' I said.

The sergeant stabbed one last evil glare at me, and they left.

Les, Charlie and Daphne were all waiting for me by Les's Wolseley just outside when the doctor discharged me a few minutes later. It was warm again, and I blinked in the bright sunshine. Then I closed my eyes and let it wash over me for a few seconds.

'Blimey, Tone,' Charlie said when he caught a glimpse of my livid bruising. 'What did they do? Hang you?'

'Tried to, Charlie,' I said. I smiled at them all. 'Thanks for coming to collect me. I'm a bit dodgy on the old pins just at the moment.'

'No problem, Tony,' Les said. 'Anyway, Daphne insisted.'

'I've brought you some chicken soup,' Daphne said. 'For your dinner. From the look of your neck, you're going to have trouble even getting that down you.'

'Thanks, Daff,' I said.

Les solicitously ushered me into the back of the car, and he and Daphne sat either side of me.

I told them as much of what had happened as I cared to on the journey back to Leyton, which meant that Ghislaine didn't get a mention.

Les looked very thoughtful. 'Miss Beaumont won't be at all happy,' was all he said.

'When is she ever?' Daphne said a bit too sharply.

'Come on, Daff,' I said. 'Be a little sympathetic. Her agent and her boyfriend . . .'

She sniffed dismissively.

*   *   *

My bare office felt sad and empty. The tray with the remains of the tea I'd drunk with Ghislaine and Jerry was still on the table, and the smell of her horrible cigarettes still lingered.

I could hear some music coming from downstairs. Nothing I recognized, but it was modern and mournful, so Jerry wasn't feeling great.

I put Daphne's Thermos with my soup in it on the table beside the tray and saw a note from Jerry lying there. I picked it up and slumped into my grandfather's old chair.

The chair groaned under me.

The note asked me to call Miss Beaumont, 'please'.

I sank down further in the comfortable old chair.

I wasn't out of the woods yet. There were no tidy conclusions, and repercussions were certain to come from Jameson and his colleagues and from Inspector Rose. My messy and muddled life would continue for a while yet, but I might, just, get away with it.

In the cinema, the credits would roll now and my mother would turn to my father and say, 'So what happens now?' He would shrug, ruffle my hair, wink at me and say, 'Life continues. As before. Only, everyone is sadder and wiser.'

Maybe Bernie would sell the diamonds for enough money for me to take Mrs Williams – Ann – to Paris. I'd always wanted to show her the place, but I'd never had the wherewithal to do it in the style I'd like: posh hotel and good restaurants with nice wine.

Perhaps I'd look up Ghislaine. Although it might be better not to. There were things that neither of us wanted to be reminded of. Monstrous things, like violent death.

Fluffy slid sinuously around the door, padded across the floor and rubbed up against my leg, purring like a low-flying bomber.

Funnily enough, though, all I could think of was something Les had said. He'd been thinking about Miss Beaumont's latest picture, the romantic historical. 'Well,' he'd said, looking more like a sad-eyed, jowly hound than ever, 'maybe you can work some magic with her, Tony, otherwise it looks like there'll be no *Hearts and Roses* for a while.'

I reached down and stroked Fluffy.

Time to pretend that I was sadder and wiser and make

some telephone calls. There was Mrs Williams – Ann – to apologize to and hadn't Manny invited me for a meal this Sunday? Or was that in another life? I could bring my own chicken soup.